SHORTLISTED FOR THE ORWELL PRIZE FOR POLITICAL WRITING 2021

LONGLISTED FOR THE WALTER SCOTT PRIZE FOR HISTORICAL FICTION 2021

'A remarkable novel, by a wondrous writer, deeply compelling, a thread that links our humanity with the colonial legacy that lies beneath, in ways that cut deep' Philippe Sands

'To read *Afterlives* is to be returned to the joy of storytelling as Abdulrazak Gurnah takes us to the place where imagined lives collide with history. In prose as clear and as rhythmic as the waters of the Indian Ocean, the story of Hamza and Afiya is one of simple lives buffeted by colonial ambitions, of the courage it takes to endure, to hold oneself with dignity, and to live with hope in the heart' Aminatta Forna

'Effortlessly compelling storytelling ... Gurnah excels at depicting the lives of those made small by cruelty and injustice ... A beautiful, cruel world of bittersweet encounters and pockets of compassion, twists of fate and fluctuating fortunes ... You forget that you are reading fiction, it feels so real' Leila Aboulela

'A tender account of the extraordinariness of ordinary lives, *Afterlives* combines entrancing storytelling with writing whose exquisite emotional precision confirms Gurnah's place among the outstanding stylists of modern English prose. Like its predecessors, this is a novel that demands to be read and reread, for its humour, generosity of spirit and clear-sighted vision of the infinite contradictions of human nature' *Evening Standard*

D0469506

'In clean, measured prose, Gurnah zooms in on individual acts of violence ... and unexpected acts of kindness. Affecting in its ordinariness, *Afterlives* is a compelling exploration of the urge to find places of sanctuary' *Daily Telegraph*

'Gurnah deftly manages the feat by spiking his stirring indictment of colonial atrocity with the intimate ordinariness of itinerant lives' *Spectator*

'Many layered, violent, beautiful and strange ... A poetic and vividly conjured book about Africa and the brooding power of the unknown' *Independent on Sunday*

'A vibrant and vivid novel which shows human beings in all their generosity and greed, pettiness and nobility, so that even minor characters seem capable of carrying entire novels all by themselves' *Herald*

'Abdulrazak Gurnah is a master of his craft ... An intricate, delicate novel, vitally necessary' *New Internationalist*

'Brings together the themes of choice, love dislocation, memory and history. The powerful stories that Gurnah tells in his novels provoke us to examine our own choices and where they have led us today' *London Magazine*

ABDULRAZAK GURNAH is the author of nine novels: *Memory of Departure*, *Pilgrims Way*, *Dottie*, *Admiring Silence*, *By The Sea* (longlisted for the Booker Prize and shortlisted for the *Los Angeles Times* Book Award), *Paradise* (shortlisted for a Commonwealth Writers' Prize), *The Last Gift* and *Gravel Heart*. He lives in Canterbury.

ALSO BY ABDULRAZAK GURNAH

Memory of Departure
Pilgrims Way
Dottie
Paradise
Admiring Silence
By the Sea
Desertion
The Last Gift
Gravel Heart

AFTERLIVES

ABDULRAZAK GURNAH

BLOOMSBURY PUBLISHING
LONDON · OXFORD · NEW YORK · NEW DELHI · SYDNEY

BLOOMSBURY PUBLISHING
Bloomsbury Publishing Plc
50 Bedford Square, London, WC1B 3DP, UK
29 Earlsfort Terrace, Dublin 2, Ireland

BLOOMSBURY, BLOOMSBURY PUBLISHING and the Diana logo
are trademarks of Bloomsbury Publishing Plc

First published in Great Britain 2020
This edition published 2021
Copyright © Abdulrazak Gurnah, 2020

Abdulrazak Gurnah has asserted his right under the Copyright,
Designs and Patents Act, 1988, to be identified as Author of this work

All rights reserved. No part of this publication may be reproduced or
transmitted in any form or by any means, electronic or mechanical,
including photocopying, recording, or any information storage or retrieval
system, without prior permission in writing from the publishers

A catalogue record for this book is available from the British Library

ISBN: PB: 978-1-5266-1589-3; eBook: 978-1-5266-1587-9

4 6 8 10 9 7 5 3

Typeset by Newgen KnowledgeWorks Pvt. Ltd., Chennai, India
Printed and bound in Great Britain by CPI Group (UK) Ltd, Croydon CR0 4YY

To find out more about our authors and books visit
www.bloomsbury.com and sign up for our newsletters

ONE

1

Khalifa was twenty-six years old when he met the merchant Amur Biashara. At the time he was working for a small private bank owned by two Gujarati brothers. The Indian-run private banks were the only ones that had dealings with local merchants and accommodated themselves to their ways of doing business. The big banks wanted business run by paperwork and securities and guarantees, which did not always suit local merchants who worked on networks and associations invisible to the naked eye. The brothers employed Khalifa because he was related to them on his father's side. Perhaps related was too strong a word but his father was from Gujarat too and in some instances that was relation enough. His mother was a countrywoman. Khalifa's father met her when he was working on the farm of a big Indian landowner, two days' journey from the town, where he stayed for most of his adult life. Khalifa did not look Indian, or not the kind of Indian they were used to seeing in that part of the world. His complexion, his hair, his nose, all favoured his African mother but he loved to announce his lineage when it suited him. Yes, yes, my father was an Indian. I don't look it, hey? He married my mother and stayed loyal to her. Some Indian men play around with African women until they are ready to send for an Indian wife then abandon them. My father never left my mother.

His father's name was Qassim and he was born in a small village in Gujarat which had its rich and its poor, its Hindus and its Muslims and even some Hubshi Christians. Qassim's family was Muslim and poor. He grew up a diligent boy who was used to hardship. He was sent to a mosque school in his village and then to a Gujarati-speaking government school in the town near his home. His own father was a tax collector who travelled the countryside for his employer, and it was his idea that Qassim should be sent to school so that he too could become a tax collector or something similarly respectable. His father did not live with them. He only ever came to see them two or three times in a year. Qassim's mother looked after her blind mother-in-law as well as five children. He was the eldest and he had a younger brother and three sisters. Two of his sisters, the two youngest, died when they were small. Their father sent money now and then but they had to look after themselves in the village and do whatever work they could find. When Qassim was old enough, his teachers at the Gujarati-speaking school encouraged him to sit for a scholarship at an elementary English-medium school in Bombay, and after that his luck began to change. His father and other relatives arranged a loan to allow him to lodge as best he could in Bombay while he attended the school. In time his situation improved because he became a lodger with the family of a school friend, who also helped him to find work as a tutor of younger children. The few annas he earned there helped him to support himself.

Soon after he finished school, an offer came for him to join a landowner's book-keeping team on the coast of Africa. It seemed like a blessing, opening a door to a livelihood for him and perhaps some adventure. The offer came through the imam of his home village. The landowner's antecedents came from the same village in the distant past, and they always sent for a book-keeper from there when they needed one. It was to ensure someone loyal and dependent was looking after their affairs. Every year during the fasting month Qassim sent to the imam of his home village a sum of money, which the landowner kept aside from his wages, to pass on to his family. He never returned to Gujarat.

That was the story Khalifa's father told him about his own struggles as a child. He told him because that is what fathers do to their children and because he wanted the boy to want more. He taught him to read and write in the roman alphabet and to understand the basics of arithmetic. Then when Khalifa was a little older, about eleven or so, he sent the boy to a private tutor in the nearby town who taught him mathematics and book-keeping

4

and an elementary English vocabulary. These were ambitions and practices his father had brought with him from India, but which were unfulfilled in his own life.

Khalifa was not the tutor's only student. There were four of them, all Indian boys. They lodged with their teacher, sleeping on the floor in the downstairs hallway under the stairs where they also had their meals. They were never allowed upstairs. Their classroom was a small room with mats on the floor and a high barred window, too high for them to see out although they could smell the open drain running past the back of the house. Their tutor kept the room locked after lessons and treated it as a sacred space, which they must sweep and dust every morning before lessons began. They had lessons first thing and then again in the late afternoon before it became too dark. In the early afternoon, after his lunch, the tutor always went to sleep, and they did not have lessons in the evening to save on candles. In the hours that were their own they found work in the market or on the shore or else wandered the streets. Khalifa did not suspect with what nostalgia he would remember those days in later life.

He started with the tutor the year the Germans arrived in the town and was with him for five years. Those were the years of the al Bushiri uprising, during which Arab and Waswahili coastal and caravan traders resisted the German claim that they were the rulers of the land. The Germans and the British and the French and the Belgians and the Portuguese and the Italians and whoever else had already had their congress and drawn their maps and signed their treaties, so this resistance was neither here nor there. The revolt was suppressed by Colonel Wissmann and his newly formed schutztruppe. Three years after the defeat of the al Bushiri revolt, as Khalifa was completing his period with the tutor, the Germans were engaged in another war, this time with the Wahehe a long way in the south. They too were reluctant to accept German rule and proved more stubborn than al Bushiri, inflicting unexpectedly heavy casualties on the schutztruppe who responded with great determination and ruthlessness.

To his father's delight, Khalifa turned out to have a talent for reading and writing and for book-keeping. It was then, on the tutor's advice, that Khalifa's father wrote to the Gujarati banker brothers who had their business in the same town. The tutor drafted a letter, which he gave to Khalifa to take to his father. His father copied it out in his own hand and gave it to a cart driver to deliver back to the tutor who took it to the bankers. They all agreed that the tutor's endorsement was certain to help.

Honourable sirs, his father wrote, is there an opening for my son in your esteemed business? He is a hard-working boy and a talented if inexperienced book-keeper who can write in roman and has some basic English. He will be grateful to you for his entire life. Your humble brother from Gujarat.

Several months passed before they received a reply, and only did so because the tutor went round to plead with the brothers, for the sake of his reputation. When the letter came it said, Send him here and we will try him out. If everything goes well, we will offer him work. Gujarati Musulman must always help each other. If we don't look after each other, who will look after us?

Khalifa was eager to leave the family home on the landowner's estate where his father was the book-keeper. During the time they waited for a reply from the banker brothers, he helped his father with his work: recording wages, filling in orders, listing expenses and listening to complaints that he could not remedy. The estate-work was heavy and the workers' pay was meagre. They were often struggling against fevers and aches and squalor. The workers added to their food supplies by cultivating the small patch of ground the estate allowed them. Khalifa's mother Mariamu did that too, growing tomatoes, spinach, okra and sweet potatoes. Her garden was next to their cramped little house and at times the paltriness of their lives depressed and bored Khalifa so much that he longed for the austere time he spent with the tutor. So when the reply from the banker brothers came, he was ready to go and determined to make sure that they would retain him. They did so for eleven years. If they were at first surprised by his appearance they did not show it, nor did they ever remark on it to Khalifa although some of their other Indian clients did. No, no, he is our brother, Guji just like us, the banker brothers said.

He was just a clerk, entering figures in a ledger and keeping records up to date. That was all the work they allowed him to do. He did not think they fully trusted him with their affairs but that was the way with money and business. The brothers Hashim and Gulab were moneylenders, which as they explained to Khalifa is what all bankers really are. Unlike the big banks, though, they did not have customers with private accounts. The brothers were close in age and looked very alike: short and solidly built, with easily smiling faces, wide cheekbones and carefully clipped moustaches. A small number of people, all Gujarati businessmen and financiers, deposited their surplus money with them and they lent it out at interest to local merchants and traders. Every year on the Prophet's birthday they held a reading of the maulid in the garden of their mansion and distributed food to all who came.

Khalifa had been with the brothers for ten years when Amur Biashara approached him with a proposition. He already knew Amur Biashara because the merchant had dealings with the bank. On this occasion, Khalifa helped him out with some information that the owners did not know he knew, details about commission and interest that helped the merchant strike a better deal. Amur Biashara paid him for the information. He bribed him. It was only a small bribe, and the advantage Amur Biashara gained from it was modest, but the merchant had a cut-throat reputation to maintain and, in any case, he could not resist anything underhand. For Khalifa, the modesty of the bribe allowed him to suppress any feeling of guilt at betraying his employers. He told himself he was acquiring experience in business, which was also about knowing its crooked ways.

Some months after Khalifa made his little arrangement with Amur Biashara, the banker brothers decided to transfer their business to Mombasa. This was as the railway from Mombasa to Kisumu was under construction and the colonial policy of encouraging Europeans to settle in British East Africa, as they called it at the time, was approved and launched. The banker brothers expected better opportunities to be opening up there, and they were not the only ones among the Indian merchants and craftsmen. At the same time, Amur Biashara was expanding his business and he employed Khalifa as a clerk because he himself could not write in roman alphabet and Khalifa could. The merchant thought this knowledge could be useful to him.

The Germans had by then subdued all revolt in their Deutsch-Ostafrika, or so they thought. They had taken care of al Bushiri and the protests and resistance of the caravan traders on the coast. They had suppressed that rebellion after a struggle, captured al Bushiri and hanged him in 1888. The schutztruppe, the army of African mercenaries known as askari under the direction of Colonel Wissmann and his German officers, was at that time made up of disbanded Nubi soldiers who had served the British against the Mahdi in Sudan and Shangaan 'Zulu' recruits from southern Portuguese East Africa. The German administration made a public spectacle of al Bushiri's hanging, as they were to do with the many other executions they would carry out in the coming years. As a fitting token of their mission to bring order and civilisation to these parts, they turned the fortress in Bagamoyo, which was one of al Bushiri's strongholds, into a German command post. Bagamoyo was also the terminus of the old caravan trade and the busiest port on that stretch of the coast. Winning and holding it was an important demonstration of German control of their colony.

There was still much for them to do, though, and as they moved inland they encountered many other peoples who were reluctant to become German subjects: the Wanyamwezi, Wachagga, Wameru, and most troublesome of all the Wahehe in the south. They finally subdued the Wahehe after eight years of war, starving and crushing and burning out their resistance. In their triumph, the Germans cut off the head of the Wahehe leader Mkwawa and sent it to Germany as a trophy. The schutztruppe askari, aided by local recruits from among the defeated people, were by then a highly experienced force of destructive power. They were proud of their reputation for viciousness, and their officers and the administrators of Deutsch-Ostafrika loved them to be just like that. They did not know about the Maji Maji uprising, which was about to erupt in the south and west as Khalifa went to work for Amur Biashara, and which was to turn into the worst rebellion of all and elicit even greater ferocity from the Germans and their askari army.

At that time, the German administration was bringing in new regulations and rules for doing business. Amur Biashara expected Khalifa would know how to negotiate for him. He expected him to read the decrees and reports that the administration issued and to complete the customs and tax forms that were required. Otherwise the merchant kept his business to himself. He was always up to something, so Khalifa was a general assistant who did whatever was required rather than a trusted clerk as he had expected. Sometimes the merchant told him things and sometimes he didn't. Khalifa wrote the letters, went to government offices for this or that licence, collected gossip and information and took little presents and sweeteners to people the merchant wanted kept sweet. Even so, he thought the merchant relied on him and his discretion, as much as he relied on anyone.

Amur Biashara was not difficult to work for. He was a small elegant man, always courteous and soft-spoken and a regular and obliging member of the congregation at his local mosque. He donated to charitable collections when a small disaster befell someone and never missed the funeral of a neighbour. No passing stranger could have mistaken him for anything but a modest or even saintly member of the community, but people knew otherwise and spoke of his cut-throat ways and his rumoured wealth with admiration. His secretiveness and ruthlessness in business were thought essential qualities in a merchant. He ran his business as if it were a plot, people liked to say. Khalifa thought of him as the pirate, nothing was too small for him: smuggling, moneylending, hoarding whatever was scarce as well as the usual stuff, importing this and that. Whatever was required, he was willing. He did his business in his head because he did not trust anyone, and also because some of his deals had to be discreet. It seemed to Khalifa that it gave the merchant pleasure to pay bribes and make devious transactions, that it reassured him when he made a secret payment for what he desired to happen. His mind was always calculating, assessing the people he dealt with. He was outwardly gentle and could be kind when he wished but Khalifa knew he was capable of real sternness. After working for him for several years, he knew how hard the merchant's heart was.

So Khalifa wrote the letters, paid the bribes and picked up whatever crumbs of information the merchant cared to let drop, and he was reasonably content. He had a flair for gossip, for receiving it and disseminating it, and the merchant did not rebuke him for spending many hours in conversation in the streets and cafés rather than at his desk. It was always better to know what was being said than to be in the dark. Khalifa would have preferred to contribute and know more about the deals but that was not likely to happen. He did not even know the combination number of the merchant's safe. If he needed a document he had to ask the merchant to get it. Amur Biashara kept a lot of money in that safe and he never even opened the door fully when Khalifa or anyone else was in the office. When he needed something from it, he stood in front of the safe and shielded the combination wheel with his body as he turned it. Then he opened the door a few inches and reached in like a pilferer.

Khalifa had been with Bwana Amur for over three years when he received word that his mother Mariamu had suddenly died. She was in her late forties and her passing was completely unexpected. He hurried home to be with his father and found him unwell and deeply distraught. Khalifa was their only child but in recent times had not seen a great deal of his parents, so it was with some surprise that he saw how weary and feeble his father looked. He was ill with something but had not been able to see a healer who could tell him what was wrong with him. There was no doctor nearby and the nearest hospital was in the town where Khalifa lived on the coast.

'You should've told me. I would've come for you,' Khalifa told him.

His father's body trembled gently all the time and he had no strength. He was no longer able to work and sat on the porch of his two-roomed shack on the landowner's estate, staring out blankly all day.

'It just came on me a few months ago, this weakness,' he told Khalifa. 'I thought I would go first, but your mother beat me to it. She shut her eyes and went to sleep and was gone. Now what am I supposed to do?'

Khalifa stayed with him for four days and knew from the symptoms that his father was very ill with malaria. He had a high fever, could not keep food down, his eyes were jaundiced and he passed red-tinted urine. He knew from experience that mosquitoes were a hazard on the estate. When he woke up in the room he shared with his father, his hands and ears were covered with bites. On the morning of the fourth day, he woke up to see his father was still sleeping. Khalifa left him and went out to the back for a wash and to boil water for their tea. Then as he stood waiting for the water to boil he felt a shiver of dread and went back inside to find that his father was not sleeping but dead. Khalifa stood for a while looking at him, so thin and shrunken in death when he had been so vigorous and such a champion in life. He covered him and went to the estate office to get help. They took his body to the small mosque in the village by the estate. There Khalifa washed him as required by custom, assisted by people who were familiar with the rituals. Later that afternoon they buried him in the cemetery behind the mosque. He donated the few belongings his father and mother left behind to the imam of the mosque and asked him to distribute them to whoever might want them.

When he returned to town and for several months afterwards Khalifa felt alone in the world, an ungrateful and worthless son. The feeling was unexpected. He had lived away from his parents for most of his life, the years with the tutor, then with the banker brothers and then with the merchant, and had felt no remorse for his neglect of them. Their sudden passing seemed a catastrophe, a judgement on him. He was living a useless life in a town that was not his home, in a country that seemed to be constantly at war, with reports of yet another uprising in the south and west.

It was then that Amur Biashara spoke to him.

'You have been with me now for several years ... how many is it, three ... four?' he said. 'You have conducted yourself with efficiency and respect. I appreciate that.'

11

'I am grateful,' Khalifa said, unsure whether he was about to receive a pay rise or to be dismissed.

'The passing away of both your parents has been a sad blow to you, I know that. I have seen how it has distressed you. May God have mercy on their souls. Because you have worked for me with such dedication and humility and for so long, I think it is not inappropriate for me to offer you some advice,' the merchant said.

'I welcome your advice,' Khalifa said, beginning to think that he was not about to be dismissed.

'You are like a member of my family, and it is my duty to offer guidance to you. It is time you married and I think I know a suitable bride. A relative of mine was recently orphaned. She is a respectful girl and she has also inherited property. I suggest you ask for her. I would have married her myself,' the merchant said with a smile, 'if I were not perfectly content as I am. You have served me well for many years, and this will be a fitting outcome for you.'

Khalifa knew that the merchant was making him a gift of her, and that the young woman was not going to have much say in the matter. He said she was a respectful girl but from the lips of a hard-headed merchant those words revealed nothing. Khalifa agreed to the arrangement because he did not think he could refuse and because he desired it, even though in his fearful moments he imagined his bride-to-be as someone abrasive and demanding with unattractive habits. They did not meet before the wedding or even at the wedding. The ceremony was a simple affair. The imam asked Khalifa if he wished to ask for Asha Fuadi to become his wife and he said yes. Then Bwana Amur Biashara as a senior male relative gave consent in her name. All done. After the ceremony coffee was served and then Khalifa was accompanied by the merchant himself to her house and introduced to his new wife. The house was the property Asha Fuadi inherited, only she did not inherit it.

Asha was twenty, Khalifa thirty-one. Asha's late mother was Amur Biashara's sister. Asha's eyes were still shadowed by her recent sorrow. Her face was oval-shaped and pleasing, her demeanour solemn and unsmiling. Khalifa took to her without hesitation but was aware that she was only enduring his embraces at first. It took a while for her to return his ardour and to tell him her story and for him to understand her fully. This was not because her story was unusual, quite the opposite, in fact, since it was the common practice of pirate merchants in their world. She was reticent because it took her a while to trust her new husband and be sure where his loyalty lay, with the merchant or with her.

'My Uncle Amur lent money to my father, not once but several times,' she told Khalifa. 'He had no choice since my father was his sister's husband, a member of his own family. When asked he had to give. Uncle Amur had little time for my father, thought him unreliable with money, which was probably true. I heard my mother say that to his face several times. In the end Uncle Amur asked that my father sign over his house ... our house, this house ... as security for a loan. He did that but did not tell my mother. That's what men are like with their business affairs, furtive and secretive, as if they cannot trust their frivolous womenfolk. She would not have let him do it if she had known. It is an evil practice, lending money to borrowers who cannot afford to repay it and then taking their houses from them. It's theft. And that's what Uncle Amur did to my father and to us.'

'How much did your father owe?' Khalifa asked when Asha fell into a long silence.

'It doesn't matter how much,' she said tersely. 'We still wouldn't have been able to repay it. He left nothing.'

'His passing must have been sudden. Perhaps he thought he had more time.'

She nodded. 'He certainly did not plan his passing very well. During the long rains last year, he suffered a recurrence of malarial fever, which he did every year, but this time it was worse than any other time before and he did not survive. It was sudden and horrible to see him in such a state before he went. May God have mercy on his soul. My mother did not really know his affairs in detail, but we soon found out that the loan was still unpaid and there was nothing left with which to make even a gesture of payment. His male relatives came to demand their share of his inheritance, which was really only the house,

13

but soon found that it belonged to Uncle Amur. It came as a horrible shock to everyone, especially to my mother. We had nothing in the world, nothing. Worse than nothing, we did not even have our lives because Uncle Amur was our guardian as the senior male relative in our family. He could decide what happened to us. My mother never recovered after my father died. She first fell ill many years before and was always ailing after that. I used to think it was sorrow, that she was not as ill as she said but allowed herself to moulder out of misery. I don't really know why she was miserable. Maybe someone made medicine against her, or perhaps her life was a disappointment. Sometimes she was visited and spoke in unfamiliar voices, and then a healer was called in despite my father's protests. After he died her misery turned into overwhelming grief, but in the last few months of her life another agony afflicted her: pains in her back and something that was eating her up from inside. That's what she said it felt like, something eating her up from inside. I knew she was going then, that this went beyond grieving. In her last days she worried about what would happen to me and begged Uncle Amur to look after me, which he promised to do.' Asha looked gravely at her husband for a long moment and then said, 'So he gave me to you.'

'Or he gave me to you,' he said, smiling to lighten the bitterness in her tone. 'Is it such a disaster?'

She shrugged. Khalifa understood, or could guess, the reasons why Amur Biashara had decided to offer Asha to him. In the first place he was making her someone else's responsibility. Then it would prevent any shameful liaison she might be tempted into, whether she had anything in mind or not. It was the way a powerful patriarch would think. Utamsitiri, Khalifa was to save her from shame and keep the name of the family clean. He was nothing special but the merchant knew who he was and marriage to him would protect her name, and therefore Amur Biashara's name, from any possible dishonour. A safe marriage to someone dependent on him like Khalifa would also preserve the merchant's property interest intact, keep the matter of the house in the family, so to speak.

Even when Khalifa knew the story of the house and understood the injustice of his wife's position he could not speak about it to the merchant. These were family affairs and he was not really family. Instead he persuaded Asha to speak to her uncle herself, asking for her portion back. 'He can be just when he wants to be,' Khalifa told her, wanting to believe that himself. 'I know him quite well. I've seen him at work. You have to put him to shame, make him give you your rights, otherwise he will pretend all is well and do nothing.'

In the end she spoke to her uncle. Khalifa was not present when she did and pleaded ignorance when the merchant politely questioned him about it afterwards. Her uncle told Asha he had already left a portion for her in his will and wanted the matter left there for now. In other words, he was not to be bothered with any further discussion about the house.

*

It was early 1907 when Khalifa and Asha married. The Maji Maji uprising was in the final throes of its brutalities, suppressed at a great cost in African lives and livelihoods. The rebellion started in Lindi and spread everywhere in the countryside and towns of the south and west of the country. It lasted for three years. As the widespread extent of the resistance to German rule sank in, so the response of the colonial administration became more relentless and brutal. The German command saw that the revolt could not be defeated by military means alone and proceeded to starve the people into submission. In the regions that had risen, the schutztruppe treated everyone as combatants. They burned villages and trampled fields and plundered food stores. African bodies were left hanging on roadside gibbets in a landscape that was scorched and terrorised. In the part of the country where Khalifa and Asha lived, they only knew of these events from hearsay. To them these were only shocking stories because there was no visible rebellion in their town. There had not been any since the hanging of al Bushiri although threats of German retribution were all around them.

The steadfastness of the refusal of these people to become subjects of the Deutsch-Ostafrika empire had come as a surprise to the Germans, especially after the examples that had been made of the Wahehe in the south and the Wachagga and Wameru people in the mountains of the north-east. The Maji Maji victory left hundreds of thousands dead from starvation and many hundreds more from battlefield wounds or by public execution. To some of the rulers of Deutsch-Ostafrika, this outcome was viewed as unavoidable. Their passing was inevitable sooner or later. In the meantime, the empire had to make the Africans feel the clenched fist of German power in order that they should learn to bear the yoke of their servitude compliantly. With each passing day that German power was pushing that yoke firmly on the necks of its reluctant subjects. The colonial administration was strengthening its hold over the land, growing in numbers and in reach. Good land was taken over as more German settlers arrived. The forced labour regime was extended to build roads and clear roadside gutters and make avenues and gardens for the leisure of the colonists and the good name of the Kaisereich. The Germans were latecomers to empire-building in this part of the world but they were digging in to stay for a long time and wanted to be comfortable while they were about it. Their churches and colonnaded offices and crenellated fortresses were built as much to provide a means for civilised life as to awe their newly conquered subjects and impress their rivals.

The latest uprising made some among the Germans think differently. It was clear to them that violence alone was not enough to subdue the colony and make it productive, so clinics were proposed and campaigns against malaria and cholera initiated. At first these served the health and well-being of the settlers and officials and the schutztruppe, but later were extended to include the native people too. The administration also opened new schools. There was already an advanced school in the town, opened several years before to train Africans as civil servants and teachers, but its intake was small and limited to a subordinate elite. Now schools were opened, intended to offer an elementary education to more of the subject people, and Amur Biashara was one of the first to send his son to one of them. The son, whose name was Nassor, was nine years old when Khalifa came to work for the merchant and fourteen when he started school. It was a little late to be doing so but that did not matter too much because the school he went to was intended to teach pupils trades not algebra, and his age was appropriate for learning how to use a saw or lay a brick or swing a heavy hammer. It was there that the merchant's son came to learn about working wood. He was in the school for four years, at the end of which he was literate and numerate and a competent carpenter.

During those years Khalifa and Asha had lessons of their own to learn. He learned that she was an energetic and obstinate woman who liked to keep busy and knew what she wanted. At first he marvelled at her energy and laughed at her opinionated summaries of their neighbours. They were envious, they were vicious, they were blasphemers, she said. Oh, come on, stop exaggerating, he protested while she frowned in stubborn disagreement. She did not think she was exaggerating, she said. She had lived beside these people all her life. He had taken her invocation of God's name and her quotations of verses of the Koran to be a manner of speaking some people had, an idiom, but he came to understand that for her it was not just an exhibition of her knowledge and sophistication but of serious piety. He thought she was unhappy and tried to think of ways to make her feel less alone. He tried to make her want him as he wanted her, but she was self-contained and reluctant and he thought she merely tolerated him and submitted to his ardour and embraces dutifully at best.

She learned that she was stronger than him, although it took her a long time to say it so bluntly to herself. She knew her own mind, often if not every time, and once she did she was firm whereas he was easily swayed by words, sometimes his own. Her memory of her father, about whom she tried to be respectful as her religion commanded, interfered with her judgement of her husband and, increasingly, she struggled to contain her impatience with Khalifa. When she could not, she spoke to him sharply in a manner she did not intend and sometimes regretted. He was steady but too obedient to her uncle who was nothing but a thief and an impious hypocrite with his lying saintly manners. Her husband was too easily satisfied and often taken advantage of,

17

but it was as He wished it to be and she would do her best to be content. She found his endless stories tiresome.

Asha miscarried three times in the early years of their marriage. After the third miscarriage in three years she was persuaded by neighbours to consult a herbalist, a mganga. The mganga made her lie down on the floor and covered her from head to toe with a kanga. Then she sat beside her for a long period, humming softly and repeatedly, and speaking words Asha could not make out. Afterwards the mganga told her that an invisible had taken her and was refusing to allow a child to grow in her. The invisible could be persuaded to leave but they would have to find out its demands and fulfil them before it would do so. The only way they could know the demands was by allowing the invisible to speak through Asha, and that was most likely to happen when it was allowed to possess her fully.

The mganga brought an assistant with her and made Asha lie down again on the floor. They covered her with a thick marekani sheet and then both began to hum and sing, their faces close to her head. As time passed and the mganga and her assistant sang, Asha shivered and trembled with increasing intensity until finally she burst out in incomprehensible words and sounds. Her outburst reached a climax with a yell and then she spoke lucidly but in a strange voice, saying: I will leave this woman if her husband makes a promise to take her on the hajj, to go to the mosque regularly and to give up taking snuff. The mganga crowed with triumph and administered a herbal drink, which calmed Asha and sent her into a doze.

When the mganga told Khalifa, in Asha's presence, about the invisible and its demands, he nodded compliantly and paid her her fee. I will give up taking snuff at once, he said, and I will just now go and perform my ablutions and head for the mosque. On my way back I will start enquiries about making the hajj. Now please get rid of this devil at once.

Khalifa did give up snuff, and he went to the mosque for a day or two but he never mentioned the hajj again. Asha knew that even while he was acting compliant Khalifa was not persuaded, was just laughing at her. It made it all the worse that she had allowed herself to agree to the blasphemous treatments her neighbours suggested. All that humming in her ears had become tiresome but she could not help it, she really did find Khalifa's lack of prayers irksome and wished for the hajj above all things. She found his quiet mockery of these desires deeply estranging. It made her reluctant to try again for a child and she found ways to discourage his ardour and avoid the disagreeable fuss he made when aroused.

His lessons fully learned, Nassor Biashara left the German trade school at the age of eighteen, besotted with the smell of wood. Amur Biashara was indulgent with his son. He did not expect him to help out in the business, for the same reason he did not require Khalifa to know the details of his many transactions. He preferred to work alone. When Nassor asked his father to finance a carpentry workshop so he could go into business for himself, the merchant was happy to oblige, both because it sounded like a good venture and also because it would keep his son out of his affairs for the moment. There will be time to initiate him into the business later.

The way of the old merchants was lending and borrowing from each other on trust. Some of them only knew each other by letters or through mutual connections. Money passed from hand to hand – a debt sold on in payment for another debt, consignments bought and sold unseen. These connections were as far away as Mogadishu, Aden, Muscat, Bombay, Calcutta, and all those other places of legend. The names were like music to many people who lived in the town, perhaps because most of them had not been to any of them. It was not that they could not imagine that they were all probably places of hardship and struggle and poverty, just like everywhere else, but they could not resist the strange beauty of those names.

The old merchants' business dealings depended on trust but that did not mean they trusted each other. That was why Amur Biashara did his business in his head, only he did not bother to keep his records straight and in the end his cunning failed him. It was bad luck, or fate, or God's plan, as you will, but he was suddenly taken ill in one of those terrible epidemics that used to occur much more often before the Europeans came with their medicines and their hygiene. Who would have thought how many diseases lurked in the filth people were so used to living with? He fell ill in one of those epidemics, despite the Europeans. When it's your time, it's your time. It might have been dirty water or bad meat or a bite from a poisonous pest that was the cause but the outcome was that he woke up in the early hours one morning with fever and vomiting and never rose from his bed again. He was barely conscious and died within five days. In those five days he never regained his presence of mind and all his secrets departed with him. His creditors came along in due course with their paperwork in good order. Those who owed him kept their heads down and the old merchant's fortune was suddenly a lot smaller than had been rumoured. Maybe he had meant to give Asha her house back and never got around to it but he left nothing to her in his will. The house now belonged to Nassor Biashara, as did everything else that was left after his mother and two sisters had taken their share and the creditors had taken theirs.

2

Ilyas arrived in the town just before Amur Biashara's sudden death. He had with him a letter of introduction to the manager of a large German sisal estate. He did not see the manager, who was also part-owner of the estate and could not be expected to make time for such a trifling matter. Ilyas handed in his letter at the administration office and was told to wait. He was offered a glass of water by the office assistant who also made probing conversation with him, assessing him and his business there. After a short while, a young German man came out of the inner office and offered him a job. The office assistant, whose name was Habib, was to help him settle in. Habib directed him to a school teacher called Maalim Abdalla who helped him to rent a room with a family he knew. By the middle of the afternoon on his first day in the town, Ilyas was employed and accommodated. Maalim Abdalla told him, I'll come by for you later so you can meet some people. Later that afternoon he called at the house and took Ilyas for a stroll through the town. They stopped at two cafés for coffee and conversation and introductions.

'Our brother Ilyas has come to work at the big sisal estate,' Maalim Abdalla announced. 'He is a friend of the manager, the great German lord himself. He speaks German as if it's his native language. He is lodging with Omar Hamdani for the moment until his lordship finds him accommodation suitable for such an eminent member of his staff.'

Ilyas smiled and protested and bantered back. His effortless laughter and self-deprecating manner made people comfortable and won him new friends. It always did. Afterwards Maalim Abdalla took him towards the port and the German part of the town. He pointed out the boma and Ilyas asked if that was where they hanged al Bushiri and Maalim Abdalla said no. Al Bushiri was hanged in Pangani, and anyway, there was not a big enough space here for a crowd. The Germans made a spectacle of the hanging and probably had a band and marching troops and spectators. They would have needed a big space for that. Their walk ended at Khalifa's house, which was the teacher's regular baraza, where he went most evenings for gossip and conversation.

'You are welcome,' Khalifa said to Ilyas. 'Everyone needs a baraza to go to in the evening, to stay in touch and catch up with the news. There is nothing much else to do after work in this town.'

Ilyas and Khalifa became good friends very quickly and within days were speaking freely with each other. Ilyas told Khalifa about how he had run away from home as a child and wandered around for several days before he was kidnapped by a schutztruppe askari at the train station and taken to the mountains. There he was freed and sent to a German school, a mission school.

'Did they make you pray like a Christian?' Khalifa asked.

They were strolling by the sea and could not be overheard but Ilyas was quiet for a moment, his lips clamped together uncharacteristically. 'You won't say anything to anyone if I tell you, will you?' he asked.

'They did,' Khalifa said delightedly. 'They made you sin.'

'Don't tell anyone,' Ilyas said pleadingly. 'It was either that or leave school, so I pretended. They were very pleased with me and I knew God could see what was really in my heart.'

'Mnafiki,' Khalifa said, not yet ready to give up tormenting him. 'There is a special punishment for hypocrites when you get there. Shall I tell you about it? No, it's unspeakable and you will have it coming to you sooner or later.'

'God knows what was in my heart, in there under lock and key,' Ilyas said, touching his chest and smiling too now that Khalifa was making a joke of it. 'I lived and worked on a coffee farm belonging to the German who sent me to school.'

'Was there still fighting up there?' Khalifa asked.

'No, I don't know how much fighting there was before, but it was all over when I was there,' Ilyas said. 'It was very peaceful. There were new farms and schools, new towns as well. Local people sent their children to the mission school and worked on the German farms. If there was any trouble it was the work of bad people who like to make an uproar. The farmer who sent me to school, he wrote the letter that got me the job in this town. The manager of the estate is a relative of his.'

Later Ilyas said, 'I've never been back to the village where we used to live. I don't know what happened to the old people. Now that I've come to live in this town, I realise that I am not very far from there. Actually I knew before I came that I would be close to my old home but tried not to think about it.'

'You should go and visit,' Khalifa said. 'How long is it since you've been away?'

'Ten years,' Ilyas said. 'Go there for what?'

'You should go,' Khalifa said, remembering his own neglect of his parents and how badly it made him feel afterwards. 'Go and see the family. It will only take a day or two to get there if you get a ride. It's not right to keep your distance. You should go and tell them that you are well. I'll come with you if you want.'

'No,' Ilyas said defensively, 'you don't know what kind of a mean and miserable place it is.'

'Then you can show them what a success you have made of yourself. It's your home and your family is your family, whatever you think,' Khalifa said more firmly as Ilyas was weakening.

Ilyas sat frowning for a moment or two and then his eyes slowly brightened. 'I'll go,' he said, becoming excited about the idea. He was like that, Khalifa was to find out. When he was taken by a plan Ilyas threw himself at it. 'Yes, you're talking sense. I'll go on my own. I've thought about it many times but managed to put it off. It takes a big mouth like you to force the issue and make me do it.'

Khalifa arranged for a cart driver who was headed in the direction of the village to give Ilyas a lift part of the way. He also gave him the name of a trading contact who lived on the main road not very far from his destination. He could stop there overnight if necessary. A few days later Ilyas was a passenger on a donkey cart headed on its bumpy way south on the coast road. The driver was an old Baluchi man who was taking supplies to the country shops along the route. He did not have a great deal to deliver. He stopped at two shops after which they turned inland on a better road, jogging along at such a good pace that they arrived at the contact Khalifa had provided in mid-afternoon. The contact turned out to be an Indian trader in fresh foodstuffs whose name was Karim. He bought food from local people and sent it to the market in the town: bananas, cassava, pumpkins, sweet potatoes, okra – hardy vegetables that could survive a day or two on the road. The Baluchi man fed and watered his donkey and then seemed to have a whispered conversation with her. He said that it was early enough for him to make a start on the return trip and stop overnight at one of the shops he had delivered to earlier, and that the donkey was willing. Karim supervised the loading of produce on the Baluchi's cart, writing the figures in his ledger and copying the numbers on a rough scrap of paper for the driver to take to his buyer in the market in town.

After the driver's departure, Ilyas explained what he was after and Karim looked dubious. He looked around him at the light, pulled a watch out of his waistcoat pocket, clicked open the cover with a flourish and waggled his head mournfully.

'Tomorrow morning,' he said. 'Today is not possible. It's only an hour and a half before maghrib, and by the time I arrange a driver for you it will be approaching dusk. You don't want to be on the road at night. Looking for trouble. You could easily get lost or run into bad people. Tomorrow morning, first thing, you shall go. I will speak to a driver tonight, but for now you will rest and let us welcome you here. We have a room for visitors. Come.'

Ilyas was shown to a small room with an earthen floor adjoining the store. Both the store and the room had rickety doors of rusty corrugated-metal sheets kept closed by iron padlocks which looked more ceremonial than secure. Inside the little room was a rope bed covered with a mat, certain to be crawling with bedbugs, Ilyas thought to himself. He noticed at once that there was no mosquito net and sighed with resignation. These were guest quarters for hardy itinerant traders but there was no choice. He could not expect Karim to invite a male stranger into his family home.

Ilyas hooked his canvas bag on the door frame and went out to look around. Karim's house was in the same yard and was a solidly built structure with two barred windows facing front, one either side of the door. It had a raised patio three steps from the ground. Karim was sitting on a mat on the patio, and when he saw Ilyas he waved him over. They sat talking for a while, about the town, about news of a devastating cholera epidemic in Zanzibar, about business, then a young girl of seven or eight came out of the house with two small cups of coffee on a wooden tray. As dusk approached, Karim pulled out his watch again and glanced at the time.

'Maghrib prayers,' he said. He called and after a moment the girl came out again, this time struggling with a bucket of water, which Karim laughingly relieved her of. He took the steps to the ground and put the bucket to one side, on a platform of stones arranged for washing feet. He gestured for his guest to come and make his ablutions first but Ilyas demurred energetically, so Karim went ahead and performed the cleansing in preparation for prayer. Then it was Ilyas's turn and he did what he saw Karim do. They went back up to the patio where the prayer was to take place, and as was customary and polite, Karim invited Ilyas to lead the prayer. Once again he energetically demurred and Karim stepped forward to lead.

Ilyas did not know how to pray, did not know the words. He had never been inside a mosque. There was not one to go to where he lived as a child, and there was not one on the coffee farm where he spent so many years later. There was a mosque in the nearby mountain town but no one at the farm or the school told him he should go there. Then at some point it was too late to learn, too shaming. By then he was a grown man working at the sisal estate and living in a town thronged with mosques, but there too no one asked him to go to the mosque. He knew that sooner or later something embarrassing was likely to happen. Karim's invitation to pray was the first time he had been caught out and he faked it as best he could, copying his every gesture and muttering as if he was speaking sacred words.

As promised, Karim arranged for another driver to take Ilyas to his old village, which was not far away. After a restless night, he came out as soon as he heard movement in the yard and was offered a banana and a tin mug of black tea for breakfast while he waited for the driver to turn up. He caught sight of the little girl sweeping the patio but there was no sign of her mother. The driver this time was a teenager who was happy to go on an outing and talked all the way about recent escapades he and his friends had engaged in. Ilyas listened politely and laughed when he was required but thought to himself: Country bumpkin.

They reached the village in an hour or so. The driver said he would wait on the main road because the path to the village was too narrow for the cart. It was only a short walk down the path he had pulled up beside. Yes, I know, Ilyas said. He took the path that led to where their old house used to be, and everything seemed as disorderly and familiar as if he had only left a few months before. It was not much of a village, a straggle of thatched houses with small cultivated fields behind them. Before he reached their old house he saw a woman whose name he could not remember but whose face was familiar. She was sitting in the cleared space outside her frail-looking wattle-and-mud house, weaving a mat from coconut leaves. A pot warmed on a trio of stones beside her feet and two chickens were pecking at the ground around the house. As he approached, she straightened her kanga and covered her head.

'Shikamoo,' he said.

She replied and waited, looking him up and down in his town clothes. He could not guess her age but if she was who he thought she was then she was the mother of children his age. One of them was Hassan, he remembered suddenly, a boy he used to play with. Ilyas's father's name was also Hassan, that was why the name came back to him so easily. The woman was sitting on a low stool and made no attempt to rise or smile.

'My name is Ilyas. I used to live up there,' he said, giving her his parents' names. 'Do they still live up there?'

She made no reply and he was not sure if she heard or understood him. He was about to move on and see for himself when a man came out from inside the house. He was older than the woman and walked haltingly up to Ilyas and looked at him closely as if his sight was poor. His face was lined and unshaven and he looked frail and unwell. Ilyas said his name again, and the names of his parents. The man and woman exchanged a look and then it was she who spoke.

'I remember that name Ilyas. Are you the one who was lost?' she said, and covered her head briefly with both hands in commiseration. 'Many terrible things were happening then and we all thought you had suffered a misfortune. We thought you were kidnapped by the ruga ruga or the wamanga. We thought the Mdachi killed you. I don't know what we didn't think. Yes, I remember Ilyas. Is that you? You look like a government man. Your mother passed on a long time ago. No one lives up there now, their house has fallen down. She had such bad luck no one wanted to live there. She left a little baby for your father to look after, fifteen or sixteen months old, and he left her for other people.'

Ilyas thought about this for a moment then he said, 'Left her for other people. What does that mean?'

'He gave her away.' The man spoke now, his voice weak and rasping with effort. 'He was very poor. Very ill. Like all of us. He gave her away.' He raised his arm and pointed in the direction of the road, too weary to say more.

'Afiya, that was her name. Afiya,' the woman continued. 'Where have you come from? Your mother is dead. Your father is dead. Your sister is given away. Where have you been?'

It was somehow what he had expected, that they would be dead. His father had been ill with diabetes all Ilyas's young life, and his mother was often unwell from unnameable ailments that afflicted women. In addition her back hurt, breathing was a struggle, her chest was thick with water and she was often retching from endless pregnancies. It was what he had expected but it still shocked him to have their deaths announced so abruptly. 'Is my sister here in the village?' he asked at last.

The man spoke again and in his tortured voice told him where the family who had taken Afiya lived. He accompanied Ilyas to the main road and gave directions to the young cart driver.

*

The small roadside village where she grew up was overlooked by a dark conical hill covered in scrub. It was always there whenever she stepped out of the house, leaning over the houses and yards across the road, but she did not see it when she was a very small child and only became aware of it later when she learned to give meaning to habitual sights. She was told that she was never to go up there but was not told why, so she populated the hill with all the terrors she was learning to imagine. It was her aunt who told her she must never go up the hill, and also told stories about a snake that could swallow a child, and a tall man whose shadow flitted across the roofs of houses when the moon was full, and a dishevelled old woman who roamed the road to the sea and sometimes took the form of a leopard who raided the village for a goat or a baby. Her aunt did not say so but the girl was sure that the snake and the tall man and the dishevelled old woman all lived on the hill and came down from there to terrorise the world.

Behind the houses and the backyards were the fields and beyond those rose the hill. As she grew older it seemed that the hill loomed even larger over the village, especially at dusk, shouldering over them like a discontented spirit. She learned to avert her gaze if she had to go out of the house at night. In the deep silence of the night she heard soft hissing whispers creeping down and sometimes they came around and behind the house as well. Her aunt told her these were the invisibles which only women heard, but however sad and insistent their whispers she was not to open the door to them. Much later she knew that the boys went up the hill and came back safely, and they never spoke of a snake or a tall man or a dishevelled old woman, and never mentioned whispers. They said that they went hunting on the hill, and if they caught anything they roasted it over a fire and ate it. They always came back empty-handed so she did not know if they were making fun of her.

The road past the village ran on to the coast in one direction and to the deep interior in the other. It was mostly used by people on foot, some of them carrying heavy loads, and sometimes by men on donkeys or on ox-carts. It was wide enough for the carts but uneven and bumpy. In the distance behind them the silhouette of mountains ran across the horizon. Their names were strange and made her think of danger.

She lived with her aunt and uncle and her brother and sister. Her brother was called Issa and her sister Zawadi. She was expected to rise at the same time as her aunt, who shook her awake and gave her a sharp little slap on her bottom to make her get up. Wake up, mischief. Her aunt's name was Malaika but they all called her Mama. The girl's first chore after she was up was to fetch the water while her aunt lit the braziers, which were cleaned and packed with charcoal from the night before. Water was not in short supply but it had to be fetched. There was a bucket and a ladle outside the bathroom door for use in there. There was another bucket by the sluice that led to the outside gutter, which was where they washed the pots and dishes, and where they poured away the water after washing clothes, but for her uncle's bath and for making tea she had to fetch the water from the huge clay tank, covered and kept under an awning to stay cool. It had to be clean water for her uncle's bath and for his tea, and the water in the buckets was only for dirty work. Sometimes the water made people ill, which was why she had to warm clean water for her uncle's bath and for the tea.

The tank was high and she was small so she had to stand on an upturned crate to be able to reach the water, and when the level was low or if the water-seller had not come to replenish the tank, she had to reach so far in that half her body was in the slippery tank. If she spoke while her head was in the tank her voice had a demonic sound, which made her feel enormous. She did that sometimes even when she was not fetching water, put her head into the tank and made gloating, groaning sounds as if she was huge. She ladled the water into two pans but only half-filled them because otherwise they were too heavy for her to carry. She took them one by one to the two braziers her aunt had started, then topped up the pans with repeated trips to the tank until the water in the pans was the right amount, one for her uncle's bath and the other for the tea.

The first she knew of anything in the world was living with them, her aunt and uncle. The brother Issa and sister Zawadi were older than her, maybe five or six years older. They were not her brother and sister, of course, but she still thought of them like that even though they teased her and hurt her as part of their games. Sometimes they beat her very deliberately, not because she had done anything to provoke them but because they liked to do it and she could not stop them. They beat her whenever it was only the children in the house and no one was there to hear her cries, or if they were bored, which was often. They asked her to do things she did not like and when she cried or refused they slapped her and spat at her. There was not much to do after her chores but if she followed them when they went out to play with their friends or to steal fruit from the neighbours' trees, they did not always like it nor did their friends. The girls called her dirty names to make the boys laugh and sometimes they chased her away. It was for different reasons but her brother and sister beat her or pinched her or stole her food, every day. She did not feel very sad that they beat her and pinched her and stole her food. It did not hurt very much and other things made her feel more sad, made her feel small and a stranger in this world. Other children were also beaten every day.

From a very young age she was required to do chores. She did not remember when it started, but she was always called to do something, sweeping or fetching water or running to the shop for her aunt. Later she washed clothes and chopped and peeled as required, and warmed the water for her uncle's bath and the household's tea. Other children in the village were required to do chores for their uncles and aunts too, in the house and in the fields. Her uncle and aunt did not have a field or even a garden, so all her chores were in the house or the backyard. Her aunt spoke to her sharply at times, but more often she was kind and told her stories. Some of these stories were terrifying, like the one about a ragged bloated man with long dirty fingernails who walked on the road at night, dragging an iron chain behind him, looking to capture a little girl and take her to his burrow underground. You can always hear him coming because of the chain dragging on the ground. Many of her aunt's stories were about dirty old people who stole little girls. When she saw Issa or Zawadi mistreating the child she rebuked or even punished them. Treat her like your sister, the poor girl, she told them.

Her mother was dead, she knew that, but she did not know why her aunt and her uncle were the ones who took her in. One day when she was in her sixth year her aunt told her, 'We took you in because you were orphaned and your father was sickening. Your mother and father lived further along the road and we knew them. Your poor mother was unlucky with her health and she died when you were very small, about two years old. Your father brought you to us and asked us to take you until he was better, but he did not become better and God took him away too. These things are in God's hands. Since then you have been our burden.'

Her aunt told her this as she was oiling and plaiting her hair after washing it, which she did every week to keep away the lice. She was sitting between her aunt's knees and could not see her face but her voice was gentle, even tender. After she was told this, she knew that they were not really her uncle and her aunt, and that her father was also dead. She did not remember her mother but it still made her sad to think of her. When she tried to imagine her she could only see one of the village women.

Her uncle did not speak to her very much, nor she to him. He frowned when she did so, even when it was only to deliver a message from her aunt. When he wanted her to come to him, he snapped his fingers or called out: You! His name was Makame. He was a big man, with a round face and a round nose and a large round stomach. He was satisfied when everything was as he wanted it. When he spoke sharply to one of his children, the house trembled and shook with his rage and everyone fell silent. She avoided his eyes because they were often hot and frightening in his glowering face. She knew he did not like her but she did not know what she had done to make him feel that way. His hands were large and his arm was as thick as her neck. When he slapped her on the back of her head she staggered and felt dizzy.

Her aunt had a habit of nodding several times when she wanted to say something firmly, and because her face was narrow and drawn and her nose was pointed, she looked as if she was pecking at something in the air when she did so. 'Your uncle is a very strong man,' her aunt told her. 'That's why he is employed as a security guard at the serikali depot. He opens and closes the gates to keep the vagrants out. The government chose him. They are all afraid of him. They say, Makame has a fist like a club. If it was not for him they would behave like hooligans and steal things.'

From her earliest memory she slept on the floor just inside the entranceway to the house. When she opened the door in the morning she saw the hill, and even when the door was closed at night she knew it was there, looming over them all. The dogs barked in the night and mosquitoes whined around her face and insects rattled and screeched just the other side of the flimsy and cracked door. Then they fell silent when the whispers began to descend from the hill all the way to the back of the house. She kept her eyes tightly shut in case she saw discontented eyes peering at her through the cracks in the door panels.

It was a small house made of mud bricks and whitewashed inside and out. There were two small rooms divided by the entranceway and a back door that opened on to the yard. A cane fence ran around this, and out there were the washroom and kitchen. The other four slept in the larger of the two rooms, mother and daughter in one bed and father and son in the other. Sometimes the younger people slept in the smaller room, which was used during the day for a sitting room or as somewhere to store things or to eat or to receive neighbours when they called. The village was a long way into the country, so there was no running water, which was why she had to fetch the water for her uncle's bath and for the tea from the huge clay tank the water-seller filled up every time it was low. The water-seller fetched the water from the village well a short distance away then he went from house to house, pulling his cart himself, and filled up the tanks of the people who paid him. Many people went to the well themselves or sent a child but her aunt and uncle could afford to pay.

One day she was in the yard helping her aunt with the washing when they heard someone calling out from the front door. Go and see who it is, her aunt said. At the door she found a man dressed in a long-sleeved white shirt and khaki trousers and thick-soled soft-leather shoes. He stood on the step, just up from the road, holding a canvas bag in his right hand. He was obviously a man from town, from the coast.

'Karibu,' she said, speaking the polite word of welcome.

'Marahaba,' he said, smiling. Then after a moment he said, 'Can I ask your name?'

'Afiya,' she said.

He smiled more widely and sighed at the same time. Then he went down on his haunches so their faces were level. 'I am your brother,' he said. 'I have been looking for you for so long. I did not know if you lived, or if Ma and Ba lived. Now I have found you, thank God. Are the people of the house inside?'

She nodded and went to call her aunt, who came out wiping her hands with her kanga. The man, now standing tall again, introduced himself by name. 'I am Ilyas, her brother,' he said. 'I went to our old home and found that my people were passed away. Neighbours told me my sister was here. I didn't know.'

Her aunt seemed perturbed by what he had said for a moment, and perhaps also by his appearance. He was dressed like a government man. 'Karibu. We did not know where you were. Please wait while Afiya goes to fetch her uncle,' she said. 'Quick, go now.'

She ran to the depot and told her uncle that her aunt said he was to come and he asked what it was about. My brother has come, she said. From where? he asked, but she just ran on before him. When they reached the house, he was a little breathless but he was polite and smiling, which was not how he usually was at home. Her brother was in the small room, cramped and cluttered as usual, and her uncle joined him there, shaking hands and beaming with delight. 'You are welcome, our brother. We thank God for keeping you safe and for leading you to our house so you can meet your sister. Your father told us that you were lost.

We did not know what to do to find you. We have done our best to look after her. She is like one of ours now,' he said, left hand on heart while his right arm was extended wide in a gesture of welcome.

'I don't know if you remember me, but I can assure you I am who I say I am,' her brother said.

'I can see the family resemblance,' her uncle said. 'There is no need for assurances.'

When Afiya came back a few minutes later with two glasses of water on a tray, she found them deep in conversation. She heard her brother say, 'Thank you for looking after her for so long. I cannot thank you enough but now that I've found her, I would like to take her to live with me.'

'We will be sorry to lose her,' her uncle said, his face shiny with dried sweat. 'She is our own daughter now, and her living with us is an expense we gladly bear, but of course she must live with her brother. Blood is blood.'

They talked together for some time before they called for her to come in. Her brother gestured for her to sit while he explained that she was to come and live with him in the town. She was to gather her things and be ready to leave with him in a short while. She collected her little bundle and was ready within minutes. Her aunt watched her closely. Just like that, not even thank you, goodbye, she said reproachfully. Thank you, goodbye, Afiya said, ashamed of her own haste.

She did not even know she had a real brother. She could not believe he was here, that he had just walked in off the road and was waiting to take her away. He was so clean and beautiful, and he laughed so easily. He told her afterwards that he was angry with her uncle and aunt but he did not show it because it would have seemed that he was being ungrateful when they had taken her in although she was not a relative. They had taken her in, that was not nothing. He gave them some money as a gift for their kindness but he did not need to, because she was in filthy rags when he found her as if she was their slave. 'If anything they should have paid you for having made you work for them like that for so long,' he said. It did not feel like

34

that to her at the time, only afterwards, after she started living with him.

That same morning he found her, he took her away with him on the donkey cart to Karim's shop. She had never travelled on a donkey cart before. They waited at the shop for a lift back and then the next day they went on another donkey cart where she sat among baskets of mangoes and cassava and sacks of grain while her brother shared the driver's bench. He took her to the small town on the coast where he lived. In the town, he rented a down-stairs room in a family home, and when they arrived he took her upstairs to meet the people who lived up there. The mother and her teenaged daughters were in and they said she was to come upstairs whenever she wished. During the time Afiya lived with her brother she slept on a bed for the first time in her life. She had her bed at one end of the room under her own mosquito net and he had his at the other. There was a table in the middle of the room where every afternoon he made her do lessons when he came back from work.

One morning, a few days after he brought her to the town, he took her to the government hospital near the seashore. She had never seen the sea. A man in a white coat scratched her arm and then asked her to urinate in a small pot. Ilyas explained the scratching was to prevent her from falling ill with fever and the urine was to test if she had bilharzia. It's German medicine, he said.

When Ilyas went to work in the morning, she went upstairs with the family and they made room for her without any effort. They asked questions about her and she told them what little there was to tell. She helped in the kitchen because that was work she knew how to do or sat with the sisters while they talked and sewed, and sometimes they sent her on errands to the shop down the street. Their names were Jamila and Saada and they became her friends from the start. Later, she had her meal with them when their father came home. She was told to call their father Uncle Omari, which made her feel she was part of the family. In the afternoon, after her brother came back from work and had a wash, she took his lunch to him downstairs and sat with him while he ate.

'You must learn to read and write,' he said. She had not seen anyone read or write although she knew what writing was because it was on the tins and boxes in the village shop, and she had seen a book on a shelf above the shopkeeper's stool. The shopkeeper told her it was a holy book you should not touch without first washing yourself as if you were preparing for prayer. She did not think she would be able to learn a book that holy but her brother laughed at her and made her sit beside him while he wrote out the letters and made her say them after him. Later she practised writing the letters herself.

One afternoon, when the people upstairs were out, he took her with him as he went to call on one of his friends. His name was Khalifa, and Ilyas said this was his best friend in the town. They teased each other and laughed and then after a while her brother said they would continue with their walk but he promised to bring her to visit again. Most mornings she went upstairs and sat with Jamila and Saada while they cooked and talked and sewed, and sometimes in the evenings when Ilyas went to the café or to be with his friends, she went upstairs and practised reading and writing her letters under the sisters' admiring eyes. Neither of them could read, nor could their mother.

Her brother did not always go out, though, and some evenings he stayed in and taught her card games or songs or talked to her about his experiences. He told her: 'I ran away from home while Ma was pregnant with you. I don't know if I really meant to run away. I don't think I did. I was only eleven. Our Ma and Ba were very poor. Everyone was poor. I don't know how they lived, how they survived. Ba had sugar and was unwell and could not work. Perhaps the neighbours helped them. I know my clothes were rags and I was always hungry. Ma lost two of my younger sisters after they were born. I expect it was malaria but I was only a child and I would not have known about things like that at the time. I remember when they both came. After a few months they fell ill and cried for days before they passed away. Some nights I could not sleep because I was so hungry and because Ba was groaning so loudly. His legs were swollen and smelled bad, like meat that was rotting. It was not his fault, that was the sugar.

Don't cry, I can see your eyes are getting wet. I am not saying this to be unkind but to explain to you that perhaps these were the things that made me want to run away.

'I don't think I really meant to run away but once I was on the road I just kept walking. No one took very much notice of me. When I was hungry I begged for food or stole some fruit, and at night I always found somewhere to creep into and sleep. Some of the time I was very frightened but at other times I forgot myself and just looked at what was happening all around. After several days I arrived in a big town on the coast, this town. I saw soldiers marching through the streets, music playing, heavy boots thudding on the road and a crowd of young people marching alongside, pretending to be soldiers too. I joined them, thrilled by the display of the uniforms and the march and the band. The march ended at the train station and I stood there to watch the big iron coaches as large as houses. The engine was groaning and puffing smoke, just like it was alive. I had never seen a train before. A troop of askari stood on the platform waiting to board the train, and I was loitering around them, just watching and listening. The Maji Maji fighting was still going on then. Do you know about that? I didn't know about it then either. I'll tell you about the Maji Maji later. When the train was ready, the askari began to board. A Shangaan askari pushed me on the train and held my wrist and laughed while I struggled but he did not let me go. He told me I was to be his gun boy, to carry his gun for him when they marched. You will like it, he said. He took me on the train until the end of the line, or as far as they had built the line at that time, and then we marched for several days all the way to the mountain town.

'When we arrived there we were made to wait in a yard for a while. I think the Shangaan thought I was no longer trying to escape him because he was not even holding my wrist. Perhaps he thought there was nowhere for me to run. I saw an Indian man standing over some cargo, giving instructions to the porters and making a note on a piece of board. I ran to him and told him that the askari had stolen me from my home. The Indian man told me, go away, you filthy little thief! I must have looked very dirty. My clothes were nothing but rags, shorts made of sacking and a torn old shirt I did not bother to wash any more. I told the Indian man, my name is Ilyas and that big Shangaan askari standing there staring at us stole me from my home. The Indian man looked away at first but then he asked me to repeat my name. He made me say it twice more then he smiled and said it too. Ilyas. He nodded and took me by the hand' – Ilyas took Afiya's hand as he said this, smiling like the Indian man and getting to his feet – 'walking towards the German officer in his white uniform who was also there in the yard. He was the chief of the askari and was busy with his troops. He had hair the colour of sand and his eyebrows were the same. That was the first German I stood close to and that is what I saw. He frowned at me and said something to the Indian man who said I was free to go. I said I had nowhere to go and when the chief of the askari heard this he frowned again and called for another German man.'

They sat down again, Afiya still smiling and her eyes rapt with pleasure at the story. Ilyas put on a scowling expression and continued.

'This other German was not an officer in a beautiful white uniform but a rough-looking man who was directing workers loading cargo, which the Indian man was counting off. When the officer finished speaking to him he summoned me to him and said sharply, What's your story? I told him, my name is Ilyas and an askari stole me from my home. He repeated my name and smiled. Ilyas, he said, that's a nice name. Wait here until I finish. I did not, but followed him in case the Shangaan askari came back for me. The man worked on a coffee farm a little way up the mountain. It belonged to another German. He took me back to the farm with him and gave me work in the animal pen. They had several donkeys and a horse in her own stable. Yes, it was a she-horse, very large and scary to a little boy. It was a new farm and there was a lot of work to do. That was why the rough German took me there, because they needed people to work.

'The farmer saw me in the pen clearing donkey dung or something like that, I can't remember exactly. He asked the man who had brought me from the station who I was. When he found out that I was stolen by an askari he was angry. We don't have to behave like savages, he said. That is not what we have come here to do. I know that was what he said because he told me later. He was pleased with what he did and liked to talk about it to me and to other people. He said I was too young to work, that I should first go to school. The Germans did not come here to make slaves, he said. Then I was allowed to attend church school, which was for converts. I stayed there on the farm for many years.'

'Was I born then?' Afiya asked.

'Oh, yes, you must have been born a few months after I ran away,' Ilyas said. 'I was on the farm for nine years so that means you must be about ten years old. I really liked living there. I worked on the farm and went to school and learned to read and write and to sing and speak German.'

He broke off and sang some verses of what must have been a German song. She thought his voice was beautiful and got to her feet to applaud him when he stopped. He was grinning with pleasure. He loved to sing.

'One day, not so long ago,' he continued, 'the farmer called me over for a talk. He was like a father to me, that man. He looked after all the workers, and if anyone fell ill he sent him to the mission clinic for medicine. He asked me if I wanted to stay on at the farm. He said I now had too many talents for a farm labourer and was I not curious to move back to the coast where there were many more opportunities? He gave me a letter to take to a relative of his here in this town who has a sisal factory. In the letter he wrote that I was trustworthy and respectful, and could read and write in German. He read the letter to me before he sealed it. That is why I have a job as a clerk in a German sisal factory, and that is why you will learn to read and write too, so that one day you will know about the world and learn how to look after yourself.'

'Yes,' Afiya said, not ready to think about the future just yet. 'Did the farmer have sandy hair like the other German in the white uniform?'

'No, he didn't,' Ilyas said. 'He had dark hair. He was slim and deliberate, never shouting at or abusing his workers. He looked like a … a schüler, a learned man, a restrained man.'

39

Afiya gave the description of the farmer a moment's thought and then asked, 'Did our Ba have dark hair?'

'Eh, probably. It was all grey when I left but I suppose it would have been dark earlier, when he was younger,' Ilyas said.

'Did your farmer look like our Ba?' Afiya asked.

Ilyas burst into laughter. 'No, he looked like a German,' he said. 'Our Ba …' Ilyas stopped and shook his head and said no more for a moment. 'Our Ba was unwell,' he said.

*

'I don't want to speak ill of the dead so soon after,' Khalifa said to Ilyas, 'but that old man was a pirate. As for the young tajiri, well, I have known him for years. He was a little boy of nine, I think, when I started working for Bwana Amur. Now he is grown into a young man of panicky spirit – and who wouldn't be with a father who kept him so much in the dark? Then all of a sudden here he is, presiding over a robbery as the creditors move in. He lost a lot in the chaos that followed his father's death. He knew nothing about the business and those other pirates robbed him. All he is really interested in is wood. He even persuaded his father to let him open that timber yard and furniture workshop. That is what he loves to do – hang around the timber yard and smell the wood. In the meantime, everything else is going to hell.

'I told you about the house. Well, we thought he was not made of the same ugly material as his father, and perhaps he would listen more kindly to Bi Asha's plea for her house, but he is greedy just like his father. He does not have any right to this house. He should have returned it to its proper owner but he firmly refuses to give it up, even though he too was surprised to discover it does not belong to Bi Asha. He could ask us to leave, I suppose, but I think he's too afraid of my wife. They are cousins, you know, almost like brother and sister, but he refuses to return the house that rightfully belongs to her family. He is just another greedy scoundrel.'

The two men took to meeting late in the afternoon or early in the evening for an hour or two at the café. They joined the general talk, which was the main purpose of gathering there, and Khalifa, who knew many people, introduced Ilyas to others and pumped him for his stories, which were often about his time in the German school in the mountain town and the German farmer who was his benefactor. Other people also had stories to tell, some of them quite improbable, but that was the café style: the broader the better. Khalifa was a well-known connoisseur of stories and gossip and was at times consulted to arbitrate between competing versions. When they had enough of the café talk, they strolled along the seashore or went back to Khalifa's porch where in the evening some of his friends came for a baraza. They were pre-occupied at the time with rumours of the coming conflict with the British, which people were saying was going to be a big war, not like the small ones before against the Arabs and the Waswahili and the Wahehe and the Wanyamwezi and the Wameru and all the others. Those were terrible enough but this is going to be a big war! They have gunships the size of a hill and ships that can travel underwater and guns that can bombard a town miles away. There is even talk of a machine that can fly although no one has seen one.

'They don't stand a chance, the British,' Ilyas said, and a murmur of agreement went through the group. 'The Germans are gifted and clever people. They know how to organise, they know how to fight. They think of everything ... and on top of that they are much kinder than the British.'

His listeners hooted with laughter.

'I don't know about kindness,' said one of the café experts, a man called Mangungu. 'For me it's their sternness and the vicious-ness of the Nubi and Wanyamwezi askari that are going to take care of the British. There is no one as stern as a German.'

'You don't know what you're talking about,' Ilyas said. 'I have met with nothing but kindness from them.'

'Listen, just because one German man has been kind to you does not change what has happened here over the years,' another man, Mahmudu, said, addressing him. 'In the thirty years or so that they have occupied this land, the Germans have killed so many people that the country is littered with skulls and bones and the earth is soggy with blood. I am not exaggerating.'

'Yes, you are,' Ilyas said.

41

'You people here don't know what happened in the south,' Mahmudu continued. 'No, the British don't stand a chance, not if the fighting is on land, but it won't be because of German kindness.'

'I agree. Their askari are ferocious and complete savages. God alone knows how they have become like that,' said a man named Mahfudh.

'It's their officers. They learn their cruelty from their officers,' said Mangungu, speaking in a tone of authority intended to settle the argument as he liked to do.

'They were fighting an enemy who was just as savage in retaliation,' Ilyas said, undaunted. 'You haven't heard half of what those people did to the Germans. They had to be harsh in retaliation because that's the only way savage people can be made to understand order and obedience. The Germans are honourable and civilised people and have done much good since they have been here.'

His listeners were silent in the face of such vehemence. 'My friend, they have eaten you,' Mangungu said eventually, having the last word as usual.

Despite such encounters it was still a great surprise to Khalifa when Ilyas announced that he planned to volunteer for the schutztruppe. 'Are you mad? What has this to do with you?' his friend asked. 'This is between two violent and vicious invaders, one among us and the other to the north. They are fighting over who should swallow us whole. What has this to do with you? You will be joining an army of mercenaries renowned for their cruelty and brutality. Didn't you hear what everyone was saying? You might be badly hurt ... worse even. Are you thinking straight, my friend?'

Ilyas was not to be dissuaded and refused to defend his decision. His only concern, he said, was to make arrangements for his little sister.

*

A whole year had raced past. For Afiya it had felt like the happiest time of her life ever since her brother came back and found her and filled her days with laughter. He really did, he was always laughing and she could not help laughing when he did. Then all of a sudden, or that was how it seemed to her, he said: 'I have joined the schutztruppe. Do you know what that is? It means protection troop, jeshi la serikali. I will be an askari. I will be a soldier for the Germans. There is a war coming.'

'Will you have to go away? Will it be for a long time?' she asked him, speaking calmly although she felt alarmed by his news.

'It won't be for long,' he said, smiling reassuringly. 'The schutztruppe is a powerful and invincible army. Everyone is terrified of them. I'll be back in a few months.'

'Will I stay here until you come back?' she asked.

He shook his head. 'You are too young. I can't leave you here on your own. I've asked Uncle Omar if you can stay with the family but he does not want the responsibility, in case ... We are not related,' Ilyas said and then shrugged. 'You can't stay here and you cannot come to war with me. I don't want to send you back to them, your aunt and uncle in the country, but there is no other choice. Now they will know I am coming back for you and they will treat you better.'

She did not know how he could send her back there, after all he had said and after he had taught her to see the cruelty of her life with them. She could not stop crying for a long while. Ilyas held her in his arms and stroked her hair and whispered reassurance. That night he let her share his bed with him and she fell asleep while he talked about the time he was at school in the mountain town. She knew he was in a hurry to leave, and she did not want him to dislike her and not come back for her so she stopped crying when he said to stop. The sisters made a dress for her as a goodbye present, and their mother gave her one of her old kangas. I'm sure you'll be very happy there in the country, the sisters said, and Afiya said yes. She had not told them anything about her uncle and aunt there – Ilyas said not to – and she did not tell them how much she dreaded going back. They also went to say goodbye to Khalifa and to Bi Asha. Ilyas knew that he was posted to Dar es Salam for training.

43

Her brother's friend Khalifa said to the girl, 'I don't know why your elder brother is going to war instead of staying here to look after you. This fight is nothing to do with him. And he's doing it in the company of murdering askari whose hands are already covered in blood. Listen to me, Afiya, until he returns, you must let us know if ever you need anything. Send a message to me at my workplace, care of the merchant Biashara. Will you remember that?'

'She can write,' Ilyas said.

'In that case, send me a note,' said Khalifa, and the two friends laughed as they said goodbye.

Everything was done in a few days and she was soon back with her aunt and uncle in the country. Her few belongings were in a small cloth bundle: the dress the sisters made for her, the old kanga their mother gave her, a small slate tablet and a packet of scrap paper that her brother had brought back from work for her to practise her writing on. She was back to sleeping on the floor in the entranceway, in the shadow of the hill. Her aunt treated her as if she had only been away for a few days and expected her to return to her chores as before. Her uncle ignored her. The daughter Zawadi sneered and said, our slave has come back. She was not good enough for the big brother in town. The son Issa snapped his fingers under her nose as his father did to summon her. Everything was a little worse than before and it hurt more. She warned herself to put up with it because her brother said to do so until he came back for good. Her aunt grumbled at her more than she used to, about how slow she was with her chores, about the expense of taking her back even though her brother gave them money for her upkeep. The son was now sixteen and sometimes he pressed himself against her and squeezed her nipples when no one was around and she was not quick enough to escape.

In the hot, dead mid-afternoon hours a few days after she came back to live with them, her aunt saw her sitting in the backyard, practising writing on the slate tablet. Her aunt had just risen from her after-lunch sleep and was on her way to the washroom. She looked on without a word at first and then came closer. When she saw that the marks were not just squiggles, she pointed to the slate and asked harshly, 'What's that? Are you writing? What does it say?'

'Jana, leo, kesho,' Afiya said, pointing to each word in turn. Yesterday, today, tomorrow.

Her aunt looked perturbed and disapproving but did not say anything. She proceeded to the washroom and Afiya hurried to put her slate away, cautioning herself to practise discreetly in future. Her aunt did not mention the slate again but she must have told her husband. The next day after he had his lunch, during which she felt an unusual tension among the family, he snapped his fingers at Afiya and pointed to the small room. As she turned to obey she saw a smile of anticipation on the face of the son. She was already in the room, facing the door, when her uncle came in with a cane in his right hand. He bolted the door and gazed at her for a moment with an expression of disgust. 'I hear you have learned to write. I don't have to ask who has taught you to do this. I know exactly who it is – someone with no sense of responsibility. No, someone with no sense at all. Why does a girl need to write? So she can write to a pimp?'

He stepped forward and slapped her on her temple with his left hand, then he swapped the cane and slapped her on the face and head with his right hand. The blows made her stagger and she reeled back as he shouted and snarled at her. Then after a long silent pause he lashed at her with the cane, deliberately missing at first but coming ever closer. She yelled with terror and did her best to escape but it was a small room and he had bolted the door. There was nowhere for her to hide so she ran and ducked and took what blows she had to. Most of them landed on her back and shoulders and made her shudder and cry out, and in the end she stumbled and fell. As she did so she put out her left hand to protect her face, and the stick landed on it with crushing force. The pain took her breath away and she gasped with shock before a scream tore through her. She lay at his feet, screaming and sobbing, while he raged at her and no one came to stop him. When he had satisfied himself, he opened the door and left the room.

Afterwards, through her tears and sobs, she knew that her aunt came to her and took her soiled dress off and wiped her down. Then she covered her with a sheet and murmured to her until she passed out. It could only have been momentary because when she came to light still glared through the window and the room throbbed with heat. She lay there all afternoon in a tearful delirium, conscious at times that her aunt was sitting against the wall nearby. In the evening she took the girl to the herbalist to have her hand bound, and the mganga told the woman: 'You should be ashamed of yourself. Everybody in the village heard him shouting and beating the child. It's as if he is out of his mind.'

'He did not mean to hurt her like this. It was an accident,' her aunt said.

'Do you think no one is keeping account?' the mganga said.

The herbalist did all she knew how to do but the hand did not heal properly. Afiya had another hand, though, and a few days after the beating she wrote a note on a scrap of paper to the man her brother had befriended in the town. She addressed the note care of Bwana Biashara as he had instructed she was to do if she needed help. She wrote: Kaniumiza. Nisaidie. Afiya. He has hurt me. Help me. She gave the note to the shopkeeper, who read it and folded it in half and gave it to a cart driver headed for the coast. Her brother's friend came back with the cart driver who delivered her note. He paid him to return the following day. She was still sore all over from the bruises and the fractured hand, and was sitting on the doorstep staring out at the hill when they pulled up outside the house. The shopkeeper had told them where to go. Her uncle was at work but he did not come back. He must have known who had arrived. It was only a small village. When she saw her brother's friend she rose to her feet.

'Afiya,' he said, and came to her and saw how she was. He took her good hand, walked her to the cart without saying a word.

'Wait,' she said. She ran inside and picked up her bundle, which was in the entranceway where she slept.

For a long time Afiya did not like to go anywhere in case they came looking for her. She was afraid of everyone except for her brother's friend who had come for her and whom she was now to call Baba Khalifa, and Bi Asha, who fed her wheat porridge and fish soup to build her strength, whom she was now to call Bimkubwa. She was sure that if her Baba had not come, her uncle would have killed her sooner or later, or if not him then his son. But Baba Khalifa came.

TWO

He picked him out with his eyes during the inspection on that first morning. The officer. That was in the boma camp where they were taken to join the other recruits who had been rounded up earlier. On the march from the depot to the boma their escort hectored and mocked and hurried them on, ahead and behind them and sometimes beside them. You're a bunch of washenzi, they said. Feeble fodder for the wild beasts. Don't swing your hips like a shoga. We are not taking you to a brothel. Straighten your shoulders, you cocksuckers! The army will show you how to stiffen that backside.

The recruits were on the march with varying degrees of consent: some were volunteers, others were volunteered by their elders who themselves were under duress, some swept up or coerced by circumstances, some picked up on the road. The schutztruppe was expanding and was eager for fighting men. Some of them talked freely, already swaggering with anticipation, familiar with this kind of work, laughing at the bullying words of their escort, eager to be admitted into the language of scorn. Others were silent and anxious, perhaps even fearful, not sure yet of what lay ahead. Hamza was in the latter category, silently wretched about what he had done. No one had forced him, he had volunteered.

They started from the recruiting depot at first light. He knew no one but to begin with he strutted with the others, made bold by the strangeness of these circumstances, out at dawn marching to the training camp at the start of an adventure. The big muscular men took the lead, striding confidently and pulling the others along behind them. One of them broke into song, his voice deep and gloaming, and some others who knew his language took it up with him. Hamza thought it was Kinyamwezi because that was what the men looked like to him. Their escort, some of whom also looked to be Wanyamwezi, smiled and even joined in at times. In a lull someone began to sing another song in Kiswahili. It was not really a song, more like a sung conversation, delivered to a jaunty marching tempo with an explosive response at the end of every phrase:

Tumefanya fungo na Mjarumani, tayari.
Tayari!
Askari wa balozi wa Mdachi, tayari.
Tayari!
Tutampigania bila hofu.
Bila hofu!
Tutawatisha adui wajue hofu.
Wajue hofu!

They sang cheerfully, half-mocking themselves with their chest-thumping gestures:

We have joined the German,
We're ready!
We're soldiers of the governor of the Mdachi,
We're ready!
We will fight for him without fear,
Without fear!
We will terrify our enemies and fill them with fear,
With fear!

Their escort laughed with them as they sang the blustering words and added obscene lyrics of their own.

Then as they marched out into the countryside and the heat rose and the sun clamped down on his neck and shoulders, and the sweat poured off his face and streamed down his back, Hamza's anxiety returned. He had volunteered on impulse, fleeing what had seemed intolerable, but he was ignorant of what he had now sold himself to, and of whether he was up to what it would demand of him. He was not ignorant about the company he had chosen to keep. Everyone knew about the askari army, the schutztruppe, and their ferocity against the people. Everyone knew about their stone-hearted German officers. He had chosen to be one of their soldiers, to get away, and as he sweated and tired, and they marched along the dirt road in the heat of the day, his anxiety about what he had done surged so powerfully at times that he grew short of breath.

They stopped for a drink of water and some dried figs and dates. They passed many paths that led off the road to villages just behind the screen of foliage but did not see anyone. It seemed they were all keeping out of sight. At one roadside, in a small clearing under a large tamarind tree, there were bunches of bananas, a small pile of cassava, a basket of cucumbers and another of tomatoes. The market had been abandoned in a hurry. People must have been surprised at their approach and not been able to gather up all their merchandise in time, opting for a safe retreat. Everyone knew the recruiting squads were out in the countryside.

Their escort halted them there and called out for the owners of the goods to appear but no one did. In the meantime the escort distributed the bananas among the marchers, only the bananas, and shouted out to the concealed traders that they should present the bill to the Kaiser's governor. The marchers were not once allowed out of sight of their escort. They were required to relieve themselves by the roadside in sight of everyone, six of them at a time, whether they needed to or not. It's to teach you discipline, their escort laughed. Get that filthy stuff out of you before we march you into camp, and cover it up with soil afterwards.

They walked all day, most of them barefoot, some wearing leather sandals. The German built this road, their escort said, just so you don't have to struggle through the jungle. Just so we can get you sister-fuckers there in comfort. By mid-afternoon Hamza's legs and back ached so much that he walked by rote and instinct, without any choice but to keep moving. Later he could not remember the final stages of that march, but like animals nearing their pens, the recruits came to life when the escort told them they were nearly there.

They arrived at the camp at dusk, walking through the outskirts of a large village where a crowd gathered to watch them trudge past. Friendly shouts and some laughter followed them until they passed through the gates into the walled boma. A long whitewashed building ran along the right-hand side of the camp. The upstairs rooms, some of which glowed with lamplight, had verandas facing the open parade ground. At ground-level beneath was a line of closed doors. There was another smaller building, which ran along the far side of the open ground facing the gate. It also had an upper storey lit against the gloom. Downstairs there was just one door and two windows, all of which were closed. To the left of the wide parade ground were two half-open sheds and some animal pens. In the corner nearest the gate there was a small two-storey building which, it turned out, was the lockup. That was where they were taken and shown into one large downstairs room with lamps hanging from the ceiling beams. The door to upstairs was shut but theirs was left open as was the main front door. The askari who had accompanied them on the march stayed, still keeping an eye on them, even though they themselves seemed worn out by the march. They were too tired for mockery and abuse, and sat by the door waiting for their relief.

There were eighteen new recruits in their group, weary and sweaty and silent now in the cramped cell. Hamza was numb with hunger and exhaustion, his heart racing with a distress he could not control. Three elderly women from the village brought a clay pot of bananas boiled with chopped tripe, which the marchers gathered round to eat as best they could, taking turns to reach in for a handful while the food lasted. When the relief guards came they took the recruits out into the dark one at a time to use the bucket latrine in an outhouse to one side of the lockup. Afterwards the guards selected two of the men to take the bucket to a cesspit outside the gate and dispose of the waste.

'Boma la mzungu,' one of the guards said. 'Kila kitu safi. Hataki mavi yenu ndani ya boma lake. Hapana ruhusa kufanya mambo ya kishenzi hapa.' This is the mzungu's camp. Everything is clean here. He doesn't want your shit inside his boma. It is not allowed to follow your savage ways here.

54

The boma gates were shut after that. By then it was fully night although Hamza could hear the murmur of the village outside the walls and then, to his surprise, the muadhin calling people for the isha prayer. Later, through the open door of the lockup, Hamza saw oil lamps moving in the dark across the parade ground but none of them approached. When he woke up during the night, he saw the whitewashed building glowing in the dark. The guards were nowhere in sight. It seemed there was no one there to watch over them. Perhaps they were outside, watching to see if they would get up to any mischief, or perhaps they knew there was nowhere safe for the new arrivals to go in the dead of night.

In the morning they were lined up for inspection facing the long white building. In daylight Hamza saw that it had a tin roof painted grey and a raised wooden deck, which ran all the way across the front of the building. He could also see that the closed doors he had seen at dusk were offices or stores. He counted seven doors and eight shuttered windows. The windows and doors in the middle of the block stood open. A flagpole was planted somewhere near the middle of the open ground, which he would later learn to call the Exerzierplatz.

The Nubi ombasha who had roused them and directed them to the parade ground strode in front of them and then behind, silently prodding with his sturdy bamboo cane to straighten the line. They were all barefoot, even those who had come in with sandals, and in their everyday clothes, while the ombasha was in military khaki, leather belt with ammunition pouches, studded boots and a tarbush with an eagle emblem at the front and a neck-shade. He was a man of mature years, clean-shaven, lean and hard despite his paunch. His teeth were stained the reddish-brown of a ghat-eater. His face was glistening, unsmiling, stern and scarred on both temples – the frightening deadpan face of the Nubi askari.

When the ombasha was satisfied that the line was straight and still, he turned towards the officer who had appeared outside the open doorway of the middle office in the building in front of which they were gathered. The ombasha stiffened his spine and shouted out that the swine were ready for inspection. Hawa schwein tayari. The officer, who was also in khaki and wearing a helmet, did not move immediately but raised his swagger stick to acknowledge the ombasha. After the momentary delay necessary for his dignity, he stepped down from the raised deck and walked towards the recruits. He started at one end of the line and proceeded slowly, pausing for a longer look at some of the men but not speaking. He tapped four in the line with his stick. The ombasha had instructed them to stand still and look straight ahead, and on no account – ever – to make eye contact with a German officer. Hamza knew he had already picked him out with his eyes. He had seen that even before the officer moved from the doorway – a slim clean-shaven man – and he could not prevent a shiver when he stopped in front of him. He was not as tall as he had looked on the deck but taller than Hamza. He only stood in front of him for a few seconds and then moved on but Hamza saw without looking that his eyes were hard and almost transparent. He left behind him an astringent medicinal smell.

Four of them were sent to the carrier corps office to be recruited as stretcher-bearers or porters, the ones the officer had tapped with his stick as he walked past. Perhaps they were too old or looked slow, or simply did not please the officer's eye. He left the rest to the direction of the ombasha. Hamza was confused and terrified and wondered if he might have preferred the carrier corps despite its degraded status. He knew that was his cowardice speaking. The porters were not spared the hardships of askari life, and in addition walked about in rags and sometimes barefoot, derided by everyone. The new recruits were marched a few feet away and made to sit down on the ground in front of the smaller building, whose central downstairs door was now standing open. The other door at one end of the building was padlocked top and bottom.

There were no trees anywhere near the perimeter wall, and no shade on the parade ground. It was early morning but because he had to sit still, the sun was already unbearably hot on Hamza's neck and head. After many minutes another German officer came out of the building, followed by a man in uniform who stood a pace or two behind him. The German officer was plump, dressed in knee-length trousers and a tunic with several pockets. On his left upper arm he wore a white band with a red cross on it. He had a florid complexion and a very large brassy moustache and pale thin receding hair, and the shorts, his girth and that big moustache gave him a slightly comical air. After regarding them for a long moment, he ordered them on to their feet, then he told them to sit and then ordered them on to their feet again. He smiled, said something to the man behind him and went back inside. The assistant, also wearing a white band with a red cross on it, nodded to the ombasha and went back into the infirmary. They were then sent in there one at a time for examination.

When it was Hamza's turn he went into an airy, well-lit room with six empty beds neatly made up. To one end was a small sectioned-off consulting room with a folding table set up to one side and an examination bed to the other. The assistant, who was slim and short and weather-beaten and had a look of experience and cynicism, smiled at him and in Kiswahili asked his name, his age, his home, his religion. He spoke to the officer in German, his tone somehow sceptical about the information he was conveying. The officer too considered these details as he received them and glanced at Hamza as if to check before he wrote them down on a card. Hamza had lied about his age, claiming to be older than he was.

'Suruwali,' the assistant said, indicating his trousers, which Hamza reluctantly removed. 'Haya schnell,' the officer said because Hamza was taking too long. He leaned forward with some difficulty and took a good look at Hamza's genitals, then with a sudden upward movement slapped him lightly on the testicles. He chuckled when Hamza jumped with surprise, and shared a smile with his assistant. Then he reached forward again, and gently and repeatedly squeezed Hamza's penis in his hand until it began to stiffen. 'Inafanya kazi,' he said to the assistant – in good working order – but the words came out clumsily, as if they were awkward on his tongue or he had a speech impediment. He let go of the penis, it seemed with some reluctance. The officer then looked into Hamza's eyes, made him open his mouth and gripped him by the wrist for a short while. Then he took a needle out of a metal tray, unstoppered a small ampoule and dipped the needle in the thick fluid. He briskly scratched Hamza's upper arm with the needle and put it in another dish, which held a clear translucent liquid. The assistant then gave a Hamza a pill to swallow down with a glass of water. He smiled when Hamza flinched at its bitterness. In the meantime the officer wrote some more on his card, looked at Hamza for a long considering moment and then waved him out, smiling slightly. That was his first encounter with the medical officer.

They were given a uniform, a belt, boots and a fez. The Nubi ombasha told them: 'My name is Gefreiter Haidar al-Hamad and I am the ombasha to train you bil-askari. You will always behave with manners and you will obey me. I have fought in the north and the south and in the east and the west, for the English, for the Khedive and now for the Kaiser. I am a man of honour and experience. You are swine until I teach you bil-askari. You are washenzi like all civilians until I teach you bil-askari. You will remember every day that you are fortunate to be askari. Respect and obey or wallahi – you will see. Unafahamu? Everybody say this together: Ndio bwana. Now, this uniform, these boots, this belt, this fez … they are most important. You wear them well na keep them clean. Clean every day, this is your first duty, bil-askari. Every day you have to check your uniform, boots, belt, and everything else is check. If is not clean you will suffer kiboko na matusi in front of everyone, hamsa ishirin. You know what this is? Twenty-five strokes of the cane on your fat buttocks. When you reach askari khasa, you will wear a tarbush like me. I will teach you and you will keep clean or wallahi – you will know. Keep your equipment clean. Unafahamu?'

'Ndio bwana.'

He explained in detail how each item was to be worn and cared for. He spoke harshly in different languages, Kiswahili, Arabic and some German, his utterances broken and incomplete. He added to them with signs and gestures that were impossible to misunderstand and repeated himself until they all nodded to show they understood. Ndio bwana. 'Shabash. This is the language of the camp, unafahamu,' the ombasha said, waving his cane in the air at them. 'If you don't understand something, this will explain.'

They were housed in a barracks block in the village just outside the walls of the boma. After that first morning their lives were taken over by exhausting daily training, which began with a bugle call at first light and went on until noon. The sessions were held inside the boma and were led by the Nubi ombasha at first, the Gefreiter Haidar al-Hamad then taken over by the shaush, Unteroffizier Ali Nguru Hassan, also a Nubi, a frowning ascetic-looking man who was hard to please. Only later, after they had been training for several days, did they come to meet the German subaltern Feldwebel Walther.

The Feldwebel was tall and solidly built, with a loud booming voice. He was dark-haired with a large moustache and brown eyes that bulged and swelled when he was irate or displeased. His lips twisted scornfully with almost every utterance he made. His training sessions were energetic and exacting, and he found much in their performance to irritate him. He kept them hard at work when he was in charge, hands cocked on his hips as he rebuked them in foul and abusive language, which poured out of him like sewage down a gutter. Even when he was silent, he struggled to contain his exasperation. He was everything Hamza had expected in a German officer. He carried a swagger stick all the time, which he tapped against his right leg impatiently, sometimes quite hard. Otherwise he only used the stick to point with or to swish through the air with great violence when his anger grew too intense to control. It was beneath the dignity of a German officer to strike an askari, and he expected the ombasha, who was present at all the sessions, to step in with blows when his words needed emphasising.

The day began with a dose of quinine followed by marching drills for several hours. It was important for the schutztruppe to make a good display, the Feldwebel bellowed at them, and marching precision was essential to that. They learned how to hold their bodies military fashion, and later how to march as individuals in front of each other and then as a group while the ombasha or the shaush or the Feldwebel shouted orders and abuse. After that they learned to hold and to use their weapons, how to lie on the ground while taking aim, how to shoot and hit the target, how to move at speed and reload. Schutztruppe askari did not retreat unless ordered to, did not panic under attack and were steadfast above all else. Unafahamu? Every order was shouted and accompanied by abuse. Ndio bwana. Every error was punished by violence or hard labour, according to its severity. Punishment was constant and public, and every few days the whole troop, recruits and veteran askari alike, were marched into the boma to witness the hamsa ishirin, the twenty-five lashes, a public flogging for one misdemeanour or another, which often did not seem deserving of such humiliation. It was to make them obedient and fearless, the ombasha told them. The flogging was always carried out by an African askari, never a German.

In the afternoons they tidied the boma and their barrack building, and performed other duties as instructed. They cleaned their weapons, their shoes and leggings, their uniforms. There were many inspections and every blemish was punished, either individually or sometimes as a whole group. They performed physical exercises to strengthen their bodies, running, forced marches and body-building drills. Most of the recruits in Hamza's group were from the local area and understood each other, but other languages were spoken in the troop: Arabic, Kinyamwezi and German mostly. Words from all these languages were churned up together with Kiswahili, some form of which was the main language of the troops.

Hamza lost himself in the exhausting routine. In the first rush of panic after joining up he had feared that he would be scorned and bullied by men who were used to violence and held only strength and toughness in high esteem. An order soon became evident in his group, and strength and agility was part of that. The enthusiasm and power of two among them, Komba and Fulani, marked them out as natural leaders and no one contested that right. Fulani had some military experience already although not of the schutztruppe calibre. He was a Mnyamwezi who had worked as a guard in a merchant's private army, and it was the merchant who named him Fulani, which means So-and-so, because he could never remember his Kinyamwezi name. Fulani liked the dash of this name and embraced it. Komba was very strong-looking and confident, a natural athlete. These two led in all the drills, chatted up the women who brought their food, traded innuendos with them and promised to visit them later in the evening. They were always served first and served plentifully. They were the ones the ombasha always praised and the Feldwebel fawned over and then reserved his worst abuse for. Komba laughed at the Feldwebel behind his back and called him Jogoo, the Cockerel. He strutted like one whenever the women were around. They all understood that the Feldwebel's assault on the two men, and Komba in particular, was a recognition of their primacy in the troop. He had to overpower them to establish his own authority without diminishing them. Hamza shuffled to defer to that order and find his own place in it, as did the rest of the troop.

The ascendancy of Fulani and Komba did not seem important or a problem to Hamza because it was the intensity of the training and the general fear of punishment that mostly preoccupied the group. No one had any answer to the scorn and violence of the Gefreiter or the Unteroffizier, and especially not to that of Feldwebel Walther. None of the instructors was addressed by name or addressed at all, just obeyed with as much alacrity as possible. Only Komba managed to get away with anything because he was an insolent dandy who made it seem that he was not conscious of causing offence or was far from intending disrespect.

Nevertheless, despite the harsh regime, Hamza found unexpected satisfaction in his own growing strength and skills, and after a while he no longer winced at the shouts of schwein and washenzi or the German words he did not yet understand, which their trainers spat at them constantly. Unexpectedly, he began to feel pride at being part of the group, not rejected and mocked as he had feared, but there to share in the punishing routines and the exhaustion and the grumbling, to feel his body becoming stronger and responding skilfully to commands, to march with the precision his instructors demanded. It took him longer to get used to the rank smell of exhausted sleeping bodies and the gases they expelled. The banter was brutal but everyone suffered from it and Hamza learned to take his share and keep his head down. When they started going out on manoeuvres he saw the terror of the villagers when the askari arrived and could not suppress a thrill of pleasure at their fright.

The officer remained a distant figure after that first morning. Their morning training was often conducted on the boma parade ground, the Exerzierplatz, and the officer sometimes came out to watch them. He did not step down from the raised wooden deck or stay watching for long. More often he was away from the boma on field manoeuvres with the regular units. They learned from the other askari that these were called shauri missions, consultation meetings to explain government policy or to hand out judgements on disputes or to carry out punishments on villages and chiefs who had offended. When their unit joined a shauri mission for training, Hamza realised there was not much consultation involved. The manoeuvres were to discipline and terrify the stupid washenzi villagers and make them obey government instructions without questioning them.

After they had been training for several weeks, the officer stepped down from the deck one morning and approached them. The moment seemed prearranged as all three of their training officers were in attendance, the Gefreiter Haidar al-Hamad, the Unteroffizier Ali Nguru Hassan and Feldwebel Walther. They were in full regalia as was the officer in his gleaming white garrison uniform. The ombasha had explained that those among their group who were scheduled for special training in the signals detachment or the band would be selected during this parade. One of their number played the trumpet, although none of them had heard him, and he intended to apply to join the musikkapelle. He asked the ombasha's permission to put himself forward. Selection for the signals detachment required the ability to read, but although Hamza could read he had not put himself forward for that. He had chosen not to do so, concerned not to draw any attention to himself, but Haidar the ombasha had seen him reading aloud to the others from the government Kiswahili newspaper *Kiongozi* during one of their rest periods. When he was explaining to them the selection process that would take place during the parade, the ombasha glanced towards Hamza as he mentioned the signals detachment.

The officer walked along the line as he had done that first morning, only this time he stopped in front of each of them in turn for a detailed inspection. At the end of this he stood a few feet in front of the troop, which stood to attention. The Feldwebel called out the trumpeter's name, which was Abudu, and he stood forward two steps as instructed. Then he called out Hamza's name and he did the same. The officer saluted and walked back to his office. The troop marched off, leaving Abudu and Hamza standing in the Exerzierplatz. They stood to attention as ordered while the late-morning sun beat on them. They both knew this was another punishing test and that if they moved or spoke there would be an unpleasant punishment to follow and the end of any further training. To Hamza it seemed a cruel caprice to no purpose but it was too late for such wisdom and there was nothing else to do but endure.

It was difficult to tell how long they stood to attention in the late-morning sun, a quarter of an hour maybe, but after some time ombasha Haidar returned and instructed Abudu to follow him while Hamza remained standing in the Exerzierplatz. Then it was his turn, and he marched ahead of the ombasha as instructed up to the open door of the office where he was momentarily blinded by the deep shade. Herein, a voice spoke from within. It was the first time he had heard the officer's voice, and Hamza felt its severity through his sinews. He stepped into a large office with two windows at the front and a desk at the end facing the door. There was a chair in front of the desk and another small table set against the wall on which stood a draughtsman's board. The officer was sitting behind the desk, leaning back in his chair. His face was leaner without his helmet and there was a wrinkle of the skin on his left upper cheek and temple below the hairline. His eyes were a piercing blue.

After a long deliberate silence the officer spoke in German and the ombasha translated. 'The Oberleutnant asks if you want to be signalman.'

'Yes, sir,' Hamza said loudly, addressing the air above the officer's head and speaking with as much conviction as he could. He did not know if being a signalman was any safer than being an askari but it was not the moment to quibble.

The officer spoke again briefly. 'Why?' the ombasha translated.

Hamza had not thought of an answer to this question although he should have done. After a moment's thought he said, 'To learn a new skill and to serve the schutztruppe as well as I can.'

He glanced quickly at the officer and saw that he smiled. It was Hamza's first sight of the sneer he would come to know well. 'Can you read?' the ombasha translated again.

'I can read a little.'

The officer made an interrogative face, asking him to clarify. Hamza did not know how to add to that. He knew all the letters and with patience could make out words if they were in Kiswahili. He was not sure if that was what the officer wanted to know so he stared above his head and said nothing. The officer spoke in German, speaking slowly and looking at the ombasha who waited until he had finished and then translated. The words came out in the Nubi's usual mangled style and because Hamza stood facing the officer, he saw on the edge of his vision that he winced slightly at times at the ombasha's excesses. It was said that the officer spoke the best Kiswahili of all the Germans.

'The Oberleutnant say why you don't learn more to read? Why you don't read everything like he can? Everything he put in front of you, kelb, and you don't learn. You have no civilisation, that is why you savage. He say you must learn. What word he say … messatik … something like that. You don't know that.'

'Mathematics,' the officer said.

'Yes, mesthamatik, you don't know that, you kelb, you savage dog,' the ombasha said.

'Nini jina la mathematics kwa lugha yako?' the officer asked, doing without the ombasha after all. What is the word for mathematics in your language? 'Do you know what mathematics is? You can't understand anything of the world's learning without mathematics, not music or philosophy, let alone the mechanics of signalling. Unafahamu?'

'Ndio bwana,' Hamza said loudly.

'You don't even know what mathematics is, do you? We have come here to bring you this, mathematics and many other clever things that you would not have without us. This is our Zivilisierungmission,' the officer said, and then gestured with his left arm towards the window at the boma outside, his lean face and thin lips creased in a sardonic smile. 'This is our cunning plot, which only a child could misunderstand. We have come here to civilise you. Unafahamu?'

'Ndio bwana.'

The officer spoke Kiswahili carefully, searching for the right vocabulary, but it was as if he was performing a language he had no control over, as if he had the words but not their emotion, wanting them to speak in a way they were not suited to. His eyes had a watchful light, which wavered between curiosity and scorn, constantly looking to see the effect his words had on Hamza. He in turn studied the officer as best he could without making eye contact. At other times, as he was to learn later, those eyes held the bright glitter of a man capable of violence.

'Only I don't think you will ever learn mathematics. It requires a mental discipline you people are not capable of. That's enough for now,' the officer said abruptly, and waved them out of his office.

Hamza found out later that day that he had been assigned as the officer's personal servant, his batman, and was required to report to his residence first thing in the morning to be instructed in his duties by the outgoing batman. His request for a posting to the signals detachment was refused. He was not told why. Komba led the mockery when the assignment became known.

'You are a shoga,' he said, 'that's why he picked you. He wants someone sweet and pretty to massage his back and serve his dinner for him. It gets cold up there in the mountains, and he will need someone to keep him warm at night, just like a little wife. What are you doing here? Anyone can see you are too pretty to be a soldier.'

'These Germans, they like playing with pretty young men, especially ones with such nice manners as you have. Kwa hisani yako,' Fulani said, waving his hand and softening his voice. If you please.

'Yes, what a dreamy little beauty you are,' Komba said, reaching out as if to stroke Hamza's cheek.

Others joined in, pretending to be him, walking with extravagant effeminacy as they play-acted serving food and massaging a back. 'When the German tires of you, you can always come back and stroke my back,' someone said. It was a long time before they tired of the game and left him alone. By then Hamza was silently cringing with humiliation and fearful that their predictions of what was to befall him would turn out to be true. He had felt himself one of them, had shared their privations and punishments, and no one among them had spoken to him in such a slighting way before. It was as if they were forcibly expelling him from their midst.

4

They had no word from Ilyas but that was nothing to worry about, Khalifa said. 'Dar es Salaam is a long way away. We should not expect to hear for a while. We'll get news when someone comes from Dar es Salaam or perhaps he'll send us a note. Sooner or later we'll hear from him.'

In the early days when she went to live with Bimkubwa and Baba Khalifa, Afiya slept on a thin kapok mattress on the floor in the same room as they did. There was a room in the backyard that was used as a store. The basket of charcoal was kept in there, and some old pots and sticks of furniture, which were bound to come in useful one day. Khalifa said he would clean it up and prepare it for her. It would need a coat of limewash to kill off the bugs but should be a comfortable room after that. There was another store room at the front of the house with its own door. 'We can move the junk in there,' Khalifa said. 'There's no hurry. First let her get used to us here. She is only a little girl. Let her get over her fears.'

'She is not a baby,' Bi Asha said, but did not insist.

Afiya was still feverish and her hand pained her, although a little less each day. Bi Asha took her to a bone-setter who massaged the hand and then put it in a cast made from herbs and flour and eggs. 'It will help the bones to heal,' he said. He took it off after a few days and taught her exercises to improve the hand's movement. He told Bi Asha, 'I don't know if she will get full use of it back. It may be there is permanent damage to the fibres in the hand.'

Bi Asha prayed for her and taught her to read the Koran. If we read together then you will not be thinking so much about your pain and God will bless you and reward you, she said. It took several weeks of daily effort for Afiya to advance enough in her learning to manage the small suras, but when she did, Bi Asha sent her to one of the neighbours, Bi Habiba, who gave lessons in her home to four other girls every morning. Bi Asha thought the company of other children would make Afiya learn better. To Khalifa she confided that she had doubts that Bi Habiba was much of a teacher. The little girls knew how to exploit her lenient ways and avoid their lessons by tricking her into telling them stories.

'What stories?' Khalifa asked. He liked stories.

'I don't know,' Bi Asha said tetchily, knowing that he had missed the point. 'I expect they are stories about the Prophet and his companions, but they should be practising reading. That's what I am paying her for.'

'Oh, good stories,' Khalifa said, exasperating Bi Asha who thought she heard something slighting in his tone. She was often irritated by his deliberate show of indifference to matters of piety.

'Yes, I hope good stories,' she said. 'Do you think I am paying for her to go and listen to gossip?'

'You're probably not paying enough for gossip,' he said, pleased with his own wit.

As the weeks passed, Afiya read more fluently and her hand healed enough for her to help with chores in the house after the class, which was for two hours or so first thing in the morning. When she came back from Bi Habiba's she gave an account of what she read that morning and sometimes had to give a demonstration to Bimkubwa. After that Afiya accompanied her to the market to buy vegetables and fruit, and perhaps meat on meat-eating days. Bi Asha taught her the cost of produce and how to pay for it, how to handle the money. When you are old enough, you'll go shopping for me, she said. Sometimes they passed the house of the merchant Nassor Biashara and saw Khalifa sitting at his desk in the office, facing the open door. The office was a downstairs room in the merchant's house. He and his family lived upstairs. Later in the morning every day, after their return from the market, a man came around from house to house selling fresh fish out of a basket. He bought from the fishermen on the beach to save his customers from having to go there and haggle among the scales and fish guts. Afiya learned how to prepare the fish: to crush the garlic and the ginger and the chillies on the grinding stone and rub the paste over and inside the flesh. She could grind the paste with one hand while steadying the stone with the other, even though she could not grip properly with her left hand. In this as in many other ways she learned to cope with her injury.

She went to see the family with whom she used to lodge when she lived with Ilyas, the sisters Jamila and Saada and their mother. They were pleased to see her and welcomed her as kindly as they had done before. They noticed her awkwardness with the hand and asked about it. She told them that her uncle beat her because she had learned to write and the mother said such ignorance was a sin. The elder of the sisters, Jamila, was betrothed by now but her father said she was too young to marry and must wait until she was eighteen, otherwise her life would be ruined by child-bearing when she had not even had her youth. Jamila said she was happy at home and did not mind waiting, nor did her fiancé. He lived in Zanzibar and they had only met once, so did not know each other well enough for Jamila to miss him. They asked about Ilyas and Afiya said she had no news. May God keep him safe, the mother said. Whenever I go past your old room downstairs I think of you two living there.

Khalifa came home for lunch every day, which was served immediately after Bi Asha said the midday prayers. Afiya was required to accompany her in prayer but Khalifa usually managed to arrive just after they finished. At first Bi Asha said the ritual words aloud so that Afiya could hear and repeat them. In prayer, she explained to her, a person is speaking directly to God and cannot break off to address someone else or do something else. So she could not stop to explain and instruct during the prayer and Afiya would have to learn by example and repetition. After lunch Khalifa pottered around their bedroom in his shirt and kikoi, and then stretched himself out on a mat for an afternoon nap. Bi Asha did the same in the bed and Afiya was left to amuse herself. She liked these quiet hours in the middle of the day when the streets themselves seemed to fall silent in the heat. She washed up the pots, cleaned the braziers and swept the backyard. Then she sat in a corner of the yard with her slate or scraps of paper and practised writing or else read from the Koran Bi Asha bought her. Everyone should have her own copy, she said, not even glancing at Khalifa who had long ago mislaid his.

The muadhin's call to the afternoon prayer was the signal for the adults to get up, Khalifa to have a quick wash and return to work for two hours or so, and Bi Asha to do a few chores in the house and then go out to call on neighbours or receive them. One day Khalifa asked Afiya if she wanted to come to the office with him or if she preferred visiting with the neighbours, so she went with him. There were three desks in the office, the large room open to the road that Bi Asha and she passed on their way to market. The desk in the middle, facing the door, was Baba Khalifa's. The one to the right of the door was the merchant Nassor Biashara's whom Afiya was meeting for the first time today although she had heard him spoken of a great deal as the greedy scoundrel or, more sarcastically, as our rich merchant. She expected to see someone very much older than he was, with mean and miserly features.

She was installed at the desk to the left of the door with a pencil and some scrap paper that Baba Khalifa found for her. Sometimes men came in to talk or do business, but mostly to catch up with the latest news and gossip. For most people it was the only way of keeping track of what was going on in the world. The visitors often said something about her. I see you have a new clerk, or I see someone in this office who looks as if she knows what she is doing. She listened to their talk of politics and government crises while she pretended to be busy with her scratchings. Their talk was often about the coming war and the ferocity of the schutztruppe, of whom they spoke with a mixture of repugnance and admiration. They are animals, those askari, she heard them say. She asked Khalifa if they were the same askari Ilyas went to fight with or if they were different.

'They are the same but also different,' Khalifa said. 'Not all of them are the fierce brutes the men were talking about. Some of them are policemen or clerks or medical orderlies, some even play music in a band. I think Ilyas will be one of those others. We are sure to have word from him soon. He must have finished his training by now and he will come home for a few days then, no doubt. We can ask him when we see him.'

The merchant did not usually say much to her. He was often busy with his ledgers and his letters or with his visitors, and in any case was not much of a talker. When there was talking going on, he was usually the listener while his visitors and Baba held forth. He wore wire-framed glasses when he wrote and Afiya had not seen anyone wearing these before. Unaware of what she was doing, she once stood staring at him as he worked. She wondered if it hurt to wear them, the way the handles curled behind his ears. Nassor Biashara eventually looked up and pushed the glasses to the top of his head. He rubbed his eyes for a few seconds then sat back and gazed at her.

'What are you staring at?' he asked.

She pointed to his glasses and Khalifa said sharply, 'Don't point at someone's face like that.'

The merchant spoke just as sharply. 'Leave her alone,' he said, and then she understood that he disliked Baba Khalifa just as much as Baba disliked him.

She had a fit of coughing in the office one day, and Nassor Biashara looked towards her with a frown of concern. Come with me, he said when her coughing did not stop. The door to their residence upstairs was just next to the office and he stood at the bottom of the stairs and called up, 'Khalida, Afiya is coming up for some water.' That was how she met the merchant's wife, and after that whenever she went to the office with Baba Khalifa, which was not every day, she went upstairs for a drink of water and sometimes a slice of rice cake. Khalida had a young baby and did not go out much, so she often had visitors, her friends and neighbours, wives and relatives of other merchants and the people who worked for them. They sat with her in their perfumed kangas and rustling chiffon dresses and talked about weddings and births and bequeathings. Afiya listened open-mouthed as they mocked people with vicious delight: men who swaggered with conceit, women who gave themselves airs, dignitaries whom rumour exposed as hypocrites, some living and some already passed on. They spared their own husbands and their relatives, but were merciless with anyone else they brought into their conversations. She did not bother to pretend that she was not listening. They laughed at her avid attention and warned each other, with winks and raised eyebrows and some coded words, not to say too much in front of the little girl. She knew when they were talking about something they did not want her to know – some people in this room have big ears – because they hummed and coughed and spoke in a roundabout way and used hand signals, laughing among themselves as they played these games. She generally worked out what they were trying to hide from her although she pretended not to. It was a long time before she realised that not everything they said about other people was true.

In this way Afiya filled her time: the class with Bi Habiba, which was in the hallway of her tiny house, the stories she told them of miraculous events befalling the Prophets of God, from Nabi Musa to Nabi Ibrahim to Nabi Issa, and above all to the Messenger of God, salallahuwaale. She visited Jamila and Saada and their mother, sat in the merchant's office while the men talked and she wrote and drew on her scraps of paper, and then went upstairs to see the merchant's wife Khalida and her friends and eat rice cake as she listened to their slanders. She did not think it at the time but later she knew that it was a period of contentment for her, those first months when she came to live with Bimkubwa and Baba Khalifa.

*

The junk in the room in the backyard was finally removed to the store at the front of the house. Afterwards the walls were limewashed and the floor was swept and washed with soapy water and the window frame was varnished and the bars were painted.

'In the time before, my father used to keep trade goods in that store at the front of the house,' Bi Asha said. 'Our tajiri Nassor has asked to keep his rubbish in there but I said no. He would

72

want to lock it and keep the key. That would be the beginning – first the store then the yard and then the whole house – and after that we would be out on the street. Nothing is beyond that scoundrel. What trade goods did my father keep in there? Whatever turned up. Everyone traded with whatever came their way: sacks of rice going cheap, which can be sold on, maize or millet after a good harvest to be shipped on, metal trays, rosewater, dates. Some of the goods were from here and some from across the sea. One year he bought dozens of clay water-pots from India, no one knew why. They remained in the store for years, and I don't know what happened to them in the end. My father was not a very good trader and somehow always managed to make wrong decisions, buy or sell at the wrong time, or at the wrong price. Anyway, he did not make any money, my poor father, and then he let Uncle Amur steal this house from him.'

A new bed with a mosquito-net frame was delivered from Nassor Biashara's workshop as a gift to Afiya from the merchant. The mattress-maker came and unstitched the worn-out mattress she slept on on the floor and filled it with new kapok. A new net was ordered from the tailor and hung glowing white in its frame. For the first time in her life, at the age of twelve, Afiya had the unexpected luxury of a room of her own. She found it a little frightening at first in her little room in the yard, but she did not say so. She bolted her door and kept one of the window casements slightly ajar as instructed. Then she tucked in the ends of her mosquito net and gradually learned to ignore the sinister rustlings that teemed in the dark.

'You don't know how lucky you are,' Bi Asha told her, but she was smiling, not scolding. 'I hope we are not spoiling you with all these comforts.'

Khalifa began to talk about how at the same age he was sleeping on a mat under the stairs in his teacher's house with several other boys and how it was worth it in the end, but Bi Asha cut him off. He is starting with his Indian stories again, she said. Khalifa smiled indulgently and went to lie down after lunch.

One morning, as Afiya was on her way to Bi Habiba's Koran class, Bi Asha gave her a kanga and showed her how to wear it.

You are growing up now. To preserve decency you must cover yourself when you go out, she said.

She knew her nipples ached and were swelling and had noticed that men's eyes fell to her chest when she walked in the streets. She realised also that Nassor Biashara preferred that she should go upstairs while his male visitors were in the office. She thought it embarrassed him the way they looked at her. She knew what was happening without anyone explaining it to her, and she accepted the kanga gratefully and covered herself as she was told.

5

The officer had the two-room apartment at one end of the upstairs block on the right-hand side of the boma. It had a small bedroom and another room with two comfortable chairs and a small desk where the officer sometimes sat down to write. There were seven rooms upstairs altogether, a replica of the downstairs layout, and there was a hierarchy to the arrangement. The two rooms at one end for the use of the commanding officer stood next to a large room in the middle of the block that was the mess, then came a room for each of the other four officers, beginning with the medical officer and ending with the Feldwebel, who had the small room at the far end because he was the lowest in rank. The other three officers in the boma had their rooms in the smaller building facing the gate, whose downstairs served as the infirmary and the padlocked store. The store contained provisions for the officers' mess: tins of European delicacies and bottles of beer and wine and schnapps and brandy. The arrangements in both blocks were very orderly. The washrooms for both were downstairs in separate buildings. The sleeping quarters for the men who served the officers were in a two-roomed outhouse behind the blocks with an attached washroom that they shared. Hamza and Julius, who served the other four officers in their block, shared one room, and the two who served the smaller block shared the other.

Julius was much older than Hamza, in his late thirties. He was the senior orderly and had served in the schutztruppe for more than ten years. He could speak a little German and understood a lot more. He was the only one of them who was allowed in the provisions store, the key to which was held by the officer in charge of supplies. Julius was given that responsibility because he could write, he explained to the others. If he took anything from the store, he had to enter it into the book kept in there. He told Hamza about his mission education in Bagamoyo but chose to be imprecise about how long he had been in school. He was proud of his education and his religion. Now and then he would say: If like me you were educated and a Christian, you would think differently about whatever. Julius was slightly wounded in a tax raid on a village and his commanding officer posted him to batman's duties while he recovered. 'This is my third year and no one has thought to move me so I must be doing it well,' he said.

The water did not run upstairs, not yet, although there were plans to introduce it, so in the morning Hamza filled the officer's washbasin with fresh water and then went to fetch his coffee from the cooking shed. The officers' meals were cooked in a shed inside the boma by women from the village, all of whom were wives of askari. By the time Hamza came back the officer was out of his inner room and dressed in his shirt and trousers, waiting for his coffee to arrive. Hamza then went into the inner room to make the bed and straighten out his clothes, often feeling the officer's eyes on him through the open door. After that he went to the mess to help Julius set the table for breakfast. The officers from both blocks ate their breakfast in the mess and met there for a formal dinner every evening. Julius explained the crockery and cutlery required and the rudiments of serving at table. Then they went downstairs to wait for the men who served the smaller block to deliver breakfast from the kitchen shed and after that Hamza and Julius laid it out in their mess and called for the officers.

After breakfast they cleared and washed the dishes, which were for the exclusive use of the officers, put them away in the cupboards, cleaned the mess and then saw to the private rooms. Hamza tidied and dusted and aired the officer's apartment, emptied and cleaned the washbasin and the chamber pot, then swept the veranda front and back and took the soiled linen in its own named bag downstairs for the laundrywoman to collect. It was a very orderly routine and he was expected to be all done by seven in the morning.

In the first few weeks of his new posting as the officer's personal servant, he joined his troop in their drill session soon after seven because he had not completed his initial training. He saw them in the Exerzierplatz earlier than that, being put through their paces by the ombasha or the shaush while he swept the veranda or ironed the officer's tunic and he longed to join them. When he could, he threw himself into the drill in an attempt to shake off the sense of unworthiness his intimate servitude to the officer made him feel. Sometimes they went out to the field for target practice or manoeuvres but he could not join them if they were going far. Just before noon he had to rush away to clean up and be ready to serve lunch to any officers who were eating in the mess on that day. By lunchtime it was often too hot to linger, and the officers bolted their food and hurried away to their rooms to rest until it was cooler. To Hamza this was a blessed part of the day when the boma and all the surrounding buildings in the settlement subsided and fell silent. Even the goats and the dogs in the village flopped down in a shady corner and panted the hot hours away. He took his time in the mess and on the back veranda because it was coolest there at that time of day, and when he retreated to the shared room downstairs he usually found Julius already asleep.

At approximately four in the afternoon, as the muadhin was calling people to the alasiri prayer in the settlement mosque outside the boma, Hamza took a cup of coffee to the officer who by then would have showered and gone to his office. The Oberleutnant instructed him to stay nearby and his post was outside on the deck, sitting on a stool, within earshot if needed. This was the routine every afternoon. He was sent on various errands to the other officers or was asked to provide whatever additional acts of comfort the officer required: a glass of water, a cup of coffee or a fresh towel. From the beginning, at some point in those afternoon hours, the officer called Hamza in and taught him German, probably to amuse himself at first but also because Hamza proved to be such a willing learner. It began with naming things.

'Fenster. You say it,' the officer said, pointing to the window. 'Tür, you say it. Stuhl, Auge, Herz, Kopf.' Door, chair, eye, heart, head, pointing or touching himself as he spoke.

Then Hamza had to repeat whole sentences: 'Mein Name ist Siegfried. No no, you say your name. Mein Name ist Hamza. Sie sind herzlich willkommen in meinem Land. You say it, but you have to say like you believe it. Sie sind herzlich willkommen in meinem Land. That's good. You say it very well. It means you are welcome to my country,' the officer said with his sneering smile.

Then he sent Hamza to the draughtsman's table on which a book of field instructions was open with a blank sheet of paper beside it. He made him copy a few lines so that he could familiarise himself with writing German words. Every day he wrote a few which he then had to read aloud without at first knowing what they meant. At every opportunity the officer spoke to him in German, which at times he found amusing, and Hamza exaggerated his bafflement to make his superior laugh. If Hamza did not understand something, the officer translated it but the next time he expected him to understand and reply. Sometimes the officer played tricks on him and made him repeat self-mocking words before laughing and explaining them. It was a game for the officer, and it pleased him that Hamza was so responsive and quick. I will have you reading Schiller soon, he said, his eyes alight with mischief.

His eyes. Sometimes while Hamza was making the bed or sweeping the front veranda or ironing a shirt, he glanced round to find those transparent blue eyes fixed immovably on him. The first time it happened, he thought the officer had said something and was waiting for a reply, but the eyes did not move and the lips did not open. Then Hamza moved away in confusion, troubled by the intensity of those eyes. He came to sense a certain stillness at times when he was near the officer, and knew that if he looked, he would find those eyes fixed on him in that same way. It was an insolent and intrusive inspection, leaving him with no choice but to allow himself to be scrutinised at such length, to be viewed as if he were incapable of returning that gaze. He learned not to look.

His success at learning to speak and read a little German delighted the officer. He displayed Hamza's achievements to the other officers in the mess, especially during and after their evening meals, when they had beer and schnapps to drink. He invited them to speak to Hamza, to try him out. The medical officer smiled benignly and looked him up and down as if searching for some evidence of his facility for German on his body. The other two officers in his block joined more willingly in their superior officer's game and asked the simple friendly questions an adult might address to a child. Wie alt sind Sie? The other officers laughed and added comments Hamza did not understand, which amused them even more. Feldwebel Walther was not amused by the officers' new game and snorted dismissively, later whispering in an angry mocking tone words that Hamza did not know but which, from the tone they were uttered in, he guessed were obscene or scornful. Julius smiled patronisingly during these exercises and told him afterwards that the officers were making a monkey out of him. Hamza left as soon as he could, to get away from their condescension and before the drinking and hilarity turned ugly.

'Don't take any notice of the Feldwebel,' Julius told him. 'He is a low-class man who should not be staying in the same building as these honourable officers. He smokes too much bangi then he goes chasing women in the village outside. His room stinks of smoke.'

Sometimes the drinking sessions went on late, perhaps when one of the officers was due to leave on a mission to discipline a village or a chief, or to go on an extended field manoeuvre. Then their voices and laughter could be heard all over the boma, and the Oberleutnant would be wracked by headaches the following morning, gripping his temples with outstretched fingers while his eyes were screwed up in agony. He always suffered like that after the late nights.

One afternoon Hamza came into the office with coffee and greeted the commanding officer as he was required to in German, but he was so engaged in what he was reading that he did not reply. The papers he held in his hand had the look of an official document, and Hamza saw the government crest on the top of the page. Eventually the officer noticed Hamza and waved him out of the office, and he did not call him back for their usual half-hour conversation class. When he came in to collect the coffee cup, the officer was leaning back in his chair with a vacant look in his eyes, deep in thought. Hamza waited to see if there were any further instructions. When there were not, he moved forward to collect the coffee tray. He was so absorbed in his scrutiny of the officer that he became careless in his movements. He stumbled against the desk and the crockery on the tray rattled noisily. The officer's head spun round, a look of rage in his eyes. 'Fuck off out of here,' he said.

There was a charge in the atmosphere in the mess that evening, which must have been to do with what the officer had been reading earlier in the afternoon. The officer must have received new orders. The talk between the officers was generally excited but at times briefly sombre, and altogether far too fluent and fast-moving for Hamza to follow with assurance. He did not think they were speaking so fast deliberately to baffle him and Julius. For a while they seemed unaware the servants were even there, but at some point they exchanged glances and must have decided that they did not want to run the risk of being understood. The commanding officer nodded at the Feldwebel who ordered Julius and Hamza to leave the mess. Hamza heard many words whose meaning he came to understand more fully later but the one he knew already was Krieg. Vita. War.

He asked Julius when they were back in their room, 'Who are we fighting?'

'Who do you think? Did you not hear them say it was going to be a big war? I thought you were a miracle German speaker,' he said, scowling with disdain. 'It could be the Belge or the Portuguese, but the British won't let them do that, so it must be all of them. We'll be fighting all of them. The Germans wouldn't say it was going to be a big war if they were talking about Wachagga or Wahadimu.'

The following morning, when Hamza brought him his coffee, the officer said with one of his sardonic smiles, 'No drill for you today. You missed a class yesterday. I want you in my office as soon as you have done your chores. We must not allow communications from the high command to interfere with your lessons.'

In time the routine changed. The officer wanted Hamza nearby more and more often. The game of teaching his servant to speak and read German absorbed him and began to turn serious. He even issued a challenge to his officers, after several drinks, betting them that he would have their young schüler reading Schiller before the monsoons arrived. Which monsoons? The other officers laughed. Maybe ten years from now.

As before, every morning Hamza filled the officer's washbasin with warm fresh water and then went to fetch his coffee. It had to be made every day from beans roasted the previous evening and pounded first thing in the morning. He did not know if the women in the cooking shed followed these instructions exactly but the officer did not complain. When he came back with the coffee the officer was still in bed in the inner room and took his coffee there when before he would have been up and dressed in his shirt and trousers. Hamza waited on the back veranda while the officer washed and then called him in to help with his boots and leggings. Once Hamza came back in too soon, when he judged that the officer was finished washing, and saw him standing bare-chested in the inner room. His torso was blotched with burn scars. Hamza retreated hastily and waited to be called back. He expected a rebuke but the officer merely talked to him as he usually did at this hour and made him reply. He called it their first conversation class of the day. Perhaps he had not seen Hamza enter. Then Hamza went into the inner room to make the bed while the officer continued the conversation as he was shaving. At times the Oberleutnant fell silent and Hamza knew without looking that he was staring at him in that strange way of his.

After breakfast he and Julius cleared the mess and saw to the rooms and their other chores, and then Hamza reported to the Oberleutnant's office. He tidied what needed tidying then waited outside for instructions. He carried messages to the other officers and sometimes to the troops outside the boma in the village. He wandered around there if he was not in a hurry, and if it was the right time he went to the mosque for prayers and the company. Every day he collected the sick report from the medical officer who refused to let his assistant bring it to the Oberleutnant because he said he was a medical orderly, not an errand boy. Many of the officers and the askari suffered from attacks of malaria from time to time, even though they all took a dose of quinine every day and slept under mosquito nets. Some were already infected before they joined up but there were also times on manoeuvres when they were unprotected and the mosquitoes could do their work. There were cases of dysentery and venereal diseases and jiggers in the toes. There were small outbreaks of typhoid, which had to be rigorously isolated and contained in the infirmary. It was from his surreptitious reading of the sick report that Hamza learned the well-kept secret of opium addiction among the Nubi non-commissioned officers.

When he made his daily call at the infirmary, the medical officer smiled at him in a knowing way Hamza had come to dislike but had to pretend not to notice. One morning as he handed over the report, the medical officer said to his assistant, speaking carefully for Hamza's benefit, 'This young man has become an obsession of our Oberleutnant's. He is going to make him a scholar. He has promised us that this young man will soon be reading to him at bedtime.'

The two men shared a smile, which the assistant allowed to slide into a leer. Sometimes when Hamza was serving in the mess and he was close to the medical officer's chair, he felt his thigh being stroked as he passed. The medical officer did it so that no one else noticed and then, when he caught Hamza's eye, gave him that same smile. Hamza asked Julius if he did that to him too and he grinned and said no.

'It's you he's after. He likes you. Didn't you know? Everyone knows that the medical officer is a basha. People say that his assistant is his wife. Even in Germany itself the soldiers are allowed to have sex with each other. One of the governors of this whole Deutsch-Ostafrika was a basha. There was a court case a few years ago when he was accused of keeping a manservant just for sex.'

'The governor himself was taken to court? Who can take the governor to court?' Hamza asked. 'Doesn't the governor own the court?'

'This is a Christian government,' Julius said with a tiny smug smile. 'No one owns the court.'

'But the governor, taken to court because he is a basha!' Hamza said, still incredulous.

'Yes, the governor himself and several of his officers. Did you not hear about that?'

'No,' Hamza said.

Julius looked pityingly at him. He considered Hamza unfortunate in many ways and told him so, not least because of his lack of a mission education and his backward religion. Hamza guessed that Julius thought himself better suited to serve the commanding officer instead of having to look after those of lesser rank, especially the bad-tempered Feldwebel, a disgraceful class of man in Julius's often-repeated opinion. He dropped his voice now as he continued, 'I have heard even the Kaiser himself,' he whispered, nodding his head meaningfully.

'No, you're adding too much salt,' Hamza said in exaggerated disbelief. 'The Kaiser himself.'

'Not so loud! Yes, only they try to hush all this up because they are afraid we will laugh at them.'

When Hamza was not running errands or sitting out of the way on the stool outside the office, and the commanding officer was not occupied with military duties in the boma or in the field, he called him in, on a whim it seemed, and made him sit at the draughtsman's table with some writing exercise. It was often copying from the field manual, which had translations of simple phrases from German to Kiswahili and a variety of instructions in German that Hamza had to copy and translate. When he did not know a word, he spoke it out loud and the officer told him its meaning. Sometimes the lesson was reversed and the officer asked for the Kiswahili word for something. What is the word for frankincense? Ubani. How do you say numb? Ganzi. What is the word for foam? Foam? Bubbles. Mapovu.

The officer sometimes interrupted his own work to have a few minutes' conversation with Hamza. He gave him an almost imperceptible nod of approval when he did well, and smiled with reluctant glee when he achieved something unexpected. You are doing very well, he told him, but you're not yet ready for Schiller. Lessons sometimes continued in the afternoon as well so Hamza felt, as he had never done before, like someone at school. They ended with the muadhin calling people to the maghrib prayer in the village outside the boma, which was usually the signal for the officer to pour himself his first schnapps of the evening.

Hamza was now visibly under the Oberleutnant's protection, and while he was not spared the bullying and abuse that was regular military practice in the boma, he was at least safe from the floggings and hard labour which were inescapable for many of the troops. He was not spared the Feldwebel's contempt, though. He called Hamza a toy soldier behind the commanding officer's back.

'Whose toy are you? You are his pretty toy, little shoga plaything, aren't you?' he said, wagging a finger in disdainful warning and once reaching out and squeezing Hamza's nipple. 'You make me sick.'

A kind of gloom descended on the Oberleutnant at times and he fell silent for long periods, or else spoke cryptic words that sounded like self-mockery. When Hamza looked up enquiringly, he said something cruel or scornful. Do you want to know exactly what I said, you slow-witted baboon? Hamza learned not to look up when he sensed this mood and, if he could, kept his distance. He had known from the beginning that the officer was capable of violence. He had seen it in the light in his eyes which glistened involuntarily, and in the tightening of the skin at his temple, as if he were suppressing a burning urge. When he was in deep concentration or sunk in despondency, he kneaded that fold of skin abstractedly. Hamza dreaded these dark moments when he was vulnerable to any humiliation the officer wished to inflict on him. He had his own ways of doing this, which involved a scornful stare, and sometimes the crash of something against the desk followed by a stream of abuse during which Hamza stood quite still while the officer raged and then gave an abrupt order for him to get out. He did his best to keep away when he suspected the onset of this mood, but this too could be viewed as a provocation if the officer called for him and he was not there or took too long in coming.

As Hamza's understanding of German improved, he took in more of what the officer was saying, at times the same thing repeatedly, often when he was writing: Why did it have to turn out like this? Why did it have to turn out like this? He would exclaim in rage at the heat or at a correspondent he was addressing: There is no point in saying the same thing over and over again – although that is what I am doing. At other times he would speak to Hamza directly, as if they were in the middle of a conversation: The stupidity of explaining ourselves and what we are doing has no limit because none of it is in the least convincing. We just say the same thing over and over again. At such moments Hamza pretended he was deaf, and perhaps to the officer he was invisible.

Then one day the Oberleutnant announced a large-scale manoeuvre in two days' time, to get all the troops combat ready. Preparations had been intensifying and field messages and telegrams had been growing more frequent. They were all waiting for the order to move. The officers held long sombre conferences and took the troops out on regular exercises. War was coming. In a quiet moment at the end of that day of frenzy when Hamza was tidying up in the officer's apartment, he sensed a sinister silence which was so thick it terrified him.

'What are you doing here? What is someone like you doing in this brutish business?' the officer asked into the silence.

'I am here to serve the schutztruppe and the Kaiser,' Hamza said, stiffening to attention and looking straight ahead.

'Yes, of course you are. What nobler duty can there be!' the officer said mockingly, coming around to face him. 'I suppose you could ask me the same question. What is a man from the lovely little town of Marbach doing here in this shithole? I was born into a military tradition and this is my duty. That's why I am here – to take possession of what rightfully belongs to us because we are stronger. We are dealing with backward and savage people and the only way to rule them is to strike terror into them and their vain Liliputmajestät sultans, and pummel all of them into obedience. The schutztruppe is our instrument. You are too. We want you to be disciplined and obedient and cruel beyond our imagining. We want you to be thick-skinned heartless braggarts who will do our bidding without hesitation and then we will pay you well and give you the respect you deserve, whether slave, soldier or outcast. Except – you are not one of them. You tremble and look and listen to every heartbeat as if all of it torments you. I have watched you from the beginning when they first brought you here. You are a dreamer.'

Hamza stood quite still, staring ahead.

'I pulled you out of that line because I liked the look of you,' the officer said, standing two paces in front of him. 'Are you frightened of me? I like people to be frightened of me. It makes me strong.'

The officer stepped forward and slapped Hamza on the left cheek then slapped him with the back of his hand on the right cheek. Hamza gasped from the shock and after a moment felt his flesh tingling with pain. The officer was now only inches away and Hamza breathed in again the astringent and medicinal smell he had caught the first morning the Oberleutnant inspected the recruits, only now he knew that it was schnapps.

'Did that hurt you? Your suffering does not concern me,' the officer said, standing very close to him. Hamza avoided eye contact and saw the stretched skin on the officer's temple ripple against his cranium. 'Answer my question. Are you frightened of me?'

'Ndio bwana,' Hamza said loudly.

The officer laughed. 'I teach you to speak and read German so you can understand Schiller and you answer me in that childish language. Now answer me properly.'

'Jawohl, herr Oberleutnant,' Hamza said, and then to himself: Scheißer.

The officer looked grim-faced at Hamza for a moment and then said: 'You have lost your place in the world. I don't know why it concerns me but it does. Well, perhaps I do know. I don't suppose you know what I'm talking about. I don't suppose you have any idea of the jeopardy that surrounds you. All right, go and do your work.' As he turned away and walked towards the inner room, he said over his shoulder, 'Get out, and make sure all my gear is ready for the manoeuvres.'

*

The war started two days later. The telegram orders arrived the morning after they returned from manoeuvres. They were to take the train to Moshi and then march to positions near the border to reinforce the defensive line. The orders were carried out with trained and practised precision. The troops marched from the boma to the town in close formation, singing their marching songs, while their officers rode ahead of them or strode beside them. The carrier corps, the wives and children and livestock, came behind them, so that by the time everyone was boarded, the train was so full that the carriers and the gun boys had to ride on the roof. After Moshi they marched north towards the border with British East Africa. That was how that part of the world was at the time. Every bit of it belonged to Europeans, at least on a map: British East Africa, Deutsch-Ostafrika, África Oriental Portuguesa, Congo Belge.

Their column of one hundred and fifty askari stretched for a mile or more with the addition of all the followers. The askari were at the front of the column with their officers riding ahead and the staff-surgeons and medical orderlies immediately behind them. That was always the formation on a march and in battle. Then came the carriers bringing equipment, ammunition, supplies and the officers' personal effects. Behind them came the camp-followers with a small group of askari under a German officer as a rearguard, to counter desertion and pilfering.

The wives and partners were not just camp-followers. When the schutztruppe marched, the whole boma settlement marched with them. For one thing, the askari would not go to war without their partners. For another, the schutztruppe lived off the land when they could and it was the women who foraged for food and information, who cooked for the troops, traded where there was trade, and kept their husbands content. It was a concession Wissman had to make when he set up the schutztruppe and it was not possible to unmake it without risking widespread mutiny and desertion.

Many of the askari in Hamza's troop were seasoned campaigners and some of them knew this area. When they were camped in askari lines in the evenings they told stories of their earlier exploits in these parts: how they subdued the disobedient Wachagga chiefs Rindi and his son Meli, and hanged thirteen of their other chiefs, how they razed villages for hiding food or for sabotage, and how they dealt with the rebellious people of Meru and Arusha who had killed German missionaries. They were all washenzi to the askari. They had to be subdued and flogged and disciplined and terrified. The more they rebelled, the worse their punishment. That was the way the schutztruppe worked. At the slightest sign of resistance, the schwein were crushed and their livestock slaughtered and villages burned. These were their orders and they carried them out with an enthusiastic efficiency that terrified their enemies and brought them respect in the eyes of fellow askari and the community. They were ferocious and merciless, wallahi.

As they told their swaggering stories and marched across the rain-shadow plains of the great mountain, they did not know that they were to spend years fighting across swamps and mountains and forests and grasslands, in heavy rain and drought, slaughtering and being slaughtered by armies of people they knew nothing about: Punjabis and Sikhs, Fantis and Akans and Hausas and Yorubas, Kongo and Luba, all mercenaries who fought the Europeans' wars for them, the Germans with their schutztruppe, the British with their King's African Rifles and the Royal West African Frontier Force and their Indian troops, the Belgians with their Force Publique. In addition, there were South Africans, Belgians and a crowd of other European volunteers who thought killing was an adventure and were happy to be at the service of the great machinery of conquest and empire. It was astonishing to the askari to see the great variety of people whose existence they had not even known about. The magnitude of what was to come was not clear this early in the war as they marched to the border, their German officers riding ahead of them on their mules, their wives and children straggling cheerfully behind, and somehow or other they were all able to find ways to sing and laugh and join in convivial displays.

Hostilities on the border began with the German commander attempting to take Mombasa a few hundred miles away. The target turned out to be too far for their supply lines and the schutztruppe was forced to retreat. For months to come, the war for Hamza and his troop was repeated patrols and raids to cut the railway in British East Africa. On the coast, the British made a landing in Tanga. In November 1914 the Royal Navy and accompanying troop ships arrived at the port and demanded its surrender. The small schutztruppe force prepared to resist, withdrawing from the town from fear of bombardment by the Royal Navy ships. The rest of the inhabitants of the town, who had nothing at stake in the war, recoiled and cowered in terror or fled to the country if they could. The point of trying to take this town was that it was the terminus of the railway, which ran to Moshi in the north.

The British landing ended in disaster. Several battalions, mostly Indian troops, were disembarked some little distance up the coast from the port. Their commanders were not sure what opposition to expect so made this cautious approach. The disembarkation was made in darkness, wading hip-deep in the sea. In the morning the troops found themselves in thick scrub and high grass without any certainty of the direction of the town. As they made their way towards what they took to be the town, they were harassed and picked off by the schutztruppe, who were reinforced by troops rushed down from Moshi on the train. The schutztruppe were expert at this hit-and-run style of war and their tactics created a panic in the troops and the carriers who took fright and ran. As casualties mounted, more soldiers ran and then after repeated panics everybody ran, and those who were still being landed ran straight back into the sea.

In the meantime the Royal Navy was firing its guns into the town, destroying buildings and killing an unknown number of its inhabitants. No one bothered to count afterwards. One of the targets the Royal Navy hit was the hospital where the wounded were being treated by the Germans, but that was the random ill luck of war. By the time it was all over and the British asked for a truce, leaving most of their equipment behind, several hundred of their troops were dead on the road and in the streets of the town. An unknown number of carriers were also killed or drowned. No one bothered to count the dead carriers either, not then nor throughout the whole war. As soon as this encounter was settled, Hamza's troop was railed up the line to Moshi and back to their old position. It was going to be that kind of war for the schutztruppe, a frenzy of rapid advances and retreats.

Despite the failure of the landing, the British Imperial machinery ground into gear, and troops began to arrive from various parts of the globe. It was certain to be just a matter of months before the conflict was over, they believed, but the German commander had other ideas. Every time the British Imperial forces thought they had the schutztruppe trapped they slipped away, leaving their sick and badly wounded for the British to look after. The schutztruppe were often exhausted and many of them fell ill, but there was also exhilaration in the swift raids and retreats that outwitted their enemies. They fed themselves on whatever they found in the villages and farms, plundering and confiscating wherever they could.

Pressed on all sides, the schutztruppe retreated in two columns, one along the lakes to the west and the other due south from Moshi. Hamza was in the column that headed due south. They dragged their big guns and equipment, their wives and servants and baggage, on the retreat across the Uluguru mountain ranges. It was in the retreat from Morogoro across the Uluguru that Komba, their platoon leader, was killed. A large piece of metal from a shell smashed into his chest and tore him to pieces. Several others in the platoon were also killed in the same action or did not come back. For the next several months Hamza's troop retreated slowly south towards the Rufiji river, constantly fighting, some of them fierce battles as in Kibati where thousands were killed.

The Rufiji was in heavy flood that year and the mosquitoes were rampant. More askari died from blackwater fever than from any other cause. Carriers were seized by crocodiles as they crossed the swamps. Hyenas dug up the dead. It was a nightmare. They finally crossed the Rufiji and afterwards fought the Battle of Mahiwa, which was the worst battle of all for Hamza's troop and for the schutztruppe. It was a costly victory for them but still they retreated, to the southern highlands and then to the Ruvuma river and the border with Portuguese East Africa. On the way they shed equipment and wives and children, leaving them behind to be interned by the British. They did not always know where they were, even with their maps, and they were forced to capture and question local people. There was always someone among the askari who could understand enough of the language to put the question, and somehow or other the infliction of sufficient pain elicited the required answer. No one needed to order the askari to do violence and brutality on the people. They knew what was needed and required no instruction. At this stage of the war, most of the soldiers engaged in combat were Africans and Indians: troops from Nyasaland and Uganda, from Nigeria and the Gold Coast, from the Congo and from India, and on the other side the African schutztruppe.

Even as the schutztruppe lost soldiers and carriers through battle, disease and desertion, their officers kept fighting on with manic obstinacy and persistence. The askari left the land devastated, its people starving and dying in the hundreds of thousands, while they struggled on in their blind and murderous embrace of a cause whose origins they did not know and whose ambitions were vain and ultimately intended for their domination. The carriers died in huge numbers from malaria and dysentery and exhaustion, and no one bothered to count them. They deserted in sheer terror, to perish in the ravaged countryside. Later these events would be turned into stories of absurd and nonchalant heroics, a sideshow to the great tragedies in Europe, but for those who lived through it, this was a time when their land was soaked in blood and littered with corpses.

In the meantime, the officers made sure to maintain European prestige. When they made camp the Germans were in separate lines from the askari, sleeping in their camp beds under mosquito nets. When they stopped by a stream, they were always upstream with the askari downstream and the carriers and animals yet further down. The officers made every effort to meet for a mess dinner every evening, where etiquette was observed as far as possible. They did not do any of the physical work associated with the askari or carriers: transporting equipment, foraging, making camp, cooking, cleaning dishes. They kept their distance, eating separately, demanding deference wherever they could. The whole schutztruppe army now, officers and men, were dressed in whatever bits of clothing they could salvage from fallen comrades and enemies, which some of the askari took as licence to adopt extravagant displays of feathers and badges, though their officers still strutted about as if they were dressed in silver buckles and gold epaulettes. The askari too had their own honour to maintain. They insisted on their difference from the carriers and considered it below their soldierly prestige to carry loads.

Of the other officers from the boma, the medical officer and Feldwebel Walther the Jogoo were still with the company. Two officers were killed on the retreat from the Rufiji and were replaced by an officer from the musikappel and a settler volunteer. Three were transferred to other companies. All of the askari who had joined up at the same time as Hamza were dead or missing or captured. After months and years of harried manoeuvres and disastrous engagements the remaining men were ragged and worn out. The medical officer had lost weight and grown a thick brassy beard. He was kept constantly busy tending to injuries and illnesses, issuing daily doses of quinine to the troops while his supplies lasted. He had to conserve supplies as best he could, so the carriers did not receive quinine any more. His orderly was still with him, lanky and phlegmatic as ever. The medical officer was even more cheerful than he had been in camp, chuckling and laughing as he saw to his grisly tasks, but it was a cheerfulness he kept going with his carefully guarded supply of brandy and other substances from his medicine chest. He had malarial fever punctually every two days which laid him out for several hours. These bouts took their toll, and each time he rose he seemed to have lost more weight and his smiles seemed to have grown weaker.

The Feldwebel was now out of his mind with rage at every irritation they encountered, his frenzy fed by bangi and the sorghum beer they confiscated from villagers. He never seemed to fall ill as all the other officers did at one time or another. His temper was so out of control that he frequently hit askari and porters with whatever was at hand: a cane, a whip or a piece of firewood. He was even more vicious than he used to be in his hatred and contempt for the local people whose land they plundered. To him they were savages and he spoke about them with greater ferocity than he showed towards the British enemy. He had a deep loathing of Hamza and abused him whenever he caught him out in any trivial, or sometimes imaginary, wrongdoing. Hamza kept out of his way whenever he could but it seemed at times as if the Feldwebel was looking for him.

Hamza was inseparable from the Oberleutnant, at his commander's insistence, which aroused some of the other officers to glowering indignation, others to mockery and the Feldwebel to more hatred. The askari assailed Hamza with their grumbles and told him to pass them on to his officer. Hamza nodded and said nothing. He was required to roll out his sleeping mat beside the officer's cot at dusk for an hour or two while he continued with what he called their conversation classes. After that Hamza was to pick up his mat and go back to the askari lines. Some nights the officer reached out to touch him in the dark. You are still there. You are so quiet, he said. Hamza did not know what he wanted of him. He felt trapped in the officer's embrace and was made queasy by the enforced intimacy although it was easier to evade it in war than it had been in the boma. In the field there was a great deal more to occupy the commanding officer as they raided and hid and searched for food and the conversation classes sometimes seemed perfunctory.

The officer lost much of his scornful and satirical aura as their difficulties increased and now he was often cold and withdrawn, sometimes silent for long periods in the grip of his dark moods. The other German officers kept up a grim camaraderie, which made the Oberleutnant's withdrawal more apparent. Their privations and way of war had weakened many of them but it had turned the officer inwards and made him hesitant where he had been so commanding before. He was more irritable with his officers and askari, and he was impatient with the villagers they plundered, sometimes issuing harsh orders to punish what he called acts of sabotage, burning their huts after confiscating all their supplies. At one village the other officers suggested the execution of an elder because he had refused to disclose an underground cache of yams, which they were only able to discover by beating a young boy and forcing him to tell them. The officer dropped his eyes before his officers' request and then nodded and walked away. The Feldwebel shot the old man in the head.

Throughout the hundreds of nightmare miles they struggled through, Hamza carried out whatever orders his officer found it possible to give under their very reduced circumstances, and as far as possible tried to provide for him. He did his best not to draw attention to himself. He marched with the troop and ran on the crouch as he was trained to do and fired his gun when he needed to but he was not sure if he ever hit anyone. He ducked and weaved and yelled like the other askari but he shot at shadows, avoiding targets. By miraculous luck he did not have to engage in close combat, and he managed to avoid shooting any of the villagers they were at times required to take reprisals on because of their treachery or deceit. He ate the stolen food like everyone else and saw the ruination of the land and hurried away as they all did. He was in a state of terror from the moment he opened his eyes at first light, but in his exhaustion he sometimes reached a stage when he was unafraid, without bravado, without posturing, detached from the moment and open to whatever might happen to him. Sometimes he lapsed into despair.

6

They talked about the war in Tanga for many weeks up and down the coast, but for most of them it was quiet after the disastrous attack. It was as everyone had anticipated: the British were no match for the schutztruppe. As word travelled down the coast from Tanga, rumour expanded and embellished the ferocity and discipline of the askari and the shambolic panic of the Indian troops, who it was assumed must have led the panic. Khalifa said they were bound to hear from Ilyas about this German victory – he would not be able to resist singing the praise of the schutztruppe – but they heard nothing from him.

The British reply to their defeat was a Royal Navy blockade of the coast. No trade was possible with Zanzibar or Mombasa or Pemba across the way, let alone the long-distance trade across the ocean. Overnight, shortages appeared as merchants hurried to hoard their merchandise, both to conserve supplies and to wait for prices to rise while keeping their goods out of the hands of the German authorities, who were sure to want to confiscate everything for themselves and their troops. Nassor Biashara, whose business had been slowly recovering from the collapse and near ruin of paying off the creditors after his father's death, now found himself in even more dire straits. He had committed himself to buying several items for wholesale distribution among customers in the interior: Indian sugar, wheat for flour-milling, sorghum and rice, all paid for and awaiting delivery. He thought he could make good his losses to the creditors with one ambitious enterprise, but the blockade caught him out.

It was not only business people like Nassor Biashara who felt the consequences of the blockade. Many things became scarcer than before: rice, coffee and tea – even though all these were grown in the country – sugar, salt-fish, flour. The schutztruppe fed themselves off the land whenever they could, and now they were at war all provisions were at their disposal. Fish was still plentiful and coconuts and bananas and cassava still grew despite the Royal Navy and the schutztruppe. For a while people bought by offering something else: a shirt for a basket of mangoes, a roll of cotton material for a ram. No one bothered much about money, just for a while. Where appropriate items of exchange were not to be had, there was always jewellery. Most families possessed some little bit of jewellery which came as dowry and was passed down the generations. Merchants and traders knew the durable value of gold and gems and could not resist them when they came on offer. For a while the panic of scarcity took over.

They had very little news of the war in the interior and what they had came through the German administration. It seemed that the experience of Tanga was enough to deter the British from making another landing anywhere on the coast, and as the period of quiet extended even though they were under blockade, so people adapted and coped, and in the greater chaos they were able to avoid paying the German authorities the taxes they normally imposed on them. Business and trade began to pick up, although Nassor Biashara's affairs were still in trouble.

'Nothing came out of your cleverness but ruin,' Khalifa said to him.

The merchant disliked the tone that Khalifa sometimes used with him, as if he were still a novice at his work. It was evident that he attempted to control his anger when Khalifa said this. He glared back with lips pressed tightly together, then looked away for a moment before he began speaking slowly. He was not yet ready for a confrontation. 'There was no cleverness in it. I just thought that we needed to do something to repair the business. How was I to know about the war and the blockade?'

'To put everything in one venture like that,' Khalifa said, 'did not show good business sense.'

'What did you expect me to do, just wait until I was impoverished? I did not put everything into that venture. We

96

still have the timber business,' Nassor Biashara said angrily. Then he took a deep breath and after a moment continued in a more measured tone. 'And anyway, if you know so much about business, where were you when all the debts were piling up in my father's time? Why did you not say something like that to him instead of grumbling at me now?'

'I did not know all his business dealings. I told you that,' Khalifa said.

'You were his clerk. You should've known,' Nassor Biashara said. 'You should have been keeping records.'

'Are you blaming me for your father's secrecy?' Khalifa asked mildly, smiling his disdain.

Nassor Biashara lowered his glasses, which were perched on his forehead during this exchange, and returned to the ledger he was once again checking through for evidence of his father's transactions, just in case he had missed something in his earlier perusals. He did not speak to Khalifa for the rest of the day and avoided eye contact. He continued in this taciturn way for a few days, speaking politely but only when it was necessary. There was not much business to do. Nassor Biashara spent more and more of his day in the tiny office he had in the timber yard. Most of the time they sat in the office and talked with whoever dropped by. They did not have another conversation like that but one day Nassor Biashara announced that he had found a tenant for the office downstairs who was going to turn it into a provisions shop, a duka. 'I am moving the paperwork to the timber yard and selling all the furniture. From now on, you will look after the warehouse as there are no books for you to keep, and what paperwork there is I will do myself. You'll also have to take a cut in pay. We all will while things are as they are.'

He delivered this announcement with some asperity, discouraging conversation. As soon as he was done with saying what he had to say, he put on his cap and went upstairs.

'He's trying to get rid of you,' Bi Asha said. 'That miserable ungrateful wretch, that small-boned thieving hypocrite, after all you've done for him and his father.' She went on in that vein for a long time while Khalifa listened gratefully to her outrage. He knew that Nassor Biashara had no choice but to cut back but he still enjoyed hearing the little tajiri being torn to pieces. It surprised him that the young man he had always known as a shy or even timorous boy was able to act so decisively. He even smiled secretly at the thought. Renting out the office was a bit of a panic measure but not very important in the end as it could always be reversed. What was there for him to do in a warehouse that was almost empty? He was afraid that Bi Asha was right, that the merchant was easing him out and soon there would be no salary. Perhaps soon there would be no merchant. Who needed a clerk in these straitened times?

But the merchant did not get rid of Khalifa. As the war receded into rumours of fierce fighting in the interior, Nassor Biashara invested in timber for the repair and reconstruction that was bound to be necessary once the conflict was over. Surely it could not continue for much longer now. He made the decision without consulting or asking for advice from Khalifa, and he kept his own records and did not wait for an incompetent clerk to do so. Khalifa, in the meantime, cleaned out and organised the warehouse to receive the timber that the merchant purchased. He too kept his own records just in case the future brought accusations of incompetence or worse.

One of Amur Biashara's old business contacts, Rashid Maulidi, who was the nahodha of a boat lying idle at the wharf, had a word with Nassor Biashara about a venture he had in mind to bring in rice and sugar from Pemba. The merchant knew without knowing the precise details that Rashid Maulidi was part of the dubious network of traders his father had patronised. He said no, it was too dangerous. If the British caught him, they would sink his boat and perhaps lock him up for years. If the Germans knew he had smuggled in supplies of rice and sugar, they would take it away for themselves and whip him with a kiboko for hoarding. Rashid Maulidi went to Khalifa who was more familiar with the kind of dealings he had in mind and explained his plan, and Khalifa listened carefully and asked Rashid Maulidi if he could bring in a consignment on credit. Was that possible? He said that his credit was good in Pemba, which was his homeland, but he was not sure if he wanted to take the entire risk himself. If something went wrong, he did not have the means to put it right and would lose his boat. Khalifa said that the merchant was a nervy young man who needed persuading. He suggested that Rashid Maulidi should get a small consignment on credit, just to demonstrate that the scheme was viable, and then they would speak to the merchant again. Rashid Maulidi brought in a modest consignment of rice and sugar as agreed, and when it was safely stored away in the warehouse, they brought Nassor Biashara to see it.

'You don't know this is here,' Khalifa said. 'You give me the money to pay for this in my name and then I sell it. After that the business pays for itself. We use the proceeds to buy more supplies. There is no need for you to be involved. Whatever profit we make, we divide four parts to you, four parts to Rashid Maulidi, two parts to me. You don't need to know anything further about it.'

There was still some haggling to do, but despite arguments back and forth that was how it ended up. Throughout the remaining years of the blockade, Rashid Maulidi brought in small supplies of whatever he could purchase in Pemba and Khalifa hid them away in the warehouse where trusted traders came to do business. It was not riches but it kept the business going and allowed Khalifa to find a new role for himself as a trader in contraband as well as a warehouse keeper. He dealt with Nassor Biashara politely, if at times irritably, and they largely left each other alone.

*

The British forces entered Tanga on 3 July 1916, nearly two years after the disastrous attempt in 1914. A small force of a few hundred Indian troops took the port without firing a shot. They found a town still bearing the scars of the Royal Navy bombardment, and the port and the Customs House buildings and jetty were in ruins, blown up by the Germans before they left. German forces in the area went to join their commander in the interior who was regrouping his forces before retreating further south. It was the end of the war for that part of the coast, though there was still the struggle for Bagamoyo and Dar es Salam to come in August. It was also the end of the blockade and a slow return to commerce with Mombasa and Pemba and Zanzibar. They now began to have more detailed news of the war in the interior. Everyone was sure the war was going to be over very soon. It will not last beyond the monsoons, they said.

Afiya was thirteen years old when the British took control of the coast. It was now more than two years since Ilyas left for Dar es Salaam and in all that time they had heard nothing from him. Baba Khalifa told her that the news from the interior was there was fighting everywhere with many casualties, German, British, South African, Indian, but most of them African. Schutztruppe askari, KAR, West African armies, many Africans are being killed to settle this European quarrel, he said. Maalim Abdalla persuaded Habib, Ilyas's fellow clerk on the sisal estate, to make some enquiries. He learned what they already knew: that Ilyas was sent to Dar es Salaam for training, but they also found out that he was trained as a signalman and posted to the Lindi District in the south. Habib could not find out any more and there was no one left to ask because the German manager was now interned by the British.

Khalifa had heard that Tabora was taken by the Belgian Force Publique and that it had been a terrible battle. The worst of the fighting had then moved south and was now in the Lindi region, exactly where Ilyas was supposed to have been posted as a signalman. He did not say so to Afiya, but he was beginning to think there was something ominous about her brother's long silence. Instead he tried to understate his concern when he spoke to her. 'A signalman is a peaceful kind of duty,' he said to her. 'He will be fine. His work will be to stand on a hill a long way from trouble and send messages on his mirrors. Don't worry, we'll hear from him soon.'

*

Afiya was now no longer a girl but a kijana, a maiden, and beginning to understand the endless resentments that were part of the sequestered lives of women. She did not call on Khalida as often as she used to, because Bi Asha said she was not to. They were scoundrels in that family, she said, and the empty-headed women friends Khalida associated with liked nothing so much as to gossip and to tear people to shreds, shame on them. Afiya knew that Bi Asha's prevailing topic of conversation was her neighbours, whose shortcomings she relished and repeatedly described. She did not make any protest at this new prohibition but when she visited her friend she did not tell Bi Asha about it, nor did she tell Khalida what was said about her and her husband or about the slander of her women friends. Apart from her visits to Khalida and to Jamila, Afiya was shut up at home day and night, or shrouded in a buibui when she went out. She could feel something in her shrinking and turning edgy as if constantly expecting a scolding. There was so much that she was now not allowed to do because it was improper. She was not to touch a boy's or a man's hand even in greeting. She was not to speak to a boy or a man in the street unless he spoke to her and was someone she knew. She was not to smile at a stranger, and always to walk with her eyes cast slightly downwards to avoid accidental eye contact. Bi Asha policed her movements, or tried to, advising her firmly on her behaviour and who she was not to see and what she was not to do.

Her friend Jamila was still unmarried and Bi Asha pronounced that the match was likely to be called off. That was what usually happened when a betrothal went on for this long. It meant someone was having second thoughts. Jamila's fiancé lived in Zanzibar and planned to move to join her after the wedding, which did not surprise Bi Asha. Who would not want to leave Zanzibar? Every disease you could name was to be found in Zanzibar, including sin and disappointment. Afiya shrugged and let the bitterness wash over her. Jamila's family did not seem to be troubled by the delay and even talked about it openly and carried on in their easy-going ways, welcoming Afiya whenever she called on them and telling her about their plans. The room downstairs that Ilyas had rented was to be Jamila's new home after the wedding and she was having it decorated in preparation.

Visiting her was not yet prohibited but Afiya sensed Bi Asha's mounting disapproval of her old friend. 'How old is Jamila now? She must be nearly nineteen. They had better get her married before she gets up to mischief. You don't know how tricky men can be and how foolish young women are. You mark my words, little girl, they are making trouble for themselves.'

I am not a little girl, Afiya said to herself and tried not to mind. In all her time with Bi Asha she had not been defiant of her wishes and the small wiles she practised for getting her own way only concerned matters of little importance. Keeping silent about her visits to Khalida was her greatest act of defiance, otherwise it was things like hiding a banana from her market shopping so she could eat it in the evening when she was sometimes hungry, or concealing a cowrie necklace that Jamila and Saada found in their mother's jewellery box and gave to her as a gift. Bimkubwa did not approve of adornments. When Bi Asha caught her out in these instances she smiled, not minding such small deceptions. Unakuwa mjanja we, she told the girl. You are becoming cunning. Baba came to her assistance at times but Bi Asha kept her sternest instructions for when she and Afiya were on their own.

When the merchant closed the office and moved to the timber yard, Baba managed to save an almost clean ledger, which he brought home for her. The pages were thick and shiny, and the cover was marbled in grey and pink. It seemed a pity to write her clumsy scribble in the beautiful pages. He also brought home past copies of *Kiongozi* wherever he found them. There were no more issues after the arrival of the British but there were still old copies circulating. Khalifa also found some copies of *Rafiki Yangu* through Maalim Abdalla. Those newspapers were her reading matter and afterwards she copied whole paragraphs for writing practice. Bi Asha was suspicious of these publications because she said they were the words of unbelievers, intended to convert people with their lies. Their desire to do evil was relentless. Sometimes Bi Asha recited a qasida while she worked, and when she was in the mood she dictated a verse and watched indulgently as Afiya wrote out the lines. Later she read the verses back to her and Bi Asha said, let me see and smiled at her cleverness. Afiya was pleased too but it was not really cleverness because she could only read slowly and her writing was laborious and clumsy when Baba's was so graceful.

'You just need to practise,' he said. 'Make a real effort.'

'You don't need to write like him,' Bi Asha said. 'He is a clerk. You are not going to become a clerk, little girl.'

I'm not a little girl.

*

In her fifteenth year, on the first day of Idd that year, Afiya wore a dress that her friends Jamila and Saada made for her as a present. The bodice was made of blue satin and fitted snugly. The neckline was round and fringed with white lace. The skirt was full and pleated, and made from a light blue poplin material with a design of tiny green blossoms. The material came from their mother who had saved it from other dresses they had made in the past. Jamila had a gift for designing dresses from odd materials and it was she who came up with the design. When Afiya tried it on at their house, the sisters smiled at each other in self-congratulation and told her it fitted very nicely. It was the most beautiful dress she had ever had. When she took it home, she hid it under her buibui and put it away in a cupboard in her room. Some instinct warned her to do so because she expected disapproval.

Most people had new clothes made for Idd: a new dress or a kanga for the women, a new kanzu and kofia or even a jacket for the men. Times were still hard though the blockade was over and she knew she was to have a dress from Bimkubwa. It was not new but one Bimkubwa had made for herself some years before and now altered so it fitted Afiya in some fashion. Afiya was slim and still growing, and the dress hung loose and baggy on her, which Bi Asha said was not a problem. You'll grow into it. When she tried it on on the eve of Idd and paraded round the house in it, Baba made a face behind Bi Asha's back, a small grimace and then a smile of sympathy.

On the first morning of Idd, Afiya did her chores and helped prepare the festival breakfast in her work clothes. At mid-morning, when they were done and just before they were ready to sit down to breakfast, she went to her room to change. She knew it was expected she would come out in the dress Bi Asha altered for her. Instead she changed into the one her friends made for her, about which she had told neither Bi Asha nor Baba. When she came out a few minutes later, Baba nodded and smiled and then silently applauded.

'That is lovely,' he said. 'Now you look like a princess instead of an orphan. Where did you get that from?'

'Jamila and Saada made it for me,' Afiya said.

Bi Asha looked on without a word for a moment, and just when Afiya thought she was going to be instructed to go back to her room and change, she too managed a smile. 'She is a young woman now,' she said.

The full weight of Bi Asha's words became slowly evident in the months that followed. Whenever Afiya made ready to go out, Bi Asha asked her to say where she was going and what she was going there for. When she returned, Bi Asha asked for an account of who she had seen and what was said. By degrees, without even realising what she was doing at first, Afiya found herself asking Bi Asha's permission before she went out. Bi Asha commented on what she wore, commending or reproving as seemed appropriate to her. The Idd dress was long-since condemned because it was too small for her, Bi Asha said. Too tight in the chest, too brazen. Afiya was even required to cover herself with a kanga when Baba was around, leaving only her face uncovered. Bi Asha seemed to know when Afiya's periods were due and always asked about them. Afiya had not yet quite got over the distaste for what happened to her during her period and she found it humiliating to be forced to describe the colour and volume of the mess.

Bi Asha's tone with her was often grating, as if a low mutter ran underneath her words. She only seemed satisfied with Afiya when she joined her in prayers or when she sat to read the Koran with her in the afternoon. To prepare for a visit to her friends, Afiya put in a lengthy spell of piety beforehand, and sometimes did so just to win some respite. She felt hemmed in and under scrutiny all the time, as if she were secretly contemplating sins. Afiya was sure that Bi Asha searched her room when she was out. She was by now resentful and guilty at the same time because she reminded herself of the kindness Bi Asha had showed her when she was a wounded and frightened child. She wanted to say to Bimkubwa that she was not a child any more but she did not

104

dare. She did not even know how old she really was because no one had bothered to record her birth.

When she said this to Baba, he said, 'Let's work it out. You know what year you were born because that was the year Ilyas ran away. So now select the date of your birth. Not everyone has this privilege. Mine was written down by my father. Bi Asha's was recorded in an accounts ledger belonging to Bwana Amur Biashara. You can choose your own date of birth. Please yourself.'

Afiya selected the sixth day of the sixth month – mwezi sita wa mfungo sita – because she liked the cadence. So from now on you'll know exactly how old you are, Baba said. Some months into her sixteenth year, the full weight of the words Bi Asha had spoken on that first day of Idd when Afiya wore the dress her friends made for her, descended on her.

'You're a young woman now,' Bi Asha said as they sat together after breakfast on another Idd day a year later. 'It's time to find you a husband.'

Baba chuckled, assuming that Bi Asha was teasing Afiya about being grown up. Afiya smiled too, thinking the same.

'I am not making a joke,' Bi Asha said dryly, and Afiya instantly realised what she should have realised in the first place. No, she wasn't. 'We can't have a grown woman sitting around the house with nothing to do. She will only get up to mischief. She needs to have a husband.'

'A grown woman! She is only a girl,' Baba said incredulously, and with such feeling that Bi Asha breathed in sharply in surprise. 'You're always calling her little girl and now she is suddenly a woman.'

'Not suddenly,' Bi Asha said. 'Don't pretend that you haven't noticed.'

'Let her have her youth before burdening her with children. What's the hurry? Has someone asked for her?'

'No, not yet, but someone will very soon, I expect. You have worked it out for yourself. She is sixteen,' Bi Asha said stubbornly. 'It's a perfectly normal age for a girl to be married.'

'It's ignorance and narrow-mindedness,' Baba said vehemently, and Bi Asha puckered her mouth in temporary retreat.

7

One night a detachment of five led by the officer and including Hamza headed for a German mission called Kilemba, which they hoped the British command had not yet reached. The British practice was to close all German outposts, farms or missions, to prevent the schutztruppe from receiving supplies there. The German civilians were treated with the courtesies befitting citizens of an enlightened combatant nation and were taken away to Rhodesia or British East Africa or Blantyre in Nyasaland where they could be interned by other Europeans until the end of hostilities. It would not do to have Europeans watched over and restrained by unsupervised Africans. The local Africans, who were neither citizens nor members of a nation nor enlightened, and who were in the path of the belligerents, were ignored or robbed and, when necessity required, forcibly recruited into the carrier corps.

The officer knew from his map that the mission used to be near here before the war, but he was not sure if it was still open or if the British had got to it already. Normally finding it would have been left to the askari troops who were expert at reconnaissance and tracking, but their commanding officer was curious about the mission station, which he had heard about from a fellow officer who had spent some weeks there recuperating during the Maji Maji war. There was also the lure of finding a German meal and some good schnapps, Hamza suspected.

They found the mission without any difficulty and arrived there in late afternoon. They had crossed from a wooded area, which rose into a stony escarpment and then descended into a grassy plain surrounded by mountains in the distance. The mission was at the top of a rise in the middle of the plain. It had a walled compound, with whitewashed buildings and a spreading fig tree. It looked serene and peaceful on the hill. The pastor was still there with his wife and two blonde-haired little girls, and stood waiting to greet them at the inner gate when they arrived. It was obvious that they were delighted to see the German troops, adult faces smiling while the children waved.

There were two small, fenced-in cultivated terraces just inside the outer gate, with pumpkins and cabbages and another crop Hamza did not recognise. The detachment waited there while the officer went forward to greet the missionary and his family and then follow them inside. A few moments later an African man came out and invited them into the compound. His brow and face were heavily lined, and there was a jagged scar on the right side of his neck. He spoke Kiswahili fluently. He told them his name was Pascal and he worked in the mission. The mission was large and had several buildings, a school, an infirmary, a chicken run and a fruit and vegetable garden. There had been fighting nearby and the people from neighbouring villages had all run away. That was why it looked so empty. Normally there were children in the school and the infirmary was always busy, treating the multitude of diseases that afflicted people in these parts: worms, sleeping sickness, malaria. The mission was allowed to stay open by the British because the pastor and his family had looked after a wounded Rhodesian officer who befriended them and pleaded for them to be left to stay and look after the local people rather than be sent to Blantyre for internment.

'Why did the people not come into the mission for safety?' an askari called Frantz asked.

'Because the pastor said not to,' Pascal said. 'He did not want the British to come back and say he was keeping ruga ruga here.'

'Do you have ruga ruga?' Frantz asked, taking on the role of spokesman.

'I don't know,' Pascal said. 'I haven't seen any. That is who we are really frightened of, not the British and the Rhodesians but the ruga ruga. Some people say they are cannibals.'

Some of the askari laughed at this. 'Who told you that?' a soldier called Albert asked. It had become the fashion among some of the askari to take German names.

'People say it,' said Pascal calmly. 'The Rhodesian officer who was here told the pastor that the ruga ruga don't take prisoners and they eat human flesh. I don't know if it's true.'

'They are just rabble-rout riff-raff, not cannibals. They are savages in their goatskins and feathers, playing at being fierce,' Frantz said after another bout of laughter. 'We use them because they have a terrible reputation and create havoc and frighten people. Do you know why they are called ruga ruga? Because they are full of bangi and are always jumping about. Ruga ruga, do you see? We are the people you should really be afraid of, the schutztruppe. We are merciless angry bastards who like to have our own way and to bully and mutilate washenzi civilians. Our officers are high-handed experts in terror. Without us there is no Deutsch-Ostafrika. Fear us.'

'Ndio mambo yalivyo,' the mission man said quietly. That's how things are. His polite indifference made it seem as if he did not really believe Frantz or else was not as awe-struck as the askari might have liked.

Later Pascal brought them food – mealie and salt-fish stew – and some plums and figs, which they ate in the lean-to where they spread their gear and mats. He sat with them while they ate with great relish. This is a feast, they said. You don't know what we've been eating out there. Afterwards Pascal fetched two other men who also worked on the mission, Witness and Jeremiah who pre-ferred to be called Juma. They were fellow Christian members of the mission community. They looked after the animals and the gardens, and Witness's wife looked after the house. She was inside serving the family and the officer their lovely German dinner at that very moment, Pascal told them. Frantz began talking about battles and the vicious events they had participated in and the other askari joined in with their own gruesome contributions. It was to frighten the mission men but they sat there and took it all in, open-mouthed. This was what they had come for, to listen to stories of askari ferocity. The more outrageous the stories became, the deeper the silence and awe with which they were received.

'The war came very close to us,' Pascal said. 'Then it went away. We have looked after a German officer and the Rhodesian man I told you about. God looked after all of them and us, and we have lost no one here at the mission.'

The temperature dropped steeply after dark. Hamza took the stone staircase to the top of the wall and felt a relentless chill wind blowing on his face. A puddle on the plain glowed eerily as it caught the light of the moon. They were to stay there the night and head back at dawn. The officer had satisfied his curiosity about the mission and the missionaries, both evidently safe in the hands of God. They left Kilemba with a gift of sausages and a bottle of schnapps for the other officers plus a supply of tobacco, which was the crop Hamza had not recognised growing on the terrace. Pascal had shown them the shed where they did the curing but he would not let the askari take any. The pastor looked after the tobacco himself and he knew how to count. He would know if any was taken. Pascal did not want the pastor to think he was a thief.

They left early and rejoined their troop without encountering any difficulties. Later that night, after the German officers had their feast, the Oberleutnant lay on his cot while Hamza sat on his sleeping mat nearby. It was time for their conversation class. The visit to the mission and the schnapps had put the officer in a good mood.

'The pastor was a decent man but maybe a little stiff,' the officer said.

'Yes, he was a decent man,' Hamza said.

'What was he thinking, bringing his wife and small children to such a distant, isolated and diseased place? She was charming and kind. The orchards were beautiful, hey? She looks after the fruit and the school. It's the coolness up here that helps, a perfect climate for fruit. But the poor woman, she was terrified by the rumours of the cannibal ruga ruga. It's just British propaganda, I told her, to reassure her. They are our ruga ruga, our auxiliaries, we would not have dealings with cannibals.'

'It was good that you were able to reassure her,' Hamza said. He had to speak from time to time otherwise the officer became irritated and told him he was having a conversation, not listening to a sermon. If Hamza did not have anything to say, he repeated the last thing the officer had said.

'It's possible, about the cannibalism, isn't it? Anything is possible when human beings go out of their minds as we have been doing, let alone those blood-crazed ruga ruga savages. That's why we use them – because they terrify our enemies with their utter savagery. Why would they stop at eating the bodies of those they kill? Can you imagine doing that, eating human flesh? I don't mean as an act of craziness in war or as a ritual of primitive people who eat their dead enemies to gain their strength, not as a custom, not as an item on your customary menu, but as a desire, as a curiosity, as an adventure. Can you imagine doing that?'

'No, I can't,' Hamza said because the officer awaited his reply.

The Oberleutnant smiled scornfully. 'No, you don't look as if you would have the daring,' he said.

*

The last few weeks of the war were a nightmare as they ran and hid from the pursuing forces. The retreat southwards drew the British and Allied Forces after them all the way to the Ruvuma. The schutztruppe did not just run and hide but were ruthless and successful in punishing the British and their allies: mainly the South Africans, the Rhodesians, the African KAR and even the Portuguese who decided it was now time to join the war, but they also took heavy casualties especially in the fighting after Mahiwa. The carriers regularly deserted in large numbers every few days, or perhaps they fell by the wayside from hunger and weariness. It was not always safe to desert. They were now in the land where the schutztruppe fought the Wahehe nearly thirty years before and then carried out the atrocities of the Maji Maji war some fifteen years later. The people who survived those times and who were now burdened with further depredations on their lives and provisions were worn down by schutztruppe violence and were not likely to show kindness to deserting carriers.

The askari remained steadfast and loyal. It was a wonder that they did. They had not been paid for months or even years in some cases, not since Dar es Salaam fell and the German administration lost the mint there. Still, it was safer for an askari to remain in the column despite the difficulties than to desert in such hostile terrain. They were short of ammunition and food, and their raids on enemy supplies and villages were no longer well rewarded. They had exhausted the land, which was now littered with starving or empty villages, their supplies repeatedly plundered by the rival armies. Beyond the Ruvuma, the schutztruppe turned westward towards the Rhodesias, deliberately leaving scorched villages behind them to thwart their pursuers, who themselves were struggling to obtain supplies and fight disease. Hamza's troop was in the thick of the retreat, and he was so exhausted by the constant movement that at times he fell asleep on his feet. The troop was all dressed in motley, including the German officers, and looked more like a rabble-rout than an army. They were now retracing their steps to the area they had been in earlier in the year, near the Kilemba mission. It was there that the final stages of Hamza's war were played out.

In the early hours of the morning, while it was still dark, he smelled the rain before his eyes were open. They woke to discover that most of the remaining carriers had deserted during the night. It was not so unexpected to Hamza or to anyone who understood what they had been muttering incessantly for days. They were exhausted by the relentless pursuit, by the heavy loads and the degrading work they were required to carry out. They were porters for hire but they had not been paid, and in addition many of them had been coerced into work they did not want to do. Casualties were high among them. They were poorly fed and badly equipped, most of them barefoot and dressed in whatever rags they could loot or steal. They died from disease and lack of care, and in the dire straits the schutztruppe were in, they must have been desperate to get away from an army facing defeat. They had been deserting day by day in small numbers but this was an organised flight, an admission that the schutztruppe could no longer ensure their survival or well-being. The Oberleutnant was furious and the other Germans joined him in his rage at the indiscipline of the carriers, as if they really believed that the ragged troop they beat and despised and overworked owed them loyalty.

'There is no choice. The askari will have to do the carriers' work,' the Feldwebel said, speaking with force as was increasingly his manner. He addressed the commanding officer, demanding his compliance with a vehemence that was close to indiscipline. The Oberleutnant shook his head and glanced at the three other Germans still with him. The medical officer also shook his head. He was very unwell now. In addition to the malaria he was exhausted and suffering from a gastric infection that repeatedly sent him into the bushes. He had no medication left to ease his suffering. The other two officers who had joined the troop in the last months of tortured retreat remained silent. They were a former music master who required the troop to exercise every morning and who waved his handgun at them while he shouted his commands, and a reserve Leutnant, soft-spoken and unwell, a settler volunteer who looked worn out by his struggles. Their silence was respectful but its meaning was clear. The askari would have to do it even though they all understood the iron protocol that an askari did not carry loads. It was a matter of honour. Just as the Europeans were immovable on the sanctity of their prestige, so were the askari. The Oberleutnant shook his head, as much in consternation and uncertainty as because he knew there was no other option. If they were to abandon their supplies and equipment then they might as well march directly to the nearest enemy outpost and surrender. It would be safer than wandering unarmed among hostile natives.

After a few minutes of fruitless reflection he gave in to the tense and silent demand of his officers and gave the order for the askari to carry the loads. The Feldwebel smiled triumphantly and took charge. He roared for the soldiers to come to attention and when they did so he called out the new order. There was a brief silence and then a breaking of ranks followed by uproar. It was a long while before order was restored by the outraged Feldwebel and the under-officers who used their canes and even their guns to force the askari into silence and then obedience. By then the rain had arrived, and the men stood in two glowering files while the officers faced them and Feldwebel Walther berated them. It was left to the under-officers to distribute the loads among the askari before they set off on that day's march. By then the rain was well set and heavy, a cold driving rain which cut into them as they trudged across the nyika towards the escarpment.

They made slow progress despite the officers' shouting and their canes. There was little respite from the under-officers' blows as the ombasha and the shaush seemed to have lost their minds too, goaded into worse ferocity by the Feldwebel. After a while the march settled into a reluctant shuffle despite the best efforts of the tiring under-officers. They stopped often, to rest or to adjust loads, and at every stop there were grumbles and scowling looks. They were not spared the usual perils of the march – the bites and the heat, the intermittent heavy rain, the aching feet from walking in worn-out boots, the exhaustion. All these were even more intolerable to the askari than usual now that they were forced to do menial work. When they finally stopped to make camp in the late afternoon, there was a tense expectation of trouble. The men grumbled in loud voices, wanting to be overheard, complaining that this slave washenzi work was not what they had agreed to when they joined up. They knew that the British were encouraging them to desert. They saw leaflets in the villages they raided for food and heard rumours from other askari. They complained that the British did not treat their soldiers with this kind of disregard. Such provocation to their dignity was intolerable. Hamza was surprised at how inconsolable their discontent was. It seemed at times close to violence, and they all knew what askari violence was capable of. In those last weeks it seemed to Hamza that there hung over the officers a fear of mutiny and massacre. He heard the Oberleutnant say softly to the other Germans, 'Everyone on the alert. There could be trouble.'

The Feldwebel saw that Hamza had heard. Their privations had made the Feldwebel lean and sinewy, his face dark from the sun, his eyes shiny with a vigilant light, his hair and beard long and dirty, his whole manner full of menace and contempt for everyone, including the Oberleutnant. To Hamza it seemed that his hatred for the officer was transmitted to him too, that in some way he exacerbated it. At that moment, when he saw that Hamza had overheard the officer's warning, his look was sharp and threatening. Hamza looked away hurriedly.

Squalls of rain turned into a thunderstorm as night fell. They had made camp in a wood, which was not normal practice but they needed cover from patrols. Some of the trees there were vast. Earlier, when Hamza put his arms around a trunk, he felt its heart beating and the sap surging up to the branches. Lightning crackled in the trees and weirdly illuminated the grove where they had sought shelter. Hamza wondered if it was safe for them to see out the storm here. He was wet through, lying on ground that was soggy and sloshy with water the earth could no longer absorb. Water dripped down on him from the trees and he felt something crawling over him but was too exhausted to move. Late into the night, he heard sounds of movement and guessed it was a small animal walking furtively about. Then all of a sudden he knew that it was the askari and lay still and silent where he was, pressing himself into the soft ground as if that way he could make himself disappear. When the lightning flashed he shut his eyes involuntarily, but in the instant before he did so, he saw the huddled shapes of men walking away into the trees. The furtive noises went on for a few minutes and then stopped and all he could hear was the splash of the rain on the sodden ground. He knew the askari were deserting but he lay still in the downpour, waiting for the dawn.

Somehow he must have fallen asleep because he woke up suddenly to shouts and commands. It was just about light and one of the under-officers, he thought it was the shaush, had discovered the desertions and was giving the alarm. Several people were quickly on their feet, shouting and looking around in agitation, not yet sure where the danger lay. Wamekimbia, wamekimbia, the shaush was shouting in a panic. They have run away, they have run away. The commanding officer asked for a head count. The Feldwebel tramped about in the rain, his sword in his hand, calling for the under-officers to count the men. Traitors, traitors, he called as he strode back and forth. Twenty-nine askari had left during the night, leaving twelve behind. Two of them were the ombasha and the shaush who had given the alarm, both Nubi and long-serving schutztruppe. The Feldwebel glared around the remaining troop and his eyes rested on Hamza, who looked away to avoid eye contact but it was too late.

'Come here,' the Feldwebel shouted, pointing at the ground two steps in front of him. Hamza stepped forward as ordered and stopped a pace or two short of where the Feldwebel pointed. 'He heard you telling us to expect trouble,' Feldwebel Walther said, addressing the Oberleutnant. The Germans were standing in a scattered group to one side facing the African troop, both the music master and the Leutnant with revolvers in their hand. 'This traitor whore of yours betrayed us. He incited them to go. He told them lies and they deserted,' Feldwebel Walther cried in rage. Then he stepped forward and with a wild swing slashed at Hamza who turned sharply to avoid the blow. It caught him on his hip and ripped through flesh and bone. He heard someone screaming and then his head hit the ground with jarring force. He heard several voices shouting and someone close by screaming dementedly. He struggled for breath, heaving desperately but unable to take in air. Then he must have passed out.

He came to for a brief dazed moment and saw the medical officer on his knees beside him and felt arms holding him. He came awake again amid angry voices and shouted orders. When he regained consciousness he found himself on a stretcher carried by two askari. It was raining and water ran down his face. He was awake for a while before he was able to arrive at that conclusion, only gradually adding together his confused impressions before lapsing into unconsciousness again. On one of the subsequent occasions he was awake, he saw the Oberleutnant walking beside the stretcher but lost him again. Hamza was hallucinating by then, perhaps he was not even on a stretcher. He saw the Oberleutnant once more, walking beside him, and asked, Sind Sie das? Is that you? His whole body was trembling and rippling and he had the taste of vomit in his mouth. The throbbing was worst on his left side but it enveloped all of him. He had no strength left to move any part of his body. He did not want to move any part of his body, and it required a great effort to open his eyes. Then they set him down on the ground and the pain shot through his leg and forced a scream out of him before he was even aware it was on its way. He came fully awake then and saw the ombasha Haidar al-Hamad on one knee beside the stretcher.

'Shush wacha kelele,' he said. 'Shush shush alhamdulillah. Not so much crying, askari.' His face was streaked with rainwater, his lips puckered as if hushing a child.

As Hamza lay on the ground with the pain pounding up one side of his body, suffocating with a feeling of nausea in his mouth, he saw the Oberleutnant some feet away, looking down at him prone on the stretcher blanket. 'Ja, ich bin es. Macht nichts,' the officer said. Yes, it's me. Don't worry.

Then Hamza passed out again. They stopped walking some time during the night. He knew that because he woke up briefly several times. It was so cold. He was wet through, trembling and shivering uncontrollably. Later he heard hyenas barking and a strange coughing he could not identify. He heard the howl of an animal having its life torn out.

It was no longer raining when they left at first light, and as the sun heated him he felt some relief. He knew now that the wetness was not only rain, that he was bleeding heavily. Flies gathered around him, in his face and on his body, and he did not have the strength to wave them away. They found a rag to cover his face, to keep away the flies. The shivering was now constant and he drifted in and out of sleep. It was night when he woke up and it took a long time to work out that he was lying on a bed in a room dimly lit by an oil lamp on a nearby table. He was trembling constantly, groaning involuntarily as spasms of pain ran through him. He was indifferent to everything else in the pain's embrace. Later he sensed the approach of dawn through the open doorway, and in a while heard someone enter and draw near.

'Oh, you've woken up,' the man said. It was a familiar voice but he was too weary to open his eyes. 'You are safe now, brother. You are in Kilemba mission. It's Pascal here – you remember Pascal. Of course you do. I will get the pastor.'

'We did the best we could to stitch you up,' the pastor said, his sunburned face bent over Hamza. Pascal translated even though Hamza could understand, their voices drifting in and out of his hearing. 'The bleeding has … some seepage. We don't know … damage inside the bone … infection. It is important … fever down … nourishment. Then we wait and hope for the best. I will tell … officer that … awake.'

The officer came in and brought a chair to the side of the bed. Hamza could not keep his eyes open and fell into and out of consciousness, but each time he opened his eyes the officer was still there at the side of the bed. He had cleaned himself up but was dressed in the ragged clothes he had worn in the field. He wore his usual mocking smile as Hamza strained to hear. He could follow the words better now. The Oberleutnant said, speaking slowly, soothingly: 'It seems that you will survive after all. What a lot of trouble you are. Now you will be lying here recuperating in this beautiful mission while … go back … troop and continue our senseless war. Zivilisierungmission … We lied and killed for this empire and then called it our Zivilisierungmission. Now here we are, still killing for it. Are you feeling a lot of pain? Can you hear me? Blink your eyes if you … Of course you can … a lot of pain, but the missionary and his people … promised me. They are good people. They will throw away your uniform so no one … you were askari and they will give you plenty of food and a good dose of prayer and you will soon be well.'

His words sounded unlikely and far away. Hamza made no effort to speak.

'Tell me, how old are you really?' the officer said, and his words suddenly came through very clearly. 'Your record says you were twenty when you joined up but I don't believe that.'

Hamza tried but it required too much effort to summon the words.

'No, I don't believe you,' the officer said. 'I can order fifty lashes for lying to an officer, a double hamsa ishirin. You could not have been more than seventeen when you joined up. My younger brother was that age when he died. In a fire in the barracks. I was in there too. Eighteen … a beautiful boy, and I think of him often.' He stroked the stretched skin on his temple and then sat stiffly for a few minutes as if he would not say any more. His hand reached out towards the bed but then he pulled it back. 'It was a terrible fierce fire. He did not want to be in the army. He was not suited to it. My father wanted it. It was a family tradition … all soldiers

118

... and my young brother did not want to disappoint him ... a dreamer. It was very clever of you to learn German ... quickly and so well. He loved Schiller, my brother Hermann. Well, you must rest now. We'll get ourselves ready to go.'

The ombasha Haidar al-Hamad and the other askari came in to say goodbye. 'You are a lucky boy,' the ombasha told him, using his regular snarling tone, his lips at Hamza's ear as if he did not want him to miss a word. 'Oberleutnant like you, that's why you lucky. Otherwise we throw you away in the forest, hamal.'

The other askari touched him on the arm and said, 'Amri ya Mungu. Mungu akueke, sisi tunarudi kwenda kuuliwa.' It is God's command. May God keep you, we are going back to be killed.

When the officer came again, all set to depart, Hamza heard everything he said. 'Do you know why I told you about my brother?' He smiled one of his old sardonic smiles. 'No, of course you don't. You are only an askari and you are not allowed to speculate on the intimate concerns of a German officer. You are piling up more strokes on your record, for insolence as well as lying and desertion' He put a book down on the table on the other side of the room. 'I'll leave this for you. It will keep you company while you recuperate and it will help you practise your German. Leave it here with the missionary when you are well enough to go. Our war will soon be over, and maybe I will come back and collect it one day. I expect the British will intern us with nigger criminals for a while, to humiliate us for being such a nuisance to them, but then they will send us home.'

*

Hamza was placed under the care of Pascal who came to attend to him several times in the day, to give him water or feed him the soup that the pastor prescribed or to clean him. Hamza had only a vague and intermittent sense of what was happening. His fever was high and there was no part of his body that did not ache. He could no longer locate the source of the pain. The wound was on his left thigh and the whole of that side of his body throbbed with a pounding pulse. He did not have any feeling in his right leg and could not move either arm. Sometimes it took an enormous effort even for him to open his eyes. The pastor came to examine him during the day and gave Pascal instructions on how to clean him and make him comfortable. The faces of the two men moved in and out of his vision, and day and night merged into one another. Hamza felt a cool hand on his brow at times but could not tell whose it was.

He woke up one night in utter darkness and realised he was the one who was sobbing in his nightmare. The ground was covered in blood sucking at his feet and his body was drenched in it. Limbs and broken torsos were pressed against him, and voices were screaming and shouting at a demented and terrified pitch. He stilled his sobbing but could not stop the shaking of his limbs or wipe away his tears. Pascal heard him and came in with a lamp. Without saying a word, he lifted the sheet to look at the dressing and then put the lamp down on the table at the other side of the room. He came back to Hamza and put his hand on his brow. He wiped away his tears with a wet cloth and then cleaned the mucus from his nostrils and his lips and made him drink some water. Finally he pulled up a chair and sat beside the bed but did not say anything until Hamza was breathing quietly again.

'You are safe here, my brother. Hawa wazungu watu wema.' These Europeans are good people. 'They are people of God,' he said, then could not restrain a smile. 'I am not the doctor but I think your fever is going down. The pastor said when the fever goes down then you are on the road to recovery. He knows about healing. I have worked for him for a long time, from down on the coast before he came to work in Kilemba. His medicine saved me when I was hurt,' Pascal said, and stroked the scar on his neck. 'He will make you better too, but we will not leave everything in his hands. We will ask God's help as well. I will pray for you.' Pascal shut his eyes and clasped his hands together and began to pray. Hamza could see him clearly, as if a film was cleaned off his eyes. He looked at Pascal sitting on the chair beside him, face weathered and lined, eyes closed as he mumbled the sacred words. Hamza looked around the room – at the table with the lamp on it, at the half-open door – and it was as if he was seeing all these sights for the first time. In the midst of his prayers Pascal reached out and took Hamza's right hand, which was lying on the bed, and lifted it up. Hamza saw his hand firmly clasped in Pascal's but could not feel it. Pascal put his other hand on his brow, and then he spoke aloud words of blessing.

'Were you remembering bad times?' he asked afterwards. 'I shall stay with you if you wish but maybe it's better to sleep. I will hear you if you call out. The door is open and I am sleeping next door. Do you want me to stay? I think tomorrow the pastor will be very happy to see your eyes shining like this.'

The next morning the pastor took his temperature and nodded approvingly at him. He removed the dressing and looked less happy but put a brave face on it. Pascal adjusted Hamza's pillows while the pastor waited. He was a thin neat upright man who held himself stiffly, just as the officer had said. When Pascal had made him comfortable, the pastor said in German, 'Verstehst du? Do you understand me? Do you want Pascal to translate?'

'I understand,' Hamza said, and was surprised by the strangeness of his own voice.

The pastor's austere face lit up in a smile. 'The Oberleutnant told us you did. That's good. Shake your head if you don't understand something I have said. I think your fever has gone down but this is only the first step in your recovery. It will take a long time,' he said severely as if Hamza might misunderstand and think himself safe. 'The bleeding must stop completely then we will get you to move a little and do exercises. For now there is still some seepage. This war makes everything difficult. We will do what we can here until we can get you to a hospital where you can be looked after properly. The most important thing is to prevent infection. Now we start you on solid food, one step at a time. Can you move your right arm? This is where we begin the exercises, with the right arm and right leg. Pascal will teach you.'

Pascal was the main nurse. He spent the night in the next room although he had his own quarters in the compound. Every morning he cleaned Hamza and helped him sit up, massaged his arms and his right leg, talking to him in his unhurried and slightly solemn way. Then he said a prayer with his eyes shut and afterwards helped Hamza eat his meal of yoghurt, sorghum and mashed pumpkin, which he told him the other African workers in the mission also ate. After that he made Hamza as comfortable as he could before leaving to attend to his other duties in the mission.

Through the open window Hamza could see part of the fig tree and part of the missionary's home. On most mornings he saw a small light-green heron standing motionless for a long time on the ridge of the roof, then for no reason he could see, it took off. He did not know why, but the sight of the heron standing motionless on the roof ridge filled him with sorrow. It made him feel so alone. In the mid-morning the pastor came to examine him. As he leaned close Hamza smelled the mingled odours of soap and moist flesh and a yeasty vegetable smell. The pastor thoroughly examined the wound, exercised Hamza's limbs, interrogated him at length and looked serious and grave whatever the result of his inspection.

Through the window Hamza heard a piano and the voices of the little girls singing and practising and heard their voices when they played on the patio. Sometime during the day, their mother, the Frau pastor, came to see him. She was a slim blonde-haired woman who looked used to hard work and perhaps a little weary but smiled easily. She usually brought him something on a tin tray: biscuits and a tin mug of coffee or a small bowl of figs or sliced cucumber. She talked to him about the months they had spent on the coast before they moved to Kilemba. Wasn't the landscape here wonderful? The chill at night kept away the mosquitoes, which was such a blessing after the coast. Both the pastor and she came from farming people and the climate here was perfect for their crops. Do you not love it here? This climate will do you good, you'll see. She asked Hamza questions and exclaimed at his German. Such excellent diction. When she left Hamza always felt better than he really was. When the Frau pastor could not bring him his biscuits or fruit at the customary time, Witness's wife Subiri came over with the tin tray, which she put down on the bedside table with a small benign murmur.

It was two weeks before he caught sight of the little girls on the patio. One afternoon, after he had regained some strength in his arms, he used the wooden crutches Pascal had made for him and, with his help, limped on one leg to the window. Hamza felt the blood rushing through his left leg and an unexpected tingling throughout his body. Out of the window he saw a corner of the patio outside the missionaries' home and the two girls sitting on a mat there playing with a doll's house. He heard the mother's voice talking to them but did not see her. They were not aware that he was watching. He placed his chair by the window and sometimes sat there throughout the morning, watching the comings and goings at the mission. As he became more mobile and could hobble out of the infirmary to catch the sun, he waved to the girls and they waved back while their mother looked on. He remembered what the officer said about how she worried for her little girls and he saw how she hovered over them. He sometimes saw the Frau pastor in the orchard by the side of her house, the girls trailing after her with their baskets.

One morning, as he sat outside on the chair he had brought out of the infirmary, the pastor came to him and stood squinting at him in the sun, regarding him without saying a word for a moment. 'We have just heard that the war is over and Germany has surrendered,' he said. 'Here in Ostafrika our commander has only just surrendered to the British with his remaining forces. It seems he did not know for three weeks that the Armistice was agreed, but now it is all over. God has kept you alive and we must thank Him for that when so many have been taken. You must always be grateful for that and that He has made this mission the instrument of His mercy.'

Pascal told Hamza that there was to be a service to pray for all who had perished and that he should come. 'It will please the pastor and the Frau pastor and will please God too. In addition to that,' he said, 'if you don't come, you will annoy the pastor. It will be better if you make him happy. He is a cautious man and would like to see you gone before the British and Rhodesians come, as they surely will. If they find you here, they will know you are a wounded askari and may even close down the mission.

If the pastor is not happy with you he will let them take you into detention, but not if you are one of his flock.'

A handful of the villagers who were part of the mission's congregation were back and the service was attended by more than a dozen people, most of them women. It was Hamza's first time in the mission's chapel, an unadorned whitewashed room with a cross on the wall and a lectern standing in front of it. He thought he understood what Pascal was doing, saving his life and at the same time looking to win Hamza's soul for the Saviour. He knew none of the hymns and sat throughout the service with head bowed while the congregation sang and the pastor prayed for the fallen.

Hamza's condition improved steadily over the weeks that followed although movement was often painful for him in the damaged hip joint and across his groin. The wound healed and he gained mobility with exercising but the pastor said there must be some damage to tendon or nerve that he was not expert enough to treat. Hamza needed crutches to get about because the leg was not strong enough to take his weight. Pascal said that it looked as if he was going to be staying for a while so they had better make him more comfortable. With the help of Witness, Pascal walled up the lean-to next to the quarters he shared with Juma, covering wattle panels with a thick paste of mud, and then he helped Hamza to move in there. You only need raise your voice for one of us to hear you, he said.

The infirmary was now back to its proper use as the local people began to come in for treatment. They heard rumours of illness everywhere at the end of the war although the worst of it had not reached Kilemba. Hamza began to help out in the work of the mission, things he could do sitting down at first: sorting tobacco leaves, cleaning vegetables, mending furniture. He found he had a certain skill with the latter and the Frau pastor and Pascal found bits of furniture for him to mend. The pastor watched his work with the tobacco leaves and the furniture and approved in his taciturn way. He was a naturally watchful man who kept his steady eyes on what was going on in the mission but did not often intervene to correct or rebuke publicly. In the evening Hamza joined Pascal and the other workers as they ate their food and talked about the chaos outside the mission's walls.

The Frau pastor said Hamza's recovery was nothing short of a miracle. He must have led a righteous life. He knew she was teasing him and exaggerating his recovery to lift his spirits, but he was thankful. The little girls, Lise the elder and Dorthe the younger, brought over their hymn sheets as he sat in the shade and taught him the words, saying them to him and making him repeat them when he could just as easily have read them himself. He did his best with the hymns but they were stern teachers and made him repeat the lines several times. On one occasion they disagreed about how to say a word, and without thinking he reached over and took the sheet from Lise so he could see for himself. She snatched it back instantly, as if without thought. It's mine, she said. In that instant as he looked at the verse he had a vague memory of the officer saying something about a book before he left. What book was that? Was that a hallucination? Did he dream about that?

'Did the Oberleutnant leave a book for me?' he asked Pascal.

'What book?' he asked. 'Can you read?'

A little, Hamza remembered, thinking of his officer. 'Yes, I can read,' he said.

'I can read too. We have some pamphlets in the chapel cupboard if you want something to read,' Pascal said. 'Perhaps in the evening we can read together? Sometimes I read for Witness and Subiri. They are such devoted worshippers.'

'No ... I mean, yes, we can read together if you wish, but did he leave a book for me? The officer,' Hamza said.

Pascal shrugged. 'Why would he do that? Was he your brother?'

The Frau pastor said to him, smiling, 'Lise told me you took her hymn sheet from her when she was teaching you. She was outraged you took such a liberty. I wondered if you wanted me to teach you how to read.'

'I can read,' Hamza said.

She raised her eyebrows slightly, briefly. 'I didn't know,' she said.

'A little,' he added humbly. 'I need more practice. Did the Oberleutnant leave a book for me?'

She looked away without replying and then said, 'I'll ask the pastor. Why do you ask?'

He had seen in the second before she looked away that her eyes lit up briefly, so he knew that he had not hallucinated, that the officer had very likely left a book, which they were keeping from him. Hamza shook his head, as if he was uncertain or making light of the matter. He did not want to make a fuss when it could be his own feverish imagination at work. 'I thought I remembered something like that but I am not sure. My memory is so confused.'

The more he thought about it, the more certain he became, and the officer's words came back to him in fuller fragments, something about a fire and his younger brother dying and how young he had been. Then he said the book was for Hamza to practise his German on, and after that something about nigger criminals. Hamza could not remember what that was about. He did his exercises and silently thanked the pastor and Pascal for caring for him and crushed any hankering desire for a book, or tried to. The wound was now completely healed on the outside although he still needed a crutch to support his weight. It had taken many weeks, past Christmas and New Year and a visit by a British officer, during which he was kept out of sight. The British officer told the pastor that an influenza epidemic was raging over the land and across the world and that thousands had already perished. There was chaos in Germany, which had banished the Kaiser and declared itself a republic. There was chaos and war in Russia after the revolution which murdered the Tsar and his entire family. The whole world was in turmoil, he said. They had food and supplies here and had better stay put for the time being until clearer orders came through.

It was the pastor who brought up the subject of the book again, but he did not do so directly. At the end of one of his regular examinations, the pastor suggested they go for a walk together to give Hamza a little exercise. It was late in the afternoon and they walked over to the gate to the mission building and then to the compound gate. The pastor stopped there, his eyes running over the plain ahead and then to the escarpment in the distance.

'Sunset gives a benign aspect to the landscape, doesn't it? Yet it is a landscape where you know that nothing of any importance has ever happened,' he said. 'It is a place of no significance whatsoever in the history of human achievement or endeavour. You could tear this page out of human history and it would not make a difference to anything. You can understand why people can live contentedly in such a place, even though they are plagued by so many diseases.' He glanced at Hamza and then smiled in a relaxed manner, at ease with his own words. 'At least, it was like that until we came and brought them words of discontent like progress and sin and salvation. The people here all share one quality, they cannot hold an idea for long. At times this can seem deceitful but it is really a lack of seriousness, an unreliability, a failure in application. That's why it is necessary to repeat instructions and to supervise. Just imagine, if we left here tomorrow they will return like bush to their old ways.'

He glanced again at Hamza and then turned to walk back. Hamza thought of him as a man torn between the demand made on him to dominate and the inner desire to give succour. He wondered if that was how it was for European missionaries working with backward people like them.

'The officer who struck you must have been out of his mind,' the pastor continued as they strolled back. 'The Oberleutnant told me about him. He said he was an officer of great competence but also a political man who was full of grievances against the nobility and the ruling class in Germany. Ours is a painfully divided country and now, after the military defeat, grumblers have ousted the Kaiser and chaos rules. It makes you wonder what a man like the Feldwebel was doing in the Imperial Army in Ostafrika. Perhaps he was attracted to violence and the schutztruppe would have given him scope for that. The Oberleutnant also told me that this officer was difficult to control – that he hated the natives so much he constantly broke the rules about what he was allowed to do to them, including his treatment of the askari. What he did to you was a crime according to schutztruppe rules. The Oberleutnant told me it was as if that man wanted to attack him when he struck you.

'Do you understand everything I have said? Of course you do. The Oberleutnant said your German was very good and I have heard you speak it myself. Perhaps it did not seem right to the other German officers that he ... befriended you, that his ... protection of you was so ... intimate. I am only guessing, I don't know, because of something else the Oberleutnant said. Perhaps his behaviour was seen as undermining German prestige. I can understand how people might think like that. I also understand that war brings about unexpected bonds.'

The pastor did not say more until they were back in the infirmary and then he stood by the window, glancing alternately out and back towards Hamza, avoiding eye contact. 'Yes, the Oberleutnant left a book for you as you asked the Frau. He told me you could read but I did not tell her that. The Oberleutnant said you were in the wrong place in the schutztruppe and now that I have seen you here for several months, I can see that too. I have watched you recover your health with the stoic patience of someone with intelligence and faith. I don't mean religious faith. I don't know that about you although I know Pascal has hopes of winning you over to the Saviour. Pascal is a great romantic and a wise man.

'When I took the book away, I did not know this about you and thought that the Oberleutnant was being reckless, that he was led by his emotions because he felt responsible for your injury. That was what made me think that he had overextended his protection of you, that it was that kind of ... solicitude that had provoked the Feldwebel to violence. The Oberleutnant said you reminded him of someone he knew in his youth, and I thought this showed too much sentiment for a German officer speaking about a native soldier. I thought the gift he left too valuable for a mere native. When my wife told me that you asked for the book, I thought again about what I had done. I did not tell her that the officer told me you could read. She believed me when I said that the book was too valuable to be left lying about, which is true. When she told me you had asked for the book, she also told me you could read. I said to her that I knew that. So then she said, you must give him the book back. It was left for him. I knew she would say something like that, which was why I had kept silent. I told her that I doubted very much if you would be able to read the book with any true understanding, which still remains my conviction. She told me that was none of my affair and I should give the book back to its rightful owner.'

The pastor smiled as he said this. 'She defeated me at every turn. Perhaps I should say, she convinced me that I was wrong to have taken it away, and so I determined to give it back to you and to explain fully why I had taken it away from you in the first place. I was mistaken. Perhaps in time you will be able to read it with as much pleasure as the Oberleutnant anticipated.'

He handed over a small book with a gold and black cover: Schiller's *Musen-Almanach für das Jahr 1798*.

THREE

8

Their boat rounded the breakwater in evening twilight and the nahodha ordered the sail lowered as he made a cautious approach into harbour. The tide was out and he was not sure of the channels, he said. It was after the kaskazi monsoon and in the period before the winds and currents turned south-easterly. Heavy currents at that time of year sometimes shifted the channels. His boat was heavily laden and he did not want to get stuck on a sandbank or to hit something on the bottom. In the end, after debating the matter with his crew, he thought it was too dark to approach the quay in safety, so they dropped anchor in shallow water and waited for morning. There were lights on ashore and a few people moving about on the quay, their elongated shadows stretched out ahead and behind them in the gloom. Beyond the quayside warehouses the town sprawled and the sky was amber from the glow of the setting sun. Further to the right the dimly lit shoreline road shaped away towards the headland which after a while ran out to the darkness of the country. Hamza remembered that from the time before, how the road ran past the house where he lived, and how then it narrowed down to the tight aperture that opened out into the interior.

Out to sea, the sky filled with stars and a huge moon began to rise, illuminating the heaving water beyond the breakwater and the frothing crest of the reef in the distance. As the moon rose higher, it submerged the whole world in its unearthly glow, turning the warehouses and the quayside and the boats tied up alongside into insubstantial silhouettes of themselves. By then the nahodha and his three crew members had eaten their meagre ration of rice and salt-fish, which they shared with him, and settled themselves to rest, stretching out in a tight cluster on the sacks of millet and lentils which were their cargo. So he lay close too, listening to their conversation and their profanities and their gloomy homesick songs while the boat pitched with the surge of the incoming tide. They fell asleep almost in unison, their breaths drawing deeply a few times and then suddenly falling silent. After the momentary stillness which followed their voices, the boat resumed its agonised creaking as the sea tugged and pulled at it in its unrest. He lay on his good side but he could not prevent the pain from returning, so he drew back from the cluster of men and put some distance between them. After a while he moved away completely for fear of making them restless with his sleeplessness. He wedged himself into a space that provided some distracting discomfort from his aches, and somehow he fell asleep.

At dawn they poled the boat in to the quayside, working silently in the mauve light. The tide was now fully in and the vessel rode high on the water. The nahodha declined his offer to help with unloading the cargo. He grinned with benign disdain, baring his stained teeth with amusement.

'Do you think this work is a joke?' he said, looking Hamza up and down in friendly mockery. 'You need skill to do this and the strength of an ox.'

Hamza thanked the nahodha who had agreed to give him passage without payment and shook hands with the crew. He walked carefully down the plank to the quayside, his whole body tense with the effort of suppressing the pain in his hip, now made worse by a night spent wedged in the boat's ribs. None of the men had asked about his pain, although they could not have failed to notice his limp. He was grateful for that because sympathy in such situations required disclosure in return. He did not look back as he walked along the almost empty quayside but he wondered if the nahodha and his crew were watching and perhaps talking about him.

He walked through the port gates, which were open and unguarded, and proceeded towards the town. He passed people heading for the port, striding on their way to work. This was not a part of town he knew well. He had lived on the edges and

134

hardly ever visited the centre, but he did not want to seem uncertain or lost so he too strode as purposefully as the pain in his hip allowed and looked out for a familiar street or building. At first the street he was on was wide and lined with neem trees, but soon it became narrower with other side-streets leading off it. As he walked further a slight panic began to rise in him. People were coming out of the side-streets, sure of their way, and he still did not know where he was. It became difficult to navigate as the crowd thickened, but also calming. He was on a busy road so his hesitation and uncertainty would not show as clearly. Sooner or later he was bound to recognise something. When he stumbled on the old Post Office building, he sat down on a step outside with relief and waited for his panic to diminish. Pedestrians and cyclists went past, mingling with the occasional car that nudged its way patiently through the crowd.

He sought the quiet streets after the Post Office, a little clearer now on where he was but still not really that sure. He walked aimlessly down cool shaded lanes and past half-open doors and overflowing gutters. He crossed wide roads past cafés crowded with breakfast customers and then slipped again down narrow alleyways where houses leaned towards each other with an intimidating intimacy. Hamza was not at ease in streets like these, with their aromas of cooking and stagnant sewage and with the echoing voices of women in their shuttered yards. He felt like an intruder. He walked on anyway, relishing the anguishing strangeness the alleys provoked in him, at once familiar and forbidding. He realised after a while that he was walking the same streets again and attracting interested glances, so he forced himself out of the circuit he had stumbled into and headed in a different direction.

It was mid-morning when he came to a yard whose wooden gates stood wide open. An earth road ran past, and across and to either side stood residential houses, which made the yard appear part of the ordinary life of the street. Something held him there for a while and then he came closer, thinking this looked a likely place to find work or at least a moment's rest. Through the open gateway came a clamour of voices and the banging of hammers and an air of honest labour. Two men were changing the wheel of a van jacked up on a pile of bricks, one was on his knees with the wheel in his hands, the other standing beside him, holding a spanner and a hammer in readiness. The big one on his knees was talking in boisterous tones. It was from him alone that the clamour came. His head was turned towards his companion whose lips were parted on the brink of laughter. The companion's head was large for his body, so large that it was impossible to overlook. Hamza glanced towards them and heard enough of the mockery and swagger and tortured laughter to recognise the familiar tones of street banter meant to be overheard. The two men paid no attention to him as he stood nearby, or perhaps pretended not to notice him.

Beyond the two men and the van, and under a young coconut tree in a corner of the yard, a boy was hammering nails into a packing crate. There were three other crates nearby already secured and an open one full of wood shavings. Another two youths, no more than boys, were carrying a hot metal pot between two poles and heading towards the building occupying the whole of one side of the large yard. From the smell he guessed the pot contained oil or varnish. The building's doors stood wide open and he could hear timber being worked inside, the sound of a saw and a plane and intermittent hammering, and he could smell the astringent perfume of wood shavings. A small door at one end of the workshop building was open, and through it he saw a man sitting at a desk, bent over a ledger, wire-framed glasses resting low on his nose. Hamza limped towards him, walking slowly, taking short steps, making every effort to disguise his injury.

The man behind the desk was dressed in a loose long-sleeved shirt of thin cotton material, and he looked cool and comfortable. His head was shaved and his scraggy little beard was flecked with grey. His embroidered cap lay on the desk beside the ledger. He was in his early thirties, sturdily built and strong-looking. Bent over his desk in the way he was, he seemed like a man completely absorbed in his own affairs, every inch the owner of the yard. Hamza stood in the doorway without speaking, waiting for the man to look up and invite him to enter the office, or to chase him away. It was a cool morning and he had become used to waiting. He stood there for what seemed several minutes, cautioning himself against showing any sign of impatience or restlessness. The man looked up sharply, as if he had been aware of him all along but had suddenly run out of patience. He perched the glasses on top of his head and looked at Hamza with the unhurried self-assurance of a man who had found his rightful place in the world. He frowned briefly but did not speak, waiting in turn for Hamza to announce himself and his business. After a moment he tilted his chin slightly, which Hamza took to be a high-handed invitation to speak.

'I am looking for work,' he said.

The man cupped his hand round his left ear, for Hamza had spoken softly.

'I am looking for work, please,' Hamza repeated more loudly, and added the courtesy because he wondered if the man wanted him to plead, wanted him to show some humility.

The man leaned back and folded his hands behind his head, flexing his shoulders, taking a moment's respite from his labours. 'What kind of work are you looking for?' he asked.

'Any kind of work,' Hamza said.

The man smiled. It was a bitter, disbelieving smile, that of a tired man about to have his time wasted. 'What kind of work can you do?' he asked. 'Labouring?'

Hamza shrugged. 'Yes, but I can also do other work.'

'I don't need labourers,' the man said abruptly in a tone of dismissal and turned back towards his ledger.

'I can read and write,' Hamza said, a hint of defiance in his voice, and then, remembering his circumstances, added: 'Bwana.'

The man looked directly at him and waited, wanting more precision, more details. 'What class did you reach?' he asked.

'I didn't go to school,' Hamza said. 'I was taught a little … then I learned by myself mostly.'

'How did you do that? Oh, never mind, can you keep book?' the man asked, pointing at his ledger, but Hamza knew he was not serious. He did not think a merchant would allow a stranger to keep book for him.

'I can learn,' he said after a long moment.

The man sighed and took the glasses off the top of his head. He rubbed the bristles on his scalp with his right palm, making them rustle softly. 'Can you work wood?' he asked. 'I could use someone in the workshop.'

'I can learn,' Hamza repeated, and the man smiled again, less bitterly this time, perhaps even a little kindly. Hamza felt a small spasm of hope from that smile.

'So you can't work wood but you can read and write. What was the last work you did?' he asked.

Hamza had not expected this question and he realised he should have done. He took so long to reply that the man pushed his glasses back on to his nose and bent over his ledger again. Hamza stood where he was, just inside the doorway, and waited while the man wrote something. He wondered if he should go before the man became irritable and ugly with him, but he was unable to move as if paralysed. Then after several minutes the man looked long and wearily at him, capped his pen, picked up his cap and said to Hamza, 'Come with me.'

That was how he so unexpectedly came to work for the merchant Nassor Biashara. The merchant later told Hamza that he took him on because he liked the look of him. Hamza was then twenty-four years old, without money and without anywhere to stay, in a town he once lived in but knew very little of, tired and in some pain, and he could not imagine what the merchant could like about the look of him.

Nassor Biashara led him out to the yard and called to the boy by the packing crates. The merchant was shorter than he looked bent over his desk but he strode out with brisk, urgent steps and was on to the boy before he had begun to move towards them.

'Take this man to the warehouse. What did you say your name was? Tell Khalifa I will be along there shortly,' the merchant told the boy, whose name turned out to be Sungura although it was not his real name. Sungura meant rabbit. It also turned out that he was not a boy but an adult man the size of a slim twelve- or thirteen-year-old whose mobile, ashen and weathered face told a different story from the impression formed on a first casual glance. There was something familiar about his features, which were angular and sharp, with high cheekbones, a pointed chin, thin nose, furrowed brow: a Khoi face. Hamza had seen many Khoi faces in recent years. In the frail-looking body of an ailing teenager the face looked a little sinister. It was more likely that it was not a Khoi face but of a kind he had not come across before, from Madagascar or Socotra or a far-flung island he had never heard of. Their world was full of strange faces since the recent war, and especially in these towns along the shores of the ocean, which had always drawn people from across the water and across the land, some more willingly than others. But perhaps it was nothing like that, and it was just the face of a man who had grown up in want and pain, or who had been afflicted with one of the many agonies which stalked human life.

Sungura led off and Hamza followed. As they passed the men fixing the van, the big one on his knees made a sucking, kissing noise and rolled his eyes in drooling suggestive fashion at Sungura, signalling barely controlled desire. His face was round and roughened by tough bristly stubble. The second man, who was dressed in ragged calf-length calico shorts, laughed and giggled foolishly, and it was clear that he was the vassal in the court of the bully of the yard. Sungura did not say anything and his expression did not change but Hamza sensed that his body cringed. Something about his manner told Hamza that he was used to this treatment, and that he was often required to carry out degrading chores. After they turned out into the road, he slowed and glanced at Hamza's hip. It was to tell him that he had seen his limp, one maimed person picking out another, and he was inviting him to set the pace.

They walked slowly through dusty crowded streets lined with shops overflowing with merchandise: cloths, frying pans and stew pans, prayer mats, sandals, baskets, perfumes and incense, with every now and then a fruit-seller or a coffee-stand. The morning was warming up but not yet hot and the crowds were still good-natured in their jostling and shoving. Carts barged their way through pedestrians, their drivers calling out in warning, bicycle bells tinkled and cyclists snaked a passage through the press of

139

bodies. Two elderly matrons shuffled on unconcernedly and the crowd parted around them as if they were rocks in the middle of a stream.

It was a relief after several minutes of walking to enter a wide, shaded lane that led to an empty clearing fringed with a cluster of warehouses. There were five of them, three in one building and the other two standing separately but side by side. Nassor Biashara's warehouse was on the corner of the clearing by the lane, standing on its own. The unpainted wooden door was half-open but it was too dark to make out anything in the gloomy interior. Sungura walked up to the doorway and called out. After what seemed to Hamza like several minutes, he had to call again before a man emerged from the shadows of the warehouse. He was a tall thin man of about fifty, clean-shaven and with greying hair. He was neatly dressed in a checked shirt and khaki trousers, more like an office-worker than a warehouseman. He looked from one to the other of his visitors, his face unfriendly and frowning, then said to Sungura, 'What are you making all that noise for? What's wrong with you, you idiot?' His tone was fussy and scornful, as if at any moment he was likely to spit out something foul. He pulled a clean handkerchief from his pocket and wiped his hands.

It had not seemed like such a lot of noise to Hamza but Sungura did not protest. 'Bwana Nassor said to bring him. He's coming himself. I'm going now,' he said and turned to leave.

'Hey, what are you talking about?' the warehouseman said but Sungura walked on without replying or looking back, his gait diffident yet obstinate. The man made a snorting noise at Sungura's retreating back and said something Hamza did not fully catch. The warehouseman raised his arm in greeting to Hamza, pushed the door open wider and pointed to a bench just inside. He sat on it as instructed and felt the man's eyes on him, studying him.

'What's this about? Are you a customer?' he asked.

Hamza shook his head.

'What did he send you for?'

'I've come to work,' Hamza said.

'He didn't tell me anything about that.'

The man he took to be Khalifa waited for him to say more and then shook his head irritably when Hamza did not. He stood still for a moment longer, bringing himself under control, then nodded slowly and repeatedly with an air of exasperated resignation. After another look followed by a deep sigh, he walked back into the shadows of the warehouse. It seemed such an unnecessary performance, a sour man by all appearances. If this was the one the merchant tajiri wanted him to work for then so be it. He would learn.

From the outside it did not seem like a large warehouse, no more than sixty paces long perhaps, the size of a six-roomed barracks block. It was built of coral stone and mortar, some of it exposed where the outer skin had eroded, and was roofed with tin. If there were any windows they were closed and only diffused light entered from under the eaves. As Hamza's eyes became used to the gloom, he saw crates and boxes on the near side, and stacks of bulging gunny sacks further inside. He thought he could smell timber and hide and perhaps engine oil, and the deep smell of weathered jute fibre. The smells brought back memories of his earlier times in this town. He looked out into the clearing. A man was walking across the far end of it but otherwise there was no movement. It was a large clearing, perhaps seeming more so because it was empty. The doors to all the other warehouses were closed. It was a forlorn, silent place, abandoned and somehow derelict although none of the buildings were damaged. It was a sight that drained resolve.

He shook his head to clear his mind of such thoughts, resisting his tendency to gloom. Grief reduces resistance, Pascal used to say. He smiled as he remembered Pascal. He was fortunate to have the prospect of work so soon after arriving in the town although he should remain cautious, not count his blessings before he was sure of the job. It had been many months of wandering, many years, and now he was making yet another start in the company of a spectral host of accusers. His return to the town was unexpected. When he fled it had seemed like an undoing of a life but for now it has ended with the futility of him returning to where he had been before, older, half-broken, empty-handed.

Hamza did not know what job the merchant wanted him for. He waited on the bench with eyes lowered from the glare, grateful for the shaded doorway, grateful for the rest. The pain in his hip was easing a little, he was sure of that. It did as the day moved on and he walked around, but he could not do that for long. He still needed frequent rests. He would just have to manage the pain better. The alternative was to allow it to overwhelm him and turn him into an invalid, as the war had done to so many. That did not bear thinking about. It had taken a long time, but he had eventually healed. Then, after leaving the mission, he had pushed himself too soon and lost track of what his wounded body could bear. He would have to manage better. As he sat on the bench he knew he was nearly worn out, distressed, on the verge of exhaustion. His head pounded and his eyes ached. He needed to sleep. His body had become used to subsisting on very little food but not yet to a permanent lack of sleep.

Hamza thought he heard faint noises from further back in the dark warehouse and wondered how Khalifa could see in the gloom, how he could move about so silently without stumbling into the merchandise. He had been sitting on the bench for a while when he saw a movement out of the corner of his eye and he was startled to see that Khalifa was standing a few feet away from him, just inside the warehouse, eyes glowing as he regarded him. Hamza looked away first, and for a while thought he could feel Khalifa's eyes on the side of his head. When he turned around again there was no one there. He was not alarmed. Khalifa seemed too fastidious and proper to be a menace, and Hamza was weary and only slightly bemused by his eccentric behaviour.

The merchant Nassor Biashara was in a hurry when he arrived, wearing a cream linen jacket and cap, on his way to do other errands. Hamza stood up from the bench, ready to carry out instructions. 'Khalifa!' the merchant called out. 'Where is he? Khalifa!'

He appeared after a moment. 'Naam, bwana mkubwa,' he said, his tone ironic and mocking. Yes, big master.

'This is our new man,' Nassor Biashara said. 'I've sent him here to help you in the stores.'

'Help me with what?' Khalifa asked insolently. 'What are you up to now?'

The merchant took no notice of this truculence, speaking in a firm business-like voice. 'Have you cleared a space for the new delivery? He could help you with that. It should be here in the next few days.'

'It's done,' Khalifa said, wiping his hands for emphasis.

'Sawa,' Nassor Biashara said. 'The van will come for the timber as soon as they've changed the wheel. It could be a while because they have to take the other tyre to the mechanic to be repaired. That van is costing me a fortune. Anyway, show him the ropes. He could help with the loading. He'll be our night-watchman from now on. Bring him to the yard after you lock up so he'll know the way. I have to go to the bank now.'

'What's your name?' Khalifa asked after the merchant left.

'Hamza,' he said.

'Hamza what?' Khalifa asked with what Hamza thought was surprising rudeness. In his turn he shrugged. He was not obliged to reply to such questions, asked in such a tone. He sat back down on the bench. 'Who are your people?' Khalifa asked, as if he thought Hamza had not understood his question.

'That is none of your concern.'

Khalifa smiled. 'I see – something to hide, eh? Never mind. You can start by sweeping up this litter,' he said, indicating the area in front of the warehouse doors, which was mostly litter-free. 'You'll find the broom behind the door … and don't make too much dust. Haya haya, you haven't come here for a rest.'

Hamza was bemused by such rudeness. He swept the yard as instructed and made a small pile of dust and litter beside the doorway, then sat back down on the bench. When the van came for the timber, Khalifa opened a barred window and the warehouse was flooded with the late-morning light. The loud-mouthed one of the pair Hamza had seen earlier in the yard, whose name was Idris, idled about in the shade of the warehouse, smoking and shouting heckling encouragement while Hamza helped his ragged partner load up the timber. This was in the form of roughly planed planks headed for the workshop. They were pale pink in colour and Hamza could not resist bending down to breathe in the scent of the wood. Khalifa stood beside the warehouse door and followed them with his eyes but did nothing to help. It only took a few minutes to load the van and afterwards Khalifa sat on the bench while Hamza sat nearby on a crate. It did not seem as if there was anything more to do. He wanted to ask Khalifa the name of the timber but the look of quivering disapproval on his face restrained him.

'Our night-watchman,' repeated Khalifa, smiling disdainfully at Hamza before looking away across the clearing. 'What is it that he has really brought you here to do? What is he up to? Has he promised you a job as a warehouse keeper? Our night-watchman! One look at you and the robbers will run as fast as they can in the other direction, terrified for their lives, eh? Our tajiri has hired a night-watchman! Why now? There has been valuable merchandise in here all these years and he never once thought of hiring a watchman before. He'll give you a sheet of marekani to cover yourself and a little stick and make you sit here all night with all the shetani and the ghosts that live here. He gets nervous about his money sometimes. It's this new equipment he's buying, I expect. You don't look like a watchman. Watchmen have bulging thighs and shining skin and big testicles. I can't think why he chose a weakling like you to be his watchman.'

Hamza smiled at this unprovoked attack but could not think of anything to say in protest. He would not have chosen himself to be a night-watchman either.

'You look ill,' Khalifa said. 'You must've prodded some better instinct in him, made him remember anxious times of his own. He gets stupid ideas sometimes. Did you hear him being the big businessman? I'm going to the bank now. What a busy man!'

Khalifa sighed heavily and leaned back against the warehouse door with his eyes shut. His face was narrow and ascetic in some way, the face of an abstemious man perhaps or one who had known bitterness and failure. Hamza sighed silently at the thought of working for such a sullen and peevish man.

'There'll be nothing here soon,' Khalifa said after a long silence, working his mouth as if preparing to spit something out.

'You should've seen this place as it was before: full of traders and people mingling and bargaining – the coffee-seller with his stand over there, carts bringing goods from the port, the fruit-seller with his gari, the ice-cream vendor with his trolley, and everywhere noise and bustle and loud talk. That place, boarded up now, was a café and there were people selling juice and cassava in the middle there. There was a stand-pipe to one side here with water clean enough to drink. Now look at this place. No one comes here. Everywhere is as dry as a bone. Those warehouses there –' he said, indicating the block of three '– a contractor has taken them over from the Bohra tajiri Alidina. What a man that was! Have you heard of the Bohra Alidina? Those were his warehouses, although he had stores and other warehouses in countries all over these parts, all the way to the Great Lakes. He was trading with India and Persia and England and Germany. Now they store cement and toilets and pipes in there when once they were full of grain and sugar and rice. You'll see, every other day the contractor sends a truck here and they load it up and take things away to furnish rich people's mansions. People were coming and going from here once all the time, buying and selling, the whole place bustling with life and trade, but now it's just where our betters store what we can't afford to have.'

Khalifa was silent again for a while, lost in his anger, glancing at Hamza now and then with a look of discontent as if expecting a response from him. 'What's wrong with you? Can't you speak?' he asked finally, and sucked in his cheeks and worked his jaws as if he was chewing something acid and sour. Hamza sat there without a word. After a while, as they waited silently, he felt Khalifa's anger recede and heard his breathing change and its measure subside. When he began to speak again it was with far less rancour than before, as if he had resigned himself to whatever had once irritated him.

'That other store, that belongs to the Chinaman.' He pointed to the other detached property. 'He keeps dried shark fin and sea cucumber and vipusa in there – you know, rhino horn – and those other things they like in China. He keeps them in there and then every few months, when he has enough, he loads it all on to a ship and sends it off to Hong Kong. I don't think it's legal but he knows how to stay out of trouble and how to keep the Customs boys happy. They like those things in China, to make their zub hard. He never rests, that Chinaman, nor does he let any of his family rest. Have you seen his house? There are trays of noodles drying in the backyard, flocks of ducks waddling about in the mud in front, his grocery kiosk is open from dawn until late at night ... and all the time he is dressed in shorts and a singlet like a labourer, working every hour of the day and night. Have you heard him speak? He sounds just like you and me ... none of that fong fong fong you expect from a Chinaman. And all his children are the same. If you listen to them speak with your eyes closed, you'd never guess that you were listening to a Chinaman. Have you heard them speak?'

'No, I haven't,' Hamza said.

Khalifa looked at him for a moment then he said, 'Don't you know the Chinaman? I don't remember seeing you before. Are you a stranger here?'

Hamza was silent for a while. 'Not really,' he said.

'Not really what? Still hiding,' Khalifa said, smiling wearily. 'Why don't you just lie? It's easier that way and you save yourself trouble. Just lie and then it's over. Otherwise it sounds like you're hiding something.'

'I'm not a stranger here,' Hamza said. 'I lived here a few years ago but then I went away.'

'Who are your people?' Khalifa asked again.

'They live a long way away,' Hamza said, lying as Khalifa had instructed him to do.

'Have you wandered far? You look as if you have,' Khalifa said, a look of mild disdain on his face. 'Tell me, were you in the war? That's what I thought when I saw you. You look like a vagrant.'

Hamza shrugged and did not reply, and Khalifa did not press him. Soon after the call for midday prayers, he locked up and they walked back to the main yard. It was now hot but not unbearably so and the walk was pleasant until they reached the busy road with the shops. The overflowing wares added to the congestion on road and pavement. The chaos and din and the irritable invective of the noon crowds forced them to shove and force themselves past people who were also intent on making their way home or else to the market or the mosque as quickly as they could. Nassor Biashara was not back from the bank yet, so while Khalifa sat outside the merchant's office to wait, Hamza went to the now silent workshop, drawn there by the smell of wood and resin. He found an elderly man sitting in a corner embroidering a cap. He looked up over his glasses and returned to his embroidery. Hamza assumed this was the carpenter having his lunch break. He spoke a greeting and made ready to retreat.

Around the workshop were various wooden items: a recliner, small tables, an ornately carved bench, a sideboard with smaller items on it – bowls, cabinets – some of them in wood the colour of bronze and some in a pale wood, many of them in states of incompleteness. It was as if the carpenter was working on several items at the same time, or else there was more than one carpenter.

The smell of wood was very strong here and Hamza wondered what kinds they were. His furniture repair work at the mission had been the fumblings of a novice, fixing what had loosened or fallen apart. He knew nothing about timber but he thought its smell wholesome, natural. He picked up a handful of shavings from the floor and inhaled them. The elderly man looked up from his embroidery and said, 'Mvule' and Hamza stored the name away gratefully. He went towards another pile of shavings, which was where the astringent smell was coming from, and before he even reached it the elderly man said 'Msonobari' and then smiled as if he was playing a game. 'Mvule lasts forever, it's harder than metal,' he said. 'Are you looking to buy?'

'No, I have come to work for the merchant,' Hamza said. The elderly man made a grunting noise and returned to embroidering his cap.

When Hamza went out to the yard again, he saw that Khalifa had gone. He sat in the shade to wait for the merchant's instructions and was still there when the leisurely return to work began in the afternoon. A man he had not seen before walked through the yard to the workshop. His hair was jet black and shiny, tied back in a ponytail. He strolled in casually, quite unhurried, and shouted obscenities at Sungura as he walked past. Hey, you little bastard, tell your mother to oil herself well. I'll be calling for her later tonight. Sungura cackled with laughter like a teased child, exposing a mouthful of tangled teeth.

Hamza sat waiting throughout the afternoon. He saw Idris and his sidekick stretch out in the van for an hour or two before making themselves scarce. He was still there when the old carpenter and his slick-haired assistant closed the workshop and left. He felt foolish waiting for so long but he had nowhere to go, and he was tired, and he did not know if the merchant even remembered his existence. The merchant returned to the yard some hours later, just as the muadhin was calling for the afternoon prayer. Sungura was the only other person there, waiting to lock up. Nassor Biashara was surprised to see Hamza waiting for him.

'What are you doing here?' he said. 'Have you been here all this time? What's the matter with you? Go home now. You can start at the warehouse tomorrow.'

9

Hamza slept by the doors of the warehouse that night because he had nowhere else to stay. He wandered the streets for a while looking for places he knew, but he recognised very little and often did not know where he was. He followed the movement of the crowds and after a while found himself unexpectedly on the shore road. He followed that with a small thrill of recognition and walked on to look for the house where he had lived in his youth, but he could not find it. He thought he had found the right area but perhaps the house was knocked down and something else built in its place. It was then a town of Deutsch-Ostafrika and was now a British colony, but that alone did not explain the disappearance of a house with a walled garden and a shop at the front. It was as if the town had grown beyond itself and some of its neighbourhoods had disappeared. He had only been away for seven years and the town could not have changed so much in that time. Or perhaps he was looking in the wrong place. He had rarely gone out of the house when he lived here before, had led a frightened life at the back of a shop, and perhaps he had forgotten the few streets he knew. Perhaps he had lost part of his memory along the way, overwhelmed by the cruelties he had lived through in the meantime. He was so tired and maybe that added to his impression that everything here was strange. Some people greeted him as if they knew him, with a smile, a friendly wave or even a handshake, but he knew they could not. They must have mistaken him for someone else. In any case, he did not know them.

He returned to the warehouse as it was getting dark. There was a streetlamp at the far corner of the clearing and although the light it cast was dim and multiplied the shadows, it also eased the unnerving emptiness to some extent. He knew there was a mosque down that far lane because he had heard the muadhin calling at noon. He went in there to wash and then joined in the prayers. People shuffled up to make space for him and he stayed for a while, for the company. When the mosque locked up for the night, he returned to the warehouse and stretched out by the door in the place he had swept earlier in the day, using the cloth bag with all his possessions in it as a pillow. He hardly slept despite his weariness. His side ached and the mosquitoes did not spare him. Cats prowled nearby, yowling out of sight and now and then glaring at him from the darkness. When he dozed he was unsettled by dreams: falling through dark emptiness, crawling over fallen bodies, hectored by a face twisted with implacable hatred. There were shouts, blows and distant hills overflowing with translucently red viscera.

He was often visited by disturbing dreams. It was a relief when he heard the dawn call to prayers and went to the mosque again to clean up.

When Khalifa arrived, he was surprised to see Hamza sitting dejectedly on the ground, leaning against the warehouse door. He stopped dead and stared, exaggerating his astonishment. 'What are you doing here so early? It's not even seven o'clock,' he said. 'Do you live nearby?'

Hamza was too weary to dissemble. 'I slept here,' he said, indicating the ground.

'He didn't ask you to,' Khalifa said. 'What are you? Some kind of hooligan, sleeping in the streets?'

Hamza did not reply. He rose carefully to his feet and looked away from Khalifa's outraged stare.

'He wants a watchman after the delivery arrives,' Khalifa said, speaking precisely as if he was explaining something to a simpleton. 'He's starting a new line in fishing equipment and he's afraid one of these fishermen will break in and steal it. They're always half-crazy with hashish, the fishermen, but I don't think they would do that. There was no need for you to sleep here. He didn't ask you to, did he?'

'I didn't have anywhere else to sleep,' Hamza said.

Khalifa glared in response, waiting for him to wheedle and moan, and when he did not, took a step towards the doors and undid the padlock while Hamza hastily moved out of the way. Khalifa opened one panel and stepped inside for a moment before he came bursting out again. 'What do you mean, you didn't have anywhere to sleep? Don't you know anyone? I thought you said you lived here.'

'Many years ago, outside of town. I don't know if those people are still alive,' Hamza said. 'If they are, I don't think they will want to hear from me.'

Khalifa was silent for a little while, irresolute, frowning, his eyes ablaze with questions. 'So you just sleep in the streets, like a vagabond? Who are your people? You can't sleep in the streets,' he said angrily. 'You'll get hurt. Don't you know anyone you can go to? Don't you have any money?'

'I've only just arrived,' Hamza said as if that were explanation enough.

'Why didn't you ask him for money yesterday? Nassor, why didn't you ask the merchant for an advance?' Khalifa asked in exasperation, and when Hamza did not answer he asked, 'When did you last eat? What are you, an idiot, some kind of a saint?' He took hold of Hamza's right wrist and slapped a coin in his palm. 'Go find yourself a café and get a cup of tea and a bun. Go, go away from here, come back later.'

Hamza had been ashamed to ask, in case the merchant refused or withdrew his offer of a job. He had not even asked what his wages were to be. He did not say that to Khalifa but went to find a café as instructed where he had a bun and a large mug of tea. When he returned Khalifa ignored him – probably, Hamza imagined, because he thought him too pathetic to bother with. Later in the morning the contractor's truck appeared and three of his men loaded up bags of cement and metal poles and then drove off, the driver leaning on the horn as if he was negotiating a crowded road. The Chinaman also turned up, fully dressed in shirt and trousers, and stopped to talk with Khalifa, who as they spoke glanced at Hamza, as if to say, Listen to him ... just like one of us, no fong fong fong from this Chinaman.

151

The van from the merchant's yard also came to deliver the crates of bowls and small cabinets Sungura had been busy packing the day before, and to collect some more timber. Khalifa showed Hamza where to stack the crates, and explained what other merchandise was stored in the warehouse and how it was distributed and organised. Here the timber, there the crates of ornamental caskets, over there the sacks of millet, and here on the shelves straw-wrapped packages of frankincense. He showed him the ledger where all the goods coming in or out were recorded. Can you read? he asked. Hamza nodded and Khalifa gave him a sharp look. Can you write? he asked. Hamza nodded again and Khalifa smiled bitterly, his suspicions about the merchant's motives for employing Hamza now confirmed. He is lining you up to take over from me, isn't he? One way or another, it was a busy morning on Hamza's second day and the clearing was a place of work rather than a silent and deserted waste-ground. It was not until very late in the morning that things quietened down and Hamza was able to rest his aching legs.

'What happened to you?' Khalifa asked him, gesturing towards his hip. His eyes ran up and down Hamza's leg, once, then went to his face. 'Is it illness? Or an injury?'

'Injury,' Hamza said.

'What happened?' Khalifa repeated. 'Were you in the war?' As he asked, he tilted his chin forward impatiently, as if growing irritated with Hamza's slowness.

'An accident,' Hamza said and looked away, ready to rise to his feet and leave if Khalifa persisted. He did not care to be interrogated.

But Khalifa laughed. 'You're a tight-lipped man with a dirty secret, I have no doubt,' he said with a grin, 'but I like the look of you. I can tell about people. Listen to me, this is not a safe place for you to sleep out in the open. You don't know who or what wanders these empty places at night, or what people come here to do in the darkness. No one would come here at night to do any good. If anything happened there would be no one to come to your help. You should sleep inside the warehouse and lock

152

yourself in, but Nassor won't let you have the keys yet until he knows he can trust you.'

He paused for a moment, waiting for Hamza to speak but he said nothing. Khalifa sighed with resignation. 'Do you understand what I'm saying to you? It's not safe to sleep in the streets,' he said. 'I have an outside store in my house that you can use for a few days. I used to rent it out to a barber. He was there for two years or so and then suddenly he left. The barber's chair and mirror are still in there. Poor fellow, I don't know what happened to him. Maybe he'll come back for them one of these days when he's ready to resume his work.

'You can use the room for a few days if you want – but only a few days. I know you're not much better than a beggar so there's no point asking for rent from you, or not yet anyway. You can stay there for a week or two maybe, until you work things out for yourself. Don't think you can just stay there forever, and I don't want you bringing women or crazy friends in there either. Just somewhere for you to sleep safely. And make sure you keep it clean, you understand?'

It made Hamza take another look at Khalifa, this generous offer, the coin earlier in the day, all that kindness alongside his irritable manner and sour looks. I like the look of you, he had said. Nassor Biashara had said that to him too. It had happened to Hamza before, that his appearance had won kindnesses for him in unexpected ways. The German officer had said that too, more than once.

*

Khalifa's house was on one level, nyumba ya chini, without an upstairs. It was joined to a taller house on one side and a lane ran on the other. Kibanda chetu, he called it, our hut, although it was not that. There was a deep covered porch at the front with the set-back front door beside it. The porch roof was supported by two thick varnished mangrove posts. The store that was to be Hamza's room was on the other side of the porch, its door opening directly to the street. It was a small room with a barber's chair and mirror on a table as promised and a wooden bench set against one wall for the customer waiting his turn. Khalifa opened the window, which had solid wooden shutters, filling the little room with light. Hamza could easily imagine the room as a barber's shop, with a customer or two sitting chatting while waiting, or a friend of the barber's visiting to fill the day's empty hours with talk. He thought he saw some hair mingled with the fluff of dust on the concrete floor but perhaps that was his imagination. Khalifa stood by the window watching him, one hand on the bars across the casement, his frown as censorious as ever but with a self-satisfied twitch to the corners of his lips. 'Does it suit Your Eminence?' he asked.

Khalifa handed over a key for the padlock and brought Hamza a broom. He swept the cobwebs and the floor, turned the mirror to the wall and rearranged the furniture to create a sleeping space. Then he sat down in the chair and leaned back against the shaving headrest, joyful at his good fortune. The street outside the door was shaded by the taller houses. Its unpaved surface was packed hard by human traffic and while Hamza sat there people walked past the window and glanced sideways through the open door. He shut the door and sat for a long time, for hours, without moving, relishing the feeling of safety he felt in the darkening cell.

He heard the muadhin calling for the maghrib prayers, the calls coming slightly out of sequence. He counted four different callers. There was always a profusion of mosques in this town, he remembered that from years ago. He thought he would go look for one, to have a wash and for the company. In so many places he had travelled there were no mosques, and he missed them, not for the prayers but for the sense of being one of many that he always felt in a mosque. He got up quickly before he lost his nerve, and went in search of one. He did not have to speak to anyone when he got there and sat quietly with downcast eyes until it was time to line up with the other worshippers. Then after prayers he silently shook hands with the men to either side of him and went on his way.

He passed shops and kiosks and cafés in the lit-up streets, with people strolling or sitting in small groups, talking or just looking at passers-by. They seemed at peace and content, and he wondered if this was because he was in a different and more prosperous part of town, or if he was walking at a different time of day when people were prone to be in this state, or if they were quiescent because they were simply bored. When he returned to the house he found Khalifa sitting on a mat in the porch, which was now lit. He motioned for Hamza to join him and poured him a small cup of coffee from his flask.

'Have you eaten?' he asked.

He went inside and came out with a dish of cooked green bananas and a jug of water, which Hamza accepted gratefully. When Khalifa's friends arrived, Hamza greeted them and stayed for a few minutes out of politeness before retreating to his store room. He lay in the dark on the bare floor for a long time, unable to sleep, his mind wandering over his earlier time in this town and over all the people he had lost since and the humiliations he had suffered. He had no choice but to accept his share of them. The worst mistakes he made in his earlier life in this town had been the result of his fear of humiliation, through which he lost a friend who was like a brother and the woman he was learning to love. The war crushed those niceties out of him and showed him staggering visions of brutality that taught him humility. These thoughts filled him with sorrow, which he thought was the inescapable fate of man.

*

In the next days Hamza felt Khalifa becoming less abrupt with him and giving him advice, which he listened to without debate. One afternoon Khalifa insisted that Hamza should ask for an advance from the merchant. They stopped at the yard on the way home and Hamza found the merchant in his office and asked him for some money from his wages while Khalifa stood outside the door, within sight but apparently out of earshot. Hamza could see that the merchant was not pleased, but he was not sure if it was Khalifa's presence or the request for money which irritated him the most.

'You've been here for three days and you're already asking to be paid. You get paid when you've done your work, not before,'

Nassor Biashara said, holding his ground. It was five days, but Hamza stood silently in front of him, adding neither plea nor supplication to his request, and in the end Nassor Biashara gave him five shillings and returned to his ledger. 'Don't make a practice of this,' he said, head bent over his accounts.

Khalifa chuckled as they walked home. 'What a miserable miser, bakhili maluun! He thinks he can treat people like dirt. He even owes money to the old lady next door who bakes millet bread. He has her bring him a mofa loaf every day and then he doesn't pay her. You should see the work that old lady does to produce one of her little loaves. She has to soak the grain overnight, pound it in the mortar, mix and knead it, then bake it in a clay oven in her backyard. After all that work, she charges twenty cents for a loaf and that miserable tajiri waits until the old lady begs for her money before he pays.'

They arrived at the house with Khalifa in good humour after embarrassing the merchant, as he saw it. 'Come in and have something to eat,' he said, overflowing with generosity. 'Hodi, we have a guest,' he called out as he opened the door.

It was his first time inside the house, and Hamza wondered if this was too much hospitality too soon. It was not usual for a complete stranger, more or less, to be invited inside a home in this way. He was already learning that Khalifa was unpredictable and that their first encounter had been misleading. His outbursts of bad temper did not last long, and he had already shown surprising generosity to him. Hamza had hardly lived properly among a family, only briefly as a child. Later he lived in the back of a shop and after that for a long time he lived a fugitive and itinerant life, so he did not really know what was done and what was not done, only what memory clung to from early childhood.

Inside the house there were two rooms, one either side of the front door, and a hallway running all the way to the back and opening out on to an interior yard enclosed by a wall. He had seen the wall from the other side while walking along the lane. Khalifa showed him into the room on the left whose floor was covered with a plaited mat and some cushions resting against the wall. It was evidently the room for receiving guests. He left

Hamza there for a moment, and when he came back asked him to come and greet the people of the house. Hamza followed him to the doorway of the yard at the back and waited there until he was called forward. A plump woman in her forties was sitting on a low stool under an awning, preparing food. A brazier with a pot on it was to the left of her, and on the other side at her feet was a clay pot covered with a straw food-cover. Her head was covered with a kanga which was tightly tucked around her brow and cheeks so that her face bulged under the pressure. It had obviously been recently tightened when Khalifa announced the presence of a guest. Some tufts of grey hair escaped this tight restraint. She looked at Hamza without speaking or smiling, staring at him intensely with a look of dislike. Khalifa introduced her as his wife Bi Asha and Hamza said shikamoo. She looked unmoved and made a noise to acknowledge his greeting.

'Is this the one you were telling me about? The one to whom you gave a room that does not belong to you? You have brought us trouble,' she said, her voice firm and querulous. She glanced at Khalifa as she said this and then returned her gaze to Hamza, her stare unwavering. 'Where is he from? Do we know where he's from? He is a complete stranger and you give him a room as if you own this house.'

'Don't talk like that,' Khalifa said impatiently.

'Just look at him. Balaa,' she said, even more loudly and with unmistakable anger. 'Nothing but trouble. You bring him here to sleep and to eat as if we are a charity when you don't have a single thing to your name. First one thing then another. Now you bring him inside so he can have a good look at us and decide what he would like to do to us. You don't know his people or where he has been or what mischief he has done, but that's nothing to you. You still bring him inside here so he can do what harm he wishes to us. Your head is full of trash!'

'Stop that kind of talk. Don't wish ill on a complete stranger,' Khalifa said.

'I'm telling you, just look at him. Hana maana, a useless man,' she said, her face twisted with rage. 'Balaa, that's what he is. Nothing but trouble.'

'All right, just serve us our food,' Khalifa said, and gave Hamza a nudge towards the inside of the house. 'Go back inside, I'll be with you in a moment.'

He went back to the guest room and sat down to wait. He was shaken by such unanticipated scorn – hana maana – but he did not examine the feeling further. He would think about it later. For now, he only wished for Khalifa to come back and ask him to leave. Perhaps Bi Asha was unwell and that made her ill-tempered, but more likely she was just a mean unhinged spirit. He thought he saw that in her eyes, a kind of frenzy. When Khalifa came in with two plates of rice and fish, he too was in a temper, as if he and his wife had had an argument. They ate quickly and in silence. Afterwards Khalifa went out to wash his hands and then called Hamza. Bi Asha was not there and he washed his hands at the sink as Khalifa instructed. When he had first looked into the yard he had noticed a girl or woman squatting on the other side of the awning, in a corner beside the door to a store or a room. He guessed she was the servant, and now as he washed his hands saw the same girl was scouring the pots by the water-pipe in the corner. Her head was covered and she did not look up, so he could not see her face. He said hello to her and she replied without looking up.

*

Khalifa and Bi Asha spoke like that to each other more often than they used to. There had always been some degree of hyperbole to her severity with him, making her seem more discontented than she really was, which gave her licence for the outrageous things she said. That was not to say she did not mean what she said or was not always after having her own way. She was, and had become accustomed to her dominance in most matters at home. Khalifa played his part as the tolerant, put-upon husband who was prepared to go along with things but who could put his foot down when necessary. Their disagreements sometimes ended in an exchange of tiny imperceptible smiles as if they had seen through each other's performances. But in recent times her tone was often sharp and suspicious when she spoke to him, and he was defensive to the point of whining when he made his excuses, or else brusque and dismissive of her.

Afiya did not understand why Baba brought the man all the way inside. It was not something he had ever done before, or not since she had been living with them. When Ilyas came visiting he never went beyond the guest room, and it was Bi Asha who came out to greet him. Baba must have known that Bimkubwa would not be happy to have a complete stranger brought inside like that. Even the fish-seller and the charcoal man, who were regular callers at the house, did not step beyond the courtyard door. The only exception she could remember was the mattress-maker who was old and had known Bi Asha since she was a child and had been repairing her mattresses ever since.

Baba should also have remembered that Bi Asha had taken a dislike to the man. This was partly because of the stories he told her about the young man: how Hamza seemed unwell, how he did not reveal anything about his people or where he had been.

'He sounds like a vagabond,' Bi Asha said dismissively.

'I think he has been in the war,' Baba said.

'Then he's probably dangerous as well, a killer,' she said, spitting out the words to provoke him.

'No no,' Baba said. 'He must have had a hard time. It could be Ilyas.'

'No yourself! Ilyas had people. You tell us this one has no people,' Bi Asha said. 'How can a decent person not have any people? He's just a dreamer.'

Perhaps Baba had not forgotten her dislike of strangers. Maybe he brought him inside to say that Ilyas too may have survived and could be on his long way back. It was three years since the end of the war and there was still no news of him. Afiya did not say it to anyone but inside she felt her brother was lost. If Baba brought that other man inside to remind them of Ilyas, then he had made a mistake because it had only provoked Bi Asha into her malign prophecy of disaster. Balaa! She was turning strange and savage with Baba, and Afiya knew she herself contributed to Bi Asha's impatience and agitation because she was nineteen and still unmarried, though it puzzled her why this mattered so

159

much to her. Afiya suspected that Bi Asha had spoken to some of her acquaintances about her availability. She had received and refused two marriage proposals already.

The first was from a man in his forties who was a clerk in the offices of the new agriculture department set up by the British administration. Afiya had never seen him or heard of him, but he had seen her walking by and made enquiries and then asked for her. Baba said no, he was a man with a reputation, and what was the rush? Afiya was present when he said that.

'What reputation?' Bi Asha asked querulously. 'He has a good government job. His proposal comes from respectable sources and he offers a good dowry. Tell me one good reason why I should not say yes to this proposal.'

'One good reason is that the proposal is not for you but for Afiya,' Baba said angrily. 'So it is up to her to accept it or not.'

'Don't give me your big talk. It's not up to her. She needs advice to make the right decision. What reputation?'

'I'll tell you later,' Baba said, and Afiya understood it was something he preferred not to say in front of her.

Bi Asha laughed mockingly and said, 'You want her for yourself, don't you? You think I'm blind. You're going to say no to any proposal because you've been waiting for her to ripen so you can have her for your second wife.'

The words thudded in Afiya's chest. She glanced at Baba whose mouth had fallen open in shock. After a moment, he said in a subdued voice, 'His reputation is that he has a great obsession with loose women ... with women who will take money from him for ... with prostitutes. That is his recreation. Spare our girl that misery and just say no.'

The second proposal had come just a few weeks ago from another older man, a café manager. Afiya knew about him because he was well known to many. His café was on the main street and she had passed it several times. Unlike the first suitor who had not married before, the café manager was fond of marrying. If Afiya were to become his wife, she would be his sixth although he never kept more than one going at the same time. He was a faithful husband to whoever was his current wife. His preference was for young orphans or girls from poor families who would be appreciative of the dowry he offered. He married them and kept them for a few years and then, when another young one caught his eye, he divorced and married again. He ran a successful café and could afford this hobby. Bi Asha did not need any persuasion to say no to this proposal.

'That predator, that filthy man. We are not so distressed that we need his disgusting dowry,' she said.

Her accusation against Baba hovered over them, and for Afiya it brought some of Bi Asha's hostility into focus. It made her feel sorry that Bi Asha feared such treachery from her and her own husband. She could not imagine that she had any grounds for fear. After his wife had said those words, Baba got up and left the house and Bi Asha and Afiya sat silent for several minutes before Bi Asha too rose and went to her room. She did not make the accusation again, but nor did she stop her persistent campaign to marry her off. Afiya wondered if that was another reason why Baba had brought the stranger inside. She had resisted the temptation to raise her head when he greeted her, but had caught a brief glimpse of him when he first entered the backyard. She knew from Baba's stories that he was a young man, so maybe he wanted to show her someone nearer her own age instead of the dissolute older suitors she appeared to be attracting.

She did not know how but word of the proposals got out, and Jamila and Saada teased her about them. Perhaps the matchmaker, whoever she was, let the word out to make mischief. Jamila was married now and carrying her first child. Khalida's friends had a good laugh at the rejected suitors, telling Afiya she deserved better and should wait for the wealthy and handsome young man who was bound to appear and ask for her. Who wants to be someone's second wife? When Khalida said that, Afiya's heart lurched and she wondered if the accusation against Baba had also somehow got out. There were no meaningful glances to accompany the words and no pregnant silence after them, so she took them to be general disdain for the idea rather than that the words were meant against a particular person.

161

10

That same afternoon, after the miserable lunch in Khalifa's house, Hamza went to the market to spend the five shillings given to him as an advance. He bought a candle for his room, and a roll of thick straw matting and a cotton sheet. He stretched out on the matting and groaned as the familiar sharp pain ran through him. After a few minutes its intensity eased and he let his body find whatever rest it could. He ran his hand over the ugly scar on his hip and massaged the healed muscle. It will get better. It was better. There was nothing else to be done. This town that he barely recognised was the nearest place to home he had. The pain will get better.

In the mornings Hamza left the house early and went to the mosque to clean up, perform a grateful prayer and then buy a jug of sweet tea at a café. After that he went to the warehouse to wait for Khalifa. Almost every day something came or went from the yard to the warehouse, and sometimes from the warehouse to the docks as the merchandise was gradually dispersed to its destinations, slowly emptying the warehouse. Almost every day, Idris and his sidekick drove up in their rattling van to deliver or collect. It seemed that whenever Idris opened his mouth something obscene came out of it and his sidekick Dubu dutifully convulsed in laughter.

It was Hamza's duty to sweep the clearing in front of the warehouse, and on windy days to sprinkle water on the area to keep the dust down. Sometimes he had to accompany the van to the yard or other locations, to help Idris and Dubu with the loading and unloading. It still left a lot of time for Khalifa and him to sit in the shade of the warehouse staring out into the empty clearing and talking. Khalifa liked to talk and Hamza was a dutiful and tireless listener. He suspected that Khalifa thought he was owed this deference. He never mentioned Hamza's encounter with Bi Asha.

'Idris is an ugly man,' Khalifa said. 'He makes my flesh shiver when he comes around. He's a filthy cruel bully, always talking dirty like some kind of oversexed beast. He treats that Dubu of his like a slave. Do you know why he is called Dubu? It's because when he was a child people thought he was stupid. He had such a big head, you see, as if he was deformed. It doesn't look so bad now but when he was a child ... Sometimes mockery like that never ends. Idris might not have given him the cruel name, but he makes him live up to it. He makes fun of him and does who knows what else to him in their spare time. He is a stupid weak man, that Dubu.

'And do you know what Sungura does in his spare time? The little rabbit is a pimp, did you know that? Did you guess? How could you not see what a little creep he is? Of course he's not one of those violent ones, but one look at him and you must have thought: He is up to something disgusting. There are two women he works for, everyone knows it. If a man wants to have one of them, he just has a word with Sungura who arranges it all. That's why he is called Sungura: small and cowardly like a rabbit, but wily. Nobody dares to touch him because those two women protect him as if he is their baby. He calls them his mothers. They're loud-mouthed shameless women who can strip a person naked with their tongues. Keep away from him as well, he's a bad influence.'

Hamza lived quietly in his store room, slipping in and out with the minimum fuss he could manage. He was not invited inside again although he could hear Bi Asha's voice, now that he knew it, whenever it rose in exasperation or urgency. Khalifa came to look for him sometimes in the evening and asked him to sit on the porch with him and whoever had stopped by for a chat. There were two men in particular who were regular callers, his baraza, Maalim Abdalla the school teacher and Topasi, a laundryman who lived nearby and was a childhood friend of both men. The porch floor was covered with a thick plaited straw mat and was lit by an oil lamp, a kandili, suspended by a hook from a ceiling beam. It shone with a soft golden glow that turned the open-sided area into an interior space. People walking past in the street murmured their greetings, as if to call them out loudly would be to intrude. All three men loved their gossip.

Maalim Abdalla was usually the last to speak. He was the wise one, often offering calming words after Topasi had delivered the latest rumours. That was why he was called Topasi, the garbage collector, because of his love of rumours. After Topasi had delivered the latest story, Khalifa did his outrage about how everything has gone to hell. Then it was Maalim Abdalla's turn to bring sagacity into their conversation.

Maalim Abdalla had started school in Zanzibar and then went to the advanced German school in the town, to train as a teacher. He knew someone who worked as a messenger at the District Officer's office, the headquarters of the British colonial administration in the town, and through him he was able to read old newspapers after they were filed away. These were copies of the government's *Tanganyika Territory Gazette* and the Kenya settler newspaper the *East African Standard*. Maalim Abdalla's knowledge of English was rudimentary, plundered from his early schooling in Zanzibar, but he made it go a long way, both in his profession and at the baraza. His sporadic access to what he called international publications gave his opinions and judgements incomparable weight, at least in his own eyes. The men's discussions were opinionated and often melodramatic, accompanied by much laughter and exaggeration. Hamza was not required to participate but they knew he was there because one or other of them would break off what they were saying to explain a detail to him. That was how he learned how Topasi had earned his nickname. More often than not Hamza was the butt of their teasing because of his reticence, but he sat with them for the company and he knew he provided a harmless distraction for them.

After the call to the isha prayers, to which none of the three friends responded, the door to the house opened slightly and

Khalifa rose to accept the tray of coffee pot and cups. Hamza did not see who delivered the tray, it would have been bad manners to stare, but he guessed it was the servant girl he had seen when he went inside. He could not imagine Bi Asha, the bad-tempered mistress of the house, doing something as menial as delivering a tray of coffee to the chatterboxes on the porch. The first time the tray came out there were only three cups on it and Hamza made that the excuse for his departure.

'He is a little saint, that one,' Khalifa said. 'Off to the mosque, I expect. Well, you won't get there in time.'

'I expect he's tired of listening to your stupid talk,' said Maalim Abdalla. 'Go, young man, go and earn some blessing.'

Some evenings later when he was at the baraza and just after the muadhin's call for the isha prayers, the door opened slightly as it had done before. Khalifa glanced at him and Hamza rose to fetch the tray. He had forgotten about his hip and could not prevent himself from uttering a small gasp of pain as he got to his feet. He reached out for the mangrove post to steady himself and moved quickly towards the door before any of the other men had moved or spoken. He took the tray and looked at the woman who stood in the shadow of the door, and saw surprise and perhaps concern in her eyes. He smiled slightly to reassure her and murmured his thanks but he was not sure if any words came out clearly. As he turned away with the tray, he saw that there were four cups on it. He set it down in front of Khalifa but he did not sit down again.

'Stay and have some coffee with your elders,' Khalifa said. 'You can catch up with your prayers later.'

'Hey, you kafir,' Topasi said. 'Don't discourage a man from saying his prayers. You are making even more trouble for yourself. You'll earn a bucket-load of sins for that and you already have a huge pile against your name.'

'Never come between God and man,' Maalim Abdalla pronounced.

Hamza smiled and did not respond, did not say that it was not for the prayers and blessing alone that he went to the mosque. It was often a relief to get away from their chatter, to get away from everyone. No one had to talk even in a crowded mosque. As he walked away he dwelt on the look of concern in the woman's eyes and wondered at the surprise and mild agitation it caused him. He had seen in his brief glimpse of the slight figure someone whose eyes and face had the clean look of honesty. He would not know how else to describe it, he knew that was what he saw. It made him feel sorry for himself in a way he did not understand, made him feel sad for the loveless years of his own life, and for the episodes of gentleness in it that had been so brief. He had assumed she was the servant girl, and maybe she was, but she was a woman of about twenty, not a girl. He wondered if, after all, she was Khalifa's wife. It was not unusual for men of his age to marry again, and to choose women who were much younger. Hamza walked the streets for an hour or more, and in that time upbraided himself for his naïve sentiment and nostalgia. It all came from his loneliness and self-pity, as if he had not seen enough in his brief life to understand that keeping his head clear and his body safe required all the wit he possessed.

Some days later he was sent for by the merchant and was asked to accompany Idris and Dubu to the port to collect a consignment. Some equipment he had been waiting for had arrived. It was Hamza's first visit to the docks since the morning he had arrived back in the town. The time had passed so quickly and somehow felt so full it was as if he had been back in the town for months. Idris was driving the van, proud as an aristocrat sweeping by in his gilded carriage past a crowd of adoring serfs, one arm resting on the open window, the other on the wheel, bouncing along the earth roads and waving to the odd acquaintance. In the meantime he kept up a slow-wheeling chatter that was mostly dirty talk. Dubu, who was sitting in the middle of the bench seat in the driver's cab, was chuckling dutifully while Hamza looked away, staring out of the window. He did not feel as repulsed by them as he had at first, although he had yet to find a way to disengage from Idris's filthy babble.

The equipment the merchant had ordered turned out to be a large propeller. Idris drove right up to the gates of one of the quayside warehouses where they found Nassor Biashara waiting for them. He was smiling, standing by the shiny propeller which stood on layers of gunny sack. All the paperwork was done, he said. Let's get the machinery to the warehouse. They put the propeller in the van and climbed in after it. The merchant rode in the front cab with Idris. Nassor Biashara was excited about his new acquisition, and he supervised its storage personally, in a space he had had Khalifa prepare in the middle of the warehouse, protected and camouflaged by less glamorous merchandise. After the equipment was stored away, he dismissed the van and waved Hamza to follow him outside. Khalifa looked annoyed and disappeared into the gloom of the warehouse.

When they were outside, standing by the warehouse door, the merchant looked around as if making sure that they were unobserved. He reached into his jacket and pulled out some folded-over banknotes. 'These are your wages for the last three weeks, and I will pay you again three weeks from now,' he said, his voice stern as if expecting a truculent response. 'I've paid you generously because you have worked well. I thought you would. From now on I want you to be the night-watchman in the warehouse. I want you to spend every night here and guard the valuable merchandise inside. You will do that for the time being and then later we'll talk about what else you can do. You will work here in the day as usual, and then you'll bar yourself in for the night. Do you understand?'

He handed over the banknotes, which Hamza accepted without a word and pocketed without counting them. The merchant smiled and nodded, no doubt amused by the pauper standing on his dignity, Hamza thought. Nassor Biashara took his cap off, rubbed his head in that characteristic gesture of his and then strode away. Hamza expected Khalifa to come striding out at once to complain about being excluded from these instructions but perhaps he was even more wounded than he had appeared. Hamza sat down on the bench by the door to wait for him and after a minute or two he called to him. When Khalifa came out Hamza held up the notes. Khalifa reached over as if to grab them and Hamza put them back in his pocket. 'I'm to be the night-watchman from tonight, and to work in the warehouse during the day,' he said.

'He is a stupid man,' Khalifa said. 'How much is he paying you?'

'I don't know,' Hamza said. 'I didn't count.'

'You are a stupid man too, but I feel sorry for you because you do it from some confused idea of being well mannered or dignified. I know the type, believe me,' Khalifa said. 'But that one is just a silly man who has never properly grown up. Why is he getting so excited about this propeller? He thinks every boatman and fisherman in the town is waiting to steal it from him. That's his new project. He spent thousands buying a boat a couple of years ago. It was going to make him money freighting cargo in the area. It didn't, and now he has spent thousands more buying a propeller because that will make him money, which it may well do, but in the meantime he acts like an idiot and he puts you in danger. You must bar yourself in after dark and don't open the door to anyone. There are drunks and hashish smokers who come to sleep in these abandoned old places. Do you understand? Whatever you hear outside, don't open the door. Let them do whatever they are doing to each other and stay inside.'

Khalifa seemed so worried for his safety that Hamza stopped himself from saying that he had seen much worse than drunks and hashish smokers in his time, instead nodding and saying he would take care. That afternoon he collected his things from Khalifa's store room, stopped at the café for a small loaf of bread and a piece of fish, and returned to the warehouse. In the night he heard cats scurrying over the roof and yowling in the lanes, and just before he fell asleep he heard someone singing drunkenly and then sobbing, calling out a name as if in an agony of yearning. He woke up in the dark and lay thinking, waiting for the dawn.

Early every evening before it got dark, he made a bed out of layers of gunny sacks on top of which he laid his straw mattress, his strip of busati. The spring and give in the sacks absorbed some of the ache in his side, except when he turned over in his sleep. Then he went to the café for something to eat, goat curry or fish or sometimes just buttered bread. Afterwards he went to the mosque to wash up and pray and then back to the warehouse, by which time it was properly dark. He lit the oil lamp he had asked the merchant to provide, barred himself in and lay down to sleep. When he could not sleep he took out one of his books from the bag and browsed through it. The lamplight was a little too gloomy for him to read the old print of the Schiller volume comfortably and he could only go over the pieces he already knew. He took the book out as much for the pleasure of handling it as for what he could read.

Then he lay in that golden lamplight and tried to ignore the tiny scurryings of mice he could not help hearing among the sacks and crates. At times he felt like a man of primeval times when the end of daylight meant a retreat to a burrow in the ground, a caveman hiding from the terrors of the night. He kept the lamp lit all night to keep those terrors at bay but he had no defence against the whispers that crept up on him on sleepless nights. Many nights he fell asleep without a struggle but on others he saw torn and mutilated bodies in his dreams and was hectored by loud and hate-filled voices and glared at by transparent gelatinous eyes. As the nights in the warehouse turned into weeks he slept for longer, even in the end until first light. Every morning he woke with surprise that he had slept so long and counted the hours of undisturbed sleep like a miser shopkeeper counting the pennies as they accumulated in his cash box. He was grateful for the benefit of the rest.

*

It took nearly a month for the mechanic who fitted propellers to get round to Nassor Biashara's dhow. The work was to be done on the sandy headland at the edge of the creek behind the port where boat repairs were usually done. The tide in the creek went out all the way to the sea, and then came surging back in late in the day. It only reached the sandy headland when it was a full moon. The mechanic's appearance was announced and then postponed four times. Several days before his actual appearance, the boat was pulled up on the headland at low tide. The crew laid lengths of mangrove logs on the beach and waited for the tide to rise when all available labour, including the merchant's workforce and any interested passer-by, joined in to haul the boat on to the rollers and as high as they could up on the sandy headland.

There it was tied to sturdy posts to prevent it from rolling back and there it stayed while the mechanic delayed further. Khalifa played no part in these efforts, only asking sarcastic questions about the elusive mechanic. The merchant paid no attention to the progress of his enterprise either, not even bothering to be exasperated by the man's continued non-appearance, as if none of it was anything to do with him. Hamza found the merchant's behaviour puzzling, but then thought that perhaps it was his way of maintaining his dignity, refusing the mechanic the satisfaction of being indispensable. The boat waited like that for several days, like a beetle stranded on its back. On the day the mechanic was available, the van came to collect the propeller and Hamza who was to go along and help. Even Khalifa could not resist the drama of the mechanic's definite appearance to fix the propeller and he too came along to observe the final rites.

Unlike the merchant, the nahodha of the boat was not concerned to maintain his dignity, and on the day the mechanic was finally available, the two of them spent the first hour hurling denunciations and abuse at each other while Dubu and Hamza sat in the meagre shade of the boat, and Idris and Khalifa remained in the cab of the van. The nahodha, who was a short, grizzled man in his fifties, with skin darkened and tanned into tough leather by the sun and sea, told the mechanic he was an ignorant idiot and a disrespectful fuckhead for wasting everyone's time. The mechanic, who was about thirty or so with a trimmed beard and a peaked cap, and who arrived on a motorcycle and knew his own importance, told the nahodha to watch how he spoke to him because he was not one of the pretty boys he liked to play with. He had his own business to attend to and if the nahodha did not like that he could go find himself another mechanic. Since there was no certainty that another would turn up any more quickly, this threat was a potent one. After a while, the bile diminished and they proceeded to install the propeller while continuing their abuse more sporadically. When the tide was in, they hauled the boat back into the water where the mechanic finished the installation. Idris drove the van back to the yard to fetch the merchant so he could be present when the mechanic fired the propeller, which he did to cheers and exclamations. By this time the nahodha and the mechanic were talking and laughing together in self-congratulation as if they had known each other all their lives, which they very likely had.

Even as they celebrated the installation of the precious propeller, the merchant's smiles were anxious, perhaps for the future of his new venture. He called Hamza over and as they stood on the sandy headland by the creek, he told him that since the propeller was now safely installed, there was no need for him to be a watchman at the warehouse and he could get his things and go back to his home. Tomorrow morning he should come and see the merchant with the warehouse keys so he could be paid off, and then maybe there might be something else for him to do but the merchant was not promising anything.

Hamza had not expected to be dispensed with so promptly. He was sorry that his warehouse duties were over. It had been a mostly peaceful time despite the lonely and anguished moods that sometimes overcame him: working in the warehouse during the day, talking with Khalifa or rather listening to him when he felt like talking, then sleeping quietly at night in the golden glow of the oil lamp and in the must and strange heat of all the merchandise ... it had given him time to rest and think and bring a little calm to his life. It had also made him live again through many regrets and sorrows, but those were with him in any case and were perhaps never to be reconciled.

The next day he told Khalifa that he was no longer the watchman. 'He has asked me to return the keys to him this morning. I think he was telling me there was no more work but I'm not sure.'

'He is a weasel, a conniving and deceitful little opportunist,' Khalifa said, delighting in the merchant's meanness. 'I expect you thought he'd give you a uniform and make you a proper security guard and build you a bathroom annexe so you could do your ablutions and say your prayers in the warehouse. You're an idiot to trust that man.' Then after a moment he growled softly and said: 'Well, you'd better come back to your store room then. Maybe another job will turn up.'

Hamza found Nassor Biashara in the furniture workshop. He was talking to the man Hamza had seen embroidering his cap several weeks ago in the timber workshop. He had been to the workshop a few times while on errands to the yard, when he had looked in to see what was going on and just for the pleasure of the smell of wood. He now knew that the old man's name was Sulemani and that he was the master carpenter in the workshop. Everyone called him Mzee Sulemani although he was probably only in his fifties. There was a younger man who worked for him, the one with the slicked-back black ponytail he was vain about and which he stroked frequently, but he was not there this morning. His name was Mehdi and he usually smelled of stale alcohol as if he had woken up after a night of drinking and had come to work without so much as rinsing his mouth. Sometimes he pressed his fingers to his temples as if his head was hurting, and Hamza thought that doing the work he did with a hangover would be a nightmare, banging and hammering and sawing. He remembered how the officer's hangovers had tormented him after the heavy-drinking sessions the Germans had indulged in. There was also a teenaged boy called Sefu in the workshop who did jobs like sanding and varnishing and who cleaned up at the end of the day. His younger brother came to help sometimes, just for something to do and perhaps to show willing in case a job came up in the future. They were the two Hamza had seen carrying a pot of varnish on his first day in the yard. Nassor Biashara himself also worked in the workshop at times. He designed all the furniture in his office but he often put the finishing touches to the small ornamental items himself.

When Hamza found them in the workshop, Mzee Sulemani was listening to the merchant with a small frown on his face when normally his brow was unlined and his expression was deadpan and aloof. The merchant finished talking to him then turned towards Hamza and held out his hand for the keys. Come with me, he said and walked away without waiting. Hamza glanced at the carpenter who looked back expressionless.

When he caught up with Nassor Biashara in his tiny office next door to the workshop, the merchant said, as if the thought had just occurred to him when it was clear to Hamza that he had been waiting to do so all along: 'You'd like to work with wood, wouldn't you? I've seen you going in there from time to time. I can always tell people who like wood. I've seen you sniffing the timber – always a giveaway. Anyway, you've finished there in the warehouse. I was just helping you out because I liked the look of you and you needed work, but you did well. How you managed to cope with that old grumbler Khalifa I don't know, but it seems he has taken quite a liking to you, which is not a habit of his. Now how would you like to work in the workshop? You can help Mzee Sulemani and he will teach you things. He is a very good carpenter. He doesn't say much but he's dependable, and you can learn a lot from him, even become a carpenter. Vipi, what do you say?'

The offer was so unexpected that for a moment Hamza could only grin with surprise. The merchant smiled back and nodded. 'It suits you much better when you smile like that,' he said. 'So it seems the idea appeals to you. Mehdi will not come back now. He has lost himself completely … all this drinking, staggering around the streets picking fights and then going home to beat his wife and his sister. I wouldn't have kept him here this long but his father was a friend of my father's so I had no choice but to keep him for their sake. This time it seems he picked one brawl too many and someone threatened to cut him with a knife. His mother has now begged him to go to Dar es Salaam to some relatives there, as if that will save him from himself. Anyway, I don't know what you're waiting for, go to the workshop and get started.'

Mzee Sulemani gave Hamza simple jobs at first, asking him to move the pieces of furniture to another part of the workshop, to hold one end of a plank while he planed or drilled, and in the meantime he watched him and instructed him. Hamza did as he was asked and apologised for the smallest mistake. The carpenter named more woods for him: mkangazi, mahogany, mvinje, cypress, mzaituni, olive. He made him smell the wood and stroke the planks so he would know them again. Hamza asked questions and allowed his enthusiasm to show, and within a few days he knew that the old man was less suspicious of him than he had

174

been at the start. At the end of the day's work Mzee Sulemani put all the tools away in a trunk himself, then padlocked it and pocketed the key. He shut all the windows and explained how he wanted the workshop left. When he called Hamza by name as he locked up at the end of the day and said, Hamza, tomorrow inshaallah, it felt like a kind of welcome: come again tomorrow. They always stopped for lunch so Mzee Sulemani could work on his embroidery although he did not eat anything. The thought of his new occupation of carpentry filled Hamza with more enthusiasm than he could remember for any other work he had done.

He told Khalifa about his new job in such excitement that he laughed and repeated the story to his baraza friends who teased the young man and called him fundi seramala. He installed himself in the store room in Khalifa's house as before and resumed his old routine: washing himself in the mosque, eating his evening meal at a café and on some evenings sitting on the porch with Khalifa and his friends while they mulled over the state of the world. That only lasted for a few days, though. One morning he was called to the door of the house by Bi Asha who sent him on an errand to the café. The young boy who usually brought their early-morning loaf of bread and buns had not come so she asked Hamza to go to the café for her. It was the first time she had spoken to him since her outburst in the yard but she acted as if nothing like that had happened between them. Take this money and fetch the bread and buns from the café – off you go. That became his job every morning. He knocked on the door and the younger woman gave him the money for the café and a basket for the bread and buns. When he came back he knocked on the door again and handed the basket over. In return he was given a slice of bread and a mug of tea for his breakfast. The woman called out his name and he went to the door to collect it. He did not think of her as the servant woman any more. She told him her name was Afiya.

He was sent on other errands: to take a parcel or a basket of food or a message to neighbours or relatives. Sometimes Bi Asha called him and lent his services to a neighbour who needed a hand with something. She was often angry with the same

175

neighbours behind their backs, recounting their endless slights of her and their repeated blasphemies. She was surrounded by blasphemers, so it seemed, and she recited scraps of the Koran as she lent Hamza to them, to provide him with some protection he hoped. She sent him on these errands in her habitual abrupt way as if she had every right to make these demands on him. Khalifa would not take rent for the room, which made Hamza a dependant of the household and under an obligation to them. He found this comforting, as if he belonged, and he did not mind being summoned back and forth. He even became used to Bi Asha's sharpness, which showed no sign of softening. It was still an improvement to be obliged to be useful rather than to be greeted as an impending disaster: Balaa. Hana maana.

*

'Mzee Sulemani is pleased with your work,' Nassor Biashara said. 'I just knew it. I knew you would be good at this. He says you have manners, which is a big word for him. It doesn't just mean politeness, it means much more than that to him.'

Nassor Biashara paused and waited. Hamza felt that he was being tested but he was not sure in what way. He waited for the merchant to explain. Nassor Biashara said, 'It's not that he has talked to me about this but it's what I think. I've known him for a long time. He never uses strong language. I don't mean bad cursing language, he does not even use the name of God the way everyone else does, wallahi and so on when we want to say we mean something. He will shush you if you say wallahi, as if you are cheapening God's name. The worst thing he can say about someone is, I don't believe him. He puts great faith in the truth, though that sounds more pompous than I meant it to. Perhaps it would be better to say he has faith in frankness, openness, something like that, without noise or show ... you're like that too. And courteous – he likes that. That is what he meant when he said you have manners. He won't say any of this to you himself so I'm telling you.'

Hamza did not know what to say. He was moved by being so well thought of and by the merchant's kindness in telling him. He felt his eyes smarting with emotion. Sometimes it troubled him that Khalifa found the merchant so abhorrent. He did not seem so bad to Hamza.

'He tells me you're living in Khalifa's house,' Nassor Biashara said, bustling with his books, his tone less confiding, less approving. 'You didn't tell me that. You're settling down nicely then. Mind you, I am not sure I would want to live with that old grumbler.'

'I don't live in his house exactly,' Hamza said. 'They let me use an outside room that used to be a barber's shop.'

'I know the house very well, and it's not really his. Or hers. How do you find Bi Asha? A bit gruff, hey? I don't know which of them turned the other the most sour but I expect it was largely her to blame. She is a woman full of grievances. You won't go and tittle-tattle about this, will you? We're related, you know. Well, I'm related to the household,' the merchant said, and then waved away any further conversation on the subject as he settled down to his paperwork.

'I hear you're related to Nassor Biashara,' Hamza said later to Khalifa. 'Or rather, he said he was related to the household.'

Khalifa considered this for a moment and then said, 'Is that what he said? That he is related to the household?'

'Why does he say household?' Hamza asked. 'Does that mean Bi Asha?'

Khalifa nodded. 'He is a weasel man, I told you that. He is a devious double-speaker who likes that kind of old-fashioned flourish talk. People like him think it's bad manners to talk about the women of the house.'

Hamza sensed that Khalifa was hesitating over saying something else so he poured him another coffee – they were sitting out on the porch that evening on their own – and asked: 'How are you related?'

Khalifa took his time, had a sip and gathered his thoughts while Hamza waited, knowing that he would get the story in due course. 'I told you I worked for his father, Amur Biashara the pirate merchant. I worked for him for many years. It was during that time that Bi Asha and I were married. Bwana Amur was a relative of hers and he ... arranged ... well, he brought us together.'

'How did you end up working for him?' Hamza asked after a long pause when Khalifa remained unusually reticent. He did not often need prompting.

Khalifa said: 'Do you really want to hear all this old stuff? You don't tell me anything about yourself and then you ask me and I can't resist. That's the curse of getting old. I can't keep my mouth shut.'

'I really want to hear about the old pirate,' Hamza said, grinning because he knew Khalifa was not going to be able to resist telling him.

*

It had been in the early stages of the kusi, the summer monsoons, when Hamza arrived in the town on that swiftly darkening evening. By then the traders from across the ocean had made their way home to Somalia and South Arabia and Western India. He did not remember much about the weather from his time in the town many years before, and many of the years after he left were arduous and spent far in the interior a long way from coastal winds. Everyone told him that these months in the middle of the year were the sweetest but he did not really understand that when he first returned. The land was still green from the long rains and the winds were mild. Later in the year, in the last third or so, it became drier and hotter, and then with the beginning of the winter monsoons, the kaskazi, came rough seas and high winds at first and then the short rains, and finally in the new year the steady winds from the north-east.

That wind brought the traders' ships back from across the ocean. Their true destination was Mombasa or Zanzibar, prosperous towns with rich merchants ready to trade, but some of them straggled into other port towns, including theirs. The arrival of the ships was anticipated weeks in advance, and popular legends of captains and crew were revived and circulated once again: the chaos they brought as they sprawled over any empty space and turned it into a campsite, the fabulous merchandise they hawked through the streets, a lot of it trinkety but some of it valuable beyond the vendors' awareness, the thick rugs and rare perfumes, the shiploads of dates and salted kingfish and dried shark that they sold as job lots to the merchants, their notorious hunger for fruit and for mangoes in particular, and their unruly violence, which in the past had led to open battles in the streets and forced people to lock themselves in their houses in terror. The sailors filled the mosques to overflowing, and perfumed the air with their sea-salted, sweat-stained kanzus and kofias, which were often tarnished brown with grime. The area around the port bore the brunt of their excesses. The timber yard and Khalifa's house were some distance into the town, and the only travellers who came their way were the street hawkers with their baskets of gum and spices and perfume and necklaces and brass trinkets and thick-woven cloths dyed and embroidered in medieval colours. Sometimes high-stepping Suri merchants who had lost their way came marching through the neighbourhood, swinging their canes high as if they were crossing enemy territory. Children trooped behind them, calling out mocking words the strangers did not understand and making farting noises with their mouths, which the Suri were reputed to find especially insulting.

If the timber yard and Khalifa's house were a little out of the way for the traders and sailors, the open ground in front of the warehouses was not. They congregated there every day, and some of them camped there during the night. Sellers of fruit and grilled maize and cassava and coffee followed them there and transformed the area to something like the buzzing tumultuous marketplace Khalifa had so longingly described to Hamza so many months before. The warehouse had been emptied of its merchandise over the past months and weeks and was now empty and ready to receive new supplies. Nassor Biashara shifted his office from the cubbyhole in the timber yard for the morning and set up another small desk just inside the warehouse doors. In the afternoon he returned to the yard to put his paperwork in order, leaving Khalifa to take charge of the delivery and stowing of the merchandise. It was a hectic time for him and he often had to work late, bustling around self-importantly with his clipboard, keeping track of the new stock. Hamza thought he was back in his element, as clerk to a pirate merchant, despatching Idris and Dubu back and forth to the port and supervising the porters who had been hired to stack the merchandise.

This was quite unlike his normal working day. Usually Khalifa locked the warehouse in the early afternoon, dropped off the keys at the timber yard and went home. If his work was light in the workshop, Hamza went with him to have lunch, which he ate in his room or on the porch. Mzee Sulemani stayed in the workshop and did not eat lunch. Hamza returned after lunch until the muadhin called the afternoon prayers when they swept the workshop and locked up. If he did not go back to the house for lunch, his portion was kept aside and he had it later on when he went home. In this way, he had become part of the household while remaining outside it in his store room. He did not go inside the house again after that first time, and when Bi Asha summoned him from the interior courtyard to run an errand as she sometimes did, her voice easily carrying to him and beyond, he waited by the outside door. When she snapped irritably at him and told him to come in, he stepped just inside the doorway and waited there until she came to him. He tried to maintain a line between being a servant, which he did not wish to be, and a dependant who had obligations to the household but who made no presumptions.

One day, during Khalifa's prolonged absence at the warehouse, Hamza knocked on the door for his lunch as was his practice and Afiya opened it. She passed him a mug of water and a dish of rice and spinach. When she did not shut the door immediately as she usually did, he sat down on the porch by the door and started to eat. He felt her presence in the shadows just inside the door. He had been living in the store room for several months by then and had not exchanged more than a few necessary words with her, although he often thought of her. After eating a few mouthfuls, sensing her nearby all the time, he said softly so that Bi Asha inside the house would not hear, 'Who gave you that name? Your father or your mother?'

'Afiya? It means good health,' she said. 'My mother gave it to me.'

He expected her to shut the door then but she did not. She stayed because she wanted to speak to him too. It had become so that he thought about her often, especially while he was alone in his room. Sometimes when she walked past and his window was open she would call out a greeting without looking in and then he would hurry to catch a glimpse of her as she walked away down the lane. Sometimes she walked past without greeting him and he caught sight of her and was stirred nonetheless. Whenever he was called to the door or when he saw her in passing, he spoke the few words it was possible for him to use without causing her offence just so that he could hear her voice, which was throaty and rich in a way he found moving.

'She called you that to wish you good health,' he said, prompting her when she did not say any more.

'Yes, and herself perhaps. She was not well,' Afiya said. 'That's what I was told. She passed on when I was very small, maybe two years old, I'm not sure. I don't remember her.'

'And your father, is he well?' asked Hamza, not knowing if he should, not sure if he should stop.

'He passed on many years ago. I didn't know him.'

He muttered condolences and addressed his bowl of rice. He wanted to tell her that he had lost his parents too, that he was taken away from them and did not know where they were and they no longer knew where he was. He wanted to ask what happened to that father she did not know. Did he pass on while she was a baby as her mother did or did he just leave her to her fate after her mother's death? He did not ask because it was only to satisfy his curiosity, and he did not know what sorrows he might release with his question.

'Does your leg hurt? I have seen you wince in pain before and I noticed that again as you sat down just now,' she said.

'It hurts, but it's getting better every day,' he said.

'What happened to you?' she asked.

He chuckled, made a brief snorting noise, trying to keep his answer light. 'I'll tell you one day.'

After a moment he heard her moving away and was sorry that he had not given her something in return for what she had given him. She came back a short while later to collect his empty bowl and to bring him segments of an orange on a small plate. 'You can come inside to wash your hands when you've finished,' she said.

When he finished he called out and went inside. He waited for her to appear at the courtyard doorway before offering her the empty plate and following behind her. She pointed to the sink against the left-hand wall of the courtyard and he went there to wash his hands. There was no sign of Bi Asha. He had guessed she was absent from the way Afiya felt free to talk to him and to invite him inside. He washed his hands at the sink and then looked around in open curiosity whereas before he had hurried to get away from Bi Asha's tetchy welcome. On the same side as the sink was the tap in the corner where he had seen Afiya washing the dishes that first time. Now he saw that the washroom was over on the back wall of the yard next to the awning and that two rooms ran along the right-hand side. He had taken one of them to be a store, in front of which stood two seredani braziers, one of which was charged with charcoal ready to be lit. The other was more substantial than he remembered it and had gauze netting and a curtain across its open window. Its door was shut. If that was her room then it was decent enough compared to customary practice. Servants sometimes only had a mat and a corner of a hallway, if anything at all. Perhaps she was not a servant and was after all Khalifa's second wife as he had at first assumed.

She followed the direction of his gaze and nodded slightly. Her kanga had slipped to the back of her head and snagged on a hairpin or a brooch there, and he saw more of her than he had seen before at such close quarters. Her hair was parted in the middle and pulled back into two braids joined together at the back. She held her kanga loosely so that he saw something of her upper body and her waist. After a moment she pulled her kanga together and adjusted it on her head. It was a familiar gesture of modesty but he wondered if she had relaxed the covering for a moment for his benefit. They exchanged smiles as he thanked her and left, but he thought she knew how he felt about her. It excited him. If she knew how he felt and smiled back at him in that way, then she could not be Khalifa's wife. That she sat with him and then invited him in to wash his hands when Bi Asha was not there, meant she was entering into a small deception. By his reckoning, which was not extensive in such matters, the situation had all the makings of a courtship and Hamza returned to the workshop in a mood of small elation.

There was an undertow to his joy however. He had little to offer her: a job that was not secure, a home that was a room granted in patronage and which could just as easily be withdrawn if his attentions offended, a bed that was a busati on the floor. His body was damaged and abused. He brought neither past joy nor future promise, just a sorry tale of abjection to add to hers when she might have looked forward to some relief from her own. There was still a chance that she was someone else's wife and he was about to become entangled in dangerous and indecorous matters. There was no talking himself out of his excitement, though, even as he also feared he did not have the will to fulfil his desire. He might in any case have completely misread the events that had just occurred. So much had been knocked out of him that at times he was paralysed by a sense of futility about anything he might wish to undertake. It was a sense he resisted daily and which the workshop and his work with wood, and the daily benign company of the carpenter, somehow helped to dissipate.

That afternoon Mzee Sulemani was in a quietly joyful mood too, humming his favourite qasidas as he worked. Perhaps he had received news that cheered him or had just completed the embroidery of his latest kofia. It added to Hamza's own sense of elation and he could not suppress his smiles, so much so that the carpenter noticed the difference in him and looked at him wonderingly without saying a word. On one occasion Hamza dropped his drill absent-mindedly and later mislaid a square, looking around irritably for it when it was right before his eyes. These were mistakes he did not usually make. On another occasion Mzee Sulemani caught Hamza's eye as he was smiling to himself and raised his eyebrows as if to ask what was pleasing him. Hamza laughed at himself for his light-headedness. After his usual fashion, the carpenter did not say anything but Hamza saw that he too was suppressing a smile. Had the old man guessed his secret? Were these things always so obvious?

'Leuchtturm Sicherheitszündhölzer.' Hamza found the box of matches tucked away in one of the drawers in the workshop and read the brand name out loud. Mzee Sulemani looked up enquiringly from his sanding,

'What did you say?' he asked.

Hamza repeated the words, Leuchtturm Sicherheitszündhölzer. Lighthouse Safety Matches. The old carpenter moved over to where Hamza stood and took the matches from him. He looked at the box for a moment and then handed it back. He walked to a shelf and took down a tin which they used for nails that needed straightening. He brought that over to Hamza who read, 'Wagener-Weber Kindermehl.'

'You can read,' the carpenter said.

'Yes, and write,' Hamza said. He could not keep the pride out of his voice.

'In German,' the carpenter said. Then pointing to the tin, he asked, 'What does that say?

'Wagener-Weber Baby-milk.'

'Can you also speak German?'

'Yes.'

'Mashaalah,' Mzee Sulemani said.

11

It had become so that she thought of him all the time. When he came to the house in the morning for the bread money, she restrained herself from speaking to him in case Bi Asha heard her. In her book of sins speaking to a man was equivalent to making an arrangement for a secret meeting with him. Hamza said, Habari za asubuhi and she said, Nzuri, and handed over the basket and the money instead of touching him or pressing herself against him. When she passed his room and could see the window was open, she had to resist the temptation to lean in and talk for a moment or hold out her hand to him. Sometimes she called out a greeting but dared not stop. She felt a small leap of elation every time he knocked on the door, and felt the beginnings of a smile on her lips, which she suppressed in case she seemed eager and flurried when she opened the door. She longed for the brief moments she saw him. She no longer called him for his slice of bread and cup of tea. It's like you are the owner's dog, she said to him one morning. She now knocked on his door and brought breakfast on a tray to him. He was always ready, waiting for her with a smile. One morning, as she was about to hand the money over for the breakfast bread and buns, she touched his hand, it seemed accidental but of course it was not, and just to make sure she held it for a brief second more. Not even an idiot could misunderstand that.

'Your leg is improving, isn't it?' she said. 'I can see from the way you move.'

'It's getting better,' he said. 'Thank you.'

The moment was coming when what needed to be said would be said but she was not sure if she should press matters forward or wait for him to act. She did not want him to think she knew how to do such things, for him to think that she had done such things before. She wished she could confide in Jamila and Saada, and many times the words were on the tip of her tongue but something held her back. She wondered if it was from fear that they would mock him and tell her to come to her senses and not act in such a self-disregarding way with a man whose people she did not know. Perhaps they would think him a penniless wanderer, not that she was anything more than that herself. She was a woman, they would say, and in the end all a woman had was her honour and was she sure he deserved the risk? She did not dare mention him to Khalida either, because she would only tell her friends who would howl with laughter and encourage Afiya to audacities she was not really up to. Anyway, what was the rush? She did not feel impatient and even liked the tense anticipation of fulfilment.

At other times she was afraid she would lose him, and he would move on as he had come, heading nowhere in particular but away from her. She had understood that much about him, from looking and listening, that he was a man who was dangling, uprooted, likely to come loose. Or at least that was what she guessed from what she saw, that he was too diffident to make the decisive move, that one day she would wait for him to come to the door for the bread money and he would not appear and would be gone from her life for ever. It was a fear that filled her with dejection, and at those moments she was determined to give him a sign. Then the moment would pass and she would be back with her own caution and uncertainty.

She thought about him so much that she was at times distracted in company. Jamila noticed and laughingly asked who she was thinking about. Had somebody asked for her? Afiya laughed too and moved the subject on and did not tell her what had happened recently at home. Just the day before Jamila caught her out in her reverie, Bi Asha had come back from one of her afternoon visits and said to her, smiling with unaccustomed archness, 'I think we are going to have some good news for you soon.'

It could only mean that a proposal was on the way. That was another fear. It had been several months since the two rejected ones, and Bi Asha had begun to murmur that they may have been too hasty and would now have acquired a reputation for arrogance in their expectations. Bi Asha's smile of relief and pleasure filled Afiya with dread. She did not ask any questions about who the suitor might be or who had made the enquiry for him. Bi Asha gave her an appraising look and came to her own conclusions, but these were probably not any cause for anxiety because the smile remained on her face. When Jamila had asked her the question, Afiya's mind was fixed on the ways she might let Hamza know how she felt. Should she write him a note? Should she lean into his window and say I can't stop thinking about you? What if he did not return her feelings? It was agony, made so much worse for her because she had time on her hands and could not speak about him to anyone.

*

Hamza also had troubles on his mind. On many occasions he walked the shore road in the direction of the house where he once lived. He was there for several years, from when he was no more than a child taken away from his first home to when he ran away to join the schutztruppe. He spent many of those years penned in the shop of the merchant who owned him, except for the several months he went with him on a long and arduous journey to the interior, walking with the porters and the guards for weeks on end across country that astonished and terrified him at the same time. The merchant was in the caravan trade, and Hamza knew later that the Germans wanted this trade to end, and wanted to be in charge of everything from the coast to the mountains. They had had enough of the resistance of coastal traders and their caravans and had dealt sternly with them in the al Bushiri wars, when it became necessary to demonstrate to the bearded rice-eating slave raiders that their time was up and German order had taken over. At the time Hamza did not fully understand much of this, even as he travelled in the interior and heard of the approach of German power. What he understood was his own bondage and powerlessness, and really he hardly understood that, but he felt how it crushed his spirit and turned him into a ghost.

In the time he lived in the merchant's shop, he hardly ever visited the town. From first light to late evening, he and another older boy stood in the shop and served the stream of customers. After dark, they closed up the premises and slept in the back. He was troubled that he could not find the house again. The shop had faced the road and there had been a walled garden along one side of the house and a stand-pipe where they had made their ablutions. There was no sign of the place now, and where he thought it used to stand was a grand-looking house painted a soft cream colour. It had an upstairs floor, a latticed veranda running all along its front and a low wall enclosing a gravelled front yard. He walked past the house several times but even after repeated visits had yet to find the courage to knock on the door and ask what had happened to the old place that once stood there. Here, many years ago, he would tell whoever opened the door, I saw my cowardice and timidity glistening like vomit on the ground. Here I saw how humility and diffidence was turned into humiliation. He did not knock and he did not say any of that, instead he circled round and headed back to the town.

There were parts of the town where he was no longer a stranger, and in the late afternoons and early evenings he walked these familiar areas. Sometimes he sat in a café and had a snack, or lingered on the fringes of a conversation or a card game. People greeted him or smiled at him or even exchanged a few words without asking him any questions or offering any information about themselves. From overheard conversations he could put names to some people and even learned brief histories of them, although those could well be exaggerations prompted by the café ambience.

Tucked away down one street he saw a group of people sitting on a bench opposite the open door of a house where a small group of musicians were rehearsing and a woman was singing. He stopped there for a while and stood in the street in the bright light of the hissing pressure lamp, which illuminated the rehearsal room and the group of people sitting and standing outside. The woman's song was full of yearning for her lover to whom she cited example after example of her devotion. The words and the voice filled him with longing, with grief and with elation at the same time. During a break in the music he asked the youth standing beside him what was happening.

'Are they rehearsing for a concert?'

The teenager looked surprised and then shrugged. 'I don't know,' he said. 'They play here and we come to listen. Maybe they play at concerts as well.'

'Do they play often?'

'Nearly every night,' the youth said.

Hamza knew he would come again.

*

Mzee Sulemani's goodwill increased after he learned that not only could Hamza read but he could read in German. He delighted in giving Hamza a sentence and asking for a German translation. He was happy to join in Mzee Sulemani's game, a small repayment for the gift of the carpentry skills he was learning from him.

Lead us on the road that is straight, make us steadfast without doubt or scepticism, without shadow or regret. How do you say that in German?' the old carpenter asked, a look of happy anticipation on his face.

Hamza did the best he could but there were times he had to admit defeat, especially with the more mystical or devotional pronouncements. Mzee Sulemani uttered some proverbial wisdom and waited with a smile while Hamza fumbled. The carpenter laughed equally at his successes and his failures and applauded him anyway. 'I only went to school to read the Koran and then just for a year. After that I was sent to work as my father and his master required.'

'His master?' Hamza asked although he thought he already knew the answer.

'Our master,' Mzee Sulemani said with composure. 'My father was a slave and so was I. Our master freed us in his will, may God have mercy on his soul. It was my father's wish that I should learn to be a carpenter and the master allowed it. So I had to stop attending school and go to work. The few suras I know, I learned by heart. Alhamdulillah, even those few have freed me from the condition of a beast.'

Mzee Sulemani described Hamza's skills to the merchant who chose to ignore this information for a while, then one day he asked, 'What is this about you being able to read and speak German? Where did you learn that? I thought you told me you did not go to school.'

'I didn't go to school. I picked it up here and there,' Hamza said.

'Where exactly? Mzee Sulemani tells me he gives you lines from the Koran and you translate them into German. You don't pick up that kind of German here and there.'

'They are very poor translations. I do my best,' Hamza said.

Khalifa was present during this exchange, and he smirked at the merchant and said, 'He has his secrets. A man is entitled to keep his secrets to himself.'

'What secrets?' the merchant asked. 'What is this about?'

'That's his business,' Khalifa said, pulling Hamza away, chuckling with the pleasure of frustrating Nassor Biashara.

That evening Khalifa told his friends at the baraza the story of Hamza's linguistic prowess and the merchant's questions and how Khalifa had frustrated him. Maalim Abdalla was a teacher and, of course, a well-known reader of newspapers in English and German. Khalifa was a former clerk to Gujarati bankers and to the pirate merchant. So it was left to Topasi, who had not had the luxury of being able to attend school, to express delight and admiration for Hamza's skills, especially for the additional fact that he had learned to do this without going to school. 'I have always said school is a waste of time. Begging your pardon, Maalim, not your school of course but many of them. You can learn just as well by not going to school.'

'Nonsense,' Maalim Abdalla said without hesitation, and no one contested the matter, not even Topasi, especially because at that moment the tray of coffee appeared and Hamza rose to collect it from Afiya. He saw from her smile in the shadows that she had been listening to the conversation. He put the tray on the porch for the old friends and went off to the mosque for isha. The others now let him go without protest or query. After prayers he walked the streets for a little while as usual and then headed back. He found that Khalifa's friends had left to go home for supper and he was sitting on the porch on his own.

'I kept some coffee for you,' Khalifa said. 'She can read and write too,' he said, indicating the door of the house, undoubtedly referring to Afiya but not saying her name. It was the first time he had made any reference to her. It had occurred to Hamza before that she moved around silently and diffidently, and Khalifa acted as if she were invisible. That could be his way of being courteous to an unmarried woman in the house, drawing a veil over her by not mentioning her name or calling attention to her. Or it could be a way of being courteous about his own wife when speaking to someone who was male and not a member of the family. Hamza did not dare to ask for fear of offending. He was not family and the womenfolk in the household were none of his business. He would find a way to ask sooner or later, he told himself, but not now. They sat with their coffee in silence for a while and then both rose at the same time. Khalifa went inside with the tray while Hamza rolled up the mat and slipped it inside the door.

*

It came to her during the night. She had heard them talking about how good his German was so she thought she would ask him for a German poem. Not even a dummkopf could misunderstand that she was asking him to translate a love poem for her, which was as good as asking him to write her a love letter.

'So you can read and write in German,' she said to him in the morning as she handed over the bread money. 'Can you find me a good poem and translate it for me? I can't read German.'

'Yes, of course. I don't know very many but I'll find one.'

At the end of the working day when she spoke to him about a poem, he walked again on the shore road and found a shaded place on the beach where he could sit for a while. The sea came over jagged rocks here and the beach was not popular with either fishermen or swimmers. He loved looking at the waves from here, just gazing for a while, following the line of the surf with his eyes, watching it come in with a muted roar and then retreat with an impatient hiss. Before leaving work he had slipped into the merchant's office while he was talking to Mzee Sulemani and picked up a piece of paper from his desk. It had the merchant's name and address printed across the top but it would be no difficulty to tear that off. A love letter had to be delivered in secret, and the smaller in size it was the more easily it was concealed.

The only German poems he knew were in the book that the officer had given him, *Musen-Almanach für das Jahr 1798*. He took the first four lines of Schiller's 'Das Geheimnis', and translated them for her:

> Sie konnte mir kein Wörtchen sagen,
> Zu viele Lauscher waren wach,
> Den Blick nur durft ich schüchtern fragen,
> Und wohl verstand ich, was er sprach.

He wrote them out on the piece of paper he had stolen from Nassor Biashara's office, trimmed it so that it was only just big enough for the verse, then folded it so it was no wider than two fingers. He knew how it would look if this scrap of paper were intercepted. If Afiya was Khalifa's wife as he feared, then at the very least Hamza would be thrown out of his room accompanied by a stream of abuse and perhaps some fully justified blows. But things had gone too far for him to hesitate any more, and the following morning as he met Afiya at the door, he slipped the square of paper into her palm. On it he had written:

> Alijaribu kulisema neno moja, lakini hakuweza –
> Kuna wasikilizi wengi karibu,
> Lakini jicho langu la hofu limeona bila tafauti
> Lugha ghani jicho lake linasema.

She was already waiting at the door when he hurried back from the café, and as she took the basket of bread and buns from him, she did not let go of his hand. She wanted to make sure he did not misunderstand her. 'I can read what your eye is saying too,' she said, referring to the last two lines of the translation: My eye can see for certain / the language her eye is speaking. Then she kissed the tips of her fingers and touched his left cheek. A short while later, when she brought him his breakfast tray, she slipped into the room and into his embrace.

'Habibi,' she said.

'Are you his wife?' he blurted out while she was in his arms and they were clinging to each other. It took her by surprise. She was relishing the moment, holding his sweet body in her arms, and he asked if she was a wife! She pulled back from him and felt his arms restraining her. 'I'm sorry,' he whispered.

'Whose wife?' she asked, alarm in her eyes too.

He hooked a thumb towards the house behind him. As his meaning became clear to her, the alarm in her eyes turned to mischief and she smiled as she sank back into his arms. 'I'm nobody's wife ... yet,' she said before freeing herself and leaving.

*

It was a Friday morning when Afiya slipped into the room and embraced him and afterwards left him speechless with joy. On Fridays they only worked half-days in the yard. Almost everywhere else also shut down at midday so that people could go to juma'a prayers in the main mosque in the town. Not everyone went, of course, despite the early release from work, only those who were obedient to God's command and those who had no choice, mainly children and the youth. Neither Khalifa nor Nassor Biashara went. Hamza did – the little saint – because he liked sitting among a crowd of people in such benign mood, listening without paying full attention to the painstakingly devout words of the imam's sermon. He had not been forced to go as a child and now it gave him pleasure to make his own choices. Then he knew, he just knew, Afiya would find a way to come to his room in the afternoon. He kept his window closed and the door slightly open, and in the glaring heat of early afternoon when sensible people stayed indoors or lay down to rest, she came dressed in her buibui on her way to somewhere. The room filled with her scent as he shut the door. They kissed and caressed and murmured to each other for an exhilarating few minutes, but when he tugged gently at her buibui whose slippery material prevented him from properly feeling her body, she shook her head and freed herself from him. Afiya said she had to go otherwise Bi Asha will miss her and make a fuss. Her excuse for coming out was to go to Muqaddam Sheikh's shop for the eggs she needed for the dessert she was making.

'What's the rush?' he said.

'She knows the Muqaddam's shop is only a few minutes away.'

'Do you have to work for her?' he asked, reluctant to let her leave.

Afiya looked surprised. 'I don't work for her. I live here.'

'Don't go,' he said.

'I must go now, I'll tell you later,' she said.

For the rest of the day he dwelt on the memory of her embraces and rebuked himself for being ridiculous with impatience. It was also the last Friday before Ramadhan and the sighting of the new moon that evening filled the day with even more excitement. Bi Asha appointed him to take word around the neighbourhood, to make sure everyone knew about the new moon so the blasphemers had no excuse for eating or drinking in ignorance during the following day. He took a long walk instead and kept out of her way, having no wish to be mocked as a pious busybody.

So much changed during Ramadhan. Work started later and many shops and premises did not open until the afternoon as people slept to shorten the day and then stayed up late into the night. The merchant considered these practices lazy and old-fashioned and asked his employees to work their usual hours, but he could not persuade all of them to agree. Khalifa took no notice of the merchant and closed the warehouse at midday and went home to sleep. Idris and Dubu and Sungura pronounced themselves exhausted with hunger and thirst at some point in the early afternoon and collapsed for a sleep in a shady place in the yard or simply slunk away. Mzee Sulemani insisted on his lunch break during which he said his prayers and recited the suras of the Koran that he knew by heart and then worked on his embroidered cap. He regretted, he told Hamza, that he could not read the Koran properly, as that was what people were required to do during Ramadhan, to read a chapter of the holy book every day until all thirty chapters were finished by the end of the month.

Eating arrangements also changed, not just the daylight hunger and thirst but how the misery was brought to an end. Ramadhan was a communal event and it was considered virtuous to make the breaking of fast after sunset into a shared meal, so instead of going off to find something in a café, Hamza was invited inside to eat the food of the household. Ramadhan food was always special as the cooks took greater trouble and had more time to plan and prepare. The delicious meals were also a reward for the stoicism of the day. Hamza broke fast with Khalifa on the porch where in the traditional way they shared a few dates and a cup of coffee and were then called inside to the modest feast Bi Asha and Afiya had prepared and which they sat down to eat with the men. It was not the quantity but the variety of dishes that made it into a feast, and they talked about the food and praised its preparation as they ate. Even Bi Asha was more mellow than she had been in the past and found teasing words to say to Hamza about his growing skills as a carpenter and his newfound fame as a reader of German. Next thing we know you'll start composing poetry, she said. Hamza just managed to resist looking at Afiya but made enough of a movement before he arrested it for Bi Asha to look towards its intended direction and then back at Hamza, who dropped his eyes and busied himself with the fish.

After the meal he sat on the porch with Khalifa where they were joined soon after by Maalim Abdalla and Topasi, and sometimes other neighbours who stopped by for a chat. Ramadhan evenings were full of talk and comings and goings. On other porches or in cafés that stayed open late, marathon games of cards or dominoes or coram went on, but on Khalifa's porch no such frivolity was entertained. There the talk was still focused on political intrigue, human foibles and old scandals. Hamza went walking the streets, which were thronged with people, and sometimes he stopped to watch one of the games or to listen to the raillery among street wits. The musicians had stopped playing after Ramadhan began but he hoped it would only be for the first few days. Every night during the previous weeks, the group he had first heard by chance played a short concert for their devoted audience of whom he had become a member. They played for sheer love, it seemed, because they never asked for money and no one offered to pay. Some nights the woman sang, and in time Hamza came to hear several of her repertoire of love songs and was moved by the longing expressed in them. He wished he could bring Afiya to listen to the music, but he did not know how he could do that or even when he could tell her about them. Now that Ramadhan was here there was no breakfast, and no need to collect the money for bread and buns from the café. He was careful not to look at her when he went to eat the evening meal inside but he knew that their exchange of glances had been intercepted by Bi Asha, who now watched him suspiciously.

Then on the first Friday of Ramadhan, at the same time as she had done the previous week, Afiya slipped into his room whose door he had left ajar. They embraced and undressed fully and made love with sinful hunger, hushing and shushing each other in case they were overheard.

'It's the first time,' she whispered.

He paused for a second and then whispered back, 'Me too.'

'You expect me to believe that?' she said.

'Maybe it doesn't make any difference,' he whispered, laughing, pleased that he had not failed and that she had taken him to be more experienced.

'We shouldn't be doing this during the fast,' she said later as they lay naked on his mat. 'The only way this can be right is if you promise to be mine and I promise to be yours. I promise.'

'I promise too,' he said, and they both chuckled at their absurd love-talk.

She reached across his body and put her right hand on the scar on his left hip. She ran her fingers over it for several seconds, stroking it and feeling it as if she would smooth its jagged contours. Just as she was about to speak he reached up and put his left hand over her mouth.

'Not now,' he said.

Gently, she took his hand away. 'All right, it's your secret,' she said, and then saw that there were tears in his eyes. 'What is it? What happened to you?'

'It's not a secret. Just not now, please, not this minute,' he said pleadingly. 'Not after love.'

She shushed him and kissed him, and after he had quietened down she held up her left hand so that it was close to his face, then she flexed her fingers as if she was trying to make a fist but the palm would not close. 'It's broken. I cannot grip with this hand,' she said.

'What happened?' he asked.

She smiled and reached for his face with her damaged hand. 'That's what I asked you and you burst into tears,' she said. 'My uncle broke it. He was not really my uncle, but I was living in his house when I was younger. He broke it because he said it was wrong for me to know how to write. He said, what will you write? You'll write ugly things, you'll write notes to a pimp.'

They lay in silence for a while. 'I am very sorry. Please tell me more about it,' Hamza said.

'He hit me with a stick. He was in a rage when he found out I could write. My brother taught me but then he had to leave so I went back to live with my uncle. When he saw I could read and write, he lost his temper and hit me across my hand, but he hit the wrong hand so I can still write. But it makes chopping vegetables hard work,' she said.

'Tell me from the beginning,' he said.

She stood up and started to get dressed, and he did too. She sat in the barber's chair while he stayed on the floor, leaning against the wall. 'All right, but after I tell you and I ask you about what happened to you, you will not push me away?'

'You are my beloved. I promise,' he said.

'I'll be quick because I have to go and help Bimkubwa with the cooking. I'm supposed to be visiting a neighbour and if I'm late she'll send someone there to fetch me.'

Then she told him how her brother came back for her when she was ten years old when she did not even know she had a brother, how she lived with him for a year and he taught her to read and write, and then he went off to war. 'My brother Ilyas,' she said.

'Where is he now?' Hamza said.

'I don't know. I haven't seen him or heard from him since he went to the war.'

'Is it not possible to find out?'

She looked at him at length. 'I don't know. We tried,' she said and then glanced down at his hip. 'Did you get that in the war?'

'Yes,' he said. 'During the war.'

*

That night after breaking fast Khalifa sat on the porch as usual but for some reason his two old friends were late in coming. Hamza sat with him to keep him company when he would rather have gone for a walk to see if the musicians were back performing again. They made casual conversation for a while and Hamza mentioned the group. Khalifa as usual knew about them and their history without stirring from his porch. 'The power of rumour and gossip,' he said with a smile. 'They stop playing during Ramadhan, only holding rehearsals indoors. The pious ones don't approve of anything festive during the holy month. They want us all to suffer and starve and rub our foreheads raw with prayers.' Then out of a lengthy silence, and without looking at Hamza, Khalifa said, 'You like her.'

When he turned to look at him, Hamza nodded.

'She is a good woman,' Khalifa said, once again looking away and speaking softly, taking any note of challenge from his voice. This was a delicate matter. 'She has lived with us for many years and Bi Asha and I have watched over her like our own. I need to know your intentions. I have a responsibility.'

'I didn't know you were related,' Hamza said.

'I promised her brother,' Khalifa said.

'Ilyas?' Hamza said.

'So you know about him. Yes, Ilyas, he lived here in this town with his little sister when he came back from his wanderings. He got a job at the big sisal factory because he could speak good German. They liked that. It was at this time that we became friends. It was soon after we were married living here. Ilyas sometimes brought the little girl when he visited us. Then when the war came he joined up, I don't know why. Maybe he had started to think of himself as a German, or maybe he always wanted to be an askari. He used to tell the story of how a Shangaan askari kidnapped him and took him to a mountain town where he was released and cared for by a German landowner. He told me once that since that encounter with the Shangaan, he had secretly thought it would be surprisingly fulfilling to be a schutztruppe. Then when the war came he could not resist. We don't know if he is alive still. It's eight years now since he went to the war and we have not heard from him since. I promised to keep an eye on her,' Khalifa said. 'I don't know how much you know about her.'

'She told me about her relatives in the country.'

'They treated her like a slave. Has she told you that? The man she called her uncle beat her with a stick and broke her hand. When he did that she sent me a note – yes, that's right. Ilyas taught her to read and write, and I told her if she was in trouble she was to write a note addressed to me and give it to the shopkeeper in the village. That's what she did, the brave little thing. She wrote a note and the shopkeeper gave it to a cart driver who brought it to me. So I went and got her and she has lived here for the last eight years. It will do her good to make her own life now,' Khalifa said. 'Have you spoken to her?'

'Yes,' Hamza said.

'That makes me happy,' Khalifa said. 'You must tell me more about your people, your lineage. What are the names of your father and mother, and what are the names of their mothers and fathers? You can tell me this later. I have seen enough of you to be reassured but I promised Ilyas. I feel a responsibility. Poor Ilyas, his life was attended with difficulties yet he lived under a kind of illusion that nothing bad could ever happen to him on this earth. The reality was that he was always on the point of stumbling. You could not imagine someone more generous nor anyone more self-deluded than Ilyas.'

Hamza had begun to think of Khalifa as a sentimental bearer of crimes, someone who took a share of responsibility for other people's troubles and for wrongs done in his time: Bi Asha, Ilyas, Afiya and now Hamza, people he quietly cared about while disguising this unexpected concern with outspoken brashness and persistent cynicism.

*

Afiya came again to Hamza's room the following Friday but this time she told Bi Asha that she was visiting her friend Jamila who had moved away from her parents' house to the other side of town, so they knew they had the whole afternoon.

'I surprise myself with my audacity,' she told him. 'Telling lies, sneaking into my lover's room in the middle of a Ramadhan afternoon, having a lover at all. I would never have thought I had it in me, but I don't know how I could not come when you are lying here a few feet away from me.'

They made love in whispers and then lay in the afternoon gloom without talking for a while. Eventually he said, 'I can't get over how beautiful this is.'

She ran her hands slowly all over him as if learning him by heart, over his brow, his lips, over his chest, down his leg and the inside of his thigh. 'You cried out,' she said. 'Was it your leg?'

'No,' he said smiling. 'It was ecstasy.'

She slapped his thigh playfully and then massaged the scar on his hip as she had done before. Tell me, she said.

He began to tell her about his years in the war. He started with the morning march to the training camp, then the boma and the drills in the Exerzierplatz, how exhausting but exhilarating it was, how brutal the culture was. He told her about the officer and how he taught him German. He told her quickly at first because there was so much to tell. She listened without interruption and did not ask questions, just giving a soft gasp now and then in reaction. When he talked about the officer she shook her head slightly and asked him to repeat what he said, and he saw that she did not want him to rush quite so much. He slowed down and provided more details: his eyes, the unnerving intimacy, the language games he liked to play. He explained about the ombasha and the shaush and the Feldwebel.

'He did this, the Feldwebel,' Hamza said. 'At the very end of the fighting, when we were all exhausted and half-mad from the bloodletting and cruelty we had been steeped in for years. He was a cruel man, always a cruel man. He cut me down in a rage, with his sabre, but maybe he always wanted to hurt me, I don't know why. It was because of the officer, I think.'

'How because of the officer?' she asked.

He hesitated for a moment. 'The officer was very protective of me. He wanted me to be close to him. I don't know why … I'm not sure why. He said: I like the look of you. I think some people … the Feldwebel and maybe the other Germans too … thought there was something wrong in this, something improper … something … too much, too fond.'

'Did he touch you?' she asked softly, wanting him to be explicit, wanting him to say what he needed to say.

'He slapped me once, and sometimes he touched my arm when he talked to me, just lightly, not touching like that. I think they thought he was … touching me. He said things like that to me, the Feldwebel, ugly accusing things. It shamed me, his obsessive cruelty, as if I had done something to deserve it.'

She shook her head in the gloom. 'You are too good for this world, my one and only. Don't be ashamed, hate him, wish ill on him, spit on him.'

He was silent for a long while and she waited. Then she said, 'Go on.'

'After I was injured the officer had me taken to a German mission, a place called Kilemba. The pastor there was a doctor and he healed me. It is a beautiful place. I was there for more than two years, helping in the mission, getting better, reading the Frau's books. When the British medical department took over, which took them a while, they told the pastor his medical training was not up to official requirements. He was not a fully qualified doctor. They wanted to upgrade the mission infirmary to a rural clinic but could not let the pastor be in charge of it so he decided it was time to return to Germany. It was time for me to move on too. I took work where I found it and then moved on, on farms, in cafés and eating houses, sweeping the streets, as a house servant … anything I could get. It was hard sometimes, with the leg, and probably in the end I overdid it, but I worked in Tabora,

Mwanza, Kampala, Nairobi, Mombasa. I had no destination in mind, or at least I did not think so at the time,' he said, smiling. 'Only now I can see I did.'

After another long silence while his words sank in, Afiya got up and began to dress.

'It must be getting late. I want to hear everything, I want to hear more about the good pastor and his mission and how he healed you, but now I must go,' she said. 'She will be angry if I'm late back because she has become suspicious. She told me someone has made an enquiry for me, but it is too late now. I am no longer available. When you come in to break fast I will still be smelling of you. I'll miss loving you until next time. As I listen to you, I also think of Ilyas. He is older than you. Did I tell you that he sings beautifully? I imagine what it must have been like for him in the war and if he is well somewhere, talking to someone like you are talking to me.'

'We can find out. We can try,' Hamza said, correcting himself. 'There are records. The Germans are good with records. Then you'll know what happened to him.'

'What can we find out? Maybe this way I don't have to know for sure, and what happened has happened. If he is well somewhere, my knowing does not make any difference to him, and if he is well somewhere, perhaps he does not want to be found,' she said. 'I must go.'

12

'Good fortune is never permanent, if it comes at all,' Khalifa said on the third night of Idd as they sat on the porch. 'It's only months that you've been with us but it seems that I have known you for longer. I have become used to you. I knew from the start that there was something alive behind your zombie appearance. You looked as if you were about to collapse in a heap in front of me when you first arrived. Now look at you. You have found work that suits you and you have even pleased that slow-witted miser of ours, only you need to ask him for a pay rise now that you've turned out to be a competent carpenter. Oh, no, you're going to be the saint who will wait humbly for his desserts to come to him!

'But listen to what I am saying: good fortune is never permanent. You cannot always be sure how long the good moments will last or when they will come again. Life is full of regrets, and you have to recognise the good moments and be thankful for them and act with conviction. Take your chances. I am not blind. I have been looking and I have seen what I have seen and I have understood, and some of what I have seen has made me anxious. I thought I would wait until you were ready to speak to me, that I would not rush you or embarrass you, and that in the meantime nothing unseemly would happen. Now that Ramadhan is over and all the holiness is behind us, now that Idd has arrived and a new year has begun, it may also be the time for you to show some conviction. If you wait too long you may lose the moment or else be drawn into something regrettable. So I am giving you a little nudge.

'Bi Asha also has eyes in her head and a mind to work things out with and, as I am sure you have noticed by now, a tongue with which to speak about them. I don't know if she has spoken to Afiya, though I expect we would know if she had. She has ideas of her own and they may not suit you. I have some idea of your feelings for Afiya, you told me of them yourself. It could be this is one of those decisive moments I am speaking of, and which I am eager for you not to miss. Am I talking in riddles or do you understand what I mean? I can see you do. I do not mean to rush you, nor am I in any hurry to get rid of Afiya. I asked you before if you've spoken to her and you said you have. If it is agreed between you, then I am happy. I like the idea, but you will need to tell me something about your people so we can be sure that no harm is done. Why don't you speak about yourself? Your silences look suspicious, as if you have done something bad.'

'Why shouldn't I lie just like you told me to before? Why should I not just make something up?' Hamza asked, provoking him because he knew where he was heading and he was confident of the outcome.

'Yes, I know I said you should just lie but this is different. This is not something to joke about, this is not about keeping the peace and moving things along. Perhaps you think I am being a meddlesome patriarch, interfering in the way a young woman might choose to live her life. I am not her father or her brother but she has lived with us since she was a child and I have a responsibility to her. It is important that we know about you so our minds can be at rest. You don't have anywhere to live, and it is likely you will continue to live here with us. I would like you to continue to live here with us, so that too is another reason we need to know more about you. You could be anybody. Of course, I don't believe for one minute that you did something bad before you came here, or no worse than the rest of us have, but I need you to tell me that. Look me in the eye and tell me. If you tell me a lie about yourself, I'll see it in your eyes.'

'You have great faith in your powers,' Hamza said.

'Try me. Tell me the truth and I'll know it at once,' Khalifa said so vehemently that it wiped the smile off Hamza's face. 'All right, let me ask some questions and you can answer as you wish. You said you lived here many years ago when you were quite young. Tell me how that came about.'

'That's not a question,' Hamza said, not yet able to give up the provoking tone.

'Don't be irritating. I know that's not a question. All right, how did you come to live in this town when you were young?' Khalifa asked irritably, not at all amused by Hamza's playfulness.

'My father gave me away to a merchant to cover his debts,' Hamza said. 'I didn't know that was what he had done until after the merchant took me with him, so I don't know what my father owed or why it was necessary for him to give me away. Maybe the merchant was punishing my father for being a bad debtor. The merchant lived in this town and he brought me here to work in his shop although he was not a shopkeeper. The shop was only a small part of his business, which was the caravan trade. He was like your merchant pirate, Amur Biashara, he did all kinds of business. He took me on one of his trips to the interior, which lasted several months. It was incredible. We went all the way to the lakes and beyond to the mountains on the other side.'

'What was his name?' Khalifa asked.

'We called him Uncle Hashim but he was not my uncle,' Hamza said.

Khalifa thought for a moment and then nodded. 'Hashim Abubakar, I know who you mean. So you worked for him. What happened to you?'

'I didn't work for him. I was bonded to him to secure my father's debts or something like that. The merchant did not explain anything or pay me. He treated me like I was his property.'

They sat silently for a while, each absorbed in his own thoughts. 'What happened to you?' Khalifa asked again.

'I could not bear to live like that any more so I ran away to the war,' Hamza said.

'Like Ilyas,' Khalifa said disdainfully.

'Yes, like Ilyas. After the war I went to the town where I had lived as a child with my parents but they were no longer there, and no one knew where they had gone. The merchant who took me away from them, Uncle Hashim, told me that several years before I ran away. He told me that they no longer lived there, but I wanted to be sure. For a long time I did not want to find them. I thought they had thrown me away and did not want me. Then after the war I tried to find them but I couldn't. So I don't have any people to tell you about. I've lost them. I lost them when I was very young and I don't know what I can tell you about them that will be of any use to a grown-up person who feels a responsibility for another person. You want me to tell you about myself as if I have a complete story but all I have are fragments which are snagged by troubling gaps, things I would have asked about if I could, moments that ended too soon or were inconclusive.'

'You're already telling me a lot. What brought you back to this town where you must have suffered such shame?' Khalifa asked.

'Shame? What shame?'

'To be bonded to another, to have your body and spirit owned by another human being. Is there a greater shame than that?'

'The merchant did not own me body and spirit,' Hamza said. 'Nobody owns anyone body and spirit. I learned that a long time ago. He had use of me while I lacked the wisdom and the skill to run away, only even then I did not know enough to keep myself safe and ran away to war. If I felt shame it was for my father and my mother, but that only came later when I was older and knew more about shame myself. I came back to this town because there was nowhere else I knew. I wandered everywhere, doing work that was slowly killing me, and in the end I just drifted back here, I suppose.

'I made a friend while I was first here. When I think back to my years, I think that he was the only friend I ever made in my life, and I felt a tug to return when I was lost and sad about many things. He was bonded to the merchant too, but when I came back the shop was gone and I couldn't find him. I didn't dare ask people about Uncle Hashim in case my father's debt had passed on to me.'

'That was wise of you. It's always best to be cautious, I know you know that. I can tell you what happened to your merchant Hashim Abubakar,' Khalifa said, smiling, happy as always to be the bringer of news, the vendor of gossip. 'The young man who ran the shop for him absconded with all the cash the merchant had hidden in the house. He ran away with the merchant's young wife too, his second wife. The pair of them disappeared, have never been heard of since. That was just before the war started so who knows what might have happened to them? So many people were lost in the war. For the merchant it was a great scandal and he sold up and went off somewhere. The last I heard of him he was in Mogadishu or Aden or Djibouti or somewhere in those parts. He was one of the last of those caravan merchants so his time was up anyway. The Germans wanted to put an end to all that and control everything themselves. What was the name of this friend who worked for Hashim Abubakar?'

'His name was Faridi,' Hamza said.

'That's exactly the young man,' Khalifa said, slapping his thigh with delight as his story was growing even more nicely viscous. 'What a rogue, hey! The money and the wife! He must have been a proper rascal, this friend of yours.'

'I was so young when I was first brought here and he looked after me like a brother. Neither of us knew anyone really, we just worked in the shop day and night. Sometimes we went to town but he did not know where he was either. We wandered around. If he absconded with the money just before the war then it must have been soon after I ran away too. The young wife he ran away with was his sister. She was also bonded to Uncle Hashim.'

Khalifa sighed at this new detail, which was now going to make his story so impossibly rich that no one would believe it. 'So that's who you are,' he said. 'I was here working for my pirate merchant and you and your friend were at the other end of town plotting the downfall of another pirate. I don't know why but it makes me happy to think of your friend Faridi running away and leaving the merchant to face the shame. We all thought it must have been the young wife who planned it. How else could he have known where the merchant hid his money? They must have been rogues, both of them, to take it all. Well, for their sakes, I hope they are never found because it was wrong to take that money, even if Faridi was a friend of yours.'

'What happened to the house? It used to be there at the end of the shore road. It had a lovely garden. I do remember that right, don't I?' Hamza asked.

'An Indian businessman bought it and demolished it to build the mansion that stands there now. Not everyone loves a garden. The businessman came with the British. When they took over from the Germans, the British brought in their own people to do business here. They brought them from India and from Kenya, and those new Indians sank their teeth in here fast and sure, and here they still are. They are taking over all the commerce and telling the government that they are British citizens and must have the same rights as the mzungus, and not be treated as if they are no better than us natives.'

*

On the fourth and last day of Idd, while there was still a trace of celebration in the morning air, Afiya pushed open the door of Hamza's store room to bring him his breakfast tray with a slice of bread and cup of tea. Because it was still Idd, she brought a festive slice of bread soaked in beaten egg and fried. He took the tray from her and put it down on the table and she was then free to slip into his arms. That was when he asked her. He had told Khalifa that he would ask her himself, because he wanted her to say that it was something she wanted too. Khalifa said that was not how things were done. He, Hamza, should speak to Khalifa who would speak to Bi Asha who would ask Afiya. Then her reply would travel back the same route. That was how things were done, and that was how things will still be done after Hamza had spoken to her, but if he wanted to ask her himself as well, he should go ahead and ask.

Afiya was in his arms when he said, 'Will it suit you if we marry?'

She pulled back to look at his face, perhaps to make sure he was not joking. When she saw how sombre his expression was, she smiled and held him tighter and then said, 'Idd mubarak, it will suit me very well.'

'I have nothing,' he said.

'Nor do I,' she said. 'We'll have nothing together.'

'We won't have anywhere to live, just this store room without even a mosquito net. We should wait until I can afford to rent somewhere more fitting,' he said.

'I don't want to wait,' she said. 'I did not think I would find someone to love. I thought someone would come for me and I would have no choice. Now you have come and I don't want to wait.'

'There is nowhere to wash. Only the mat to sleep on. You will live like an animal in a burrow,' he said.

She laughed. 'Don't exaggerate,' she said. 'We can wash and cook inside, and make love on the floor whenever we want. It will be like a journey together and we will find our way even if our bodies smell of old sweat. She has been wanting me to go for years. She said she did not like the way he looked at me. Ever since I became a woman. She said he wanted to make me his wife – Baba Khalifa. She said men are animals like that. They have no restraint.'

'I didn't know,' Hamza said. 'You told me this is your home.'

'Bi Asha has a bitter heart. She hated that I was a young woman. She wanted me to go but she hated when a young man looked at me. Even a glance in the street was enough to start her accusations. She said it revolted her, the way men looked at me. She said I encouraged it when I did no such thing. She wanted me to go but she wanted an older man to come and take me for his second wife. She did not want me to feel attractive and young, but to be taken by someone who would use me for his pleasure, who would degrade me with his cravings. It's the bitterness in her, it makes her mean. She was not like that to me when I was a child. She was fierce as you see her now but she was not mean. It was when I grew into a woman that she became like this.'

'I didn't know,' he said again. 'Did someone come for you?'

She shrugged. 'Twice. I didn't know one of them. The other was the manager of the café on the main road. He saw me walking by. He has seen me walking by for years, ever since I was ten years old. That's how they are, men like that, they have money and they want a young woman to play with for a few months. They see you

209

walking in the street, and they say who is that woman and they come for you because they can. That's what Baba Khalifa said.'

'But you said no.'

'I said no and Baba Khalifa said no. She said it was because he wanted to keep me for himself. That was when she first came out with it. She accused him of that, for many days. When he brought you that day, when he brought you inside, I think he wanted me to see you. I don't know if he really meant to do that, maybe he just liked you. But I saw you, and each time I saw you I felt a little more longing for you. I didn't know it would be like that. That's why I don't want to wait, and why this room is not a burrow.'

'Has she spoken to you about us? Khalifa said he did not know if she had.'

'Two days ago she said don't bring shame to our house, but she has said that before.' Afiya smiled at him. 'Too late now.'

When he found out from Hamza that they planned to live in the store room, Khalifa would not hear of it. Hamza could not repeat what Afiya had told him about her persecution, and after stuttering helplessly he said Bi Asha's name. Khalifa shrugged and then shook his head emphatically. 'You will come and live in the house with her, with us,' he said. 'Not out there like vagrants. Inside will be more comfortable for you. That room may be adequate for a jaluta like you who is used to wandering like a hooligan. It is not suitable for a daughter of our house.'

'We will find our own place to rent,' Hamza said. 'Maybe it's best to wait for a while until I can afford something better.'

'What is there to wait for?' Khalifa asked. 'You can move in here now and when you are ready to rent, off you go.'

'Well, we'll see,' Hamza said, reluctant to be forced inside, to be forced to live intimately with Bi Asha's distemper.

The couple married fourteen days later. Their wedding was so quiet that the merchant Nassor Biashara and the people at the timber yard did not know about it until after it happened. Khalifa invited the imam and his baraza friends for a meal, and Bi Asha did the same for her women neighbours. They hired a cook to come to the house to prepare a biriani and he took over the backyard for that. The women were in Bi Asha and Khalifa's bedroom, with the bed upended and pushed against the wall. The men gathered in the guest room where the imam invited Hamza to ask for Afiya in marriage. Since the ceremony was an agreement being entered into in front of witnesses, it was customary at this point to state what mahari or dowry the man intended to offer and for the bride or her representative to consider whether this was satisfactory. Such matters would have been discussed well beforehand but were confirmed in front of witnesses. Hamza had nothing to offer as mahari. He told this to Khalifa who said the decision to take him without was up to Afiya. Since she waved that conversation away – we'll have nothing together – this part of the ceremony was quietly ignored, and Hamza simply asked if Afiya would accept him for her husband and Khalifa accepted in her name. The news was conveyed to Afiya and Bi Asha's guests in the other room who welcomed it with ululations. They were then served the meal and that was the end of the festivities.

Khalifa allowed them no choice but to move in. He was utterly insistent, and Afiya shrugged and said they could try it. There was always the store room if it did not work out. Hamza moved his few belongings into Afiya's room: his small shoulder bag, which contained the copy of *Musen-Almanach für das Jahr 1798* the Oberleutnant had left for him, another book by Heinrich Heine, *Zur Geschichte der Religion und Philosophie in Deutschland*, which the Frau gave to him as a parting present, his mat and his clothes.

Afiya's room was bigger than the store room, and it was comfortable and within easy reach of the washroom. There was a curtain across both the window and the door, which she often kept open for the breeze to enter until bedtime. The head of the bed was pushed hard against one wall, with just enough room left for them to slip in on either side. A rectangular wooden frame was suspended from the ceiling for the mosquito net. There was an old rickety thin-panelled cupboard against the opposite wall, and when he saw it for the first time Hamza told her he would make a new cupboard for them in the workshop. That would be her mahari. Inside the cupboard there was a small locked box painted in green and red diagonal stripes. She opened it for him and showed him its treasures: the notebooks she had used when her brother taught her to read, the marbled ledger that Baba gave her, a gold bracelet Ilyas bought for her for Idd during the one year they lived together, now too small for her to wear, a picture postcard of the mountain overlooking the town where he had worked on the German's farm and then gone to school, and the tiny scrap of the Schiller poem Hamza had translated for her.

Afiya's room opened out on to the yard, which was where the household's cooking was done, and where they ate and washed, and where the women of the house spent several hours of the day. It was their part of the house and male strangers did not go there. Hamza was not a stranger any more but he did not feel like a member of the family either. After what he had heard about Bi Asha's bitterness, he was nervous about the arrangement and how she would take his presence in the yard. He greeted her when he came upon her and she made some kind of acknowledgement without eye contact but there was no conversation between them. He felt her resistance in the air and cringed with discomfort and self-dislike. He did not want to be there. As soon as he was up in the morning he used the washroom, drank his tea in the yard with Khalifa who joined him and insisted on this arrangement, and left the house together with him. When he returned in the afternoon the yard was unoccupied and Hamza went straight to their room where Afiya was waiting for him. In the evening Bi Asha and Afiya prepared supper in the yard and sometimes women neighbours called so he made sure to be out of the room so they could talk without being overheard. That was what he understood manners required. After several days of these unsettled jitters Afiya told him to stop scurrying out of the way.

'Usijitaabishe,' she said. 'Don't worry yourself. He asked you to live here, so just ignore her and she'll get used to it.'

'She doesn't want me here,' he said. 'Balaa, remember? She thinks I will bring disaster.'

'She was just being cruel,' Afiya said. 'She is not that cranky.'

His anxiety about Bi Asha did little to diminish his pleasure in the new intimacies Afiya and he now came to know when they were alone together. Luck had preserved him through the war and brought him into her life, and the world always moves on despite the chaos and waste in its midst.

Nevertheless, living in the yard was a tense affair. Even when he made casual conversation with Bi Asha he was always aware of an edge to her words as if she were likely to say something wounding the next moment. When she spoke sharply to Khalifa he ignored her, as if she had said nothing. Even when she spoke about everyday matters, the price of fish or the quality of the spinach available in the market, it seemed these things too caused her bitterness and discontent. He did not know how long he would be able to bear such ill-tempered patronage.

The merchant Nassor Biashara said to him, 'Aha, why do you look so gloomy? My wife told me that you married a few days ago, and you did not even invite any of us to the wedding. You should be looking joyful! Or is it maybe you're not getting enough sleep? He-he-he. I know Afiya, or I did when she was young. My wife tells me she is now a very lovely woman. My congratulations. It's all working out for you, eh? You deserve it. Look at you. You have a good job and now a good woman to help you bear the burdens and it's me you have to thank for it. I'm not asking for gratitude, you have worked hard, but it was all down to me. I saw you and I thought: Why not give this dopey young man a chance? He looks like a loser but maybe given an opportunity he could come good. I have an intuition about people, you see. I saw something there in that shambles you presented to the world. Now look at you. Are you still living in that store room? I hope not, not with your new wife. I hope you've found yourself somewhere decent to live ... You live with those two grumblers! That is not a sensible start to your married life. What do you mean, you can't afford to rent a place of your own? What are you talking about? Do you need to rent a mansion with a steam bath and a walled garden and a latticed veranda? What do you mean, you would like a pay rise? I pay you enough, don't I? I treat you decently. I am not made of money, you know. You are not going to become greedy now just because you have a wife. Has Khalifa put you up to this?'

When Mzee Sulemani heard about the wedding he said to Hamza, 'Ask the miser for a pay rise. It's the least he can do after all the work you have been doing here since that drunkard Mehdi left. Alhamdulillah, may you be blessed with many children. Can you say that in German?'

'Mögest du mit vielen Kindern gesegnet sein.'

Mzee Sulemani chuckled with pleasure as he always did when Hamza delivered one of his translations.

FOUR

13

It was a time of ease for Hamza compared to preceding years. The strain in their living arrangement with Bi Asha and Khalifa lessened as the weeks and months passed by or maybe they became inured to it. They found ways of avoiding each other without seeming to be at loggerheads, of not seeing Bi Asha's accusing looks and not hearing her growling undertones. Hamza learned to keep out of her way so well that often he only saw her briefly when he came home from work in the afternoon, although her voice was never far away. Afiya was always the first up, but Hamza was usually awake, unable to sleep deeply once it was light. She made the tea while he washed and then he left the house before Khalifa and Bi Asha came out of their room.

When he arrived at the yard, Nassor Biashara was always already there. They greeted each other and the merchant gave him the key to the workshop without any conversation and sometimes without even looking up from his precious ledgers. After Mzee Sulemani arrived, the three of them met briefly to discuss the schedule of the day's work and Nassor Biashara sometimes joined them in the workshop, putting finishing touches to bowls and cabinets or passing a critical opinion on a new design. He was making plans to build padded sofas and needed to employ an upholsterer in due course, but for the time being he was experimenting with the frames. The demand for furniture was constantly rising. His freight business was also expanding, and contrary to Khalifa's predictions, investment in the propeller had proved to be a great success, attracting more business than could be conducted by one boat and requiring the purchase of a larger motorised vessel. Nassor Biashara liked to call it his steamer. The merchant's affairs were flourishing so much that he designed a signboard, which he carved and painted himself and had Sungura fix on the yard gates: Biashara Furniture and General Merchandise.

'I think we'll have to extend the workshop and bring in new equipment,' he said, looking at Mzee Sulemani first, whose expression remained blank, and then at Hamza who nodded in support. 'This is a big yard, isn't it? We could build a new workshop right across here, properly equipped to win government contracts – school desks, office furniture, that kind of thing. We can keep the old workshop for home orders and vanity stuff. What do you think?'

The more he spoke about the new workshop, which he did often in the following weeks, the more he addressed Hamza whom he was lining up to run it, so it seemed. The British mandate government had announced an expansion in school-building and a literacy drive, which was the source of Nassor Biashara's excitement about a government contract. The administration was also expanding its activities in agriculture, public works and health care. If nothing else it would show the Germans how to run a colony properly. All these departments and projects needed offices and offices needed desks and chairs. Hamza nodded with carefully judged enthusiasm as Nassor Biashara, who now preferred to be called a businessman and not a merchant, talked himself into the new venture. Sooner or later Hamza would ask for a big pay rise but for the time being he bided his time.

He delayed going back for lunch to allow Khalifa and Bi Asha to eat first. By the time he arrived they were usually finished and making ready for their mandatory siesta. He ate lightly, some rice and spinach and whatever fruit was in season. Sometimes he had a paratha, a small piece of fish and a bowl of yoghurt and then went back to work. In the afternoon after he returned he had a wash and lay down to rest for an hour or so, and if she was in Afiya joined him in their room and they talked and reprised the day. Often she was out visiting then, seeing her friend Jamila who was now a mother, or Khalida, Nassor Biashara's wife, or else attending one of the stream of obligatory functions that filled women's daily lives: memorial gatherings after funerals, betrothals, weddings, sickbeds, visiting a mother and her newborn.

In the evening Hamza strolled the streets and met the people he had come to know and befriend, especially one of the musicians in the group he went to listen to whenever he could. His name was Abu and he was a carpenter as well, a few years older than Hamza. They met after the maghrib prayer in a café by the bridge across the creek and talked with others who were regulars there and who made room for him. Hamza was not much of a talker, in a gathering of big talkers, so he was always welcome. The tone of their conversation was light-hearted and irreverent, often salacious, and it seemed to him they vied with each other to see who could make the most outrageous banter. At times the comedy was so low and so irresistible that his sides ached from laughing and yet afterwards he knew that nothing of any consequence had been said and that he had wasted his time in shameful frivolity. Some evenings Hamza went with Abu to the rehearsal room and sat with the musicians for an hour or so while they played and practised.

Then he returned to the house – he was not yet able to call it home – and sat with Khalifa and Maalim Abdalla and Topasi while they pondered the state of the world and turned over and analysed the latest outrages and gossip. At that time the administration had started publishing a Kiswahili monthly magazine *Mambo Leo*, to inform those who could already read about world and home affairs, about good practices in farming, about medical hygiene and even sports news. Khalifa bought a copy, which he passed on to Hamza and Afiya when he finished with it. Maalim Abdalla came to the baraza with his own copy and informed his friends about whatever interesting item in there had caught his eye, which often needed dismantling and debunking and exposing. At other times he came with an old copy of the *East African Standard*, the settler newspaper from Nairobi that his friend who worked in the District Commissioner's office borrowed for him on an extended loan. Some of the stories in the *Standard* provided compelling discussion material for the three sages, especially the heated exchanges between settlers who wanted to remove all Africans from Kenya and make it what they called A White Man's Country, and those who wanted to remove all Indians and only allow in Europeans but keep the Africans as labourers and servants, with a sprinkling of some savage pastoralists in a reserve for spectacle. The propositions and their defenders sounded so strange that it was if the settlers were living on the moon.

Hamza left them after collecting the coffee tray from Afiya and went to the mosque for isha. Off you go, little saint, Khalifa always cheered him away. When he returned, he went straight to their room where Afiya joined him for the sweetest part of the day. They talked for hours, reading old newspapers, catching up with each other's lives, looking into the future, making love.

*

One night she woke up with a start beside him. She gripped his upper arm and whispered his name. 'Hamza, shush, shush … stop now.'

His face was wet and his body was drenched in sweat. There was a sob still in his throat as he came awake. They lay quite still in the dark, Afiya's grip firm on his upper arm. 'You were crying,' she said. 'Is it him again?'

'Him, yes. Sometimes it's him, sometimes the officer. Or else the pastor. It's always them,' he said. 'Only it's not the person so much, it's the feeling they bring.'

'What feeling? Tell me.'

'A feeling of danger, terror. Like great danger is bearing down and there's no escape. Such noise and screams and blood.'

Then they lay still again in the dark for a long time. Much later she asked, 'Is it always the war?'

'Always. Before, when I was a child, I was often troubled by nightmares,' he said. 'Animals consuming me while I lay prone, unable to move. It did not feel like danger somehow, more like defeat, like torture. Now when the nightmares come, they terrify me. Like what is coming at me will crush me with great pain, will make me suffer torments and I will drown in my own blood.

220

I can feel it filling my throat. That is the feeling I dread, not the person. But sometimes it is him, the Feldwebel. I don't understand why seeing the pastor should make me feel like this. I don't know how he comes into it. He healed me. I stayed on his mission for two years.'

'Tell me some more about him,' she said. 'Tell me about the tobacco sheds and the fruit trees and the books the Frau lent you to read.'

She sensed him smiling in the dark. 'You were listening then. I thought you'd fallen asleep when I told you about the Frau pastor. The pastor was a very thorough man and the tobacco shed gave him much pleasure, I think. There he was in full control. He always wanted to be right, he could not help it. It was as if he had to force himself to listen to other people, to teach himself to be kind. It made you wonder that he chose to be a missionary. I think it was she who taught him to be forbearing when his natural inclination was to be stern. She was effortlessly good and thoughtful and generous. I will never forget her. She lent me books, yes. She gave me their address in Germany. She said I should send them news now and then. She wrote it in that Heine book I told you about.'

'Maybe you will write one day,' she said. 'Maybe you will be able to forget that terrible time one day even if you don't forget her. Sometimes when I am away from the house I think I will come home and find that you are gone, that you have left me and disappeared without a word. I don't know if I understand everything about you yet and I am so terrified that I will lose you one day. I lost my mother and father before I even knew them. I don't know for sure if I remember them. Then I lost my brother Ilyas who appeared like a blessing in my childhood. I could not bear to lose you too.'

'I will never leave you,' Hamza said. 'I too lost my parents when I was a child. I lost my home and very nearly my life in my blind desire to escape. It was not much of a life until I came here and met you. I will never leave you.'

'Promise me,' she said, stroking him and signalling her readiness for him.

＊

Five months after their wedding, Afiya miscarried her first pregnancy. She told Hamza when she missed her second month but instructed him not to speak about it. Who was he going to tell? he asked. They could not help smiling and indulging in pleasant fantasies about the Forthcoming, as they began to speak of the life within her, speculating on gender and names. She did not even dare call it a pregnancy, reminding him that Ilyas had told her that their mother miscarried more than once. She waited for nine days after her third month before announcing to Hamza that it was now certain.

'It's a boy,' she said.

'No, it's a girl,' he said.

The following afternoon, on the tenth day after her third missed period, Bi Asha spoke to Afiya. At first she glanced at her lower abdomen and then she looked into her eyes for a long moment.

'Have you fallen?' she asked.

'I think so,' Afiya said, quite surprised that she had guessed when they were so careful to keep things to themselves.

'How many months?' Bi Asha asked.

'Three,' Afiya said hesitantly, not wanting to sound too definite in case it aroused Bi Asha's disdain.

'About time you fell,' she said, with not a hint of gladness in her voice. 'Only … women often lose their first.'

The next day, as she was hanging out the washing in the yard, Afiya felt something wet on her thigh. She hurried to her room and found that her underclothes were dark red with blood. Bi Asha, who was also in the yard at the time, followed her into her room and helped her to undress. She fetched some old sheets and made Afiya lie down.

'Perhaps you won't lose it,' she said. 'The clothes are not very bloody. Just rest and let's wait and see.'

The bleeding continued for the rest of the morning, steadily staining the sheets Afiya lay on. She remained still throughout, slowly becoming resigned to the loss. When Hamza came back for lunch, Bi Asha at first tried to keep him out of the room. These were matters for women, she said, but he brushed her restraining hand away and went to sit with his wife.

'We celebrated too soon,' Afiya said through her tears. 'I don't know how she knew. She said I would lose it. She wished that on me.'

'No,' he said. 'It's just bad luck. Don't pay any attention to her.'

The worst of the bleeding was over by the next morning although there was still some spotting. After three days there were no signs of blood but Afiya was exhausted and without strength and trying hard not to feel sad. Bi Asha told her she must rest but she shook her head, got up and did what chores she could manage. Somehow word of her misfortune got out as word always did by some means, and her friends Jamila and Saada came to visit and Khalida, who never visited because of Bi Asha's feud with her husband, sent words of commiseration and an offer of whatever help she required. In the meantime Bi Asha fussed bossily over her, preparing a soup made from maize, including the silk, which she said was good for Afiya, and meals that she said were appropriate for her feeble condition: sautéed liver, steamed fish, milk jelly, stewed fruit. She was like the Bi Asha Afiya had known as a child, her voice still hard-bitten but her strokes kindly.

This period of grace lasted while she convalesced. After three weeks the special meals stopped and the sharp edge began to return to Bi Asha's voice. The loss of the pregnancy made Afiya feel more of a wife to Hamza. He was tender with her for days afterwards, holding on to her even in their sleep, his hand resting on her shoulder or her thigh. He softened his voice when he spoke to her as if loud tones would upset her. After several days of this treatment and his abstemiousness from making love to her, she reached for him and whispered to him that his attentions were now overdue. He was worried that she was hurting, he said, but she soon demonstrated that he had no reason to be concerned. It was strange also that the loss made her feel more independent of the constraints of the house, a grown-up person, almost a mother. She went out to the market every morning and made decisions about what to prepare for the household's lunch without consulting Bi Asha beforehand. She bought what looked best and what took her own fancy, nothing unusual, just bananas that looked dark green and plump or yams or cassava freshly dug from the soil or newly harvested pumpkins that glistened with wax. To her surprise, Bi Asha did not make any objection, only now and then scolding her and mocking her if she thought a purchase too expensive or if a dish went wrong. Where did you get this okra? It's rotten, that kind of thing.

Most afternoons Afiya went to visit Jamila and Saada, who now ran a small dress-making business from home, and she sat with them and took on small unskilled tasks they allowed her to do: sewing on buttons, measuring and cutting the lace and ribbons that everyone loved to have on their dresses. In time they gave her more complicated tasks, and gradually she learned how to measure material from a dress a customer wanted copied, how to cut it to best effect, and to choose the lace and the ribbons and the buttons from the Indian haberdasher's shop to which her friends took her. Since all the customers were acquaintances and neighbours of the sisters, they charged only a pittance for the work they did. It was as much to fill the empty hours after the daily household chores as for the money that they did it, gladly doing something that engaged them and required skill, to ease the frustration of the hemmed-in lives they were forced to endure.

Afiya fell pregnant again several months later, just over a year after their wedding. She told Hamza after her second missed period and they waited chastely until they were safely past the third month before beginning to speak of the Forthcoming, and then only between themselves.

It was at about this same time that Bi Asha's pains started – not that she did not suffer occasional aches and pains like everyone else did, but this was different. They were preparing lunch when Bi Asha rose from the kitchen stool to fetch a fan because she was feeling hot and a sudden excruciating pain stabbed her in the lower back. It was so sudden and so fierce that she had no choice but to collapse on the stool again with a cry of alarm.

'Bimkubwa,' Afiya cried and rose to her feet with arms outstretched. Bi Asha held on to the extended hands and uttered an unaccustomed whimper. Afiya kneeled down beside her, holding her trembling hands and murmuring softly, 'Bimkubwa, Bimkubwa.' After a few minutes of silent panting Bi Asha heaved a great sigh and then arched her back to test if the pain was still there. Afiya helped her to her feet and she took a few steps around the yard without any mishap.

'Lo, that was like someone had cut me in half,' Bi Asha said, her hands massaging her sides just above the pelvis. 'Go and fetch a mat for me. I'll lie here on the floor for a while. It must have been a spasm.'

Later that evening, Bi Asha asked Afiya to massage her back as she had always done since she was a child. She stretched out on a mat in her room while Afiya kneeled beside her and massaged her from the shoulders to the hips. Bi Asha groaned with contentment and afterwards thought she felt much better. But the pain did not go away. She complained daily about the ache in her sides, which sometimes caught her so unexpectedly that she could not prevent a cry. As time passed she became worse. The pains began when she rose from her bed and stayed with her most of the day, then they came to her during the night as well while she lay trying to rest.

'You should go to the hospital to have that checked,' Khalifa said. 'You can't just go on groaning and doing nothing about it.'

'No, which hospital? They don't treat women there,' she said.

'What nonsense! I'm talking about the government hospital,' Khalifa said, inclined not to take her complaints too seriously. 'They've been treating women there since German times.'

'Only pregnant women,' she said.

'That is no longer true if it ever was. The government wants all of us to be healthy so we can work harder. It says so in *Mambo Leo*.'

'Stop your drivel, you hopeless man. You think you're funny,' she said. 'Leave me alone.'

'What about the Indian doctor?' he suggested. 'We can get him to come here. He makes house calls.'

'He is just a waste of money. He'll take my money and give me coloured water, which he will say is medicine.'

'Not at all,' Khalifa said, smiling and teasing her. 'You're just afraid of the jab. You know he gives everyone a jab for almost any condition. Some people become so addicted to the jab that they refuse to pay unless he gives them one. We'll get him to come and see you. He'll give you one injection and you'll soon be better.'

It was evident now that it was not Bi Asha's back that was hurting but something inside, in the soft part above her hips. She sat on a mat in the backyard for long periods, her eyes closed, emitting an involuntary groan every so often. Her expression was scowling and sullen, and the unmistakable source of her misery was her own body. Afiya tried to anticipate the chores Bi Asha might have thought were hers. Bimkubwa, let me do it, she said when Bi Asha was taking a broom to the backyard or gathering clothes and bedding for the laundry, but she was proud and pushed her away, saying, I am not an invalid.

Her appetite diminished and she began to lose weight. After one or two mouthfuls of cassava or rice she gagged, unable to swallow. Afiya prepared bone soup for her and mashed some fruit with yoghurt and sat with her while she ate, in case she needed help. In the end Bi Asha's pride gave way and the pain forced her to her bed, groaning and almost delirious. Khalifa pleaded with her to go to the hospital or at least to see the Indian doctor but Bi Asha said no, she did not need that kind of attention. She did not want strange men poking at her with that instrument they wore around their necks and then put on your heart to drink your blood. Instead she asked for the maalim, the hakim.

'What do you think he'll do? Say a prayer and make you better. You're an ignorant woman,' Khalifa said, turning to Afiya for support, hoping she would add her own words of persuasion. 'You are not important enough for the hakim to come to you. He only goes to the houses of the eminents and the moneybags. His prayers are not cheap. There is something wrong with your body. You need to see a doctor.'

'Perhaps we can call the doctor to come here,' Afiya suggested. 'He visits patients at home sometimes. I know he does.' She did not say she knew because the doctor had visited Khalida when her son was ill with jaundice, in case the name provoked Bi Asha into further resistance.

Bi Asha smiled her derision. 'Then he can charge us even more for his rubbish. Go to the hakim's house and explain to him the pain I am enduring. Ask him what he advises I should do.'

Afiya went to the hakim's house as instructed. It was by a mosque and beside an old cemetery. Its continued use had been forbidden by the Germans many years before for fear of infection and contamination, and their threat to dig it up was only averted by the outbreak of war. The British administration did not renew the threat but upheld the prohibition on new burials, ordering that the cemetery grounds be kept clear of undergrowth to prevent the spread of malaria.

Afiya was shown into a downstairs room just beside the front door. She was nearly six months into her pregnancy so she sank carefully to her knees and squatted as comfortably as she could while she waited for the hakim to appear. There were thick straw mats on the floor and a book-stand on which rested a copy of the Koran and an inactive incense burner beside it which nevertheless gave off a scent of ud. The window, which was barred, was wide open and a soft light filtered in through the overhanging branches of the neem tree outside, which was the sole survivor from the clearing of the adjoining cemetery.

The hakim was an elderly and ascetic man of considerable eminence and respectability. He was dressed in a brown sleeveless robe and wore a close-fitting white cap. Afiya had not spoken to him before and was a little awed by his air of assured self-possession. He did not smile or beckon but slipped silently to his place beside the book-stand and listened without speaking while Afiya described Bi Asha's condition. When she had no more to say he asked after Bi Asha's age and her general health. His voice was deep and pliant, accustomed to addressing multitudes. Then he said Afiya should come back in the afternoon, to collect something he will prepare to bring relief to the ailing woman.

When she went back in the afternoon he gave her a small porcelain plate with a gilded border on which were written lines of the Koran in a dark brown ink. He explained that the ink was an extract of the flesh of the walnut, which itself has medicinal qualities. He also gave her an amulet. His instructions were for

227

her to pour half a coffee-cupful of water, very carefully, on to the plate until the holy words dissolved. She was not to stir or add anything to the liquid and once the writing was dissolved she was to pass the plate to the ailing woman to drink. The amulet was to be strapped to her right ankle. Afiya was to bring the plate back in the morning so that he could prepare it for her to collect another dose in the afternoon. Afiya accepted these objects with both hands and then handed over the small purse Khalifa had given her for the hakim who accepted it without checking the amount. This treatment went on for several weeks without diminishing Bi Asha's pain.

As the days went by, word got out that Bi Asha was very unwell and neighbours and acquaintances began to call on her. She received them in the guest room because she did not want to be thought seriously ill, but then she began to allow her visitors to come to her bedside. It was they who persuaded her that she should see the mganga who lived nearby. I've seen her before, it did no good, Bi Asha said. No, not that one, her visitors persisted, people speak well of this one. She knows medicines.

The mganga came to the house and was closeted with Bi Asha for a long time, asking her questions while she examined her. Bi Asha asked that Afiya should stay with her. The mganga was a very thin woman of uncertain middle age, her eyes kohled and intense, her movements commanding and precise. She talked almost constantly while she was with Bi Asha, even ventriloquising some replies to the questions she addressed to her. After her first examination she left some herbs which Afiya was to steep in warm water and give to Bi Asha to drink before bed. It will help her to sleep, the healer said. The mganga came every day after that and rubbed potions and balm on the painful areas, which made Bi Asha groan with contentment and pronounce herself much improved. She made Bi Asha lie on her back on the floor and covered her completely with a thick blue calico cloth for several minutes. Then she made her lie on her left side and ripple her body from head to toe. She made her repeat this on the right side, while she read prayers over her and sang words Afiya did not understand. This ceremony was performed for four days and afterwards the healer left instructions for the food Bi Asha was to eat, even if only a spoonful or two every day. Still, the pain did not go away and the mganga whispered to Afiya that perhaps they needed to call in a spirit healer in case it was not the patient's body that was the problem, in case an invisible had taken her.

'I told this to her,' the mganga said. 'Only a spirit healer will be able to hear what the invisible desires before releasing you. But she shook her head as if she knows better. Without a spirit healer, how can she know what the invisible wants? You have to know how to make it speak.'

Afiya did not tell Khalifa about this conversation because she knew he would scoff, but she told Hamza who said nothing. In time Bi Asha was so bedridden that she needed to use a bedpan, and it was then that Afiya saw the blood in her urine. There were small lumps of faeces in the pan as well so at first she was not sure where the traces of blood came from, until the next time when she had a pan with only urine and tiny clots of blood in it.

'Bimkubwa,' she said, holding out the pan. 'There's blood – dark blood.'

Bi Asha turned her face to the wall, evidently not surprised.

'Bimkubwa, you must go to the hospital,' Afiya said.

With her face still turned away, she shook her head and then shivered all over in a fit of trembling. Afiya told Khalifa who went without further hesitation to fetch the Indian doctor, but he was not able to come until the following morning because he had been called away. The doctor was a short plump man in his fifties, silver-haired and mild-mannered. He was dressed in a white shirt and khaki trousers like a government man. He asked Khalifa to leave the room and Afiya to remain. At first he asked questions and looked to Afiya to corroborate the replies. All the defiance had gone out of Bi Asha and she answered him in a defeated voice but without reluctance. How long had she seen blood in her urine? What did she have for breakfast, for lunch? Was she able to keep food down? Where did it hurt most? Did she know if any relative had suffered similar pains in the past, her mother or her father? Then he examined the places in her side where it hurt most. Afterwards he told Khalifa and Afiya that at first he thought the blood in the urine was bilharzia in the bladder, but it was more likely that her kidneys were failing. The kidney failure could itself be the result of untreated bilharzia, so she would have to go to the hospital to be tested for that. It was possible, though, that matters were even worse than that because he felt a lump in her side that might well be something dangerous. They should not have waited so long.

She was X-rayed at the hospital and found to have an advanced growth in her left kidney and a smaller one in her bladder. She also had the bilharzia worm but it was quite certain that the growths were advanced and very likely malignant. The Indian doctor told them that the hospital had asked her to return for further X-rays in case there were more growths, but he said it was up to her to decide. There was no treatment possible for the growths they found but he was able to give her medication for the bilharzia. To Khalifa he said it would now be a matter of a few months only and the best he was able to offer was pain-killing injections. Khalifa thought it was right to tell her so she could prepare herself and her affairs. He told her that the doctor offered to give her pain-killing injections if she wished, and he could not help smiling as he told her that. Doctor Sindano, he said. He wondered, without saying anything to Bi Asha but voicing the thought to Afiya, if now was the moment to reconcile his wife with her nephew Nassor Biashara, undeserving though he was. It was not right to leave such rancour behind. He did not say this to Bi Asha because the news she had received was already too much for her. He had not thought she would go before him. She was always so strong.

Afiya went round to see Khalida, Nassor Biashara's wife, to tell her about Bi Asha's illness. She was heavily pregnant now, nearing the end of her term, and the stairs in their house exhausted her. 'Baba asked me to tell you this,' Afiya told her, making it clear that the information was also an implied invitation to visit the dying relative.

Khalida came to the house for the first time that afternoon. She kissed Bi Asha's hand as she lay in her bed and sat on a stool beside her, making the kind of conversation people did by a sickbed. It was a low-key reconciliation, and neither Khalida nor Bi Asha made any drama out of it. After about an hour Khalida wished her better health and left. Bi Asha heaved a great sigh after she left, as if at the end of an ordeal. All resistance went out of her as she lingered with them in her last days. She drifted in and out of delirium, muttering incomprehensibly, sometimes in tears.

14

Afiya delivered her child at home, attended by the midwife who had had a hand in the arrival of scores of other babies in the town. Like many others, Afiya preferred to go into labour in the presence of women she knew than to suffer the attentions of complete strangers, so despite the administration's Maternity Health campaign she did not go to the new clinic for the birth. The midwife was sent for as soon as her waters broke, as was Jamila who had promised to be with her during the birth. Her labour started in late afternoon and went on through the night and into the late morning of the next day. Hamza was sent to the room used to receive guests, where Khalifa also took refuge. No one slept much during that tense time. They left the doors open so they could hear Bi Asha, and Khalifa was up and down to her as she called out for him, groaning with weariness. The backyard door also stood open and the dying woman's groans mingled with Afiya's intermittent gasps of pain. Hamza sat on the back doorstep for a while in case help was needed and because he felt so useless sitting inside. When the midwife came out and saw him there she chased him away. It will be a long night yet, she said, and it was not seemly for the husband to be sitting so expectantly by. He did not know what was unseemly about it but he obeyed and returned to the guest room.

A neighbour came in the morning to look after Bi Asha so Khalifa could go to work, and the women persuaded Hamza to go too. There was nothing for him to do and they would send for him when there was news. He went reluctantly, feeling bullied by the women when he wanted to be nearby while Afiya was in pain, and within reach when the Forthcoming arrived. No call came throughout the morning and he could hardly keep his mind on the work. Khalifa appeared at the workshop just after the noon call to prayers, anxious for different reasons to be back, and they went home together. It was the good neighbour looking after Bi Asha who told them that Afiya had given birth to a boy. Hamza found her lying in bed, exhausted but triumphant, while Jamila stood grinning nearby and the midwife silently went about her work.

'We were just cleaning up before sending for you,' Jamila said.

They called the baby Ilyas. That was decided before his arrival, Ilyas if it is a boy, Rukiya if it is a girl.

After the birth, Bi Asha appeared to fall into a deep doze, not quite fully asleep but not awake either. She did not take any food and did not seem to wake when the neighbour or Khalifa rolled her over to remove the towelling they wrapped around her middle as a nappy. Her breathing was deep and laboured but she no longer made the weary groans of recent days. On the third day after the birth, Jamila prepared lunch for the household and then went back to her own family. She said she would come again the next morning. Afiya was already on her feet and she resumed her household chores while the baby napped. Later that afternoon, without coming awake once since the baby's arrival, Bi Asha passed away in unaccustomed silence.

For the next few days they were engaged in the obligatory observances of her passing, and it was only after they were over that the household began to assume its new shape without Bi Asha. In public, Khalifa wore the sombre face of a mourning husband out of respect for Bi Asha, and even at home some puff seemed to have gone out of him although they had known for months that she was passing away.

'It is so final, that is what is surprising, what I did not properly understand,' he said, 'that this person is gone forever.' He looked at Hamza and then could not resist a touch of mischief. 'Unless you believe the fairy story that all the dead will one day come back to life?'

'Shush, Baba, not now,' Afiya said.

'Well, we have to make some changes anyway,' he said. 'We can't have the two of you and the little one in that store room in the yard while I live like a lord inside an empty house. So this is what I suggest now. You two move inside and take the two adjoining rooms, and I'll move out into the yard. You will need the space and I would like some fresh air. What do you think? We'll get some new furniture for the other room so you can sit there and receive your guests, and the little prince can play and invite his guests.'

Afiya suggested that they punch a hole through into the front store room and make that part of the interior of the house, then they could still keep the guest room for visitors or if someone came to stay. Who would that be? The words remained unspoken but they all knew she meant in case of the elder Ilyas's return. They debated these suggestions for a while before deciding what best to do while Hamza reminded both of them that it was not their house and they had better talk to Nassor Biashara before knocking down any walls. It is now indisputably Nassor Biashara's house and he might well want us to leave, he said. Khalifa waved this away, He wouldn't dare, he said.

Despite his level-headed practical manner, though, something seemed to have gone out of Khalifa. He went to the warehouse in the morning and grumbled about the waste of time every day. He sat with his friends on the porch in the evenings and spoke his outrage with more restraint than he used to, and even tutted at Topasi when his gossip became too fanciful when before he would gleefully have elaborated on it. To Afiya and Hamza he said he needed to make new plans, do something more useful than sit on a bench outside a warehouse for the rest of his life. There are all these schools the government is opening up, perhaps I can become a teacher, he said.

Nassor Biashara also had new plans. Building works on the new workshop were under way and new machines were on order. 'It will take some months for the workshop to be ready,' he said to Hamza. 'And when it's ready I want you to run it. When the machinery comes, I will arrange for someone to come from Dar es Salaam to train you. Mzee Sulemani will continue in the other workshop making our regular items. In the meantime, we will need to find a new carpenter to work with him on the sofa and armchair line … maybe young Sefu is ready, what do you think? Or how about your friend Abu? He is a carpenter, isn't he? I think he just does odd jobs for people at the moment. Ask him if he wants a regular job working for me. You will also need an assistant to work with you, someone properly trained, maybe more than one if we get going. Perhaps that's a better job for Sefu. He's young, he'll learn quickly.'

'Abu will come with me, he'll learn just as quickly as I will. Sefu already works with Mzee and knows what's required there,' Hamza said.

'As you wish,' Nassor Biashara said.

'Pay rise?' Hamza suggested.

'I will increase your pay. In fact, I will double it once you start the new workshop. Find yourself somewhere to rent and get away from that miserable house.'

'What about Khalifa?'

'He can find somewhere to rent too,' Nassor Biashara said.

'Are you trying to get him out of the house?'

'I would love to do that. I could get a good rent for that property,' he said.

'Rent it to me then,' Hamza said.

Nassor Biashara laughed in surprise. 'You are a sentimental fool,' he said. 'Why do you want to worry about that old grumbler?'

'Because he is Afiya's Baba,' Hamza said.

'I'll think about it,' Nassor Biashara said. 'What makes you think you'll be able to afford it?'

'You are a good businessman. You'll not want to make your new workshop manager miserable by charging him an unreasonable rent.'

'You're turning into a conniving little manipulator! First you charm that old grumbler so that he takes you into his house, then you seduce his daughter and bamboozle the old carpenter with your German translations, and now you are trying to blackmail me,' Nassor Biashara said. 'I told you, I'll think about it.'

*

The construction of the new workshop progressed at speed. Nassor Biashara was as excited about his new plans as he had been by the arrival of the propeller a few years before. This will be another brilliant idea, he said, and even Khalifa did not mock. Mzee Sulemani looked on indulgently and turned his attention to training their young apprentice to take over when Hamza was no longer available to him. After the gleaming equipment arrived and was connected to electric power, an Indian machinist and carpenter arrived from Dar es Salaam to train Hamza and Abu. His father's company was the importer and distributor of the machinery and also the owner of a sawmill and a transport company. He demonstrated for Hamza and Abu over three days with Nassor Biashara hovering in the background. After three days and repeated test runs with the saws and the grinders and the frets, the Indian machinist made ready to go, promising to return when required and certainly at the end of the year for a service check. Take your time. Don't take any risks with the machinery, he said. Nassor Biashara expected this new partnership to grow and for the sawmill to be the supplier of timber for the new enterprise, and he showered the young man with thanks and goodwill.

These were contented years for Afiya and Hamza. Their child was well, learned to walk and to speak and seemed to have no blemish. When he was still a baby, Hamza took him to the hospital for the recommended vaccinations and watched diligently over his health. Child deaths were not uncommon but many of the illnesses that took them away were avoidable, as he knew from his time in the schutztruppe which took good care of the health of the askari. In the year of Ilyas's birth, the British were in the early stages of the mandate awarded to them by the League of Nations to administer the old Deutsch-Ostafrika and prepare it for independence. Although not everyone noticed at the time, that last clause was the beginning of the end for European empires, none of which had dreamed hitherto of preparing anyone for independence. The British colonial administration took the mandate responsibility seriously rather than just going through the motions or worse. Perhaps it was just a lucky confluence

237

of responsible administrators, or it was the compliance of the people who were exhausted after the rule of the Germans and their wars and the starvation and diseases which followed, and were now willing to obey without defiance so long as they were left in peace. The British administrators had no fear of guerillas or bandits in this territory and could get on with the business of colonial administration without resistance from the colonised. Education and public health became their priorities. They made a big effort to inform people about health issues, to train medical assistants and open dispensaries in far-flung parts of the colony. They distributed information leaflets and conducted tours by medical teams to instruct people on malaria prevention and good childcare. Afiya and Hamza listened to this new information and did what they could to protect themselves and their child.

They also made some changes to the house. With Nassor Biashara's permission, they punched a doorway in the wall of the old store room and made that part of their bedroom, which was now large and airy with windows looking out over the street. When Ilyas was old enough to get about, he had the run of all the rooms and the yard and even Khalifa's room. Khalifa loved him to totter in there and climb up on the bed with him.

One of Hamza and Afiya's sadnesses was their failure to provide Ilyas with a brother or sister. Twice in the next five years Afiya was pregnant and then miscarried in the third month. They learned to live with this disappointment because everything else was going so well, or that was what Hamza said to Afiya when she was made sad by her failure to keep another pregnancy. Another disappointment was the continuing silence about the elder Ilyas. There was still no word from or about him. It was now six years since the end of the war and it caused Afiya much anguish that she could not decide whether to give up hope and grieve or keep thinking of him as alive and on his way home. After all, she lost him for nearly ten years once before and then he turned up like a miracle.

'Everything *is* going well,' Hamza insisted. The new workshop was a success and in his prosperity Nassor Biashara was generous to them. 'I'll ask Maalim Abdalla to make enquiries again.'

Maalim Abdalla was now headmaster of a large school and had good contacts with the British administrative office through his friend in the District Officer's staff. He offered Khalifa a job as a primary school teacher of English but he was still dithering, not really sure if he wanted the bother of disrespectful twelve-year-olds. He was kept pleasantly busy in the warehouse with the growing prosperity of the business, and so much at ease in the new arrangement at home with his room in the yard that his contentment was evident in his appearance. He was not really sure if he wanted to start a new profession at his age. He was busy being a grandfather. He always had a little something for Ilyas: the sweetest banana in the market, a segment of ripe red-fleshed guava, a flapjack. Where is my grandson? he called as he came in. In their favourite game Ilyas sometimes hid while Khalifa pretended to look for him although his hiding places were often easy to guess.

He was a handsome slim boy, and it became evident as he grew up that he was drawn to silence. His silences did not seem troubled although Afiya was not always sure and wondered if there was a sorrow in him he did not yet know how to speak. Hamza shrugged and did not say that sorrow was impossible to avoid. At times Ilyas sat in the same room as he did while Hamza lay stretched out on a mat and neither of them spoke for long periods. It seemed to Hamza that this silence was a place in which his son found refuge.

When he was five years old the world economy went into a great Depression, not that he knew much of it. Ilyas grew up in these years of austerity when Nassor Biashara's affairs once again went into decline, and everything in everyday life became scarce and expensive. Government plans for new hospitals and schools were abandoned, and workers were laid off and went hungry in towns and villages and on the land. It seemed that bad times never left them for long. Nassor Biashara did not lay off any of his workers but he reduced their wages and quietly reopened the smuggling business he had run during the war, buying supplies from Pemba and bringing them in without paying customs duties and then selling on at inflated prices. They all had to live.

With time on his hands, Khalifa began to teach Ilyas to read. You'll be going to school soon, so might as well get started now, he said. Ilyas listened open-mouthed to Khalifa's stories, which he mixed in with reading and writing exercises to keep the boy interested. Once upon a time, he would begin, and Ilyas's eyes would lighten and his mouth slowly slacken as he was drawn into the tale.

'A monkey lived on a palm tree by the sea.'

It was a story Ilyas knew but he did not smile or grin in recognition, only his eyes softened in expectation.

'A shark swam past in the water nearby and they became friends. The shark told the monkey stories of the world he lived in across the water in Sharkland, about its luminous landscape and happy population. He told him about his family and friends and the celebrations they held at certain times of the year. The monkey said how wonderful his world sounded, and how he wished he could see it, but he could not swim and if he tried to get there he would drown. It's all right, the shark said, you can ride on my back. Just hold on to my fin and you'll be quite safe. So the monkey climbed down from the tree and sat on the shark's back. The journey across the water to ...'

'Sharkland!' Ilyas filled the gap Khalifa left for him.

'The journey to Sharkland was so exhilarating that the monkey exclaimed, You're such a good friend to do this for me. It made the shark feel bad and he said, I have a confession to make. I am taking you to Sharkland because our king is ill and the doctor said that only a monkey's heart will make him better. So that's why I'm taking you there. Without any hesitation the monkey said, Why didn't you tell me?'

'I didn't bring my heart with me,' Ilyas declared, grinning with delight as he supplied the line.

'Oh, no, the shark said. What shall we do now? The monkey said, Take me back and I'll fetch it from the tree. So the shark took the monkey back to the tree on the shore, and he rushed up the palm and the shark never saw him again. Don't you think that was a clever little monkey?'

Ilyas did not remember much of his early days at school, but later his teachers praised him for his neat work and his obedient manner. They sometimes pointed him out to others as an example: Look at Ilyas, why can't the rest of you sit quietly and get on with your sums. Despite that, the other children did not persecute him or take much notice of him. He stood by and watched the boisterous play of the other boys, and at times was dragged in to take part if an extra body was needed to make up a team.

He suffered his small share of the unavoidable indignities of childhood. Once he misjudged his need to urinate and underestimated the distance from classroom to toilet. On another occasion he was found to have picked up lice from another boy in the class and had to have his head shaved. On his way home one day he stubbed his toe on a protruding rock and as he fell a piece of broken bottle cut into his calf. When he reached home his foot was covered in blood and Afiya wept at the sight of his injury. She strapped his calf and walked him to the hospital where his eyes roved over the hospital grounds while they waited outside the clinic, returning again and again to the casuarinas swaying so elegantly in the breeze.

One day he got lost. He went with his father to watch a boat race at the waterfront. The boats were coming into the finishing line and Hamza was craning his neck for a glimpse of the outcome when he realised that Ilyas was no longer beside him. He rushed in all directions looking for him but could not see him. In the end, frantic now that he had lost their precious little boy, he hurried home in the hope that someone who knew the child had found him wandering the streets and had taken him there, but he was not home either. So he headed for the Government Hospital to see if by chance his son had been injured and he found him sitting silently under the serene casuarinas, watching them sway elegantly in the breeze. Hamza sat beside him and breathed in deeply a few times to calm himself.

'Is there something wrong with him?' Afiya asked Hamza, who shook his head emphatically.

'He forgets himself sometimes, that's all,' he said. 'He's a dreamer.'

'Like his father,' Afiya said.

'He looks like his mother to me.'

'Do you think he looks like my brother Ilyas?'

He shook his head. 'I don't know, having never met the elder Ilyas.'

'No,' she said. 'Our Ilyas is much more handsome. I'll ask Baba.'

Her lost brother was never far from her thoughts and Hamza sometimes wondered if it had been a mistake to name the boy after him, if that made the absent one ever-present and refreshed the anguish of his loss. The memory of him more often than not made Afiya sad although at times she remembered the happy times she had spent with him. After they spoke of him she sometimes fell silent in a way he was beginning to recognise and it took a while for her to extricate herself from such recollections.

'I wish we knew what happened to him,' she said. 'I wish I knew how to find out for sure, but I don't. You are the one who has travelled and worked everywhere and fought wars in many lands. Sometimes when I hear you talk about the people and places you saw, it makes me bitter that I have been penned here all my life.'

'Don't be unhappy. It's not as you imagine out there,' he said, holding her while she shed gentle tears in the dark.

He asked Maalim Abdalla once again if there was any news from his friends in the British administration and he said no. No one was interested in a missing askari. There were so many unaccounted dead that it was impossible to get information on an individual. The number is not even known, hundreds of thousands of them most likely, among them carriers on both sides and civilians in the south who starved or died from the influenza epidemic. Among the askari also many died from diseases. It is a long time now since his sister lost touch with him, the maalim said. I fear it can only mean one thing.

Afiya heard from Khalifa about a campaign to recruit young mothers to train as midwife assistants. The new maternity clinic was a big success, although expectant mothers only went for the antenatal events and most of them refused to deliver there.

They wanted to recruit more midwife assistants to provide a comprehensive service, including visiting mothers at home. The candidates were required to be literate enough to write basic notes and read simple manuals, and to be fluent in Kiswahili. It was thought their experience of childbirth would benefit other expectant mothers to whom they would also be able to communicate with nuance rather than just issuing instructions and prohibitions. When she told Hamza he was enthusiastic. You fit all the requirements, he said. There is such a need for it, and you yourself will learn new skills.

*

Ilyas was eleven years old when the whispers started. He was used to playing alone, he was an only child. Maybe his temperament inclined him that way anyway, his contented silences, as they seemed to Hamza. In his games he made a variety of blameless objects play major roles in his stories: a matchbox became a house, a small pebble was the British warship he saw in the harbour, a discarded thread-spool was the locomotive that growled into the centre of the town. As he manoeuvred these objects he told their stories in an intimate voice only audible to him and his playthings.

Early one evening, just as it was turning dusk, Hamza came home from an afternoon stroll by the sea. That was his routine, a late-afternoon walk by the sea and then directly to the mosque for the maghrib prayer. On this occasion he was a little early so he decided to go home first. He was on his way to the washroom in the backyard to perform his ablutions before heading to the mosque when he saw Ilyas sitting on a stool near the side wall, facing away from the doorway. He did not seem to notice Hamza's arrival. He was speaking in an unfamiliar whisper, his face lifted, not narrating a story or pretending to be a house or a rabbit but apparently addressing someone tall standing before him. Hamza must have made a noise or his presence might have disturbed the air because Ilyas looked round quickly and stopped speaking.

Perhaps, Hamza thought afterwards, he was memorising a poem or a passage from his English class. His teacher was fond of that method of learning, making his pupils copy the poems into their exercise books, learn them by heart and then recite them while he corrected their pronunciation and awarded marks. It was a frugal and pleasant use of the teacher's time. He preferred his pupils should think of the poems as something they would treasure for life – or that was what he told them whenever there were signs of rebellion. Some of his choices surprised Hamza when he read them. He was not familiar with them or with English poems in general but they seemed to him demanding or even incomprehensible material for children of his son's age. Hamza himself had only a modest grasp of English but knew he was a more fluent reader than Ilyas. He was not sure what any eleven-year-old would make of 'The Psalm of Life', or 'The Solitary Reaper'. On the other hand, the pastor had thought Schiller and Heine were too much for him but Hamza had found something in them in his own way. So after he saw Ilyas whispering in that way for the first time and had time to reflect on the sight, he guessed the boy was practising a recitation for class.

He came home again at the same time the next evening but Ilyas was out somewhere and not in the backyard speaking strangely. Hamza checked that for a few days just to be sure. Their sleeping arrangement was that Afiya and he slept in the old front store room, which now had a door to the bedroom once occupied by Bi Asha and Khalifa. Ilyas slept in the inner room, which also had a desk made for him by his father where he could do his schoolwork. The door between the two rooms was rarely closed although a curtain hung in the doorway to give the parents privacy when they wished it. Hamza stood beside the doorway some nights, listening intently for Ilyas's whispers, but heard nothing. He did this for several nights in a row until he was sure that what he had heard that evening at dusk was the boy practising a recitation.

Khalifa was now approaching sixty and spoke of himself as a man on his last legs. He did wobble a little at times, when he made a sudden turn or rose to his feet after sitting cross-legged for a long time, but it still provoked Afiya when he said that. She told him not to wish misfortune on himself or one of these days his wish might be granted. It also provoked Maalim Abdalla, who was now an eminent officer in the Education Department, a school inspector and no longer a teacher. He liked to tell Khalifa that he would not talk about being on his last legs if he had a proper job to do instead of secreting smuggled goods in a warehouse. They were still there on the porch most evenings, Khalifa, Maalim Abdalla and Topasi, giggling over racy gossip, catching up with the world and exposing its endless excesses. Hamza sat with them for a while at times, and sometimes brought them their tray of coffee as he used to, sharing that duty with Ilyas, but he liked to spend part of the evening inside, sitting in the guest room listening to Afiya talk about her day at the clinic and browsing through the old newspapers that Khalifa and Maalim Abdalla passed on to them. Several new ones had appeared in recent years: in Kiswahili, in English and even in German for the settlers who chose to remain after the war. Ilyas sometimes sat with them, listening or reading, but he was usually the first to go to bed.

'There's something here about pensions and back-pay for the schutztruppe,' Hamza said, reading in the German newspaper one night. 'It says there is a campaign to persuade the German government to resume paying pensions now that its economy is coming out of the Depression. You remember, they stopped them a few years ago.'

'No, I don't,' Afiya said. 'Did you ever receive any money?'

'You had to produce a certificate of discharge. I didn't have one of those. I was a deserter,' Hamza said.

'Will my brother Ilyas receive a pension? Maybe we can find him like that.'

'If he's still alive.' Hamza regretted the words as soon as he said them. Afiya put her hand to her mouth as if to stop herself from speaking, and he saw her eyes suddenly brimming. She had spoken about the possibility before and it was he who had asked her not to give up hope. Now it was he who spoke abruptly about his passing.

'It makes me feel so bad that we don't know,' she said in a broken voice.

'I'm sorry ...' he began but she hushed him and glanced towards Ilyas who was still in the room, his eyes large with hurt and fixed on his mother.

'Anyway, you were not a deserter, you were injured, slashed by a maddened German officer. Does it not say anything there about a pension for the injured?' she asked.

He understood that she was making conversation to distract Ilyas, so did not say that the pastor had told him that in the German Imperial army he would have been court-martialled and shot for running away and discarding his uniform. He did not know if that was true or if it was the pastor once again cutting him down to size. He was in no state to run when he left his company and it was the pastor himself who had ordered the uniform to be burned, for fear that the British would send him and his family to a detention camp for giving aid to a schutztruppe. Hamza did not want their pension anyway. 'It says that the General is still working hard for his troops in Berlin, so maybe everybody will get their pension,' he said. 'The settlers here love the General.'

During school holidays and on days when Afiya was at the midwife clinic, Ilyas came to the timber yard with his father. Sometimes he stayed all morning, at others he wandered off on his own for a while and then returned when he was ready to go home. Mzee Sulemani greeted the boy with smiles and let him do small jobs in the workshop. He even taught him how to embroider a cap. When Idris was in full flow with his filthy talk he had a captive audience in Ilyas now as well as Dubu, and it seemed at times that he exerted himself to even lower depths to entertain the boy. Nassor Biashara, who still worked from his small office despite his prosperity, was often forced to intervene and silence his foul-mouthed driver. You're poisoning the boy's mind with your dirty talk. Ilyas grinned at the drama and waited for more. On their way home for lunch they went to the market to buy fruit and salad, and some afternoons after work the boy joined Hamza on his walk by the sea for a while before heading back to the house. They did not talk much, that was not their way, but sometimes Ilyas held his father's hand as they walked.

After the baraza on the porch concluded, Khalifa usually locked the front door and went to his room in the backyard. On his way to bed he sometimes stopped for a word if they were still up but often he went by with just a wave. One evening he said Hamza's name as he walked past but did not stop. Afiya and Hamza looked at each other in surprise at his abrupt tone of voice. She mouthed, What have you done? He shrugged and they shared a smile. He hooked a thumb towards the porch. Perhaps they bickered over something out there. Better go and find out.

Hamza found Khalifa sitting cross-legged on his bed, and he lowered himself carefully as he always had to at the foot, so that they faced each other.

'I wanted to have a word with you on your own after what Topasi just told me,' Khalifa said. 'It's all right but I wanted to have a word first to see what you know. It's about the boy, about Ilyas. People are talking about him. He walks long distances into the countryside on his own. People find it strange that a twelve-year-old town boy should walk for miles into the countryside on his own.'

'He likes walking,' Hamza said after a moment, smiling but also troubled that the boy was the subject of discussion in this way. 'He often walks with me while I limp along. Maybe he likes to stretch his legs properly at times.'

Khalifa shook his head. 'He talks to himself as he walks. He walks along the wide country paths talking to himself.'

'What! What does he say?'

Khalifa shook his head again. 'He stops talking when someone comes near. No one has heard what he says. You know that for many people that is a sign of ...' He paused, unable to say the word, his face puckered with repugnance for the imputation.

'Maybe he is reciting the poems his teacher sets them at school. I've heard him do that. Or maybe he is making up a story. He likes to do that. I'll tell him to be careful.'

Khalifa nodded then shook his head yet again, his eyes turning to Afiya who stood just inside the room. He waved her in and waited while she closed the door. 'You have not told him,' he said, and she shook her head. 'Two days ago I was resting here late

247

in the afternoon,' said Khalifa, addressing Hamza and lowering his voice to a whisper. 'I am not usually here at that time of day, as you know. The window into the yard was open but the door to this room was closed. I heard someone talking, very close, an unfamiliar voice, a woman's voice. I could not hear the words but the tone was grieving. I thought for a moment that it was her, Afiya, but then instantly I knew it was not. It was not her voice. I thought it was a guest with a sad tale talking to her, then I remembered I had heard Afiya calling out to Ilyas as she left the house a short while before. It was alarming. Someone was in the house unannounced.

'I got up from the bed to have a look but I must have made a noise because the voice immediately stopped. I opened the curtain and there he was, Ilyas, sitting on a stool by the wall. He was surprised, not expecting me to be there. Who was talking to you? I asked him. No one, he said. I heard a woman's voice, I said. He looked puzzled and then shrugged. I don't know. What are you smiling at?'

That last question was addressed to Hamza who said, 'I can just picture it. That is his favourite reply to any question he does not want to answer. I don't know ... what are you so worried about, Baba? He must have been pretending to be a grieving a woman in a story he was making up.'

Khalifa shook his head emphatically, beginning to show signs of impatience. 'I spoke to Afiya when she came back. I told her about the unfamiliar voice I had heard. You weren't there, Hamza. It was a strange old voice, grieving and complaining at the same time. I saw as soon as I began that she knew about this voice. Tell him.'

Hamza was now on his feet, leaning against the bedpost, facing Afiya. 'I have heard him,' she said, coming closer, keeping her voice down. 'He has always done this, playing those games where he speaks all the parts. Two times now I have heard him speaking in the way Baba describes, a grieving voice, here in the backyard. He did not see me standing at the door and I waited because I did not want to shock him or make him feel bad. I thought it was like sleepwalking and I should let him wake up when he was ready.

One night when you were sleeping, I heard a noise from his room and found him wincing and turning and moaning in that voice.'

'Something is troubling that child,' Khalifa said.

Hamza turned to him with a look of rage on his face but he did not speak for a moment. He knew they were waiting for him. 'Maybe he was having a bad dream. Maybe he has a rich imagination. Why are you talking about him like this, as if he is ... unwell?'

'He walks on country roads talking to himself,' Khalifa said, raising his voice in irritation. Afiya instantly hushed him but he was not finished. 'People are talking about him, and it is they who will make him unwell if we don't find help for him. Something is bothering that child.'

'I will talk to him,' Hamza said with a note of finality. He glanced at Afiya and began to move towards the door.

Don't panic him, she said when they were alone.

I know how to speak to my son, he said.

Only he was not sure how to speak to him about this, and days passed without him doing so, withstanding Khalifa's questioning glances with a deadpan expression. There were no further reports of Ilyas's strange whispers for a few days and Hamza was tempted by the thought that perhaps the episode was over and they were safe. Then on Saturday, when Hamza was heading to the music club, Ilyas asked if he could come too. The club belonged to the players he had first heard several years ago. By now they were an orchestra and they gave a free performance to a small audience on Saturdays. They only played for an hour and were finished by five o'clock, then continued their rehearsals behind closed doors. They walked home by the sea and because Hamza had relished the music and was warmed by the absorbed silence of Ilyas beside him, which made him think that he too had relished it, they stopped when they saw an empty bench at the waterfront and sat down to look out to sea as the sun set behind them. Hamza tried to think of an opening that would allow him to approach the subject of voices. He tried and rejected several before eventually he said, 'Do you have schoolwork to do this weekend?'

'I have to revise for an algebra test on Monday.'

'Algebra? That sounds complicated. I never went to school, you know, so I didn't learn any algebra.'

'Yes, I know. This is not really difficult, we are only doing very simple algebra at the moment,' Ilyas said. 'I expect it will get very difficult later.'

'No poems to learn then? Hasn't your English teacher given you any to learn this week?'

'No, he makes us recite the same ones again and again,' Ilyas said.

'Is that what you recite when you take your long walks in the country? The poems?' Ilyas turned to look at Hamza as if he was waiting for his father to explain. Hamza smiled to show that this was not a rebuke. 'I've heard about your long walks and how you say things aloud. Are you reciting those poems?'

'Sometimes,' Ilyas said. 'Is it wrong?'

'No, but some people think it's strange. They say you're talking to yourself. So when you practise your poems or you're making up a story, it's better to do it at home or at school. You don't want ignorant people to say you're crazy, do you?'

Ilyas shook his head and looked defeated. Just at that moment the burning disc of the sun dipped below the town's skyline behind them and Hamza was able to change the subject. In a few moments it was dusk and they were on their way home.

*

The Italians invaded Abyssinia in October 1935 and brought talk of war back into their midst. They captured Addis Ababa in May 1936 and alarmed the British enough to begin a recruiting drive over the next two years for their colonial army, the King's African Rifles, which they had largely disbanded during the austerities of the Depression. Not only was the administration concerned about Italian intentions towards their colonies, they were worried about the German remnant in the old Deutsch-Ostafrika, which they expected to be anti-British and pro-Hitler. They also feared that Italian violence against Abyssinian resistance, which included chemical weapons used against civilians, would stir up the Somali and Oromo and Galla people who had not fully reconciled themselves to British rule on the northern frontier. War and rumours of war filled the newspapers.

Ilyas's whispering malaise, which so alarmed his mother and Khalifa, subsided for several months after that conversation with Hamza by the sea. They were relieved that it had turned out to be no more than a brief episode of childish behaviour. Then talk of war and recruitment of an army brought the whispering back. Afiya found her son slumped on the floor beside his bed late one evening, his hands over his ears.

'What is it? Is your head hurting?' she asked, kneeling beside him. She saw there were tears running down his face. He was thirteen now and it was an unusual sight to see tears on his face.

He shook his head. 'It's the voice,' he said.

'What voice? What voice?' Afiya said in alarm, knowing they were back in trouble again when she had thought they were safe.

'It's the woman. I can't make her stop.'

'What is she saying?' Afiya asked but Ilyas shook his head and said no more. He sobbed in gentle gasps and seemed unlikely to stop, so in the end Afiya helped him to his feet and made him lie on his bed. To her relief he was very soon asleep, or pretending to be. When she asked him the next morning if he was all right, he said curtly that he was well. Is the woman still there? she asked but he shook his head and went off to school.

It was only a brief respite. Another episode occurred a few days later when they woke in the middle of the night to hear his cries. He was calling out his name, Ilyas, Ilyas, but in a woman's voice. Hamza climbed into bed with him and held him in his arms while he struggled. When he calmed after what seemed like hours, Hamza asked him, 'What does she want?'

'Where is Ilyas?' the boy said. 'She says, where is Ilyas? Again and again.'

'You are Ilyas,' Hamza said.

'No,' he said.

Khalifa said to Afiya, 'He is asking for your brother Ilyas. I knew it was a mistake to call him that. All this war talk has brought it back. Maybe he is blaming himself. Or you. Maybe that's why he speaks in a woman's voice. He is speaking for you. There is no one here who can help him. If you take him to the hospital they will ship him to an asylum a hundred miles from here and put him in chains. We have to look after him ourselves.'

After that the voice came every night asking for Ilyas. 'We have to do something,' Afiya said. 'Jamila thinks maybe we should see if the hakim can help him.'

'She grew up in the country,' Khalifa said mockingly, addressing Hamza. 'They believe in all that witches and devils business. You're a religious man so maybe you might also see if the hakim can give you a little powder to chase the demons away.'

'Why not?' Hamza said although he had no faith in that kind of religion. So Afiya once again visited the hakim as she had when Bi Asha was unwell and came back with a gilded plate with verses from the Koran written on it. She ran some water on the plate to dissolve the words and made Ilyas drink it. The signs did not abate even after repeated doses of dissolved holy words. Now Ilyas no longer left the house. He was losing weight and sleeping long hours in the day because his nights were disturbed. Afiya was distraught and grew increasingly desperate. One night, as Ilyas lay gently moaning his name, she said aloud and in agony, Oh my God, I can't bear this torture. It was after that night she decided to call a shekhiya whose name was given to her by the mganga neighbour who had come to see to Bi Asha in her last days.

'What will she do?' Hamza asked.

'If he has been visited the shekhiya will tell us.'

'Visited by what? I told you, she grew up in the country. We're going to do witchcraft in our house,' Khalifa said, going to his room in disgust.

The shekhiya entered the house in a cloud of incense, so it seemed. She was a small pale-complexioned woman with a sharp-edged handsome face. She greeted Afiya brightly and began talking cheerfully as she took off her buibui, which released another cloud of incense and perfume, and then she settled herself down on the mat in the guest room. 'That sun is fierce out there. I stopped to rest wherever I found some shade but look at me, I'm covered in sweat. It makes you long for the kaskazi to arrive and bring us a breeze. So, my child, are you well, and is your household well? Alhamdulillah. Yes, I know, your loved one is troubled otherwise you would not have called me. Haya, bismillahi. Tell me what has been troubling him.'

The shekhiya listened with eyes cast down as Afiya described the episodes and the voices, her fingers toying with a brownstone rosary. She wore a red shawl of flimsy material and a loose white shift that covered all of her. Only her face and hands were exposed. The shekhiya did not ask any questions while Afiya spoke but raised her head now and then as if struck by a detail. Afiya circled the events back and forth, not sure if she had managed to convey the force of what she was describing, until in the end she began to feel that she was rambling and stopped.

'He calls out the name Ilyas, which is his name as well your brother's who did not come back from the last war. You don't know if he is lost or still living and stranded somewhere. His father was also in the war but came back,' the shekhiya said, and waited for Afiya to confirm. 'I will now see the boy.'

Afiya called out and Ilyas came in, looking frail and a little nervous. The shekhiya smiled brightly and patted the mat beside her for him to sit down. She gazed at him for a moment, still smiling, but did not ask him any questions. She closed her eyes for what seemed a long time, her face solemn and composed, and once she raised her hands, palms outwards, but did not touch him. Then she opened her eyes and smiled again at Ilyas, who shuddered. 'Haya, you go and rest now,' she said. 'Let me speak alone with your mother.

'There is no doubt that your son has been visited,' the shekhiya said. 'A spirit has mounted him. Do you understand what I am talking about? It is a woman and that makes me hopeful. Women visitors talk, the males sometimes just blunder about angrily. She speaks to him – that too makes me hopeful. From what you have told me she has not hurt him and from feeling the boy here beside me, I don't think the visitor means him harm but we have to find out what she wants and what will placate her and then provide that if it is possible. If you are willing, I will bring my people here and we will purify the boy here in this room and listen to what his visitor demands. The ceremony will not be cheap.'

Several people came to know of the coming ceremony and none but Khalifa mocked as Hamza had feared they would. Mzee Sulemani asked about Ilyas but did not say anything about the ceremony. Hamza did not imagine that the old carpenter would approve. I will pray for his health, he said. Nassor Biashara knew the details from his wife who had heard about them from Afiya herself. He too asked after Ilyas and said with a shrug, Might as well try everything. Hamza knew that they now had no choice but to go through with the ceremony even though he himself had deep doubts about it. He had heard about it in the schutztruppe where there were regular ceremonies in the boma village every week among the Nubi families, but he knew that Afiya had become distraught and frightened about it, had driven herself frantic with anxiety. She was making herself ill.

He did not argue or scoff about the ceremony as Khalifa did. He had his own guilty idea that it was his trauma which was the source of what was tormenting his son, an aftermath of something he had done during the war. He could not think what it could be so there was no logic to this sense that it was something in his past which generated the evil air. Then there was the lost Ilyas. They had named their son after him and somehow established a connection between them, made the boy bear the tragedy of Afiya's loss, share in her guilt that their efforts to locate her brother or discover his fate had failed.

The Frau's address was in the copy of Heine's *Zur Geschichte der Religion und Philosophie in Deutschland*. When the pastor saw Hamza with it, he said, 'What are you doing with that book?'

'The Frau lent it to me,' he said.

'She lent you Heine!' The memory of his shocked surprise still made Hamza smile with glee even after all these years. 'And what have you made of it so far?' the pastor asked.

'I am making very slow progress,' Hamza said humbly, knowing how it provoked the pastor when the Frau praised his ability to read German, 'but I was interested to learn that there was a time in Germany when men made the sign of the cross when they heard the nightingale sing. They took her for an agent of evil, as they did everything that gave pleasure.'

'That is exactly what I would've expected of an ignorant reader,' the pastor said. 'You can only understand the frivolous in Heine while his deeper thought escapes you.'

When the pastor decided to return to Germany and Hamza made ready to leave too, the Frau gave the book to him and wrote her name and address on the title page. It was an address in Berlin. Write and tell me when something good happens to you, she said. Hamza had thought of writing to her before to ask if there was a way of finding out about Ilyas from the records in Germany. He was discouraged by the audacity of the idea. Why would she bother to find out? How would she know about the records of the schutztruppe askari? Who cared what happened to a lost schutztruppe? In addition, he was discouraged by his own lack of a return postal address. Recently the Biashara Furniture and General Merchandise Company had acquired a post office box so now that problem was solved. He composed a brief letter to the Frau, reminding her of who he was and explaining his search for his brother-in-law. Did she know how they could find out what had happened to him? He copied the letter on to a sheet of the company's headed paper, addressed an air-mail envelope and took it to the Post Office on the same day. That was in November 1938.

*

After the isha prayer on the evening of the appointed day, soon after Hamza sent off his letter, the shekhiya arrived at the house with her entourage. She was dressed in black from head to toe and her eyelids and lips were kohled. Her woman singer and the two male drummers were dressed more casually in ordinary clothes. She closed the window and lit two scented candles. She then sprayed the room with rose water and started the incense burners, one of ud and the other of frankincense. She waited until the room was filled with scent and fumes before she summoned Ilyas and Afiya and asked them to sit against the wall. No one else was to come in although she did not close the door to the room. She sat cross-legged in front of Ilyas and Afiya with eyes closed. Then the drummers began, beating a gentle rhythm while the woman singer hummed.

Hamza sat on his own in their bedroom, the door open in case he was required. He remembered that the ceremonies lasted a long time and sometimes became loud and disorderly and people were hurt. Khalifa sat on the porch with his friends and tried to ignore the drumming and the singing. More people walked past than usual that evening, curious for a glimpse of what was going on, but they were disappointed. Both the front door and the window were closed, so all they saw were three elderly men sitting on the porch pretending that nothing unusual was happening inside.

The drumming went on for an hour, for two hours, monotonous and getting louder. The singer raised her pitch but her words were as incomprehensible as before, if they were words at all. The shekhiya was reciting prayers but they were inaudible in the din and rhythm of the drums. She kept the incense burner fuming, adding coals from a pot she kept beside her. At some point during the second hour, Afiya's head dropped and Ilyas's followed a few moments later. She began to mutter and after a while that became a word: Yallah. Yallah. By the third hour both Afiya and Ilyas were rocking back and forth in a trance as was the shekhiya. Suddenly Ilyas fell over on to his side and Afiya screamed. The drummers and the singer took no notice, nor did the shekhiya stop speaking her prayers.

By this time Khalifa had shut up the house and was sitting on the bed in his room, Hamza beside him, waiting for the drama to come to an end. Just before midnight, the drumming stopped and the two men approached the room. They saw Ilyas lying on his side on the floor while Afiya was leaning against the wall, her eyes wide open in exaltation. Without turning around, the shekhiya waved the two men into the room while the drummers and the singer rose wearily and went into the yard to eat the food they had asked to be prepared for them.

The shekhiya then told them, 'The visitor lives in this house. She was already here when the boy was born. Someone died soon after he was born, and the visitor left that one and mounted the boy. She is waiting for Ilyas and in her anguish she will trouble the boy. There will be no cure until you find him or find out about him, only then will the visitor learn to live with the affliction of his absence and stop tormenting the boy. Until you have that knowledge you will have to call me whenever the boy suffers a crisis and we will perform another ceremony to placate the visitor. She does not mean to harm the boy. She is in anguish herself. She wants to see Ilyas.'

After that the shekhiya collected her fee and the gifts she had requested and at that late hour left the house with her entourage, leaving a perfumed silence behind her.

Hamza helped the exhausted Ilyas to his feet and to their bed in case he needed attention in the night. I will sleep in the boy's bed, he said. He went back to check that all was well and saw Khalifa standing in the doorway of the guest room.

'What nonsense! All the perfume and drumming and stupid wailing!' he said. 'That woman knows a source of income when she spots one. She has worked out what Afiya wants to hear: Find your brother. The story about a love-besotted devil is the kind of rubbish even Topasi will not believe. Anyway, maybe that will calm the boy down and settle his nightmares or whatever they are. The only bit that made sense was that thing about the devil being in Asha all along. That comes as no surprise to me.'

*

The shekhiya ceremony took place a few weeks before the arrival of the kaskazi with its dry steady winds, just before the beginning of the school year. There were no further episodes of voices during those weeks and the boy gradually lost the tense expectant look that was characteristic of him at the time. He was subdued and withdrawn at first but his manner was obliging and affectionate. It seemed that the treatment had done enough to rid him of the voices and the fear they induced in him, at least for the time being. Khalifa said it was because the old witch had terrified the boy and that had made him give up his whispering nonsense. Afiya kept an anxious eye on her son, secretly fearful that the treatment could not possibly have been a cure.

His school had a new headmaster at the beginning of that year. He was also Ilyas's English teacher and he did not ask his students to memorise poems. Instead he had a zeal for handwriting and for writing in general. They had a writing exercise in every class, painstakingly copying out in their best hand the short passages the teacher wrote out on the blackboard. No more of those lazy tedious lessons when one boy after another stood up to recite the same poem while the teacher sat contentedly at his desk. They had to write a story to a given title for homework every week, to be collected by the class captain first thing on Monday mornings. Ilyas took to this new regime with a passion. With the teacher's encouragement, his stories grew longer with every new attempt, and were written in a careful hand that the teacher showered with praise. Over the months of that year, his stories featured monkeys, feral cats, encounters with strangers on country roads, a cruel German officer who ran berserk with a sword and even a story about a fifteen-hundred-year-old jinn who lived in the neighbourhood and visited a fourteen-year-old boy. He wrote his stories with dedication and unmistakable pleasure, sitting at the desk Hamza had moved to the guest room so his son could work undisturbed. Ilyas sat there for hours, writing in his note-taking book first before copying the finished product into his homework book on the Sunday night. They all read his stories: Afiya, Hamza and Khalifa. When he was especially pleased with one he sometimes asked to read it aloud to them.

'That boy has a rich imagination,' Khalifa said admiringly. 'It's such a relief that he has taken up writing instead of whispering.'

'Like I said, maybe that is what he was doing all along,' Hamza said smugly. 'Making up stories.'

Afiya looked doubtfully at both of them. Had they really already forgotten that blood-curdling voice, the tears and the pain-wracked cries in the middle of the night? Was that just stories waiting to be told? To her it had seemed like torture. She did not think she could bear the endless drumming and those incense fumes of the shekhiya and her entourage again. For now the boy seemed excited and confident in his new accomplishments, but she remained fearful of a recurrence of the monstrous voice.

15

One mid-morning in March the following year a policeman on a bicycle rode up to the Biashara Furniture and General Merchandise timber yard. It was raining lightly, hardly spotting his khaki, the end of the vuli rains, the short rains. The policeman was of medium height, with a thin mild-looking face and a small nervous twitch around his left eye. He leaned his bicycle under cover and entered Nassor Biashara's office.

'Salam alaikum,' he said politely.

'Waalaikum salam,' Nassor Biashara replied, leaning back, his spectacles on his forehead, suspicious. There was never a good reason to be visited by a policeman.

'Is Hamza Askari here?' he asked in a voice as mild as his appearance.

'There is a Hamza here but his name is not Askari,' Nassor Biashara said. 'He was one a long time ago. What do you want with him?'

'That must be him. Where is he?'

'What do you want with him?' Nassor Biashara asked again.

'Bwana mkubwa, I have work to do and so do you. I don't want to waste your time. He is wanted at HQ and I have to take him there,' the policeman said politely, even smiling. 'Kwa hisani yako, please call him for me.'

Nassor Biashara rose to his feet and led him off to the workshop where the policeman informed Hamza that he was to follow him to Police HQ at once. What has he done? Nassor Biashara asked, but the policeman took no notice, facing Hamza and pointing to the door with his left arm outstretched.

'What is this about?' Hamza asked.

'It's not my business, let's go. I am sure you will soon find out,' the policeman said.

'You can't come here and arrest a man and not even tell him what it is about,' Nassor Biashara protested.

'Bwana, I have work to do. I am not here to arrest him, but I will if he does not come with me willingly,' the policeman said, his right hand reaching for the handcuffs hooked to his belt.

Hamza raised his hands placatingly. They walked through the streets, Hamza slightly in front, the policeman wheeling his bicycle just behind. They drew glances but no one addressed them. At Police HQ another officer wrote Hamza's name in a book and pointed to a bench where he was to wait. He tried to guess what this summons was about. The policeman had asked if he was Hamza Askari so it was something to do with the schutztruppe. He never called himself Askari. Were they going to detain him after all these years? There were rumours that some of the German settlers in the country were making ready to leave. The growing talk of war between the British and the Germans raised fears of the detention of enemy aliens.

After what felt like an hour but was probably less, he was called and taken down a short corridor to an office. A European policeman with thinning hair, bristling moustache and glittering eyes was sitting behind a desk. He was not in police uniform but was dressed in a white short-sleeved shirt, khaki shorts, white stockings and polished brown shoes, the uniform of a British colonial official. Another policeman in khaki uniform but without his hat was sitting at a small desk near him, ready to take notes. The British officer pointed to a chair without speaking. He waited while Hamza settled down and then waited a moment longer.

'Is your name Hamza?' he asked in Kiswahili, his voice rasping and menacing, seeming to come out of the corner of his mouth. There was a brief and unexpected glint of amusement in his eyes, then he repeated the question in a gentler voice. 'Hamza?'

He thought he recognised a contained violence in that tone that he had heard so often from the German officers. He had not had much to do with British officials and this police officer was the first one he was meeting in this town. 'Yes, I am Hamza,' he said.

'Hamza, can you read?' the British officer asked, speaking again in that rasping voice.

'Yes,' he said in surprise.

'In German?' the British officer asked.

Hamza nodded.

'Who do you know in Germany?' the police officer asked.

'I don't know anyone,' Hamza said, and remembered the Frau even as he made this denial.

The police officer held up an envelope. It had been opened. 'This is addressed to Hamza Askari, using the Post Office Box number of Biashara Furniture and General Merchandise. Is this you?'

She had replied! He stood up and reached out for the letter. The uniformed policeman also stood up.

'Sit down,' the British officer said firmly, looking from one man to the other.

'It's my letter,' Hamza said, not sitting.

'Sit down,' the officer said more mildly, and waited until Hamza sat. 'How do you know this woman?' he asked, speaking her name.

Yes, she replied! 'I worked for her many years ago,' he said, and the officer nodded. There could be nothing irregular about a native working for a European. The officer took out the letter and seemed to read it through silently.

'It's my letter. Why are you keeping it from me?' Hamza demanded loudly.

'For security reasons. Don't raise your voice at me or you will not see this letter, ever,' the officer said in fluent German. 'Why would a respectable German woman write to you and how is it that someone like you can read a letter written in such sophisticated language? What other letters have you exchanged with her?'

'I have not received a letter from anyone in my whole life,' Hamza replied in Kiswahili, understanding now why the police officer was interested in his letter. 'We have been waiting for news of my brother for many years. He was an askari. I know a little German so in the end wrote to the Frau to ask for her help. Does it say his name in that letter?'

The officer held out the letter and Hamza stood up to take it. 'Tell me what it says,' the officer said.

Hamza read it silently through, and then read the letter again. It was a long letter, two pages, and he took his time, making a pretence of struggling to understand it all. 'It says he is alive and in Germany,' he said. 'Alhamdulillah, she managed to find out. Someone who helped the Frau found his name mentioned twice in the office dealing with askari records, in 1929 when he applied for his pension and 1934 when he applied for a medal. So he's alive, alhamdulillah, but she does not know any more. She says she will keep asking. It's unbelievable. She says my letter took a long time to reach her because they have moved but it did, and then she had to get in touch with ...'

'That's enough,' the British officer said, cutting off his babble. 'I have read the letter. What is all this about a book by Heine? Have you read this book?'

'Oh, no, madam gave it to me,' Hamza said. 'It was a joke, I think. She knew it was too difficult for me. I lost it many years ago.'

The British officer considered this for a moment and then decided to let it go. 'Affairs with Germany are very tense at the moment. If there are further exchanges with anyone living there we will investigate and may withhold correspondence. There could be consequences for you. Be aware that we will keep a close watch on you and on this address from now on. You may go.'

Hamza pocketed the envelope and strolled back to the timber yard, relishing the anticipation of how he would break the news to Afiya later. They crowded around him when he returned to the yard and he made light of it, saying he was questioned by a British officer about his time in the schutztruppe. He wanted to keep the news of the letter for Afiya first. 'They must be checking up on old askari,' he said, 'to recruit them for the KAR. I told them I was injured so that was that.'

He waited for them to come home for lunch. Khalifa no longer worked at the warehouse, spending his mornings at home or dropping in at one café or another to share the news of the day, and then he went to the market for fruit and vegetables as instructed by Afiya, who worked at the maternity clinic in the mornings. Ilyas was back from school when she came home to prepare their lunch. They did not usually eat until two in the afternoon. Hamza waited until after lunch, eating the matoke and fish with silent relish, then he washed his hands and called for attention.

'What are you up to?' Afiya said, smiling. 'I knew there was something.'

Hamza pulled the envelope out of his shirt pocket and they all knew at once what it was. None of them ever received any letters. He read it to them, simultaneously translating as he did.

Dear Hamza, It was such a lovely surprise to receive your letter. It was such a long time ago and we often talk about our time in Ostafrika and the mission. I am glad to hear you are well and that you are now a carpenter and a married man.

Your letter took a long time to reach us because we no longer live in Berlin but now live in Würzburg, so it had to be forwarded to us. We were very sorry to hear about your brother-in-law and started enquiries immediately. It is very fortunate that a friend of ours works in the Foreign Affairs Office in Berlin and he found two references to Ilyas Hassan in the schutztruppe records, which are held in that Office, so your relative is here in Germany. Such a striking name, I think there could only have been one Ilyas Hassan in the whole of the schutztruppe. The first reference to the name was in 1929 when he applied to receive his pension, and the second was in 1934 when he applied to receive the campaign medal for the Ostafrika campaign. He made both these applications in Hamburg so it is likely that he is living there. Many foreign people do because they work on the ships, so maybe that is his work too. He was unsuccessful with the pension application because he did not have discharge papers. He was also unsuccessful with the application for a medal because it was only awarded to Germans and not to askari.

These recent years have been difficult years for Germany, and as a foreigner I expect that life has not been easy for your brother-in-law, but at least you know now that he is alive. Our friend was not able to find out when he came here and where he was before that. I expect there is more information available and we will make further enquiries. We will let you know if we learn any more, and will give him your address when we find him. It would be so very good if you were able to be in touch again.

By the way, when our mail was forwarded from the mission, there was a letter from the Oberleutnant, your old officer who brought you to us. He wrote to us after he was repatriated to Germany in 1920 when we ourselves were already here. It seems he was detained first in Dar es Salaam and then Alexandria. He asked after you and I was able to write to him and tell him that you made a full recovery and your German had progressed in leaps and bounds, and that you were a devoted reader of Schiller. The pastor sends his regards and would like to know how you got on with Heine. That is how he remembers you, not as the man whose leg and perhaps his life he saved, but as the askari who presumed to read his Heine. That was his copy I gave you. Please accept our best wishes to you and your family.

*

They never received another letter. Hamza replied to thank the Frau but perhaps the letter did not leave the country. If it did and she replied with more news, perhaps her letter did not get past the watchful police officer. In September that year war was declared between the United Kingdom and Germany and that was the end of postal services between the two countries. In the town they were very distant from this war and only knew about it as news for a while, despite the deployment of KAR through Tanga towards the campaign against the Italians in Abyssinia. Khalifa did not survive the war. He passed away quietly one night in 1942 at the age of sixty-eight. When his body was taken in the bier for the funeral prayers, it was the first time he had entered a mosque in decades. He left nothing for anybody apart from a few rags and a pile of old newspapers.

264

Ilyas finished Standard VIII in 1940 but there was no further schooling available in the town, and Standard VIII was achievement enough in many people's eyes. It was good enough for training as an officer of some kind in a government department, health or agriculture or customs. Ilyas enlisted in the KAR in December 1942 soon after Khalifa's passing and a few months after the defeat of the Italians in Abyssinia. He was in his nineteenth year. He had been talking about joining up for more than a year but Khalifa so vociferously opposed this move that Ilyas did not dare disobey. This is nothing to do with you, he said to Ilyas. Isn't it enough that your father and your uncle were stupid enough to risk their lives for these vainglorious warmongers?

After Khalifa's passing, Ilyas wore his parents down with his pleas. The British administration promised to send qualified veteran KARs for further studies at the end of the war and Ilyas could not resist the lure. He was sent to Gilgil in the highlands in Kenya Colony for training and then was posted to Dar es Salaam for garrison duties with the coastal regiment for the rest of the war. He did not take part in any fighting but he learned a great deal about the British and their pursuits. He also learned to ride a motorcycle and drive a Jeep, and even to tinker successfully with its engine. He played football and tennis and went fishing with a speargun and flippers. For a while he even smoked a pipe.

At the end of the war, the promised further studies became training as a school teacher in Dar es Salaam and afterwards Ilyas found work in a school in the city and rented a room in Kariako Street. These were the years when new stirrings of anti-colonial sentiment were spreading, informed by the successful campaign in India and the triumph of Nkrumah in the Gold Coast and the defeat of the Dutch in Indonesia. Students politicised by their university experiences in the African Association in Makerere University College and by their involvement in student organisations in England and Scotland, were active in this movement. They and everyone else who knew about it were alarmed by the settler leanings of the new colonial administration. Ilyas was not yet drawn into these activities although he would be later. In these years, when he was in his late twenties, he played sports and taught school, and as time passed he began making a name for himself writing stories in Kiswahili, which were sometimes published in the newspapers. In the 1950s the colonial administration introduced a new radio service. It aired news and music programmes and features on improvements in health, agriculture and education. The news soon became strident accounts of Mau Mau atrocities in Kenya, which were so persuasive that mothers threatened their children's misbehaviour with the appearance of the rebels.

For a few days every vacation, Ilyas went to see Hamza and Afiya. Parts of the town now had an electric supply, including their old house. He strolled the streets with some pleasure but he soon became restless and longed to return to the city. His parents loved his stories from there, asking to hear details of his classroom achievements and the success of his publications in the newspapers. Afiya gasped with amazement at his sporting exploits, exaggerating her surprise, which flattered Ilyas and made him feel proud that he had prevailed against his timidity as a youth. He asked about his uncle Ilyas, if they had any more news. He always asked, not expecting any. His father told him that he had written again to the Frau pastor but received no reply. Stories of the wartime destruction in Germany were only slowly reaching them, and he was fearful that the Frau and the pastor might not have survived. Hamza was by now in his fifties, slowing but content and well, managing the Biashara timber yard for Nassor who was now no longer a businessman but a magnate with a variety of trading outlets – pharmaceutical companies, furniture stores and most recently electrical products, including radios. Hamza and Afiya owned one.

A popular feature on the radio service was a story programme that invited contributions from listeners. The assistant to the producer of the programme drew his boss's attention to one of Ilyas's stories. The producer asked to meet him. He was a big genial Englishman with a large face and a coppery moustache. He was dressed in the colonial uniform of white shirt, khaki shorts, white calf-length socks and brown shoes. The exposed parts of his arms and legs were muscular and covered with coppery hair, just like his face.

'My name is Butterworth and I am on secondment from the Department of Agriculture,' he told Ilyas. 'I am not an expert on either radio or stories. They might as well have sent me to the National Authority for Anchorages and Tunnels but you have to muck in and get on with it. Now I know I like stories to have some element of instruction to them. This one here about the experiences of a school teacher will do very well. Can you do another with something about farming in it?'

Mr Butterworth was also a reserve KAR officer and when he learned that Ilyas was a veteran, he found ways of showing favour to him. That was how he was given the opportunity to read his own stories on the radio and become a minor celebrity. Mr Butterworth was relieved of his secondment in the mid-1950s and was transferred to the West Indies but by then Ilyas was in and making his own way in his new profession. In time he came to be a full-time member of the production team of the broadcasting service, working mainly in the newsroom and writing stories when he found the time. The mid-1950s were the years of TANU's march to independence under the leadership of Julius Nyerere, the mission- school boy who had at one time considered ordination into the Catholic Church before he became a radical activist for Independence. By the elections of 1958, it was evident that the British colonial administration was in disarray and on the retreat. The elections of 1960, held under the supervision of the colonial administration, gave TANU and Nyerere 98 per cent of the elected members of Parliament. These were not results produced out of a hat by a corrupt electoral commission but ones achieved under the grumbling surveillance of reluctant colonial officials. There was no way to argue against that and by the next year the British were gone.

In 1963, two years after Independence, which both his parents lived to see, Ilyas was awarded a scholarship by the Federal Republic of Germany to spend a year in Bonn learning advanced broadcasting techniques. He was thirty-eight years old. The Federal Republic of Germany was what was popularly known as West Germany, a federation of the regions occupied by the US, the British and the French after the war. The part of Germany occupied by the Soviet Union became the German Democratic Republic. The GDR was highly active in colonial politics, and along with other Soviet East European allies provided sanctuary, training and arms to insurrectionist liberation movements in many parts of Africa. It had positioned itself as the champion of decolonising nations, and the Federal Republic scholarships were gifts intended to match those of the German Democratic Republic and to win support from poor nations at forums like the United Nations. Ilyas was interviewed and assessed and was delighted to be awarded the scholarship. He had never travelled anywhere, apart from those months in Gilgil where he did his basic training. Now he was travelling as a mature man with his eyes open and curious.

He spent the first six months in Bonn in an intensive course in German language. He enjoyed his time there, attending every class, practising for hours, walking the streets every day to see whatever there was to see, wandering into shops and exhibitions, sending postcards to his parents and friends at work. He lived in a three-storey building that provided accommodation for mature students. There were six large rooms with shared bathroom facilities on each floor. It was not far from the university cafeteria and was altogether comfortable and suited to Ilyas's needs. It seemed he must have inherited something from his father because he made rapid progress in German, and his teachers praised him for his competence in it.

At the end of the first six months he began the broadcasting part of the program. As part of it, he was expected to work on a journalistic project requiring research and recorded interviews. He was given a budget and six hours of consultation time with a supervisor for technical assistance. He knew about this before he came and already knew what his subject would be. He chose to work on the whereabouts of his uncle Ilyas. He had copied the Frau pastor's address from his father's volume of Heine, and while he was still on the language course began reading about Würzburg. He learned that 90 per cent of the city was destroyed in an air raid on 16 March 1945 by hundreds of British Lancaster bombers dropping incendiary explosives. There was no pressing military imperative behind the raid, which was intended purely to demoralise the civilian population. He found a contemporary map of the reconstructed town in the university library and searched for the street named in the Frau's address. The details of the wholesale destruction made him doubtful that it would still be there, but it was. When his German was good enough, he wrote a note explaining that he was the son of Hamza the askari and wished to extend his father's greetings to the pastor and Frau. He wrote his address on the left-hand corner of the envelope. Ten days later his letter came back unopened with Nicht bekannt unter dieser Adresse written across the bottom of the envelope. Not known at this address.

His assigned supervisor, Dr Köhler, frowned as Ilyas began to describe his project. 'A war in Africa fifty years ago,' he said. 'Germany gets no rest from her wars.'

Dr Köhler was in his early forties, tall and fair-haired, a striding smiling presence in the department, and Ilyas was disappointed by his disapproval. He waited for a moment before continuing and then explained that the schutztruppe he was trying to trace was his uncle who had come to Germany after the war in Ostafrika. Dr Köhler lifted his chin and then gave a small nod for him to continue. Ilyas explained about the pastor who had saved his father's leg and perhaps his life, and the mission in Kilemba, and the letter from the Frau pastor about his uncle. He told Dr Köhler about the letter he had written to the Würzburg address and that it was returned. Dr Köhler shrugged. Ilyas thought he understood what that shrug meant.

'A pastor means he is a Lutheran,' Dr Köhler said. 'A Lutheran minister in Catholic Würzburg should not be too difficult to trace. How do you intend to proceed?'

'I was planning to go there to see if there are any records about the street or anything about the pastor or the Frau.'

'The sooner the better,' Dr Köhler said with a glimmer of enthusiasm. 'Where will you look for these records?'

'I don't know. I'll enquire when I get there,' Ilyas said.

Dr Köhler smiled. 'If I were you, I would begin at the Rathaus. As you know, you can claim your travel and subsistence expenses for trips associated with your project but only afterwards. Our bureaucracy is very thorough about funds ... oh, about everything. German bureaucracy is the envy of the world. I hope you have enough money to spend and then claim. This is your project and you proceed as you wish, but I would like us to meet like this once a week for you to give me a report. Yes, go and check the Rathaus in Würzburg. It was a lovely town but I have not been there since the war.'

Ilyas took the train from Bonn to Frankfurt and changed there for Würzburg. At the Rathaus he was directed to the Civil Registration Office where he found out that the street the pastor and his family lived in was completely destroyed and the pastor, the Frau pastor and a daughter were presumed dead in the fire that followed the raid. There were two daughters, he remembered, but one was evidently no longer living with her parents then. That was all the record held in that office contained, their names, the street they lived in and its destruction. The woman in the office explained that if the person he was looking for was a Lutheran pastor, then he should check the Lutheran archive for Bavaria in Nuremberg.

He reported his findings to Dr Köhler who advised him to make a phone call to the archive before going there. In the meantime, he showed him a Compact Cassette recorder released by Phillips only a few months before. The department had acquired two of them, he said, and why did Ilyas not take one with him in case he was able to record a conversation with the archivist? He made his phone call and took another trip to Bavaria, travelling through Frankfurt and Würzburg again. He had not known how close he was to Nuremberg on his previous trip. The archivist was a lean elderly man in a dark suit, which was a little loose on him. He took Ilyas into a room with a long table on which he saw a small stack of papers. The archivist sat at one end of the table with some papers of his own, presumably to keep an eye on him. If you need any assistance, please do not hesitate to ask, he said.

Ilyas read in the papers that after his return from Ostafrika, the pastor was attached to the Evangelical Lutheran Church of St Stephan in Würzburg. The church was totally destroyed in March

1945 and rebuilt in the 1950s. He also taught part-time at the Julius-Maximilians-Universität Würzburg. He taught a course in Protestant Theology. The Frau's occupation was not recorded. Both had perished with their younger daughter in the bombing raid. Do you know what happened to the other daughter? Ilyas asked the archivist who shook his head but did not speak. Among the papers was a brief cutting from a newspaper or magazine about the mission in Kilemba, just a couple of paragraphs about a clinic and a school and the pastor's name. There was no photograph and the title and date of the publication had been cut off. Ilyas asked the archivist if he knew the source of the cutting.

He came over to where Ilyas was sitting and looked at the cutting for a moment. He said, 'Most likely *Kolonie und Heimat*, the old one before it was taken over by the Reichskolonialbund.'

'What is that?' Ilyas asked.

The archivist looked stern, almost contemptuous of his ignorance. 'It was the bund, the Gleichschaltung for the recolonising movement. There was a campaign to get back the colonies taken away by Versailles.'

'What is that word? Gleichschaltung?' Ilyas asked. 'Please, I would be very grateful for your help.'

The archivist nodded, perhaps mollified by his manner of asking. 'It refers to the way the Nazi government brought organisations together under one administration. It means ... coordination, control. The Reichskolonialbund brought together all the recolonising associations and put them under the control of the party.'

'I knew nothing about a recolonising movement,' Ilyas said.

The archivist shrugged. Dummkopf. 'They revived *Kolonie und Heimat*, which was a publication from Imperial times. I think this cutting is from the old one,' he said, and returned to his place at the table while Ilyas wrote up his notes. It was then that he realised he had forgotten to switch on the Phillips Compact Cassette recorder. He did not think he could ask the stern man to repeat what he had said about the Reichskolonialbund. As he was taking his leave, it suddenly occurred to Ilyas to ask, Were you in Ostafrika? They were standing at the outside door when he asked and the archivist said yes and turned away before Ilyas could ask any more.

Dr Köhler was also surprised to hear that Ilyas had not heard of the recolonising movement. 'It was a big thing, a real grudge for the National Socialists to exploit. I remember the marches. Did you use the Compact Cassette? Oh, that's a pity. You are making a radio programme so it would be good to have some clips from someone like the archivist. Maybe on your next search.'

Ilyas found out that the archives of the Reichskolonialbund were in Koblenz, not at all far from Bonn, a beautiful old city at the junction of the Rhine and Moselle rivers. He rang ahead with his request to look at the *Kolonie und Heimat* archive and was met by a woman archivist who led him to a large room with lines of shelving stacks. She said her office was next door if he needed her. In the archives he found out that the Reichskolonialbund was established in 1933 and incorporated into the National Socialist Party in 1936. *Kolonie und Heimat* was revived in 1937 and was as much a magazine as a photo-journal. As he searched the copies he saw many photographs of colonial homesteads and ceremonies, taken before the loss of the colonies, but also photographs of events that were organised by the Reichskolonialbund to campaign and agitate for the return of the colonies. In the rallies and on platforms, members wore the uniform of the schutztruppe and carried a specially designed flag. In a November 1938 issue he saw a grainy photograph of a group standing on a stage, two adult Germans in uniform, a German teenager in a white shirt and black shorts, standing before a microphone, and behind him and to the left of the frame, an African man in schutztruppe uniform. Behind them was the flag of the Reichskolonialbund, a corner of which displayed the swastika. The caption to the photograph described it as the Hamburg Reichskolonialbund Gala but did not name the four figures. He asked the archivist if it was possible to find the original photograph or any details of the source or occasion. This time he remembered to switch on his Phillips Compact Cassette.

'We have many of the original photographs but I am not sure where they are exactly or if they are properly classified,' she said apologetically. 'I have some deadlines to meet, but if you give me a few days I will get back to you. I have the telephone number of your department at the university.'

A few days later he was back in Koblenz and, with the Cassette running, the archivist helped him go through the boxes of photographs which were collected by year. They found the original photograph with ease. On the back of it was a label with the name of the photographer and those of the figures in it, which the picture editor must have decided to leave out of the caption. The label also said that the event was a rally after the screening of a film about a Deutsch-Ostafrikan community, shown in Hamburg. The African man in schutztruppe uniform was named as Elias Essen. Those eyes, that brow.

He asked the archivist for a copy of the original and sent it to his mother. She replied in a few days to say it was his uncle Ilyas.

He was in Bonn and lived within walking distance of government offices, including the Foreign Affairs Office, and his accreditation as both a student on a broadcasting program funded by a Federal Government scholarship and a journalist by profession gave him access to many officials. Even when they were not able to supply him with the information he required, they were often able advise on where he should be looking. He wrote home to let his parents know about the progress of his search, but some of his finds were too inconclusive to announce in a letter.

He made trips to Freiburg to the Institute of Military History, to Berlin to the archives of the Colonial Association, to the Institute of Oriental Languages in Berlin to meet linguists and search their archives for the language training of policemen and administrators who were to run the regained colonies. Some of the researches were to consolidate the information he had already gathered, some to provide more context and background. He met military enthusiasts, amateur and professional historians, his Phillips Compact Cassette recorder running whenever the person he was speaking to allowed it, and gradually he was able to assemble a sketch, a story, which still required lengthier and more determined research to fill out in detail, but was quite adequate enough for his radio project. Dr Köhler was delighted with the effort and thought that the poor-quality sound the Compact Cassette produced somehow enhanced the emotional power of the proceedings.

He waited until he returned home before telling his parents the full story of what happened to Uncle Ilyas. This was what he told them. Uncle Ilyas was wounded at the Battle of Mahiwa in October 1917. (I was there, Hamza said. It was a terrible battle.) He was taken prisoner and held in detention first in Lindi and then in Mombasa. (So he was only a day away from us here, Afiya said.) After the war, the British repatriated the German officers to Germany but released the schutztruppe askari any old how, just let them out and allowed them to look after themselves as best they could. Ilyas was not sure where or when Uncle Ilyas was released. He could not find out anything about that. He might have ended up anywhere on the coast or even across the ocean. Nor was he sure what kind of work he did after his release. At some point he worked on ships as a waiter or a general servant of some kind. For sure he worked on a German ship and was in Germany in 1929 as they knew from the Frau's letter and from what Ilyas saw in the Foreign Affairs Office record. By this time he had changed his name to Elias Essen and was making a living as a singer in Hamburg. He was remembered as Elias Essen, a performer in low-life Hamburg cabarets who wore the military uniform of an askari on-stage, including the tarbush with the Imperial eagle badge. He married a German woman in 1933 and had three children. Ilyas knew that because one of the entries on his record was the appeal his wife made against eviction from their rented property, and she provided details of her marriage and the birth of her children and her husband's record as a veteran of the schutztruppe. Another entry was his application for a campaign medal in 1934, but they knew about that already because the Frau had told them. What they didn't know, because the Frau did not know it either, was that Uncle Ilyas was marching with the Reichskolonialbund, a Nazi Party organisation. The Nazis wanted the colonies back, and Uncle

Ilyas wanted the Germans back, so he appeared on their marches carrying the schutztruppe flag and on platforms singing Nazi songs. So while you were grieving for him here, Ilyas said, Uncle Ilyas was dancing and singing in German cities and waving the schutztruppe flag in marches demanding the return of the colonies. Lebensraum did not only mean the Ukraine and Poland to them. The Nazi dream also included the hills and valleys and plains at the foot of that snow-capped mountain in Africa.

In 1938 Uncle Ilyas was living in Berlin, and perhaps just as the Frau was making her enquiries on their behalf, he was arrested for breaking the Nazi race laws and defiling an Aryan woman. Not for marrying his German wife! That marriage took place in 1933 and the race laws were not passed until 1935 so could not be applied to them. It was for an affair he had with another German woman in 1938. That is what the rule of law means. He broke the law fair and square in 1938 but he did not in 1933 because the race law was not yet passed. Uncle Ilyas was sent to Sachsenhausen concentration camp outside Berlin and his one surviving son, who was called Paul after the General in the Ostafrika war, voluntarily followed him there. It is not known what happened to his wife. Both Uncle Ilyas and his son Paul died in Sachsenhausen in 1942. The cause of Uncle Ilyas's death is not recorded but from the memoir of an inmate who survived, it is known that the son of the black singer who voluntarily entered the camp to be with his father was shot trying to escape.

So what we can know for sure, Ilyas told his parents, is that someone loved Uncle Ilyas enough to follow him to certain death in a concentration camp in order to keep him company.

ALSO AVAILABLE BY ABDULRAZAK GURNAH

GRAVEL HEART

'A captivating storyteller, with an oeuvre haunted by memory and loss. His intricate novels of arrival and departure ... reveal, with flashes of acerbic humour, the lingering ties that bind continents, and how competing versions of history collide' *Guardian*

Salim has always believed that his father does not want him. Living with his parents and his adored Uncle Amir in a house full of secrets, he is a bookish child, a dreamer haunted by night terrors. It is the 1970s and Zanzibar is changing. Tourists arrive, the island's white sands obscuring the memory of recent conflict: longed-for independence from British colonialism swiftly followed by bloody revolution. When his father moves out, Salim is confused and ashamed. His mother explains neither this nor her absences with a strange man. When glamorous Uncle Amir, now a senior diplomat, offers Salim an escape, the lonely teenager travels to London for college. Struggling to find a foothold, and to understand the darkness at the heart of his family, Salim must face devastating truths about himself and those closest to him – and about love, sex and power.

'Gurnah writes with wonderful insight about family relationships and he folds in the layers of history with elegance and warmth' *The Times*

'Exile has given Gurnah a perspective on the "balance between things" that is astonishing, superb' *Observer*

ORDER YOUR COPY:

BY PHONE: +44 (0) 1256 302 699
BY EMAIL: DIRECT@MACMILLAN.CO.UK
DELIVERY IS USUALLY 3–5 WORKING DAYS.
FREE POSTAGE AND PACKAGING FOR ORDERS OVER £20.
ONLINE: WWW.BLOOMSBURY.COM/BOOKSHOP
PRICES AND AVAILABILITY SUBJECT TO CHANGE WITHOUT NOTICE.

BLOOMSBURY.COM/AUTHOR/ABDULRAZAK-GURNAH

BLOOMSBURY

THE LAST GIFT

An astounding meditation on family, self and the meaning of home by the Booker-shortlisted author of *Desertion*

Abbas has never told anyone about his past – before he was a sailor on the high seas, before he met his wife Maryam outside a Boots in Exeter, before they settled into a quiet life in Norwich with their children, Jamal and Hanna. Now, at the age of sixty-three, he suffers a collapse that renders him bedbound and unable to speak about things he thought he would one day have to.

Jamal and Hanna have grown up and gone out into the world. They were both born in England but cannot shake a sense of apartness. Abbas's illness forces both children home, to the dark silences of their father and the fretful capability of their mother Maryam, who began life as a foundling and has never thought to find herself, until now.

'Gurnah is a master storyteller ... A subtle and moving tale of a family coming to terms with itself: one to read at leisure and absorb at length'
Aminatta Forna, *Financial Times*

'Gurnah writes with wonderful insight about family relationships and he folds in the layers of history with elegance and warmth' *The Times*

'A well-made novel about identity and, at a time of forbidding public rhetoric about immigration, Gurnah's sensitive and sympathetic portrayal of his cast feels welcome' *Sunday Times*

ORDER YOUR COPY:

BY PHONE: +44 (0) 1256 302 699
BY EMAIL: DIRECT@MACMILLAN.CO.UK
DELIVERY IS USUALLY 3–5 WORKING DAYS.
FREE POSTAGE AND PACKAGING FOR ORDERS OVER £20.
ONLINE: WWW.BLOOMSBURY.COM/BOOKSHOP
PRICES AND AVAILABILITY SUBJECT TO CHANGE WITHOUT NOTICE.

BLOOMSBURY.COM/AUTHOR/ABDULRAZAK-GURNAH

BLOOMSBURY

DESERTION

The breakthrough book from the highly acclaimed author of *By the Sea*

Early one morning in 1899, in a small town along the coast from Mombasa, Hassanali sets out for the mosque. But he never gets there, for out of the desert stumbles an ashen and exhausted Englishman who collapses at his feet. That man is Martin Pearce – writer, traveller and something of an Orientalist. After Pearce has recuperated, he visits Hassanali to thank him for his rescue and meets Hassanali's sister Rehana; he is immediately captivated. In this crumbling town on the edge of civilised life, with the empire on the brink of a new century, a passionate love affair begins that brings two cultures together and which will reverberate through three generations and across continents.

'Rich in detail and filled with acute observations, this novel movingly examines the absences eating away at the core of all of its characters' *Sunday Telegraph*

'As beautifully written and pleasurable as anything I've read ... Gurnah's portrait is the work of a maestro' *Guardian*

'This is an impressive and deeply serious book, a careful and often heartfelt exploration of the way memory inevitably consoles and disappoints us' *Sunday Times*

ORDER YOUR COPY:

BY PHONE: +44 (0) 1256 302 699
BY EMAIL: DIRECT@MACMILLAN.CO.UK
DELIVERY IS USUALLY 3–5 WORKING DAYS.
FREE POSTAGE AND PACKAGING FOR ORDERS OVER £20.
ONLINE: WWW.BLOOMSBURY.COM/BOOKSHOP
PRICES AND AVAILABILITY SUBJECT TO CHANGE WITHOUT NOTICE.

BLOOMSBURY.COM/AUTHOR/ABDULRAZAK-GURNAH

BLOOMSBURY

BY THE SEA

A staggering novel of displacement and loss from the critically acclaimed author

On a late November afternoon Saleh Omar arrives at Gatwick Airport from Zanzibar, a far away island in the Indian Ocean. With him he has a small bag in which there lies his most precious possession – a mahogany box containing incense. He used to own a furniture shop, have a house and be a husband and father. Now he is an asylum seeker from paradise; silence his only protection. Meanwhile Latif Mahmud, someone intimately connected with Saleh's past, lives quietly alone in his London flat. When Saleh and Latif meet in an English seaside town, a story is unravelled. It is a story of love and betrayal, of seduction and of possession, and of a people desperately trying to find stability amidst the maelstrom of their times.

'Rarely in a lifetime can you open a book and find that reading it encapsulates the enchanting qualities of a love affair ... one scarcely dares breathe while reading it for fear of breaking the enchantment' *The Times*

'An epic unravelling of delicately intertwined stories, lush strands of finely wrought narratives that criss-cross the globe ... astonishing and superb' *Observer*

ORDER YOUR COPY:

BY PHONE: +44 (0) 1256 302 699
BY EMAIL: DIRECT@MACMILLAN.CO.UK
DELIVERY IS USUALLY 3–5 WORKING DAYS.
FREE POSTAGE AND PACKAGING FOR ORDERS OVER £20.
ONLINE: WWW.BLOOMSBURY.COM/BOOKSHOP
PRICES AND AVAILABILITY SUBJECT TO CHANGE WITHOUT NOTICE.

BLOOMSBURY.COM/AUTHOR/ABDULRAZAK-GURNAH

BLOOMSBURY

ADMIRING SILENCE

Masterfully blending myth and reality, this is the story of a man's escape from his native Zanzibar to England to build a new life

He thinks, as he escapes from Zanzibar, that he will probably never return, and yet the dream of studying in England matters above that.

Things do not happen quite as he imagined – the school where he teaches is cramped and violent, he forgets how it feels to belong. But there is Emma, beautiful, rebellious Emma, who turns away from her white, middle-class roots to offer him love and bear him a child. And in return he spins stories of his home and keeps her a secret from his family. Twenty years later, when the barriers at last come down in Zanzibar, he is able and compelled to go back. What he discovers there, in a story potent with truth, will change the entire vision of his life.

'I don't think I've ever read a novel that is so convincingly and hauntingly sad about the loss of home, the impossible longing to belong' Michèle Roberts, *Independent on Sunday*

'Abdulrazak Gurnah's fifth novel, *Admiring Silence*, is his best to date … There is a wonderful sardonic eloquence to this unnamed narrator's voice' *Financial Times*

'Through a twisting, many-layered narrative, *Admiring Silence* explores themes of race and betrayal with bitterly satirical insight' *Sunday Times*

ORDER YOUR COPY:

BY PHONE: +44 (0) 1256 302 699
BY EMAIL: DIRECT@MACMILLAN.CO.UK
DELIVERY IS USUALLY 3–5 WORKING DAYS.
FREE POSTAGE AND PACKAGING FOR ORDERS OVER £20.
ONLINE: WWW.BLOOMSBURY.COM/BOOKSHOP
PRICES AND AVAILABILITY SUBJECT TO CHANGE WITHOUT NOTICE.

BLOOMSBURY.COM/AUTHOR/ABDULRAZAK-GURNAH

BLOOMSBURY